Valentine

Valentine

A Novel

Elizabeth Wetmore

HARPER LARGE PRINT

An Imprint of **HarperCollins***Publishers*

"Oklahoma" from *Winter Stars* by Larry Levis, © 1985. Reprinted by permission of the University of Pittsburgh Press.

HarperCollins books may be purchased for educational, business, or sales promotional use. For information, please e-mail the Special Markets Department at SPsales@harpercollins.com.

FIRST HARPER LARGE PRINT EDITION

ISBN: 978-0-06-297934-6

Library of Congress Cataloging-in-Publication Data is available upon request.

20 21 22 23 24   LSC   10 9 8 7 6 5 4 3 2 1

For Jorge

Often, I used to say: I am this dust; or, I am this wind.
And young, I would accept that. The truth is, it
    was never the case.
I have seen enough dust & wind by now to know
I am a little breath that always goes the distance
Longing requires, & to know even this will fail.

LARRY LEVIS

Valentine

Gloria

Sunday morning begins out here in the oil patch, a few minutes before dawn, with a young roughneck stretched out and sleeping hard in his pickup truck. Shoulders pressed against the driver's side door, boots propped up on the dashboard, he wears his cowboy hat pulled down far enough that the girl sitting outside on the dusty ground can see only his pale jaw. Freckled and nearly hairless, it is a face that will never need a daily shave, no matter how old he gets, but she is hoping he dies young.

Gloria Ramírez holds herself perfectly still, she is a downed mesquite branch, a half-buried stone, and she imagines him facedown in the dust, lips and cheeks scoured by sand, his thirst relieved only by the blood in his mouth. When he startles and shifts roughly against the truck door, she holds her breath and watches his jaw clench, the muscle working bone against bone. The sight of him is a torment and she wishes again that his death will come soon, that it will be vicious and lonely, with nobody to grieve for him.

The sky turns purple in the east, then blue-black, then old-bucket slate. In a few minutes it will be stained orange and red, and if she looks, Gloria will see the land stretched tight beneath the sky, brown stitched to blue, same as always. It is a sky without end, and the best thing about West Texas, when you can remember to look at it. She will miss it when she goes. Because she can't stay here, not after this.

She keeps her eyes on the pickup truck and her fingers begin to press themselves lightly against the sand, counting one, two, three, four—they are trying to keep her from making any sudden moves, to keep her quiet, to keep her among the living for another day. Because Gloria Ramírez might not know much on this morning, February 15, 1976, but she knows this: if he hadn't passed out before he sobered up enough to find his gun or get his hands around her throat, she would already be dead. Fifty-two, fifty-three, fifty-four— she waits and watches, listens as some little animal moves through the mesquite, and the sun, that small, regular mercy, heaves itself over the earth's edge and hangs burning in the east. And her fingers keep on.

Daylight reveals miles of pumpjacks and oil-field litter, jackrabbits and barbed-wire fences, clumps of mesquite trees and buffalo grass. In piles of caliche and stacks of old pipeline rat snakes and copperheads and rattlers lie entwined, their breath slow and regular, waiting for spring. When morning has come all the way in, she sees a road and behind that, a farmhouse. It may be close enough to walk to, but it's hard to say. Out here one mile can look like ten, ten could be twenty, and she knows only that this body—yesterday, she would have called it *mine*—sits in a pile of sand, somewhere in the oil patch, too far from town to see the water tank with her town's name painted on the side, Odessa, or the bank building, or the cooling towers at the petrochemical plant where her mother works. Soon, Alma will come home from a night spent cleaning offices and break shacks. When she steps into the one-bedroom apartment that still smells of last night's hominy and pork, and Tío's cigarettes, when she sees that the sofa bed where Gloria sleeps is still made up from the day before, Alma might feel worried, maybe even a little afraid, but mostly she will be pissed off that her daughter is not home where she belongs, again.

Gloria scans the pumpjacks moving up and down, great steel grasshoppers, always hungry. Did he drive them as far as Penwell? Mentone? Loving County? Because the Permian Basin is eighty thousand square miles of the same old, same old, and she could be anywhere, and the only true things are her thirst and pain, and the roughneck's occasional sighs, his teeth grinding and body shifting, the click and hum of the pumpjack just a few yards away from where she sits.

When a bobwhite begins to call its own name, the sound gently pries the morning open. Gloria looks again at the farmhouse. A dirt road slices the desert in half, a straight line moving steadily toward a front porch she is already starting to imagine. Maybe it's close enough to walk to, maybe a woman will answer the door.

He has not moved when her fingers push the last number into the sand, a shaky one thousand. Gloria turns her head slowly back and forth, and understanding that it is her silence as much as anything else that's keeping her alive, she wordlessly considers the pieces of her body as they appear to her. Arm. Here is an arm, a foot. The foot bone's connected to the heel bone, she thinks, and the heel bone's connected to the anklebone. And over there, on the ground next to the wooden drill platform, her heart. She turns her head this way and that, gathering the body, covering it with clothes that lie torn and strewn around the site, as if they are trash, disregarded and cast aside, instead of her favorite black T-shirt, the blue jeans her mother gave her for Christmas, the matching bra and panties she stole from Sears.

She knows she shouldn't, but when it is time to go Gloria cannot help looking at the roughneck. Thin wisps of blond hair crawl out from under the felt edge of his cowboy hat. Skinny and gristle tough, he is just a few years older than Gloria, who will be fifteen next fall, if she survives this day. Now his chest rises and falls regular, just like anybody else's, but otherwise he is still. Still asleep, or pretending to be.

Gloria's mind skitters into this thought like a horse into a hidden skein of barbed wire. Her mouth falls open then jerks itself closed. She is oxygen starved and gasping, a fish torn from a lake. She imagines her own limbs disconnected, fleeing into the desert to be picked clean by the coyotes she heard calling to each other all through the night. She imagines her bones blanched and worn smooth by the wind—a desert filled with them—and this makes her want to shriek, to open her mouth and howl. Instead, she swallows hard and sits back down in the sand, shutting her eyes tight against both the roughneck and the sun brightening, interminable sky.

She must not panic. To panic is the worst possible

thing, her uncle would say. When Tío tells a war story—and since he came home last year, every story is a war story—he begins the same way. Know what you call a soldier who panics, Gloria? KIA, that's what. He ends his stories the same way, too. Listen, an army man never panics. Don't you ever panic, Gloria. You panic and—he forms his index finger into a pistol, presses it against his heart, and pulls the trigger—bang. And if there is only one thing she knows for sure on this morning, it is that she doesn't want to die, so she jams two fists hard against her mouth and she tells herself to stand back up. Try not to make a sound. Move.

Then Gloria Ramírez—for years to come, her name will hover like a swarm of yellow jackets over the local girls, a warning about what not to do, what never to do—stands up. She does not go back for her shoes, when she thinks of them, or the rabbit fur jacket she was wearing last night when the young man pulled into the parking lot at the Sonic, his forearm hanging out the open window, sparse freckles and golden hair glistening beneath the drive-in's fluorescent lights.

Hey there, Valentine. His words took the ugly right out of the drive-in, his soft drawl marking him as not from here, but not that far away either. Gloria's mouth went dry as a stick of chalk. She was standing next to the lone picnic table, a shaky wooden hub in the midst of a few cars and trucks, doing what she always did on a Saturday night. Hanging around, drinking limeades and begging smokes, waiting for something to happen, which it never did, not in this piss-ant town.

He parked close enough that Gloria could see the oil patch on him, even through the windshield. His cheeks and neck were wind-burned, his fingers stained black. Maps and invoices covered his dashboard, and a hard hat hung on a rack above the seat. Empty beer cans lay crushed and scattered across the truck's bed, along with crowbars and jugs of water. All of it added up to a pretty good picture of the warnings Gloria had been hearing her whole life. And now he was telling her his name—Dale Strickland—and asking for hers.

None of your damned beeswax, she said.

The words were out before she could think about them, how they would make her seem like a little girl instead of the tough young woman she was trying hard to be. Strickland leaned farther out the open window and looked at her real puppy-dog like, his eyes bloodshot and ringed with shadows. She stared directly into them for a few seconds. The blue turned pale then slate, depending on how the light hit his face. They were the color of a marble you fought to keep, or maybe the Gulf of Mexico. But she wouldn't know the Pacific Ocean from a buffalo wallow, and this was part of the problem, wasn't it? She had never been anywhere, never seen anything but this town, these people. He might be the start of something good. If they stayed together, he might drive her down to Corpus Christi or Galveston in a few months, and she could see the ocean for herself. So she gave him her name. Gloria.

He laughed and then turned up the radio to prove the coincidence, Patti Smith singing Gloria's name on the junior college radio station. And here you are, he said, in the flesh. That's fate, darlin'.

That's *bull*shit, darling, she said. They've been playing that album every two hours since last fall.

She had been singing it for months, waiting to hear the album, *Horses*, on the radio and enjoying her mother's conniptions every time Gloria sang, *Jesus died for somebody's sins but not mine*. When Alma threatened to drag her to mass, Gloria laughed out loud. She hadn't been to church since she was twelve years old. She made a fist, held it in front of her mouth as if it were a microphone, and sang the line again and again until Alma went into the bathroom and slammed the door.

The Sonic was dead as hell on this Valentine's night. Nothing and nobody—just the same skinny, jacked-up carhop who came straight from her day job and pretended not to see the same old delinquents pouring Jack Daniel's into paper cups half full of Dr Pepper; the girl only a couple of grades ahead of Gloria who sat on a barstool behind the counter, flipping switches and repeating orders, her voice blurred by the heavy speakers; and the cook, who occasionally stepped away from the grill and stood outside smoking while he watched cars cruise the drag. And now, a tall, big-shouldered old lady let the bathroom door slam shut behind her, wiped her hands on her pants, and walked briskly toward a truck where an even older man, pole skinny and bald as an egg, sat watching Gloria.

When the woman climbed in beside him, he pointed at the girl, his head bobbing slightly as he spoke. His wife nodded along with him, but when he stuck his head out the window, she grabbed his arm and shook her head. Gloria leaned against the picnic table and snugged her hands in the pocket of her new jacket, glancing back and forth between the couple and the young man, who sat with his arm hanging out the open window, fingers tapping steadily against the side of his truck. Gloria watched the two old buzzards arguing in the truck and when they again looked at her, she pulled one hand from her pocket. Slowly, slowly she uncurled her middle finger and held it in the air. Fuck you, she mouthed, and the horse you rode in on.

She looked again around the Sonic parking lot and shrugged—nothing to lose, everything to gain—and she climbed into the young man's pickup truck. The cab was warm as a kitchen, with the same faintly ammoniac smell of the industrial cleaners that lingered on her mother's hands and clothes when she came home from work. Strickland turned up the music and handed her a beer, cracking it open with one large hand while his other curled around the steering wheel. Well, what do you know, he said. Gloria, I think I love you. And she pulled the heavy door closed.

The sun is lingering just above the truck's wheels when she finally walks away from him. She does not look behind her. If he's going to wake up and shoot her, she does not want to see it coming. Let the bastard shoot her in the back. Let him also be known as a coward. As for Gloria, she will never again call herself by the name she was given, the name he said again and again, those long hours while she lay there with her face in the dirt. He spoke her name and it flew through the night air, a poison dart that pierced and tore. Gloria. Mocking, mean as a viper. But not anymore. From now on, she will call herself Glory. A small difference, but right now it feels like the world.

Glory makes her way across the oil patch, walking, stumbling, and falling past pumpjacks and mesquite scrub. When she crawls through a hole in the barbed-wire fence and walks into an abandoned drilling site, an awkwardly written sign gazes flat-faced down upon her, warning of poisonous gases and the consequence for trespassing. YOU WILL BE SHOT! When a stray piece of glass or a cactus spine pierces her foot, she watches her blood gather on the tough, impermeable ground and wishes it were water. When a coyote howls and a second answers, she looks around for a weapon and, seeing nothing, grabs hold of a mesquite branch and tears it from the tree. She is surprised by her strength, surprised she is still moving, surprised by the aching dryness in her mouth and throat, and a new pain that began as a small pricking in her rib cage when she first stood up. Now it has moved down to her belly, turned hot and sharp, a steel pipe set too close to a furnace.

When she comes to a set of railroad tracks, she follows them. When she loses her balance, she grabs onto a barbed-wire fence and falls hard into a pile of caliche rocks laid out in a long line. She studies the gravel lodged in the palms of her hands. His skin and blood are under her fingernails, a reminder that she fought hard. Not hard enough, she thinks, as she picks up a small stone and places it under her tongue, like Uncle Victor might, if he were thirsty and wandering through a desert, wondering how far away home was. At one end of the rock pile, a small marker with the words *Common Grave* is mounted on a steel cross. A second grave lies a few yards away, small and unmarked, the grave of a child or, perhaps, a dog.

Glory stands up and looks behind her. She is closer to the farmhouse than the truck. The wind riffles the air, a finger drawn through the grass, and she notices for the first time how still the morning has been. As if even the buffalo and blue grama grasses, thin and pliant as they are, have been holding their breath. It's a small wind, scarcely noticeable in a place where the wind is always blowing, and surely too light to carry her voice back to him. If she speaks, he will not hear. Glory Ramírez turns and looks toward the place where she has been. For the first time in hours, she means to say something out loud. She struggles to find some words, but the best she can manage is a small cry. The sound comes forth briefly and pierces the quiet and disappears.

Mary Rose

I used to believe a person could teach herself to be merciful if she tried hard enough to walk in somebody else's shoes, if she was willing to do the hard work of imagining the heart and mind of a thief, say, or a murderer, or a man who drove a fourteen-year-old girl out into the oil patch and spent the night raping her. I tried to imagine how it might have been for Dale Strickland:

The sun was already crawling toward high sky when he woke up, dick sore and dying of thirst, his jaw locked in a familiar amphetamine clench. His mouth tasted like he had been sucking on the nozzle of a gas can, and there was a bruise the size of a fist on his left thigh, maybe from hours pressed against the gearshift. Hard to say, but he knew one thing for sure. He felt like shit. Like somebody had beaten both sides of his head with a boot. There was blood on his face and shirt and boot. He pressed his fingers against his eyes and the corners of his mouth. Turned his hands over and over looking for cuts, then pressed them against the sides of his head. Maybe he unzipped and examined himself. There was some blood, but he couldn't find any obvious wounds. Maybe he unfolded himself from the front seat of his pickup truck and stood outside for a minute, letting the harmless winter sun warm his skin. Maybe he marveled at the day's unseasonable warmth, its unusual stillness, just as I had earlier that morning when I stepped onto my front porch and turned my face to the sun and watched a half dozen turkey buzzards gather in large, slow circles. The work of mercy means seeing him rooting around in the bed of his truck for a jug of water and then standing out there in the oil field, turning 360 degrees, slow as he could manage it, while he tried to account for his last fourteen hours. Maybe he didn't even remember the girl until he saw her sneakers tumbled against the truck's tire, or her jacket lying in a heap next to the drilling platform, a rabbit skin that fell just below her waist, her name written on the inside label in blue pen. *G. Ramírez*. I want him to think, What have I done? I want him to remember. It might have taken him a little longer to understand that he had to find her, to make sure she was okay, or maybe to make sure they were clear about what had happened out there. Maybe he sat on the tailgate, drinking musty water from his canteen and wishing he could remember the details of her face. He scuffed a boot against the ground and tried to bring the previous night into focus, looking again at the girl's shoes and jacket then lifting his gaze to the oil derricks, the ranch road and railroad tracks, the scarce Sunday traffic on the interstate and behind that, if you looked real hard, a farmhouse. My house. Maybe he thought the house looked too far to walk to. But you never know. These local girls were tough as nails, and one who was mad? Hell, she might be able to walk barefoot through hell's fires, if she made up her mind to do it. He pushed himself off the tailgate and squinted into the jug. There was just enough water to clean up a little. He bent down in front of the driver's mirror and ran his fingers through his hair, made a plan. He would take a piss, if he could manage it, and then drive over to that farmhouse and have a little look-see. Maybe he'd get lucky and the place would be abandoned, and he'd find his new girlfriend sitting out there on a rotting front porch, thirsty as a peach tree in August and happy as hell to see him again. Maybe, but mercy is hard in a place like this. I wished him dead before I ever saw his face.

⌣

When the time comes and I am called to take the stand, I will testify that I was the first person to see Gloria Ramírez alive. That poor girl, I will tell them. I don't know how a child comes back from something like this. The trial will not be until August, but I'll tell those men in the courtroom the same thing I will tell my daughter when I think she's old enough to hear it.

That it had been a bad winter for our family, even before that morning in February. The price of cattle was falling by the minute, and there had been no rain for six months. We had to supplement with feed corn, and some of the cows foraged for licorice root to help them abort their calves. If not for the oil leases, we might have had to sell some of our land.

That most days, my husband drove around the ranch with the only two men who hadn't left us for more money in the oil patch. The men threw silage off the back of the truck and fought screwworms. They pulled out half-dead cows that got tangled in barbed wire—they are stupid animals, don't let anybody tell you different—and if an animal couldn't be saved, they shot it between the eyes and let the buzzards do the rest.

I will tell them that Robert worked all day, every day, even Sundays, because a cow can die just as easily on the Sabbath as any other. Other than the fifteen minutes it took him to choke down a plateful of pot roast—you spend half the day cooking it, and they eat it in less than five minutes—I hardly ever saw my husband. What we need is a tougher brand of cow, he'd say as he stacked his fork and knife on his plate and hand it to me on his way out the door. We need some Polled Herefords or Red Brangus. How do you think we're going to afford that, he'd say. What are we going to do?

When I think back on that day and finding Gloria Ramírez on my front porch, my memories are stitched together like pieces of a scrap quilt, each a different shape and color, all bound together by a thin black ribbon, and I expect it will always be this way. Come August, I will testify that I did the best I could, under the circumstances, but I will not tell them how I failed her.

I was twenty-six years old, seven months pregnant with my second baby, and heavy as a Buick. With the second one, you always get bigger faster—so say the women in my family—and I had been feeling lonely enough that I occasionally let Aimee stay home from school with some invented malady, just to have a little company. Two days earlier, we had called the school secretary, Miss Eunice Lee.

As soon as I hung up the phone, Aimee Jo started mimicking Miss Lee's crabby old face. Some people say she's a direct descendent, and I don't believe it for a minute, but I will tell you this: if it *is* true, she sure didn't inherit the general's good looks. Bless her heart. My daughter scrunched up her face and pretended to hold the school's phone next to her ear. Well, thank you for calling, Mrs. Whitehead, but I do not care to know the details of Miss Aimee Jo's BMs. I hope she feels better real soon. Y'all have a happy Valentine's Day. Bye-bye! Aimee wiggled her fingers in the air, and the two of us just fell out laughing. Then we started a batch of yeast rolls to eat with butter and sugar.

It was a small thing, me and Aimee standing together in the kitchen while we waited for the dough to rise, the whole day stretched out in front of us like an old housecat, the two of us laughing so hard at her impression of Miss Lee that we nearly peed ourselves. But I sometimes think that when I am on my deathbed, that Friday morning with my daughter will be one of my happiest memories.

On Sunday morning, we were playing gin rummy and listening to church services on the radio. Aimee was losing, and I was trying to figure out how to throw the game without her catching on. While I waited for her to draw the four of hearts, I passed cards and dropped hints. Won't you be my valentine? Won't you be my heart? I said. Oh, my heart! I can hear it beating—one, two, three, *four* times, Aimee Jo. Back then, I did not believe it was good for a child to lose at cards too often, especially a little girl. Now I think differently.

We listened to Pastor Rob finish a sermon about the evils of desegregation, which he likened to locking a cow, a mountain lion, and a possum in the same barn together, then being surprised when somebody gets eaten.

What's that mean? my daughter asked me. She pulled a card from the deck, looked at it for a few seconds and laid her cards on the table. I win, she said.

Nothing you need to know about, little girl, I told her. You have to say *gin*. My daughter was nine years old, just a few years younger than the stranger I was about to find standing at my door, waiting for me to pull open that heavy door, to help.

It was eleven o'clock. I am sure of this because one of the deacons—one of those Hard Shell types that doesn't believe in having any fun—gave the sending prayer. I don't suppose any serious Baptist would think too kindly about us playing cards while we listened to church services on the radio, but that's how it was. After eleven, it's the oil reports, then the cattle markets. That month, you listened to rig counts and new leases if you wanted to hear good news. If you wanted to sit down in your recliner and have yourself a good cry, you listened to the cattle markets.

The girl knocked on the front door, two short and sturdy raps that were loud enough to startle us. When she knocked a third time, the door trembled. It was brand-new, made of oak but stained to look like mahogany. Two weeks earlier, Robert had it shipped down from Lubbock after we had our same old argument about whether we ought to move to town. It was a familiar argument. He thought we were too far away from town, especially with another baby coming and the oil boom getting under way. It's busy out here now, he argued, drilling crews driving all over our land. No place for women, or little girls. But this fight got ugly and we said some things. Threats, I guess you could say.

Of course, I was tired of watching flatbed trucks tear up our road, tired of the stink, a cross between rotten eggs and gasoline, tired of worrying that some roughneck would forget to close the gate behind him and one of our bulls would end up on the highway, or Texaco would dump wastewater in the unlined pit they built too close to our well. But I love our house, which Robert's grandfather built fifty years earlier with limestone he hauled in little by little, in the back of his truck, from the Hill Country. I love the birds that stop over every fall on their way to Mexico or South America, and again in the spring on their way back north. If we moved into town, I would miss the pair of mourning doves that nest under our porch and the kestrels that hover just a few feet above the pale earth, their wings beating madly in the seconds before they swoop down and fetch up a snake, and the sky going mad with color twice a day. I would miss the quiet, a night sky uninterrupted by anything except the occasional glow of red or blue when casinghead gases are being flared off.

Well, this is my home, I told him. I'm not leaving.

At some point, I punched Robert in the chest, a thing I had never done before. He couldn't hit me back because I was pregnant, but he sure could throw a fist into our front door three, four times. Now I had this pretty new door, and because she had lain in bed listening to us scream at each other in the kitchen, Aimee Jo got a new bicycle, a little Huffy with pink streamers and a small white basket.

We heard the three loud raps and Aimee said, Who's that? When I thought about it later, when I saw how badly Gloria had been beaten, I was surprised she was able to muster it, to make that thick oak tremble beneath her fist. I hauled myself out of the recliner. We were not expecting company. Nobody comes out this far without calling first, not even the Witnesses or Adventists, and I hadn't heard a truck or car coming up our road. I bent down and picked up the Louisville Slugger that Aimee had left on the floor next to my chair. You stay put, I said. I'll be right back.

I opened the door just as a little capful of wind picked up, disturbing a cluster of flies that had settled in her hair, on her face, in the wounds on her hands and feet, and my gorge rose. Christ Almighty, I thought and looked up the dirt lane leading from our house to the ranch road. All quiet, aside from a noisy flock of sand hill cranes wintering next to our stock tank.

Gloria Ramírez stood on my front porch tottering like a skinny drunk, looking for all the world as if she had just crawled down from the screen of a horror movie. Both eyes were blackened, one swollen nearly shut. Her cheeks, forehead, and elbows were scraped raw, and vicious scrapes covered her legs and feet. I snugged my fingers around the baseball bat and yelled at my daughter. Aimee Jo Whitehead, run to my bedroom and get Old Lady out of the closet, and bring it here right now. Carry it the right way.

I could hear her moving through the house, and

I yelled that she was not to run with my rifle in her hands. When she walked up behind me, I kept my body between her and the stranger on the porch. I reached behind me to take my dear old Winchester from my daughter's small hand. Old Lady, I'd named that rifle, after the grandma who gave it to me on my fifteenth birthday.

What is it, Mama, rattlesnake? Coyote?

Hush up, I said. Run to the kitchen and call the sheriff's office. Tell them to bring an ambulance. And Aimee, I said without taking my eyes off the child in front of me, you stay away from those windows or I will beat you to within an inch of your life.

Not once have I beaten my daughter, not once. I got whipped when I was a little girl, and I swore up and down I'd never do it to my own kids. But on this morning, I meant what I said and Aimee believed me, I guess. Without a word of argument, she turned and ran to the kitchen.

I looked again at the child faltering on my porch then glanced away for long enough to scan the horizon. It's flat enough out here that nobody can sneak up on you, flat enough you can see your husband's pickup truck parked next to a water tank and know he's still too far away to hear you shouting for him. You can drive for miles out here without the road turning or lifting, not even a little bit. I stepped farther onto the porch. I couldn't see anybody who might want to hurt us, but I couldn't see anybody who might want to help us either.

And now, for the first time since we moved to Robert's family land, I wished to be elsewhere. For ten years I had been keeping an eye out for snakes and sandstorms and twisters. When a coyote killed one of my chickens and drug it through the yard, I shot him. When I went to draw a bath for Aimee and found a scorpion in the tub, I stepped on it. When a rattlesnake curled up underneath the clothesline or next to Aimee's little bicycle, I took a hoe to it. Daily, it seemed, I was shooting something or chopping it to pieces or dumping poison down its burrow. I was always disposing of bodies.

Imagine me standing on my porch with one hand on my belly, the other using Old Lady as a crutch while I try to remember what I had for breakfast—cup of Folgers, piece of cold bacon, the cigarette I sneaked when I went out to the barn to gather eggs. Imagine my stomach turning itself inside out when I bend down to face the stranger on my porch, when I swallow hard and push the salt from my mouth, when I say, Where are you from, honey? Odessa?

Imagine that hearing the name of her hometown

breaks whatever fearsome spell the girl is under. She rubs at her eye and winces. When she begins to speak the words come rough, like grains of sand blown through a screen door.

Can I have a glass of water? My mother is Alma Ramírez. She works nights, but she will be home by now.

What is your name?

Glory. Can I have some ice water?

Imagine the girl might be asking after my okra patch, calm as she seems, remote, and it is this horror hiding behind indifference that finally causes something to tear loose, to break apart from the rest of me. In a few years, when I think she's old enough to hear it, I will tell my daughter that my lower belly cramped and went cold as a block of ice. A steady hum started in my ears, faint but growing louder, and I remembered a few lines of a rhyme I had read back in high school, the winter before I left school and married Robert—*I heard a fly buzz—when I died*—and for a few cramping, cold and miserable seconds, until I felt the unmistakable kick, I thought I was losing the baby. My vision dimmed and I remembered another verse, stray and unconnected to anything. How strange it was to be thinking of poems now, when I had not given them so much as a passing thought all these years since I had become a grown woman, a wife and mother, but now I recalled: *This is the Hour of Lead—Remembered, if outlived.*

I stood up straight and shook my head gently, as if doing so might help me clear away all that was happening right in front of me, as if I could clear away the terrible fact of this child and whatever hell she had endured, as if I could step back into my living room and tell my daughter, It's just the wind, honey. Don't pay any attention, it's not calling our name today. How about another game of gin? You want to learn how to play Hold'em?

Instead, I leaned heavily on the rifle and rested my other hand on my belly. I am going to get you a glass of ice water, I said to her, and then we'll call your mama.

The girl gently shifted from side to side, a halo of sand and dirt rising up around her face and hair. For a few seconds, she was a dust cloud, a sandstorm asking for help, the wind begging for a little mercy. My hand reached out to her, as the other stretched behind me to lean the rifle against the doorframe. She leaned hard to one side, a reed in the wind, and when I turned back to grab her—to keep her from falling off the porch or maybe just trying to keep myself upright, I will never be able to say for sure—she ducked her head slightly. Dust filled the sky behind her.

A pickup truck had turned off the ranch road and

was starting toward our house. When it passed our mailbox, the driver swerved suddenly, as if briefly distracted by a quail darting across the dirt road. The vehicle skidded toward our stock tank, then straightened out and kept on. The driver was still at least a mile off, rumbling steadily up our road, kicking up dirt and ruddying the air. Whoever he was, he drove like he knew exactly where he was going, and he was in no real hurry to get there.

⌒

These were my mistakes: When I saw the truck coming up the road, I did not allow the child to look behind her so I couldn't ask, Have you ever seen that truck before? Is that him?

Instead, I scooted her inside and handed her a glass of ice water. Drink it slow, I told her, or you'll throw up. Aimee Jo stepped into the kitchen, her eyes growing big as silver dollars when the girl began quietly to say over and over, I want my mom, I want my mom, I want my mom.

I chewed a couple of saltine crackers and drank a glass of water, then bent over the kitchen sink and splashed my face for long enough that the pump switched on and the odor of sulfur filled the basin. Y'all stay right here,

I told them. I've got to take care of something outside. When I come back, we'll call your mama.

My stomach hurts, the girl cried. I want my mom. And my anger was sudden, filled with bile that burned my throat and, later, made me feel ashamed of myself. Shut up, I yelled at her. I sat both girls down at the kitchen table and told them not to move. But I never asked my daughter if she had called the sheriff. My second mistake. And when I stepped outside and picked up my rifle, when I carried it to the edge of the porch and readied myself to meet whoever was coming up our road, I did not check to make sure it was loaded. My third mistake.

Now. Come and stand with me at the edge of my porch. Watch him drive slowly into my yard and park not even twenty feet from my house. Watch him slide out from behind the steering wheel and look around our dirt lot with a long, low whistle. The truck's door slams closed behind him and he leans against the hood, looking around as if he might like to buy the place. The sun and air pluck gently at him, lighting the freckles on his arms, riffling his hay-colored hair. Late-morning sunshine turns him gold as a topaz, but even from where I am standing I can see the bruises on his hands and face, the red borders around his pale blue eyes. When a gust of wind passes through the yard, he crosses his arms and shrugs, looking around with an easy smile, like the day has just become too good to believe. He is barely past being a boy.

Morning—he glances at his watch—or I guess it's afternoon, just about.

I stand there clutching the rifle stock like it is the hand of my dearest old friend. I do not know him, but I understand right away that he is too young to be one of the surveyors who sometimes drives out to make sure we're keeping the access road open and clear, or a wild-catter who has stopped by to shoot the shit and see if we might be interested in selling our land. He looks too young to be a deputy volunteer either, and that's when it occurs to me that I did not ask Aimee if she called the sheriff's office.

What can I do for you? I say.

You must be Mrs. Whitehead. This is a real pretty place y'all have out here.

It's all right. Dusty, same as always. I keep my voice steady, but I am wondering how he knows my name.

He chuckles gently, a stupid, arrogant sound. I guess so, he says. Good for my line of work, though. It's easier to work a rig when Mother Nature keeps things nice and dry.

He stands up straight and takes one step forward, his palms facing up. His smile is steady, a needle on a cracked kitchen scale.

Listen, ma'am, I've had a little trouble this morning. I wonder if you will help me?

He steps toward the porch, and I watch his feet move closer. I look up, and he's holding his hands high above his head. When the baby kicks me hard in the ribs, I rest a hand on my belly and wish I could sit down. Two days ago I fired my gun at a coyote trotting through the yard with his eyes on the chicken coop. At the last second, I took my eye off the bead sight at the end of my muzzle and missed him, and then Aimee started hollering about a scorpion, so I set the gun down and grabbed my shovel. And now I cannot recall whether I replaced the cartridge. Old Lady is a Winchester 1873, which my grandma believed to be the finest gun ever made. Now I smooth my thumb across the worn-smooth wooden stock as if she might tell me herself: yes or no.

Son, what do you want? I say to the boy who is barely a man.

He looks fine standing out there in the sunlight, but his eyes narrow. Well, I'm real thirsty and I'd like to use your telephone to call—

He takes another step toward the house but stops

abruptly when he sees Old Lady. He can't possibly know, I tell myself, that it might not be loaded. I tap the barrel gently against the pecan planking, one, two, three times, and he cocks his head, listening.

Mrs. Whitehead, is your husband at home?

Yes he is, of course he is, but he's sleeping right now.

His smile gets a little wider, a little friendlier. A cattleman asleep at noon?

It's 11:30. I laugh, and the sound is bitter as juniper berries. How stupid it sounds! How alone it makes me seem.

He giggles a little, real high-pitched, and my stomach roils at the sound. His laughter is a false cut.

Lord, Mrs. Whitehead, did your husband tie one on last night too?

No.

He sick? Too much Valentine's candy?

He is not sick—I press one hand against my belly, thinking, slow down, little baby, quiet—can I help you with something?

I told you, I've had some trouble. My sweetheart and I drove out here last night for a little celebration. You know how it is—

I see, I tell him, and smooth my hand back and forth across my stomach.

—and we drank too much, had a little dustup. Maybe

she didn't like the heart-shaped box of chocolates I bought for her, and I might have passed out—

Did you.

—guess you could say I lost my valentine. Shame on me, huh?

I watch him talk, and I am holding on to my old rifle for dear life, but my throat feels like somebody just wrapped his hand around it and started to squeeze real slow. Behind him, and barely visible on the horizon, I catch a glimpse of a cherry-red car racing down the highway. It is more than a mile away, and from this distance, the car looks as if it is flying across the desert. Come and visit me please, I think as it approaches the turnoff to our ranch, and my throat aches a little. The car hesitates, a small wobble on the horizon, and then speeds away.

The young man keeps telling his little story, still smiling, blond hair glowing in the sun. He is standing less than ten feet from me now. If there's a bullet in the chamber, I won't miss him.

When I woke up this morning, he tells me, she had already hightailed it out of there. I'm afraid she might be walking around in the oil patch and that ain't no place for a girl, as I'm sure you know.

I don't say a word. Listening is what I do now. I listen, but I don't hear anything except him, talking.

I hate to think of her getting into some trouble out there, he says, stepping on a diamondback or running into the wrong kind of person. Have you seen my Gloria? He lifts his right hand and holds it out to his side, palm down. Little Mexican gal? About yay high?

My throat slams shut, but I swallow hard and try to look him right in the eye. No sir, we haven't seen her. Maybe she hitched a ride back to town.

Can I come in and use your phone?

I shake my head real slow, back and forth. No.

He pretends to look genuinely surprised. Well, why not?

Because I don't know you. I try to speak this lie as if I mean it. Because now, I do know him—who he is and what he's done.

Listen, Mrs. Whitehead—

How do you know my name? I am nearly shouting now, pushing one hand against the baby's foot, which hammers against my rib cage.

The young man looks surprised. Well, it's right there on your mailbox, ma'am. Listen, he says, I feel bad about what happened out there, and I'm real worried about her. She's a little crazy, you know how these Mexican gals can be. He stares at me intently, his blue eyes just a shade darker than the sky. If you've seen her, you should tell me.

He stops talking and gazes past me toward the house for a few seconds, a broad grin spreading across his face. I imagine my daughter peeking out the window at him. Then I imagine the other girl looking through the glass, her blackened eyes and torn lips, and I do not know whether to keep my eyes locked on him or turn my head to see what he sees, know what he knows. So I stand there, me and my maybe loaded gun, and I try to listen.

I want you to step back, I tell him after a thousand years of silence have passed. Go stand next to the tailgate of your truck.

He doesn't move. And I told you that I want a drink of water.

No.

He looks up at the sky and lays his hands on the back of his neck, fingers threaded. He whistles a few bars of music and though the song is familiar, I can't name it. When he speaks, he is a man, not a boy.

I want you to give her to me. Okay?

I don't know what you're talking about. Why don't you go on back to town?

You step inside the house now, Mrs. Whitehead, and get my girlfriend. Try not to wake your husband, who is sleeping upstairs, except he's not, is he.

It is not a question, and suddenly, Robert's face rises

wraithlike before me. You did all this for a stranger, Mary Rose? You risked our daughter's life, our baby's life, yourself, for a stranger. What the hell is wrong with you?

And he'd be right. Because who is this child to me, anyway? Maybe she got into his truck willingly. I might have done the same ten years earlier, especially for a man this pretty.

Lady, I don't know you, he says. You don't know me. You don't know Gloria. Now I want you to be a good girl, and set down that gun and go inside that house, and you bring her out here.

I feel the tears on my cheeks before I'm aware that I have begun to weep. There I stand, with my rifle, that useless piece of beautifully carved wood, and why should I not do as he asks? Who is she to me? She is not my child. Aimee and this child whose feet and fists kick and flail, they are somebody to me. They are mine. This girl, Gloria, she is not mine.

When he speaks next, the young man is no longer interested in asking questions, or talking. Bitch, he says, you listen here—

I try to listen for something other than his voice—a phone ringing in the house, a truck coming up the road, even the wind would be a welcome noise, but everything on this particular piece of flat and lonely earth has gone silent. His is the only voice I can hear, and it roars. Do you hear me, you stupid bitch. You hear me?

Gently, I shake my head. No, I don't hear you. Then I pick up the rifle and snug it against my shoulder, a right and familiar sensation, but now it feels like somebody has poured lead into the barrel. I am as weak as an old woman. Maybe it is loaded, I don't know, but still I point it at his pretty, golden face—because he doesn't know either.

I don't have one word left in me, so I flick my thumb across the safety and sight him through the aperture, my vision blurred by tears and the sorrow of knowing what I will say if he asks even one more time. Well, come on then, mister. I will take you to the ground myself, or die trying, if it means standing between you and my daughter, but Gloria? Her you can have.

We hear the sirens at the same time. He is already turning around when I lift my gaze from the bead sight. We stand there and watch the sheriff's car coming fast up the road. An ambulance is right behind him, kicking up enough dust to choke a herd of cows. Just this side of our mailbox, the driver overcorrects and slides off the road. The vehicle bounces off the barbed-wire fence and skids into the flock of sand hill cranes, who rise up shrieking. They take flight, all noise and thin legs and thwapping disorder, a hue and cry.

For a few seconds, the young man holds himself still as a frightened jackrabbit. Then his shoulders slump forward and he rubs his fingers against his closed eyes. Well, shit, he says. My daddy's going to kill me.

A lot of years will pass before I think my daughter is old enough to hear it, but when I do, I will tell her the last thing I remember seeing before I leaned back against the doorframe and passed out cold on the front porch. Two little girls, faces pressed against the kitchen window, mouths agape and eyes wide open, only one of them mine.

Corrine

Well, it's a murderous little shit, the skinny yellow stray with lime-colored eyes and balls the size of silver dollars. Somebody dumped it in the dirt lot behind the Shepards' house at the end of December—a Christmas present that wore thin quick, a bad idea from the get-go, Corrine told Potter at the time—and no creature has been safe since. Songbirds have perished by the dozens. Finches, a family of cactus wrens nesting under the storage shed, too many sparrows and bats to count, even a large mockingbird. In four months, the stray has doubled in size. His pale fur glows like a chrysanthemum.

Corrine is kneeling in front of the toilet when she hears the panicked cry of another small animal in the backyard. The birds shriek and beat their wings against the ground, and the garter snakes and brown racers die quietly, their light bodies barely disturbing the hard-packed dirt in her empty flowerbeds. This is the sound made by a mouse or squirrel, maybe even a young prairie dog. Critters, she thinks, that's what Potter used to call them. And her throat closes up.

Holding her thin brown hair with one hand, she finishes bringing up the contents of her stomach, then sits with her cheek pressed against the bathroom's cool wall. The animal cries out again and in the silence that follows, she tries to piece together the details of last night. Did she have five drinks or six? What did she say, and to whom?

The ceiling fan rattles overhead. The meaty stink of salted peanuts and Scotch drifts toward the open window, and Corrine's eyes are wet from the force of her sick. All this, and that bald spot on the crown of her head getting bigger by the day. Not that this particular detail has anything to do with how drunk she got last night, but still—it is part of the inventory. As is the small square of toilet paper dangling from her chin. She flicks it into the toilet bowl, closes the lid, and lays her forehead against the porcelain while she listens to the tank fill back up.

Sloppy as a bag of fishing worms left out in the sun, Potter would tell Corrine if he were here. Then he'd fix her a Bloody Mary, heavy on the Trappy's hot sauce, and fry up some bacon and eggs. He'd hand her a piece of toast to sop up the bacon grease. Back in business, he'd say. Pace yourself next time, sweetheart. Six weeks since Potter died—went out in a blaze of glory!—and this morning she can hear her husband's voice so plainly he might as well be standing in the doorway. Same old goofy smile, same old hopeful self.

When the phone in the kitchen rings, the sound tears a hole in the quiet. There's not one person in the world Corrine cares to talk to. Alice lives in Prudhoe Bay and only calls on Sunday nights when long distance rates are low. Even then, Corrine, who hasn't forgiven her daughter for the blizzard that shut down the airport in Anchorage and kept her from Potter's funeral, always keeps the conversations short, talking just long enough to reassure her daughter that she is fine. I am just fine, she tells Alice. Staying busy with the garden, going to church on Wednesday nights and Sunday mornings, going through your daddy's things so the Salvation Army can pick them up.

Every word of it is bullshit. She hasn't boxed up so

much as a T-shirt of that old man's. Out back, the garden is nothing but packed dirt and bird carcasses, and after forty years of letting Potter drag her to church, she isn't about to give those sanctimonious bitches another minute, or another nickel. In the bathroom, his leather shaving kit still sits open on the vanity. His earplugs are on his nightstand, alongside an Elmer Kelton book and his pain medicine. The jigsaw puzzle he was working on when he died is still spread out on the kitchen table, and his new cane leans against the wall behind it. A stack of life insurance forms, along with six banker's envelopes from the credit union, mostly fifties, a few hundred-dollar bills, lies on a gold plastic lazy Susan in the center of the table. Sometimes Corrine thinks about setting the envelopes on fire, one by one, with the money still inside.

The phone rings again, and Corrine presses her eyes against the palms of her hands. A week earlier, she broke off the volume dial in a fit of pique. Now, with the ringer stuck on high, the god-awful off-key chime pierces every nook and cranny of the house and yard, screaming when it could have asked. The voice on the other end is equally unpleasant when Corrine finally snatches up the phone, when she says testily, Shepard residence.

Because of you, a woman shouts, I got fired last night.

Who? Corrine says, and the woman sobs and slams the phone so hard that Corrine's ear rings.

The stray cat is standing outside the sliding-glass door with a dead mouse in his mouth when the phone rings again. Corrine snatches it up and yells into the receiver, Go to hell. The cat drops his victim and bolts across the backyard, scaling her pecan tree and launching his large, ugly body over the cinder-block fence and into the alley.

⟳

They were making plans for their retirement when Potter's headaches started the previous spring. He was fully vested in his pension, and Corrine had been collecting hers since the school board forced her out a few years earlier, in the wake of some ill-advised comments she made in the teacher's lounge. Maybe we can drive up to Alaska, Potter said, stop in California and see that redwood tree that's big enough to drive a truck through.

But Corrine had her doubts. You can't even get the sun up there for half the year, she told him, and what the hell is in Alaska? Moose?

Alice, said Potter. Alice is up there.

Corrine rolled her eyes, a habit she'd picked up from thirty years of working with teenagers. Right, she said, shacking up with whatshisname, the draft dodger.

Two days after they put down a deposit on a brand-new Winnebago thirty feet long and with its own shower, Potter had his first seizure. He was mowing the front yard when he fell to the ground, teeth clattering, arms and legs jerking madly. The lawn mower rolled slowly toward the street and came to a stop with its back wheels still on the sidewalk. Ginny Pierce's kid was riding her bike in circles on the Shepards' driveway, and Corrine heard her hollering all the way from the bedroom, where she'd been reading a book with the swamp cooler turned up high.

They drove five hundred miles to Houston and rode an elevator for fifteen stories to sit in two narrow chairs with vinyl cushions and listen while the oncologist spelled it out for them. Corrine sat hunched over a spiral notebook, her pen bearing down on the paper like she was trying to kill it. Glioblastoma multiforme, he said, GBM, for short. For short? Corrine looked up at him. It was so rare, the oncologist said, they might as well have found a trilobite lodged in Potter's brain. If they started radiation therapy right away, they might buy him six months, maybe a year.

Six months? Corrine gazed at the doctor with her mouth hanging open, thinking, Oh no, no, no. You are mistaken, sir. She watched Potter stand up and walk over to the window where he looks out at Houston's soupy brown air. His shoulders began to move gently up and down, but Corrine didn't go to him. She was stuck to that chair as surely as if someone had driven a nail through one of her thighs.

It was too hot to drive home, so they went over to the Westwood Mall, where they sat on a bench near the food court, both of them clutching bottles of cold Dr Pepper as if they were hand grenades. At dusk, they walked to the parking lot. They drove with the windows down, the wind blowing hot against their faces and hands. By midnight the truck stank of them—the remnants of a cup of coffee Corrine had spilled on the seat the day before, her cigarettes and Chanel No. 5, Potter's snuff and aftershave, their mutual sweat and fear. He drove. She turned the radio on and off, on and off, and on, pulled her hair into a clip, let it back down, and turned off the radio, turned it back on. After a while, Potter asked her to please stop.

City traffic made Corrine nervous, so Potter took the loop around San Antonio. I'm sorry, she told him, for adding time to our drive. He smiled wanly and reached across the seat for her hand. Woman, he said, are you apologizing to me? Well. I guess I really am dying. Corrine turned her face toward the passenger window, and cried so hard her nose clogged up and her eyes swelled nearly shut.

⌒

Not even nine o'clock, and it is already ninety degrees outside when Corrine looks out the living-room window and sees Potter's truck parked on the front lawn. It was his pride and joy, a Chevy Stepside V8, with a scarlet leather interior. It has been a dry winter and the Bermuda grass is a pale brown scarf. When the breeze picks up, a few blades of grass that weren't flattened beneath the truck's wheel tremble under the sunlight. Every day for the past two weeks, the wind picks up in the late morning and blows steadily until dusk. Back when Corrine gave a shit, that would have meant dusting the house before she went to bed.

On Larkspur Lane, the neighbors stand in their front yards, water hoses in hand, staving off the drought. A large U-Haul turns the corner and stops in front of the Shepards' house, then backs slowly into the driveway across the street. If you really want to know, Corrine would gladly explain to anybody who cared to ask, I am not a drunk, I'm just drinking all the time. There is a world of difference between the two.

No one will ask, but they will sure *talk* if she doesn't move Potter's truck off the lawn, so Corrine swallows an aspirin and puts on a skirt suit from her teaching days, an olive-green number with brass buttons shaped like anchors. She puts on pantyhose, perfume, lipstick, and sunglasses then creeps outside wearing her house slippers, as if she has just returned from church and is settling in for a busy day at home, doing something.

The day is lit up like an interrogation room, the sun a fierce bulb in an otherwise empty sky. Across the street and down the block, Suzanne Ledbetter is watering her St. Augustine. When she sees Corrine, she switches off her hand sprayer and waves, but Corrine acts as if she doesn't see. She also pretends not to see any of the neighbor kids who have spilled out of houses and across lawns like pecans from an overturned basket, and she barely registers the crew of men who have climbed out of the moving truck and are standing around the yard across the street.

When she opens the door to Potter's truck and spots a cigarette lying on the bench seat, broken but repairable, Corrine gasps with gratitude. Quick, quick, she shifts the truck into reverse and pulls it squarely onto the driveway, then fetches up the cigarette and makes for the front door, pausing for just long enough to turn on the faucet. A water hose is stretched across the lawn like a dead snake, the rusty nozzle lying facedown in the dirt beneath the Chinese elm she and Potter planted twenty-six years earlier, the spring after they bought the house. Ugly and awkward, the elm reminds Corrine of dirty hair, but it has survived droughts, dust storms, and tornadoes. When it grew three feet in a single summer, Potter, who had a nick-name for everything and everyone, started calling it Stretch. When Alice fell out of it and broke her right wrist, he started calling her Lefty. Every other damn thing in the backyard is dead, and Corrine couldn't care less, but she can't bear to let this tree die.

And even if she wanted to, Corrine knows, if she lets the tree go, or she makes a habit of parking Potter's truck on the grass, or people see her in the front yard wearing the same clothes she wore to the Country Club last night, they might start feeling sorry for her. Pity. It makes her want to kick the shit out of someone—namely Potter, if he weren't already dead. She thumps his funeral wreath and slams the front door behind her. In the kitchen, the phone rings and rings, but she is not picking up. No way, no how.

⁓

At three o'clock in the morning, they stopped to gas up at the Kerrville truck stop and wandered into the restaurant for coffee and an ice cream cone. After they ordered, he told her that radiation therapy was just a bunch of poison they pumped into your veins. It burned you from the inside out, made you even sicker, and what kind of months would those be?

I won't do it, Corrine. I'm not having my wife wipe my ass, or run my steak through a blender.

Corrine sat across from her husband with her mouth hanging open. You always told Alice that getting hurt was no excuse to quit playing a game—her voice rose and fell like a kite in strong wind—and now you're going to die on me? A couple sitting in the adjacent booth glanced their way then stared down at their table. Otherwise, the restaurant was empty. Why on earth had Potter chosen to sit here? Corrine wondered. Why must she share her grief with total strangers?

This is different, Potter said. He studied his ice cream for a few seconds. When he looked out the window, Corrine looked too. Between the diesel stations and eighteen-wheelers and a neon sign advertising hot showers, it was bright as high noon out there. A trucker pulled away from the diesel pump, honking twice as he merged onto the frontage road. A cowboy leaned against his tailgate and gulped down a hamburger, his belt buckle sparkling in the light. Two cars filled with teenage girls rolled slowly through the parking lot.

Potter and Corrine leaned back in their booth and looked at the ceiling. The plaster tiles directly above their heads were covered with piss-colored water spots and a smattering of holes about the size of No. 8 buckshot, as if some jackass had thought it might be funny to discharge his weapon while people were trying to eat their supper. When there was nothing left to look at, they looked at each other. His eyes filled with tears. Corrie, this is terminal.

What in the hell are you talking about? Corrine knocked her fist on the table, and coffee sloshed out of their mugs. Get up and fight! like you always said to Alice, and me too, on occasion.

Well, it didn't do me no good, telling y'all that. Speaking low and fast, Potter leaned toward his wife. Alice still ran off to Alaska with that boy. You still walked away from teaching, the minute things got hard. All that work, Corrine—when we met, you were the

only person I had ever known who went to college—
and you gave it up to stay home and read your poetry
books.

Her face was crimson with fear and rage. I think I
told you a dozen times that I was sick to death of it all.

Baby, I don't think you understand how serious this
is. He reached across the table, but Corrine snatched
her hand back and folded her arms across her breasts.
Don't you dare call me *baby*, Potter Shepard, or I will
kill you myself.

I'm already dying, honey.

Screw you, Potter. You are not. Never let me hear
you say that again. And they sat in stupefied silence
while the coffee went bone-cold and the ice cream
turned soupy.

When they pulled into the garage the next morning,
they were greeted by the same musty smell of cardboard boxes and Potter's old army tent, the same click
and whir when the motor on the deep freeze switched
on, the same old tools gathering dust on Potter's tool
bench. Nothing was different in any way, except they
hadn't slept in nearly twenty-four hours, and Corrine
looked like she had aged ten years, and Potter was
dying.

While she made a skillet of corn bread and warmed
up some pinto beans, he set a jar of chow-chow and

a plate of sliced tomatoes on the kitchen table. He pointed at the heat shimmers on the other side of the sliding-glass door. The heat in August, she said, it's a special kind of hell. It's a wonder any of us survive it. He laughed gently, and the two of them fell silent.

After breakfast, they set the dishes in the sink and went into the bedroom, where he turned the swamp cooler on high and she pulled the draperies closed. They crawled into bed, Corrine on her side, Potter on his, and in that strange midday dusk they lay next to each other, fingers twined and minds numb with terror. They waited for whatever was coming next.

⌒

Thinking it might help with her hangover, she tries to make herself a fried egg sandwich, but she sees the yolk wobbling in her cast iron skillet, a watery yellow eyeball, and her stomach roils. Instead, she holds her hair back, lights her cigarette on the stove burner, and leans against the icebox while she waits for the nicotine to help bring the previous night into focus.

It had been a slow night at the Country Club and by midnight, everyone had gone home except Corrine and the bartender, Karla, along with a few diehards, men with nowhere to be and no one waiting for them once they got there. She'd be damned if she was going to make small talk with any of these fools, so she watched Karla polish glassware while the men talked football and oil prices—1976 looked like it was going to be a damned good year for both—and discussed Carter and Ford—hated them both, one was a dipshit and the other was a pussy. Nixon had been their man, and now, with Watergate in the rearview mirror, the men were beginning to understand that they'd not only lost their leader, they'd lost their war against chaos and degeneracy. Black Panthers and Mexicans, Communists and cult leaders, people who fucked right in the middle of a street in downtown Los Angeles, for chrissakes.

Talking shit, Corrine mused, same as any other group of men anywhere else on the planet. She figured she could parachute into Antarctica in the dead of night, and she'd find three or four men sitting around a fire, filling each other's heads with bullshit, fighting over who got to hold the fire poker. After a few minutes, it was all just low, male murmuring.

Karla! Corrine thinks now as she stubs her cigarette out in the kitchen sink. It was Karla who called earlier, or maybe Ginny's kid, who calls almost every morning to see what Corrine is doing, and whether she might not like some company.

⌒

On the last day of 1975, they stood on the back patio after supper and watched the stray carry a white-throated sparrow across the backyard. It was a female, rarely seen this far south, and they had been listening to its sweet, singular song—*Old Sam Peabody, Peabody*—since early November, just a few days after they brought Potter home from the hospital. For the last time, he said when they were still sitting in the hospital parking lot. Corrine hadn't even got her key in the ignition when he leaned over and tried to pat her knee. I gave it a shot, for you, he said, but this is the last time. No more treatments, no more doctors.

He didn't feel up to driving to church for the New Year's party, and she had never wanted to go in the first place, and by four o'clock, they'd eaten supper and put on their sweatpants. While Corrine enjoyed her cigarette, Potter leaned heavily on his new cane. The cat sat atop their cinder-block fence like he owned the place, his fur turning gold in the last bit of daylight. Potter said that he couldn't help admiring him. Most strays didn't last a week before they were run over on Eighth Street, or some little boy shot them with his .22. The black stripes across the cat's face made him look a bit like an ocelot, he observed. He'd probably be good company, Potter said, if you got him fixed.

We ought to poison the little bastard before he kills every living creature on the block, Corrine said. She handed her cigarette to Potter, who held it stiffly between his thumb and index finger. He had quit twenty years earlier, and they'd been fighting about her habit since. But all his griping hadn't mattered a bit, she thought sadly as she walked over to sweep up the bird carcass. She was going to outlive him after all.

⌒

While Karla polished glassware and cut limes, Corrine smoked one cigarette after the other. She ran her thumb across the names and phone numbers carved into the mahogany bar. On one side of the room, large plate-glass windows overlooked the golf course. The wildcatters who bankrolled the project in the late sixties had originally planned on eighteen holes, but construction ceased abruptly amid a sudden glut in the oil markets.

While a bulldozer and irrigation pipes sat rusting on what would have been the tenth, club members made do with nine holes. And now, seven years later, with the price of oil ticking up, they might finally get those other nine.

When Corrine folded her beverage napkin and slid her glass to the edge of the bar, Karla brought another Scotch and Coke. Was it her fifth, sixth? Enough that she hooked her toes around the bar rail when she reached for her drink, enough that Karla set a bowl of cocktail peanuts on the bar in front of her.

One man said, just as plain as day, What we have here are two competing stories, a textbook case of he said, she said.

A second sipped his beer and set it down hard against the bar. I saw that little Mexican gal's picture in the newspaper, he said, and she didn't look fourteen.

Corrine paused on the number she had been tracing with her finger. They were talking about Gloria Ramírez, the girl she and Potter had seen at the Sonic. We watched her climb into that truck, Potter said, and we sat there like somebody had sewn our pants to the seat.

You okay, Mrs. Shepard? Karla was watching her from the other end of the bar, dishrag in one hand, empty mug in the other.

Yes ma'am. Corrine tried to sit up a little straighter, but her toes lost their grip and her elbow slipped off the edge of the bar.

The men looked at her briefly and then decided to ignore her. It was the best thing about being an old lady with thinning hair and boobs saggy enough to prop up on the bar. Finally, she could sit down on a barstool and drink herself blind without some jackass hassling her.

That's how they are, a third man said, they mature faster than other girls. The men laughed. Yes, sir! A *lot* faster, said another.

Corrine felt the heat climbing up her neck and spreading across her face. Potter must have talked about Gloria a dozen times, usually late at night when the pain was so bad he got out of bed and went into the bathroom and she could hear him moaning. All the things he wished he'd done. Could've, would've, should've, she had told him. That's all we needed, you picking a fight with a man half your age.

But Potter insisted that he had known right away something wasn't right. He'd worked alongside young men like that for twenty-five years, and he knew. But they sat there and watched the girl climb into that truck, and then he and Corrine drove home. Two days later, when they saw the man's mug shot in the *American*, Potter said that he was a coward and a sinner. A day after that, when the newspaper published Gloria Ramírez's school picture, he sat in his recliner for a long time looking at her straight black hair and tilted chin, the gaze she directed at the camera, the little smile that might have been a smirk. Corrine said there ought to be a law against putting that girl's name and picture in the local paper—a minor, for God's sake. Potter said she looked like a girl who feared nothing and nobody, and that was probably all gone now.

While Karla eyed the tip jar, Corrine downed her drink in several long, throat-searing gulps. She signaled for another. Karla Sibley was barely seventeen, and she had a new baby at home with her mama. She was still trying to decide whether to cut Corrine off when the old woman pushed her barstool away from the bar, wobbled mightily and tugged at her shirt until it hung straight against her large chest and hips.

Never mind, Karla, she said. I've had enough. She turned to the men. That girl is fourteen years old, you sons of bitches. You gentlemen have a thing for children?

She drove herself home, keeping her eyes on the centerline and Potter's truck ten miles under the speed limit, and it was after three when she finally lay down on the sofa. She pulled an afghan over her legs—she still couldn't sleep in their bed, not without Potter—and though she would struggle to piece it together, at least until the first rush of nicotine hit her bloodstream the next morning, she had fallen asleep replaying what she said to the regulars and the last words she heard before she slammed the heavy door behind her, Karla whining at the men, It's not *my* fault, I didn't bring it up. You can't tell that old lady anything.

Fourteen years old. As if there might have been some moral ambiguity, Corrine thinks bitterly, if Gloria Ramírez had been sixteen, or white. She carries her ashtray to the kitchen table and sits down at the table, where she fiddles with a loose puzzle piece and glares at the envelopes filled with money. Potter had worked on the puzzle for hours, his left hand sometimes shaking so hard he had to prop his elbow on the table and form a brace with his right. All those hours, all that effort, and still he had completed only the border and a couple of brown and gold cats.

When the stray wanders across the patio and sits outside the sliding-glass door, staring at her, Corrine picks up Potter's cane and shakes it at him. She might give the little son of a bitch a pretty good knock on the head, if he doesn't quit coming into her backyard and killing everything.

⌒

In late February, the cat caught a large male grackle and tore it to pieces, and Corrine nearly slipped on the shiny blue-black head when she took out the trash. The next morning they found a warbler—its head a tidy tuft of gray and black, the bright yellow breast a shock of color against the concrete. Potter paused and watched its feathers tremble in the wind. By then, he had begun to stammer sometimes. Cor—, Cor—, Cor—, he would say, and Corrine wanted to clap her hands over her ears and shout, No, no, no, this is a mistake. But it had been a good morning, no seizures, no falls, and when Potter spoke it was the same voice she had been hearing for thirty years.

Well, he said, if you got him fixed and set some food out, he might stop killing things. He might be pretty good company.

Hell, no, Corrine said. I need something else to take care of like Jesus needed another nail.

Wish you wouldn't blaspheme like that, Potter said. But he laughed anyway and they looked out across the yard where the cat was lying under the pecan tree. His weird green eyes were fixed on a small lizard that was running along the cinder-block fence.

It was midmorning and sunlight had turned the fence the color of ash. A small wind ruffled the cat's gold fur. On the other side of the dirt lot behind their house, an ambulance wailed down Eighth Street. Corrine and Potter listened as the sound moved downtown toward the hospital. What in the world are you going to do without me? Potter asked, and when Corrine told him, with no small amount of sorrow, that it had never occurred to her, not once in their marriage, that she would outlive him, Potter nodded gently. It don't seem fair, he said.

Corrine started to correct her husband's grammar—it *doesn't* seem fair—same as she always did, but then she thought about his occasional mistakes, his tuneless whistling, his habit of giving a nickname to every goddamn creature that crossed his path, and she sighed deeply. She would miss the sound of his voice. Not fair, indeed! She nodded at him and turned away before he could see her starting to cry.

Potter touched her arm and hobbled over to the shovel that leaned against the house. You might surprise yourself, he said, after I'm gone.

I doubt that very seriously, she said.

In recent weeks, he had started to bury some of the animals they found in the backyard, when he felt up to it. This time, it took him nearly ten minutes to break through the hard-packed dirt and caliche. Corrine asked if he wanted a hand and he said no, no, he could do it. He dug a foot-deep hole next to the back fence, set the warbler in it, and covered it up. Buried it, Corrine still mutters when she thinks about that bird, like the damned thing mattered. Toward the end, her husband had become more sentimental than usual. Right up until the minute he wasn't, the bastard.

A week later, Potter woke up early and rolled over to face Corrine. He felt good, he said. Like the tumor never happened, almost. He left his cane in the kitchen and went outside to sweep the back patio. He fetched his shears from the garage and trimmed the hedges next to the front porch. After he gathered up the skinny limbs and carried them to the dumpster, he admired his work and Corrine yelled at him for walking around without his cane. If she had been paying attention, she wouldn't have allowed it for a minute. But Potter grabbed her around the waist and nuzzled her neck, saying, baby you smell so good, and she let him pull her into the bedroom for an hour or two.

After, Potter said he wanted a T-bone for supper. He

would grill and they could have a couple of baked potatoes with all the fixins—and butter, not that margarine she had been pushing on him for the last decade. If they took a pecan pie out of the freezer now, he said, it would defrost in time for dessert. After supper, he put on a Ritchie Valens album and danced her around the living room, and so what if it had been years since they had thought to dance with each other? They could do it now, he said. Later, it would occur to Corrine that she should have known, right then and there, what he was up to.

On the table next to his chair in the living room, the newspaper from February 27, the day he died, is folded to the crossword. A single word is penciled in. Four letters, to walk or drive across a shallow place. Ford. On the table next to her chair sits a book of poetry that she has not touched in months, preferring instead to read articles on cancer and healthy eating, even one about a doctor down in Acapulco, an idea that Potter had immediately vetoed. She wanders back into the front hallway and lets her fingers drift across the walnut case of his AM/FM radio, twisting the knobs back and forth. On pretty nights, when the wind was blowing from the north, they would carry it out to the front porch and listen to the country station out of Lubbock. To the day he died, only Corrine, Potter, and the doctors knew about his illness. Any day, they kept promising each other, they would tell Alice and a few people from church, but then Potter went and jumped the gun. Goddamn him.

The doorbell is mounted on the wall directly above the radio, and when it rings, Corrine nearly comes out of her skin. She stands frozen in place, heart pounding, her right hand still on the radio's dial. The bell rings again and then she hears Debra Ann Pierce's peculiar knock, three evenly spaced raps in the center of the door, three staccato knocks on the left side, three on the right, then the child calling, Mrs. Shepard, Mrs. Shepard, Mrs. Shepard, as she does at least once every day.

Corrine opens the door, wedging her large body between the doorjamb and door. She squeezes her thighs together, as if given half a chance the child might try to dart between her legs, like a small dog.

Are you the one who's been calling me all morning, Debra Ann Pierce? Corrine's voice is a rasp and her tongue feels like someone put a coat of paint on it. She turns her head toward her shoulder and coughs.

No, ma'am. Debra Ann is wearing a hot pink T-shirt

that says *Superstar* and a pair of orange terrycloth shorts that barely cover the tops of her thighs. In one hand she holds a horny toad, which she rubs between the eyes with her index finger. Its eyes are closed, and Corrine wonders if this child has been carrying a dead animal around the neighborhood, but then the little creature starts squirming in the girl's hand.

You should let that poor thing go, Corrine says. It's not a pet. Little girl, I had a late night and I'm tired, and my phone has been ringing off the wall this morning.

Where did you go?

That's none of your business. D. A. Pierce, why are you calling my house?

It wasn't me, I swear.

Do not swear, Corrine says and regrets it immediately. What the hell does she care what this child does, as long as she gets off the front porch and leaves Corrine be?

Yes, ma'am. Debra Ann reaches around and pulls her shorts out of her butt crack. She looks across the street and frowns. Are those Mexicans moving *here*?

Maybe, says Corrine. That, also, is none of your business.

Some people ain't going to like that one bit—Mr. Davis, Mrs. Ledbetter, old Mr. Jeffries—

Corrine holds up her hand. You stop that. Those men have as much right to be here as you and me.

They do not, the girl says. This is *our* street.

What do you think Mr. Shepard would think if he heard you talking like that?

The girl looks down at her bare feet and flexes both big toes a few times. She adored Potter, the only adult who never corrected her grammar or undercut her plans, who listened attentively to her tall tales about her imaginary friends Peter and Lily, who flew in from London and regaled D. A. with stories about the London Bridge and the Queen of England. Not once had Potter suggested that she was too old for make-believe friends, never did he tease.

Corrine pats the several pockets of her suit jacket and discovers a box with one cigarette. Well, hot damn. She pulls it out of the box and lights up, blowing the smoke just above the girl's head. Where's your daddy today?

Working in Ozona—Debra Ann pushes out her bottom lip and blows upward so hard her bangs tremble—or Big Lake. The girl turns the horny toad around and holds it close to her face. I'm gonna take you home with me, she whispers ominously and grabs hold of her eyebrow. She yanks several hairs out and flicks them into the hedge next to the porch. There are small bald patches in each brow, Corrine sees now. In the days after Debra Ann's mother left town, Corrine carried food over to Jim while Potter and D. A. sat on the couch and watched cartoons. At Potter's funeral, the girl had leaned over the casket and peered into Potter's face for so long that Corrine wanted to knock her in the head with the flat of her hand and say what the hell do you think you're looking at, little girl?

Debra Ann tries to see if the toad will fit in the pocket of her shorts, but it starts clawing at her hands. I thought you might like some company, she tells Corrine. We could finish Mr. Shepard's puzzle.

I do not care for any company, thank you.

The girl gazes at her, and after a few seconds Corrine sighs. Well, I'm out of cigarettes. Do you want to ride your bike up to 7-Eleven and buy me a pack?

D. A. nods and smiles. She is missing two baby teeth, one canine up top, one canine on the bottom, and the gaps are red and inflamed. The remaining teeth are yellow and dingy, and there are pieces of food, bread maybe, along her gum line. Her black hair is jagged and matted at the ends, as if she started to comb it out and got bored, and Corrine could swear she sees a few nits. Wait here, Corrine says and goes inside to fetch her purse. When she hands the girl a dollar bill, D. A.'s eyes widen with pleasure.

Here's fifty cents for a pack of Benson & Hedges, she says, and fifty cents for your time. Make sure you get the right brand—Ultra Lights.

D. A. shoves the bill into her shorts pocket and asks if Corrine has a shoebox so she can leave the horny toad on the porch. Corrine tells her no, there is a stray running around killing anything it can catch, and the child takes off running across the lawn, the toad clasped in her left hand. When Corrine yells at her not to talk to strangers, D. A. lifts the animal above her head and waggles it in the old woman's direction. Even from a distance, Corrine can see thin streams of blood leaking from both the creature's eyes, its last and most desperate line of defense.

Potter had written his letter on a yellow legal pad he found in Corrine's desk. He had tried hard not to nickel-and-dime the Almighty, he wrote. He had prayed for help only a handful of times that he could remember—when his B-29 lost an engine over Osaka, when Corrine had some trouble with the morphine in the moments after Alice was delivered, when they all had pneumonia in the winter of 1953. In 1968, he prayed for the price of oil to go back up, and he might have prayed to catch a bigger catfish once or twice when they were fishing Lake Spence, but he was mostly joking. And now, Potter wrote, he was counting on the Almighty not to nickel-and-dime him—because he was not willing to ride this train to the end of the line.

He wrote that he would miss their long drives and their camping trips, and the way Corrine moved her feet up and down against his calves at night after they had crawled into the tent because she was always cold and he was always warm. He would miss all the little critters they listened to, as they lay in the tent with their sleeping bags zipped together.

There were some things he regretted. He wished he had gone to college when he came home from the war, even if it had meant accepting help from the government. He wished they had gone to Alaska to see Alice, and he had sent their daughter a letter saying as much. But most of all, he wished he'd done things differently on Valentine's night. All this, from a man who had hardly written so much as a grocery list since he came back from flying bombers over Japan.

He left the letter on the kitchen table, along with several envelopes that contained ten thousand dollars in cash. He had been worrying for weeks that the life insurance company would find some way to cheat Corrine out of the policy, and she correctly guessed this was emergency money he had stashed somewhere. At the bottom of the note, a sentence had been added, scrawled quickly with a red pen. *Make sure Dr. Bauman writes hunting accident on the death certificate.*

Twenty minutes later, when the sheriff's deputy came to the front door, and before Corrine even had a chance to ask where they had found him, the deputy told her there had been an accident, a terrible accident, the kind of accident you never saw coming. It happens more often than you would think, he said.

⌒

When Debra Ann returns fifteen minutes later, her mouth is ringed with chocolate and she is no longer carrying the horny toad. She clutches Corrine's cigarettes in one grubby hand while she explains that her daddy won't be home until eight o'clock, and she thinks there might be some leftover goulash at home, but she isn't sure. Maybe Lily and Peter ate it all. Debra Ann leans toward Corrine and cranes her neck as she tries to see down the hallway, the smell of mildew rising from her hair and clothes. Stomach lurching, Corrine holds out her hand for the cigarettes. She knocks the box against her palm, nods gently while Debra Ann jabbers on about the horny toad, how the clerk at the 7-Eleven made her let him go before she could come into the store, and although she told the animal to stay put in her bicycle basket, of course he was gone when she came back.

They are wild animals that will give you warts, Corrine told her. Get a better pet next time.

I saw Mr. Shepard's cat out there in the alley behind your house.

That is not Mr. Shepard's cat.

Well, he used to feed it.

Oh, he did not.

I know for a fact that Mr. Shepard used to let it sleep in the garage sometimes when it was cold outside.

Oh, bullshit, says Corrine. We didn't even have so much as a sleet storm last winter.

It still got cold, says Debra Ann. He might be good company.

Corrine tells the child that she does not want to feed anything, or water it, or clean up its shit or pull ticks off its ears, or vacuum fleas out of her draperies when it gets into the house. I'll tell you what, D. A., she says, if you can catch that cat, you can take it home with you.

I wish I had a cat that wanted to come live with me, Debra Ann says, but my daddy only wants pets that will live in a box. I wish we had something to eat other than goulash. I wish—but Corrine interrupts and asks if D. A. remembers what Corrine's old daddy himself used to say.

Wish in one hand and poop in the other, see which one gets full faster? she says glumly.

Yes, ma'am, Corrine says as she steps backward into the house and gently pushes the door closed in the child's face.

While the phone rings a dozen times, Corrine fixes herself an iced tea with a smidge of bourbon. When she's sure Debra Ann isn't hanging around the yard, she heads back outside for a porch-sit and a smoke. She will stay low, sitting on the concrete step next to the hedges, where she can see what's going on without anyone noticing her.

At least once a week since Potter died, Suzanne Ledbetter shows up at Corrine's door with a casserole and an invitation to participate in some damned crochet circle or one of those god-awful recipe swaps where each woman makes the recipe and writes down her observations on a 3x5 notecard before passing it along to the next woman, who also makes the recipe and adds her notes to the card. And so it goes. In this way, the women are able to make a good recipe even better, says Suzanne Ledbetter.

Corrine has learned over the years to say no thank you to get-togethers and recipe swaps. Still, by the time she sits down on her front porch with a drink in one hand and an unlit cigarette in the other, she has a freezer full of casseroles. And a head full of bullshit too, she thinks as she lowers her bottom onto the concrete step and scoots over to peer through her scraggly hawthorns. Across the street, two young men are carrying a large television console into a rust-colored brick ranch that is a mirror image of Corrine and Potter's—nine hundred square feet, three bedrooms, one full bath plus a powder room off the dining room. The kitchen window faces the backyard, same as Corrine's, and the same sliding-glass door leads to a back patio, she imagines, though she never knew the previous tenants, three young men who kept a large mutt chained to a dead pecan tree in the front yard and who, mercifully, took the dog with them when they moved out in the middle of the night.

A white sedan pulls up, and a young girl and her mother start taking several small boxes from the back seat. The woman is heavily pregnant, swollen as a deer carcass on a hot road, and there is no sign of a mister. When the car is empty, the woman stands in the front yard while the child hops around the dead tree. She is the spitting image of her mama—white-haired and round-faced—and from time to time she walks over and hangs on the woman's maternity smock as if one or the other of them might lift off the ground and drift across the sky, should she let go.

The woman—she looks too young to have a girl that big—rubs her daughter's back while they watch three young men carry furniture and boxes up the driveway, through the open garage, and into the house. They are still boys, Corrine sees now, no more than fifteen or sixteen years old, with sneakers, crew cuts, and cowboy hats in varied shades of brown perched on their heads. Two middle-aged men, wearing the same brown steel-toed boots that Potter used to lace up before he headed out to the plant in the mornings, stand by the front door measuring and re-measuring the doorframe against a massive mahogany door that is leaning against the house like a drunk. Corrine swirls her pinkie in her drink and looks at the pregnant woman with amusement. The front door that's already there wasn't good enough for her? Well! She sucks the liquor off her finger.

One of the men holds up his hands in the shape of a door, showing how wide, how tall, and the woman shakes her head. One hand moves to her forehead, the other to her belly, and then, as the man points again at the doorframe, her upper body drifts toward the door, a boat listing ever so slightly, then sinking fast as she folds in half. A cry rises up from the men. Corrine sets down her drink and smacks her lips. By the time she has hauled herself to her feet and pulled on her slippers, the woman is on her hands and knees in the front yard, her belly skimming the dirt. The child hovers anxiously around her mother's head. Words in both Spanish and English fly around the yard like sparrows. A man runs into the kitchen and returns with a plastic cup filled with water.

Corrine introduces herself and points at her house across the street while the girl, Aimee, plucks at her mother's maternity blouse. She is a jowly child with eyebrows and eyelashes so pale they are nearly invisible. The mother, Mary Rose, gasps as her blouse rises and falls with a contraction, and Corrine thinks she might have seen her back at the high school, just another girl who dropped out and got married. It's impossible to remember them all.

Corrine tries and fails to remember a single useful detail from the hazy twilight sleep of her labor with Alice, some thirty years ago. Can I drive you to the hospital?

No, thank you. I can drive myself. Mary Rose

presses both hands against her belly while she looks up at Corrine. I saw the wreath on your front door. I'm sorry for your loss.

My husband died in February. I just haven't taken it down. Corrine narrows her eyes and looks at the men and boys who stand quietly in a row, shifting back and forth on their feet, eyeing the rancher's wife who has gone into labor in the middle of their weekend job, whose husband is well known to them and theirs.

It was a hunting accident, Corrine says. She might as well have swallowed a shovelful of scorpions, the way those words tear at her throat, poisonous, claws out.

A hunting accident. Mary Rose rolls over and sits up, and Corrine is surprised to see tears in the woman's eyes. I am *so* sorry. Listen, we're still waiting for them to turn on the electricity and I don't want my daughter sitting around the waiting room by herself. Would you mind if she came to your house for a few hours, just until my husband returns from a livestock auction in Big Springs?

No, ma'am, Corrine says without hesitation. I cannot have anybody in my house right now, sorry. Can I call your mother, or maybe a sister?

No, thank you, Mary Rose says. They've got their hands full already.

I want to stay with you, the child whines at her mother. I don't even know her.

I'd be happy to drive you to the hospital and wait with—Corrine pauses while the child glares at her and clutches her mother's smock—Aimee.

I don't want her in a waiting room with a bunch of strange men, Mary Rose says.

The women look at each other for a few seconds, the younger woman's lips a tight seam. She pulls herself to her feet and tells her daughter to run and fetch her car keys, and the little ditty bag she has set in the hall closet. After Aimee scampers into the house through the open garage, Mary Rose asks the foreman to lock up behind them when they have emptied the moving van, and when Corrine starts back toward her own front porch, already longing for the rest of that bourbon and iced tea, hoping that cat didn't stick its nose in her glass and lick the ice, Mary Rose yells at her, too. Thanks for nothing, she says, but Corrine pretends not to hear. She keeps walking and when she is safely across the street, she dumps her drink in the hedge and goes inside to fix herself a fresh one.

⌒

It's not quite dark outside when the phone rings again. Corrine, who is well into that bottle of bourbon, rushes to the kitchen and grabs the phone with both hands.

Every goddamn thing in this house buzzes, rattles, or rings. She wraps the cord around the phone's base and props open the door between the kitchen and garage with her foot. The loose skin on her arms wobbles madly when she lifts the phone over her head. The phone soars into the garage, strikes the concrete and rings twice when it lands next to the Lincoln Continental that she has forsaken in the forty days since Potter chose to remove himself from what he had once described as his situation. It was *our* situation, goddamn you.

The kitchen is quiet now, save for the ticking of the wall clock next to the kitchen table. Corrine narrows her eyes at it, considering. Empty liquor bottles lie atop the full trash can, along with a stack of unopened doctor's bills. She picks up a full ashtray and slowly dumps it on the envelopes in the center of the table. Cigarette butts roll slowly across the pile and fall onto the puzzle pieces. The icemaker dumps a batch of ice cubes. Outside the sliding-glass door, the western sky is the color of an old bruise. A mockingbird perches on the back fence, its voice persistent and sad.

Fetching up the trash can and stepping outside, Corrine jerks the sliding door closed with such force that Potter's cane clatters to the linoleum and rolls in front of it. The thin sole of her house slipper gives way when it presses against a soft body and she cries out, jumping backward and looking down to see a small brown mouse. She closes her eyes and sees Potter standing by the back fence, sees him struggling with the shovel while he digs the hole, sees him set the animal gently inside.

She wishes she could do that, bury a little creature, act as if it matters. But the ground is hard and her arms are flabby, and she has to stop and catch her wind when she carries groceries in from the truck. She isn't nearly as good as Potter, never has been. She grabs a shovel out of the garage anyway and slips the blade under the soft, small body. Nearly choking with rage, she carries the mouse into the alley and flings it into the open dumpster. They could have talked about it, how and when he would die. Potter said he wouldn't have her taking care of him, and she had promised she wouldn't ask him to hang on until he was unrecognizable to himself, or her. But in the end, he had chosen to go it alone.

The plant whistle blows, the longer, more plaintive wail that signals an accident, and she stands for a few seconds with her hand on the steel dumpster. She has spent a lifetime listening to that whistle and wondering what happened. But these particular fears, that her husband might be lying facedown in a puddle of benzene, that he was working in the area where the explosion occurred, that he didn't move quickly enough, these worries are now the province of Suzanne Ledbetter and a thousand other women in town. Not Corrine's. In the field behind her house, the cat stays low, its green eyes steady and vacant, as it watches a yellow rat snake race down the dry flood canal where D. A. Pierce and the other little girls on the street used to ride their bikes, ditching them to sunbathe on the steep concrete slopes, before the city got wise and put up a chain-link fence.

Beyond the canal, the 7-Eleven and A&W Root Beer share a parking lot with the bookmobile, a thirty-foot trailer with perilously unstable metal bookcases and shag carpeting that smells like mildew. Six months earlier, an industrial-sized Quonset hut was built on the lot, a windowless steel building called the Bunny Club—a strip club sharing a parking lot with the mobile library—and it is a damned miracle, Corrine thinks, that any girl in Odessa makes it out alive. For twenty years she watched these local girls at the high school, most of them aspiring to little more than graduating before some boy knocked them up. On any given Monday morning, she might walk into her classroom and listen to sad, vicious rumors about the hospital or jail, or the unwed mothers' home in Lubbock. She attended more shotgun weddings than she could shake a stick at, and she still runs into those same young women at the grocery store, older now, but still clutching pale and round babies to their chests, still shifting them from one skinny, freckled arm to another while they scream at older kids who dart up and down the aisles like manic squirrels.

Corrine is still standing in the alley when a truck speeds up the main drag and turns into the lot. Its wheels spin and squeal as the driver turns doughnuts in the parking lot. Several men are standing in the truck's bed, shouting and roughhousing and hanging on for dear life. One of the men throws a bottle at the flood canal, and the glass shatters when it strikes the concrete. When another of them falls from the back of the truck and hits the pavement with a cry, the others laugh and holler. He stumbles after the truck, hands outstretched, and when he draws close to his friends, the truck stops abruptly. He has his hands on the tailgate when somebody tosses two bags onto the pavement and the driver hits the accelerator.

The truck circles around a third time as a man leans over the side of the truck bed with a piece of steel pipe in his hand. The truck speeds up and he leans out a little farther, one hand holding on to the truck's roll bar, the other waving the pipe back and forth. Corrine opens her mouth to yell *Stop*, just as the man who stands in the lot lifts his hands over his head as if to say, I give up. The pipe catches him square in the back, and he falls to the pavement like an egg knocked from its nest.

Lord, have mercy, Corrine yells and runs for the house. She is moving fast, praying there will be a dial tone when she plugs the phone back into the wall when her foot catches on Potter's cane and she pitches forward, landing facedown on the kitchen table. Puzzle pieces fly through the air like brown bats rising from an old water tank, and as Corrine settles onto the kitchen floor, she is aware of the clock ticking on the wall. She is also aware of her face and hands, her knees and shoulders, all shot through with a pain so sudden and big that it might as well be everything in the world.

When they were younger, Potter used to joke that Corrine would go out with a bang. There would be a holdup while she was standing in line at the bank and she would refuse to hand over her purse. Or she would flip the bird at some good old boy who was having a worse day than her, or maybe blow a tire while she was driving too fast on the loop. Maybe her seniors would beat her to death with their copies of *Beowulf*, or they would sneak out during a pep rally and cut her brake lines after a particularly brutal pop quiz. But nope. Here she is, sprawled out on the kitchen floor like an old heifer, boobs and belly in the kitchen, feet and ass still on the patio.

If things had worked the way they ought to have, Potter would have buried her. He would grieve, of course he would, but he also would have gone on living—playing cards down at the VFW, driving out to the plant to say hello, puttering around the garage or the backyard. He would have put together his god-damned puzzles and listened to Debra Ann talk about childish things—the imaginary friends she was too old for, how many bottle caps she found in the alley, missing her mama and wondering when she was coming home. He would never tire of listening to that child, and even if he did, he wouldn't say so. If Potter were here, D. A. Pierce and the little girl from across the street, Aimee, would be sitting at the kitchen table with two bowls of Blue Bell ice cream, and that damned cat would dine nightly in the garage, probably on cans of tuna fish. But here Corrine is, and what the hell she will do next, she cannot even begin to imagine.

Tomorrow morning, she will survey the damage—a small cut above her left eyebrow and a goose egg on her right temple, a bruise the size of a grapefruit on her forearm. Her hip will be out of whack for weeks, and she will use Potter's cane to get around, but only in the house or the backyard, where no one can see her. In the front yard when she waters the tree, and in the grocery store where she picks up a few items for Mary Rose and delivers them, along with one of Suzanne Ledbetter's casseroles that she digs out of the deep freezer in the garage, Corrine will stand up straight and grit her teeth and act as if nothing hurts. When the phone rings, she will answer, and when she hears Karla's voice on the line, she'll ask how she can help.

And what of Potter's puzzle pieces that flew across the linoleum, several of them skittering so far beneath the icebox and stove that there will be no retrieving them? In a few weeks, when Corrine starts packing up his things for the Salvation Army, she will scribble a note for whoever might get the puzzle next, a little warning that some of the pieces might be missing. Because as Potter has told her a hundred times, there is nothing in this world worse than working that hard, for that long, only to discover that you never had all the pieces to begin with.

Tonight, she rises up from the kitchen floor and plugs the phone in. She calls the police station downtown and tells them that she didn't see a license plate or notice the color of the truck, and she can't really describe the men, other than to say that they were drunk, and white, and sounded like they were still boys.

The man is long gone when she returns to the alley. Everything hurts. But it's a pretty night with lots of stars and Mars glowing in the southern sky. There's a light wind blowing from the north. If she carries the radio out to the front porch and sets it on the window-sill, she might get the radio station in Lubbock. They've been playing a lot of Bob Wills since he died, and it will be good company.

She is still sitting out there when a truck pulls into the driveway across the street and a man who must be Mary Rose's husband steps out. He hurries around to the passenger side, where he picks up his sleeping child. And now Corrine is struggling to her feet, moving as fast as her bruised old body can carry her. She has a knot on her forehead the size of a silver dollar, and there's not enough Chanel No. 5 in the world to cover up the stink of cigarettes and booze, but she hurries toward the man who shifts his daughter from one hip to the other and grabs a flashlight off the dashboard before starting toward the house, its uncovered windows gazing emptily across the front yard and street, still waiting for somebody to turn on the lights.

Wait, she shouts. Wait! The little girl's hair glows

white under the streetlight and Corrine crooks a finger around her bare foot as it swings next to her daddy's knee. When the young man tries to step around her, Corrine gently touches his arm. Is the baby all right? How's Mary Rose? She is breathing hard and holding the stitch in her side. Listen, she gasps, tell your wife if she needs anything, anything at all, she can count on me. All she has to do is ask, and I will be right there.

Debra Ann

On a different Saturday afternoon, in a different year, she might never have seen the man. She might have been playing H-O-R-S-E at the prairie dog park or hanging around the practice field at Sam Houston Elementary, or riding her bike to the buffalo wallow to look for trilobites and arrowheads in the dry lakebed. Back when it was full of water, Debra Ann and her mama sometimes drove out there to watch people get saved. It's something to do, Ginny always said, as she spread an old bath towel on the hood of the car, and Debra Ann climbed up, careful not to let her legs touch the hot metal. They would lean against the windshield, passing a bag of chips back and forth while the saints stood on the bank singing *are you washed in the blood of the lamb* and the sinners waded in barefoot, stepping right through the pond scum, faith alone keeping them safe from water moccasins and broken glass. And if a preacher smiled and waved them over, Ginny would shake her head and wave back. You're fine the way you are, she told Debra Ann, but if you feel someday like you've just got to be saved, do it in a church. At least you won't get tetanus. When they were bored, Ginny packed up the car and they drove back into town for a Whataburger. Where will we go next? she'd ask her daughter. You want to drive out and see the graves at Penwell? You want to go to Monahans and walk on the sand hills? Shall we drive over to the cattle auction in Andrews and pretend we're going to bid on a bull?

But this spring, Ginny's not here, and everybody is talking about the girl who was kidnapped and attacked. She was raped—the adults think D. A. doesn't understand, but she's no dummy—and now the parents on Larkspur Lane, including her daddy, have agreed that no child is to leave the block without adult supervision, or at least without telling somebody where they're going. It's insulting. She hasn't been supervised since she was eight years old, and she's spent most of the spring ignoring the rules, even after her daddy sat at the kitchen table and drew a map for her.

The northern edge of the approved roaming zone is Custer Avenue, and the empty house on the curve marks the southern border. The western border is the alley behind Mrs. Shepard's and Debra Ann's houses, where Mrs. Shepard stands and frowns at the trucks coming and going from the Bunny Club. It's a titty bar, D. A. knows this too. At the other end of the block, where Casey Nunally and Lauralee Ledbetter live, Mrs. Ledbetter keeps a close eye on everything and everyone. She thinks nothing of grabbing a kid's handlebars and firing off a series of probing questions. Where are you going? What are you doing? When was the last time you bathed? The other girls are two years younger than Debra Ann, still too young to break any rules, she guesses, or maybe they're just afraid of their mamas.

She finds the man the same way she finds most of her treasures. She looks. She rides up and down the alley behind Mrs. Shepard's house, steering around beer cans, carpenter's nails, and beer bottles with ragged edges. She dodges rocks big enough to send a girl flying over her handlebars and headfirst into the side of a steel dumpster or cinder-block fence. She keeps her eyes peeled for loose change, unexploded firecrackers, and locust shells, swerving hard when she sees a snake, just in case it's a baby diamondback. She catches horny toads by the dozens, cradling them in her palm and gently rubbing the hard ridges between their eyes. When they fall asleep, she gently slips them into the mason jar she keeps in her bicycle basket.

In the alley behind Mrs. Shepard's house, she balances on her bike pedals and looks across the field. Everything that lies before her is off-limits—the dried-out flood channel, the barbed-wire fence and dirt lot, the house on the curve that has sat empty since the Wallace boy was killed when a radio fell into the bathtub with him in it, and finally, the flood channel where the canal narrows and disappears into two steel pipes wide enough that Debra Ann can stand up in them. Beyond all that forbidden territory is the strip bar, which opens every day at 4:30. She has been spanked only a few times in her life, and never very hard, but when her daddy got a call from Mrs. Ledbetter in March that she'd seen his daughter riding her bike back and forth in front of the building, trying to peek inside the front door every time some man walked in or out, his face turned white and he smacked her so hard her bottom hurt for the rest of the day.

D. A. rides along the flood channel, and when she is just a few feet from the sharp curve by the empty house, she ditches her bike, climbs onto a metal milk crate, and peers over the cinder-block fence before crawling up and straddling it for a few seconds. When she jumps into the backyard she hits the ground hard, first with a grunt and then with a cry as her knee strikes the hard-packed dirt. At the last second, she rolls and manages to avoid a small pile of caliche that would surely have landed her sobbing on Mrs. Shepard's porch while the old woman fetched her rubbing alcohol and a pair of tweezers.

Three Chinese elm saplings stand dead in the center of the yard, and a bunch of two-by-fours, bleached nearly white by the sun, lean against the back of the house. Several tumbleweeds rest against the sliding-glass door as if they knocked for a long time, and finally gave up. In the top corner of the glass, a small sticker warns: *Forget the dog. This house is protected by Smith & Wesson.* Last July, when all the girls still roamed free, she and Casey and Lauralee had sneaked into this same yard to set off a box of M-80s they found under the bleachers at school.

Every house on Larkspur Lane is more or less the same, and at this house, as at Debra Ann's, two small bedroom windows look out across the backyard. The windows are stripped of any curtains or blinds and they gaze nakedly across the grass, indecent and sad, like the small dark eyes of Mr. Bonham, who lives one block over and sits on his front porch all day threatening people if they let so much as one bicycle wheel touch his damn lawn. The sun's glare makes it impossible to see into the house, but it doesn't take much to imagine that electrocuted boy watching from the other side of the glass, his hair still standing on end. It's enough to give you the shivers, said Lauralee when they were last here.

D. A. is hungry and needs to pee, but she wants to take a closer look at the empty field that lies between the alley and the flood channel. Thankfully, the construction-paper fortune-teller she keeps in her basket agrees. *Do Not Hesitate!* When she asks a second time, just to make sure, snugging her index fingers and thumbs into the four slots and counting to three, the fortune-teller is clear. *Yes!* Sometimes she asks the fortune-teller questions whose answers she already knows, just to verify that it's the real deal.

Am I taller than an oil derrick? *No.*

Will Ford win the election? *Not Likely.*

Will my daddy ever order anything but strawberry ice cream at Baskin-Robbins? *No.*

From this end of the alley, Debra Ann can see a narrow sliver of the gentlemen's club on the other side of the flood channel. It is mostly empty this time of the day, so only a few pickups and winch trucks are spread out across the parking lot. Two men, one tall and one very short, are standing next to a flatbed truck. The tall one rests his foot on the truck's bumper while they talk and pass a liquor bottle back and forth. When the bottle is empty, he steps back into the club while the short one tosses the bottle into the steel dumpster. After a quick look around, he hops the fence and moves quickly across the field, running sideways down the flood channel's concrete berm and disappearing into the largest of the drainage pipes.

D. A. drags an old Maytag box into the middle of the field and uses a box cutter she found in Mrs. Shepard's garage to carve out a window just a little bigger than the distance between her forehead and her nose. She climbs into the box and waits. A few minutes later, the man pokes his head out of the drainpipe. He looks left and then right, then left again, like a prairie dog checking for a king snake before it leaves the burrow, then crawls out of the pipe, headfirst, as if he is being born into the day. When he stands up straight and stretches, D. A. claps her hand over her mouth to keep from laughing. Never has she seen such a little man. He is short and skinny and sorrowful as a scarecrow, with wrist bones like bird skeletons, and he can't weigh more than a hundred pounds dripping wet. If not for the stubble on his chin, he might just be an older kid.

At the end of the flood channel, he crouches and looks both ways up and down the canal, then leans forward and runs up the steep embankment. Once he reaches the top, he walks quickly along the fence until he comes to a place where the barbed wire lies flat. Debra Ann knows this spot. She hops it all the time, a shortcut to the bookmobile or 7-Eleven.

He stops at the dumpster behind the club to take a piss. After he buttons his pants and knocks on the back door of the gentlemen's club until it swings open, Debra Ann squirms her shoulders and hips and slides awkwardly out of the box. She brushes the dust from her T-shirt and then rears back and pitches a rock. It travels halfway across the field and lands with a solid enough thud to raise some dust. She can't figure out why the man is living down there unless there's something wrong with him. Her daddy says you'd have to be half stupid, half crazy, or half dead not to find work in Odessa right now. Everybody's hiring. Maybe the man is all three—stupid, crazy, sick—but whatever his story, he poses no danger to her. She feels it down deep in her soul, feels *convicted* in the same way she believes that nothing bad can happen as long as she steps between cracks in the sidewalk and eats her veggies and doesn't talk to any men she does not already know. D. A.'s confidence has been shaken this spring by Ginny's leaving, and it is a relief to study this man and *know*: he will not hurt her.

She spits in the dirt and picks out her next rock. This one lands in a small thicket of mesquite trees next to the spot where the land begins to curve toward the flood channel. I'm going to get one over the canal before summer is over, she says out loud.

ᔓ

Every day for a week, she rushes home from school to watch him. The first three afternoons she gathers information—What time does he leave? Is it always the same? Does he always go to the titty bar? Then she waits for her chance to get a closer look.

It is nearly five o'clock and the sun beats like a fist against the top of her head. Her mouth and throat are so parched that they ache. The heat presses against her chest and stifles her breath, and because she sweated through her T-shirt an hour ago, she doesn't have any sweat left to cool her off. When she pulls the fortune-teller from the pocket of her shorts, it is dry and brittle against her hands. Should I check out his camp? *Yes.* Should I check out his camp? *Do not hesitate!*

The drainpipe is tall enough that she only has to bend a little when she steps in and sees a trash bag with dirty underwear and socks hanging out of it. Next to the bag, a small stack of pants and shirts lies neatly folded. A pair of boots sits next to a wire milk crate that has been turned upside down to make a small table, upon which rests a ceramic bowl and razor, along with two manila envelopes. One has the words *PFC Belden, Discharge* written on it in black marker. *Medical* is written on the other.

Ten feet in, the man has constructed a wall to close off the rest of the pipe, which carries water all the way to a field outside town when it floods. These days, that means never. The last time this channel flooded, D. A. still had training wheels on her bike. On closer examination, she recognizes an old appliance box from the previous summer, one the girls had abandoned after it was battered by a dust storm. Lauralee's awkward, loping cursive is still clear on the side—the word *Hideout* with a large smiley face and two hearts with arrows through their centers.

A backpack and neatly rolled sleeping bag are stacked against the cardboard wall. Debra Ann walks to the man's table and gently runs her finger across a crack in his shaving bowl. She picks up his razor and his small black hair comb, turning them over in her hands while she looks again at the envelope with his discharge papers. He's probably a hero, she decides. He was probably injured in the war. Ever since her mama left town, D. A. has been looking for something to do with her weekends. She's been looking for a project, and this man might be it. Maybe he is there to help her become a better girl, not the kind who drives her mother so crazy she feels like she has to leave town without telling anybody where she's going, or how long she'll be gone. Will Ginny be home before the fireworks show on the Fourth of July? *Yes.*

∾

She leaves his first gift in a brown paper bag at the mouth of the drainage pipe and scampers back to her box to wait and see what will happen next. The man opens the bag carefully, as if he expects it to be filled with tarantulas, or at least a couple of cow patties. When he instead pulls out a can of creamed corn, a package of gum, and a brown crayon with a dull tip, he smiles and looks around. There is a note too, folded in half, the edges sticky and stained with candy, and Debra Ann can see his lips moving as he reads it. *Don't worry, we'll take care of you. Write down what you need & put it under the big rock next to the fence. Don't tell anybody. D. A. Pierce.*

She watches him sharpen the brown crayon with his pocketknife, and later, when he knocks on the back door of the bar and steps inside, she runs down the concrete embankment to fetch the note. It reads *Blankit cookpot can opener matches, thx & bless you, Jesse Belden, PFC, U.S. Army.*

On the Monday after Easter, she brings everything he needs in a paper sack from Piggly Wiggly. In it, she has packed two hard-boiled eggs, a piece of corn bread wrapped in foil, a slice of ham, and a half-thawed casserole with most of Mrs. Shepard's name picked off the label. COR is all that's left, and that's not enough for the man to trace it back to anybody in particular. She also brings him two ripe tomatoes, and a handful of chocolate bunnies from the Easter basket her daddy left on the kitchen table.

While he reads the note, she watches with joy from her spot in the field, her lips moving along with his. *Happy Easter, Jesse Belden, PFC, U.S. Army, you are a great American. Do you like okra and pinto beans? Sincerely, D. A. Pierce.*

At the beginning of May, three weeks since she first saw him, D. A. waits until he goes into the pipe and then climbs down into the drainage ditch with a bag of food and two cans of Dr Pepper. She shines her flashlight into the pipe. Are you in here? Her voice drifts through the dark. I won't tell anybody you're here. Do you need help?

Later, when they know each other a little better,

Jesse Belden will explain that he had been resting on the bare concrete because it was cooler, counting his money and thinking about how to get his truck back from Boomer, the cousin who says that Jesse owes him two months' rent and groceries. Jesse will tell her that he had been lying with his good ear to the ground—the world is so much quieter that way—and that's why D. A. was practically standing on him before they saw each other.

Well, didn't we scare the living daylights out of each other? Jesse says.

I nearly pissed myself. She watches him carefully, waiting for him to scold her for cussing, which he does not do. Jesse might be a grown man, but he sure doesn't act like it. He might be a little stupid, she thinks, and he is surely ignorant of the ways people talk to kids. He tells her that his eyes had been dry as the dust he sleeps on every night, dry as the half-dead snake that old tomcat drug up one morning and laid at the opening of the flood pipe, but they still managed to fill with water when Debra Ann shined her flashlight in his face and asked, What do you need? And Jesse, who had not said anything more than yes sir or no sir for days, whose ribs were still sore from the blow to his back when he was standing in the parking lot, practically begging his cousin to stop the truck, Jesse said, I want to go home.

She doesn't tell him that she has been watching him for weeks. She says, Yes sir, and promises she will always sit on his right side, where her words will be as clear to Jesse as the cold streams he tells her about, back home in eastern Tennessee, where he used to live with his mama and his sister Nadine.

⌒

He is twenty-two years old and she is ten, and they are skinny as ocotillo branches. They both have a small scar on their right ankle, his from a bad infection he got in Southeast Asia, hers from a firecracker that exploded before she could sprint away from it. They eat baloney sandwiches and watch the cat chase sunflower shells they spit on the concrete. They talk about getting a collar for the cat, so if he gets lost somebody can call Debra Ann's house and tell her to come get him.

She brings chocolate bars that melt in her pocket and they lick the warm liquid directly off the foil wrapper. When she asks him why he works at a strip bar, the back of his neck turns scarlet and he looks at his feet. Without his truck, he can't get to his job in the oil patch. They only let me mop the floors and take out the trash, he says, but I used to work with my cousin mucking saltwater tanks.

He doesn't tell her that he came to Texas because there aren't any jobs in Tennessee and Boomer swore he was making money hand over fist. Nor does he tell her about a two-week stop at the VA hospital in Big Springs where he slept in a good bed and ate some pretty good food, and talked to a doctor who eventually walked Jesse out to his truck and handed him an envelope and said, You are twenty-two years old, son, and lucky you came home in one piece. There isn't one thing wrong with you that some hard work won't fix. He doesn't tell D. A. that he felt the weight and shape of the man's class ring against his T-shirt. How far is it to Odessa, Jesse asked him, and the doctor pointed west. Sixty miles and be sure to lock up your truck at night, he said, and Jesse wished the man could be his father.

D. A. tells him that she went looking for the cat yesterday and saw Mrs. Shepard's Lincoln parked in her driveway, which was strange because Mrs. Shepard only drives her dead husband's truck now. There was no answer when she knocked on the front door, and Debra Ann guessed she was taking a nap, but then she tugged open the garage door to see what she could find in the deep freezer and found Mrs. Shepard sitting in Mr. Potter's old truck with the motor running. How come you're out here? D. A. asked, and Corrine sat for a few more seconds without moving, then sighed and said Jesus Christ and turned off the motor. How come *you're* out here?

I'm looking for a sharp knife.

Corrine pointed to a workbench covered with gardening tools and dust. Bring it back when you're done, she said. Don't run with it in your hands.

Have you seen the cat?

No, I have not seen that goddamned cat. Now will you please get out of my garage?

Jesse and Debra Ann chew blades of St. Augustine that she pulled out of Mrs. Ledbetter's lawn and saved in plastic bags. They drink a gallon of orange juice that one of the bartenders gave Jesse. They play poker with a deck of cards she pilfered from Mrs. Shepard's kitchen drawer. He shows her a small leather bag filled with agates he found near the Clinch River, which is so close to his family's hollow that you can hit it with a rock. Pick out your two favorites, he says. They're good luck.

Before the war, he tells her, his hearing was so good that his uncle used to brag that Jesse could hear a doe swat a horsefly off her ass from a hundred yards away. He could hear a tick let go of a dog's ear, and a catfish farting from the bottom of a swimming hole. He doesn't tell her that when he came home after three years overseas, he walked a little ways into the woods and stood real still, waiting. And when the sounds finally came—a branch striking the dirt after the wind had shaken it loose from the tree, a whitetail tearing up the woods, a rifle report from the other side of the hollow—he couldn't tell if he was really hearing those sounds, or just remembering them. Thrum of cicadas, frogs belching by the creek, two crows fighting off a blue jay trying to steal their eggs, buzz of mosquitoes and yellow jackets, the splash a rainbow trout made when Jesse pulled it from the river—maybe he heard all these noises when he came home from the war, maybe he just wished he did.

D. A. tells him she always checks the toilet bowl before she sits down because she has heard stories about water moccasins climbing up through the sewer pipes and curling themselves around the rim. There was a girl in Stanton who sat down in the middle of the night to pee, and a four-foot-long water moccasin crawled up and bit her right on the cooter.

The cooter? Jesse starts laughing his ass off. Yeah. D. A. laughs. She swole up like a deer tick. She takes a deep breath and fills her round cheeks with air, then reaches over and flips the cat onto its back, feeling around in its fur. When she finds a lump, she pulls out a fat gray tick, fully engorged and big as her thumbnail. Like this, she says and squeezes it with her fingernail until it pops and blood spurts all over her fingers.

She tells him that she has consulted her fortune-teller and her mother will be home in time for the Fourth of July fireworks show. Next time she comes, she will bring it with, so he can ask some questions of his own. Will he get his truck back from Boomer? Will he be home in time to fish the Clinch River before it gets too cold and the fish stop biting? She tells him that she visits the bookmobile so often the two old ladies who work there, unmarried sisters from Austin, have threatened to put her on the payroll. They let her check out as many books as she wants, and some mornings, she is already sitting on the rickety metal stairs when the sisters pull up in their Buick. Sometimes, Debra Ann says, one of the sisters tosses her the keys to the trailer and lets her unlock the front door, and then Debra Ann lies on the wet-dog-smelling carpet in front of the swamp cooler and reads all day long.

Every book has at least one good thing, she tells Jesse, because she's pretty sure he can't read, not really. Love stories and bad news and evil masterminds, plots as thick as sludge, places and people she wishes she could know in real life, and words whose loveliness and music make her want to cry when she says them aloud.

She stands up and wipes the tick's blood on her shorts, stretches her arms over her head and recites some of the most beautiful words she ever read. *The crickets felt it was their duty to warn everybody that summertime cannot last forever. Even on the most beautiful days in the whole year—the days when summer is changing into autumn—the crickets spread the rumor of sadness and change.* Now see here, she tells Jesse, I can't even imagine a place where there is autumn, but I guess I can understand sadness and change as good as anybody else. Me too, he says.

⌒

When school lets out in late May, she visits him every day, at least for an hour before he goes to work at 4:30. While the cat naps on Jesse's army pack, they sit next to each other on two milk crates D. A. found next to the dumpster behind 7-Eleven. The front porch, Jesse calls it, and she says it's a pretty good porch, but she is already hatching a plan to invite him over for lunch one day when Mrs. Ledbetter is out running errands. She wants to show him a real porch, let him sit down in a real chair at a real kitchen table, so he can see what is possible.

She brings two forks and it takes them less than five minutes to eat the casserole she stole from Mrs Shepard. Even the frozen parts are good, he says. They taste like something a person made with care and love. When they finish eating, she sets a piece of notebook paper on the cardboard box between them. She hands him a pencil, momentarily embarrassed when she notices the metal band at the bottom of the pencil is covered with small bite marks. Write down everything you need, she says. I'll bring it if I can.

Could you write it? He hands the paper and pencil back to her. I'm tired.

He could use an old bedsheet. It's already too hot out for the blanket she brought him last month. He loved those cigarettes she brought, even if he won't smoke them in front of her. Some more of them would be nice, and maybe some more of that corn bread, if she can get it, and those pinto beans and chow-chow.

You wash a meal like that down with a cup of buttermilk, he says, and you're standing in tall cotton.

What's the best meal you ever had? she asks.

Pot roast and potatoes, probably. Maybe the steak they gave me at the base the night I came home from overseas.

Favorite snack?

Chocolate-chip cookies that my mama makes from scratch.

Me too, she says, and they fall quiet for a little while. She stares at his face as if trying to memorize it. I'm going to bring you a toothbrush, she says, and Jesse laughs. The only person who ever gave a tinker's damn about whether or not he brushed his teeth had been his sergeant, and he rode Jesse's ass all the time. Now he's back home in some place called Kalamazoo. That sounds like a made-up place, D. A. says, and Jesse tells her that he used to think so too, but then he looked at an atlas and there it was, barely an inch from Canada.

When the plant whistles at quitting time, Jesse says he has to go to work soon, but he could use a flea collar for the cat if she can get one, and a few more cans of tuna fish. Another jug of water, maybe some bug spray. She writes it all down for him, and when she spots a scorpion coming out of the pipe where he puts his trash, Jesse walks over and stomps it with his boot. D. A. looks down at her thin plastic sandals, the pale-pink nail polish she let Casey put on for her, and she imagines the scorpion scuttling over the lip of her sandal, the tail rising to deliver the hot, agonizing sting. She thinks how nice it is when somebody saves you from something, even if you don't need to be saved.

꙳

She can ride her bike the entire length of Larkspur Lane, even around the curve, without touching her handlebars, not even once. She can turn twenty-six cartwheels in less than a minute and hang upside down on the monkey bars until she nearly passes out. She can stand on her hands for thirty seconds, on her head for one minute, and on one foot for ten. These, she demonstrates on the hot concrete at the bottom of the flood canal. She can slip a candy bar into her pocket at 7-Eleven, smuggle a casserole out of Mrs. Shepard's house in her backpack, and, if her T-shirt is baggy enough, listen to a lecture from Mrs. Ledbetter with a can of chili tucked in the waistband of her shorts.

In a different year, a normal one, she might feel guilty about stealing. But since Ginny left, Debra Ann has thought about what it means to live an upright life. She keeps the kitchen clean and makes sure her daddy gets some rest on Sundays. She checks on Mrs. Shepard and plays with Peter and Lily—she knows they're imaginary, and she does not care, they have pointed ears and wings that shine in the sunlight, and they fly in from London when she is having a bad day, when she can't stop picking at her eyebrows and wondering where her mama is, and why the hell she left in the first place. D. A. has given a lot of thought to the matter of petty theft, parsing her lessons from a week of vacation Bible school last summer, and she knows: Stealing is better than letting a man go without food and company.

When Jesse leaves for work every afternoon, she rides her bike over to Casey or Lauralee's house on the off chance they might be home. She rides home and sits cross-legged on the floor in the garage so she can rifle through Ginny's old cedar chest. She tries to listen to the Joni Mitchell album she found in the kitchen trash can, but it reminds her of driving all over West Texas with Ginny, killing time and seeing what there was to see. She reads an article in *Life* about the bicentennial celebration in Washington. She eats a piece of buttered bread with sugar, carefully wiping up the sugar she spilled on the counter. That done, she walks over to Mrs. Shepard's house with a can of Dr Pepper and bag of chips, and when she sees that Mr. Shepard's truck is gone, she crawls into the hawthorn hedge and lies down in the gently stippled shade, and thinks about Ginny until her cheeks and chin are muddy with dirt and tears. It's a good place to cry—cool and private, no eyewitnesses.

People get old and die. Mr. Shepard was already sick when he had his hunting accident, even if he didn't want to talk about it. His hair fell out, he started to walk with a cane, he forgot things, and toward the end, he couldn't always say Debra Ann's name. Everybody knew.

Men die all the time in fights or pipeline explosions

or gas leaks. They fall from cooling towers or try to beat the train or get drunk and decide to clean their guns. Women are killed when they get cancer or marry badly or take rides with strange men. Casey Nunally's daddy was killed in Vietnam when she was just a baby, and Debra Ann has seen photographs hanging in their hallway—a high school portrait taken just a few months before he left for basic training, a wedding photo taken when he was on leave, and the girls' favorite, a snapshot of him taken at the Dallas/Fort Worth airport. He wears his dress greens with a single patch sewn to the top of his left sleeve, and he holds his baby daughter up to the camera, his grin wide and toothy.

I never knew him, Casey says. To her, David Nunally is the flag that Mrs. Nunally keeps folded in her cedar chest. He is three medals resting in a small wooden box lined with purple satin, and paint peeling off the wood trim on their house. He is Mrs. Nunally's job at the bowling alley, the grocery store, the department store, and her praying for help in a dozen different churches, each a little stricter than the one before. He is Casey wearing the long skirts of all Adventist women and girls, even in the summer, and church on Saturdays instead of Sundays. He is Casey saying to Debra Ann, Everything would be different if—

When people die, there is proof and protocol. The

undertaker dressed Lauralee's grandmother in her favorite wig and blouse. He tried to hide her cancer with a thick layer of face powder and arranged her hands so they rested just beneath her breasts, one pale and wrinkled hand crossed over the other. Lauralee reported that her grandma's cheek was cool and rubbery, and Debra Ann had already taken Casey's hand to guide it into the casket when Mrs. Ledbetter grabbed both girls by the tender, fatty part of their arms and squeezed hard, when she leaned down and breathed in Debra Ann's ear, What in the world is wrong with you?

But Ginny Pierce is not dead. She left—left town, left a note and most of her clothes, left Debra Ann and her daddy. So Mrs. Shepard pats her arm and offers to trim her bangs for her, and Mrs. Nunally purses her lips and shakes her head. On Sunday mornings, her daddy makes breakfast for them. Sunday afternoons, they grill steaks and drive over to Baskin-Robbins. When they come home, he sits in the living room playing albums or wanders down the block to sit in Mr. Ledbetter's backyard and drink a beer.

When Ginny comes home, Debra Ann doesn't want the house to be such a mess that her mom turns around and walks right back out the door again, so she straightens up and tries to figure out how to help Jesse get his truck back. She worries about her dad, who doesn't sleep enough, and Mrs. Shepard, who sometimes pretends she isn't home, even when Debra Ann lies down on the front porch and hollers, I can see your tennis shoes under the door! She waits for her mama to call, jumping every time the phone rings and then sighing when she hears her daddy's voice on the other end. She practices what she'll say when her mother finally calls home. She will keep her voice causal, as if Ginny is calling from the customer service desk at Strike-It-Rich to see if they need ice cream. When she calls, Debra Ann will sound friendly but not too eager, and she will ask the question she has been hanging onto since February 15, when she wandered home early from the basketball courts and found Ginny's note pinned to her pillow.

When are you coming home?

Ginny

Sunday morning, February 15—It will be cold comfort, knowing she is not alone. Plenty of other women have gone before her. By the time she pulls into the fire lane at Sam Houston Elementary, two suitcases and a shoebox of family pictures hidden in the trunk, Ginny Pierce knows plenty of stories about those other women, the ones who ran off. But Ginny is not the running-off kind. She will be back in a year, two at the most. As soon as she has a job, an apartment, a little money in the bank—she is coming back for her daughter.

Mama, why are you crying? Debra Ann asks, and Ginny tells her, It's just my allergies, honey, and D. A. shakes her head in the same manner she does everything, fiercely—It's February, too early for allergies—as if that settles it. And Ginny swallows the stone in her throat. Could you scoot over here for a minute, honey? Let me see your face?

Her daughter is nearly ten. She is going to remember this day—the two of them sitting together in the front seat of the getaway car, a shaky and capricious Pontiac Ginny has been driving since high school. D. A. will remember her mother reaching out suddenly and pulling her across the front seat until they are sitting with their shoulders pressed together. Ginny will remember pushing her daughter's fine brown hair out of her eyes, the smell of oatmeal and Ivory soap, the chocolate on her chin from the Valentine's candy she's been eating all morning, and the shine on her cheeks from the suntan lotion Ginny swiped across her face before they left the house. When she reaches for her daughter to rub in a smudge of lotion on her chin, Ginny's hand trembles and she thinks, Take her. Make it work somehow. But Debra Ann scoots away, saying, Quit it! Because to her, this is still like any other Sunday morning and her mother might be nagging her about any of the usual things. To her, even Ginny's tears have become old hat.

The car door, when it slams closed, nearly catches Ginny's finger. A backpack slung over one shoulder, D. A.'s basketball striking the concrete and rolling onto the dusty playground, a hand thrown casually in the air, her daughter walking away from the car. Bye, Mama. Bye, Debra Ann.

⌒

Ginny's grandma never much cared to talk about the women who made it out alive, but the stories about the ones who died trying? They are bright and enduring, as if somebody took a branding iron and seared them into Ginny's memory.

In the spring of 1935 a cattleman's wife served lunch to a dozen ranch hands and then hanged herself on the front porch. She didn't even wash the dishes, Grandma said, just set them in the sink, took off her apron, and walked upstairs to change into her favorite shirtwaister. As if that were the story, the sink full of dishes. Later that afternoon a cowherd came up to the house to fill a water barrel and found her—a kitchen chair knocked over on the front porch, the wind slowly turning her round and round, back and forth, one bare foot peeking from beneath her skirt. It took them two days to find that missing shoe, her grandma said, and Ginny imagined a brown leather slipper, kicked far out into the yard and covered over with sand.

Another woman left a note saying that she had to see something green, anything at all, a dogwood, a magnolia, a little St. Augustine grass. She saddled up her husband's best mare and dug in her heels, and they were flying fast across the desert when they ran into a barbed-wire fence just this side of Midland. It's easy to get turned around out there, Grandma said, if you don't know where you're going.

Even those women who toed the line couldn't escape Grandma's stories. They got lost in sleet storms on their way home from church. They ran out of food and firewood in the middle of a blizzard. They buried babies that had been picked up and flung against the earth by a twister, and children who wandered into the yard during a dust storm and suffocated on the dirt from their own front yards. Sometimes Ginny thought her grandma didn't know how to tell a story with a happy ending.

On the other side of Ginny's windshield, the I-20 lies stretched out like a dead body. Up above, the sky is bland and unblinking. Nothing out here but that open road she's been dreaming about, though at the moment she can barely see it. She turns on the junior college radio station, and Joni Mitchell's voice fills the car, achingly beautiful, clear and certain as a church bell, or a plainsong, and it is unbearable. Ginny cannot turn it off fast enough. Now there is only the persistent thrum of road noise, and a worrisome little screak under the hood. When she presses down on the accelerator and the noise grows louder, she holds her breath and crosses her fingers.

At the turnoff to Mary Rose Whitehead's house, Ginny switches on the blinker, takes her foot off the gas, and considers the turn. She imagines herself driving up the dirt road and knocking on the door of the woman she once stood outside the high school with, both of them waiting, Mary Rose for her mother and Ginny for her grandma, to pick them up and take them home for good.

The final bell had not yet rung, and they stood alone in the parking lot, their purses stuffed with gym suits and the contents of their school lockers, both of their noses red and sore from crying in the nurse's office. Mary Rose was turning a small metal padlock over and over in her hand. She was seventeen years old and as of thirty minutes ago, pregnant enough that somebody took notice. I thought my life was taking forever to get started, Mary Rose said, but not now. Do you know what I mean? Ginny, barely past her fifteenth birthday, shook her head and stared at the ground. She tried to imagine what her grandmother was going to say about this, Ginny making the same mistake as the daughter she had lost to a car accident a decade earlier.

Mary Rose leaned down and scratched her ankle. She stood back up, reared back, and hurled the lock against the side of a pickup truck. The girls watched it bounce off the door without leaving a mark. Well, Mary Rose said, I guess we're in it now.

Yes we were, Ginny thinks, and she pushes the accelerator to the floor.

ॱ

Still, when all the shouting and tears and threats were done, the baby was perfect. Ginny and Jim Pierce could hardly believe it. Look what they did. They made a person. A daughter! So they dug their King James out of a moving box and hunted up a fine, strong name. Deborah, *Awake, awake, utter a song!* But the county clerk spelled it *Debra* and they didn't have the three bucks to resubmit the paperwork, so Debra it is—and Jim went to work in the oil patch while Ginny played house.

Afternoons while her daughter napped, Ginny liked to sit quietly and look at magazines with photographs of places she had never even heard of. She thumbed through art books that she found at the bookmobile, filled with photographs of murals and paintings and sculptures. She turned the pages slowly, marveling that somebody thought to make these things in the first place, wondering if the artists ever imagined someone like her looking at their work. Ginny loves her daughter, but she feels like she's sitting in the bottom of a rain barrel, and there's a steady drizzle filling it up.

And it is for this reason—more than the men on the street who holler every time she steps out of her car to gas up, or the unceasing wind and relentless stench of natural gas and crude oil, even more than the loneliness that is briefly staved off, sometimes, when Jim comes home from work, or Debra Ann climbs into her lap even though she is too big to stay for more than a minute—that Ginny takes five hundred dollars from their joint account and one of the road atlases from the family bookcase, and drives out of West Texas as if her life depends upon it.

⌒

There was a man who ran a cow-calf operation on the same piece of land where he lived with his wife and three children. During the 1934 drought, the price of cattle fell to twelve dollars a head, not even worth the cost of moving them to the stockyards in Fort Worth.

They shot them in the forehead, Grandma said, some-times the government men who came to make sure the ranchers had thinned their herds out, but more often, the ranchers themselves, who didn't feel it was right to ask a stranger to do their dirty work. The men stood over the bodies with kerosene-soaked rags in their hands, pausing awkwardly, as if everything might change if only they waited a few more minutes, days, weeks. Sighing, they lit the rags and then stood back and shook their heads. But there was always one old bull that wouldn't die, who bawled and staggered as shot after shot struck his tough old skin, his flank, his heart girth. There was always one old cow everybody thought was dead, but then she rose up and wandered off across the field, smoke rising from her flanks, the stench of singed hair drifting behind her. All this, Grandma said, and the wind blew all day, every day.

Some men down from Austin arrived one morning to find a pile of cattle still smoldering in an open field. The rancher was dead in the barn. His wife lay a few feet away, fingers still curled around the pistol, and the front door of the main house was standing wide open, the wind slamming it madly against the frame. The men found the children locked in an upstairs bedroom, where the oldest, a boy of seven, handed the men an envelope with train fare and a scrap of catalog paper.

A brief note was scribbled underneath the name and address of a sister in Ohio: I love my children. Please send them home.

Ginny's grandma was a toothy old woman, a believer in hellfire and hard work and punishment that fit the crime. If the devil comes knocking on your front door in the middle of the night, she liked to say, chances are you flirted with him at the dance. When she delivered the punch line, she clapped her hands twice sharply, just to make sure Ginny was paying attention.

I'm not going, the oldest boy told the cowhands. I'm staying right here in Texas. Well, all righty, one of the men said. You can come home with me, then.

So there's your happy ending, Virginia.

⌒

She is less than thirty miles from Odessa when the whine under the hood of her car sharpens and grows louder, a steady keen that does not abate even when she slows to fifty, then forty-five, then forty. Eighteen-wheelers blow their horns and pass on the right, the wind shaking her car and nudging it toward the median. And then the sound stops. The car shudders once, as if shaking off its troubles, and she drives on, fifty, fifty-five, sixty miles per hour.

The sun stares down on her, flat-faced and bland. By now, Debra Ann has probably beaten every girl in the neighborhood at basketball. Or she is sitting on the bleachers, looking through her backpack for the sandwich that Ginny packed. Or she is walking home, the basketball a steady heartbeat against the sidewalk. D. A. is going to be fine for a couple of years. She is the best part of each parent—the boy who was a second-string quarterback and the girl who loved Joni Mitchell, two kids who hardly knew each other when they drank too much Jack Daniel's at the homecoming dance and took a drive through the oil patch during the worst sleet storm of 1966, a story as common as dust on a windowpane.

What kind of woman runs out on her husband and her daughter? The kind who understands that the man who shares her bed is, and will always be, just the boy who got her pregnant. The kind who can't stand thinking that she might someday tell her own daughter: All this ought to be good enough for you. The kind who believes she is coming back, just as soon as she finds someplace where she can settle down.

⌒

Come to think of it, country and western singers, those purveyors of sad songs and murder ballads where a good woman gone bad gets her just desserts? They've got nothing on Grandma—or Ginny, as it turns out.

It was 1958, and Ginny's parents had been dead for less than a year. The boom had finally begun to level off, and there were fewer strange men around town, fewer roughnecks and roustabouts driving in to spend their paychecks and raise hell, but Ginny was still young enough to hold her grandma's hand for no particular reason, just because. The two of them were making their way to the drugstore, cutting across the lawn at City Hall on their weekly sojourn to pick up her grand-daddy's pills and maybe a licorice whip for Ginny. It was early summer and the wind held still for a few minutes, here and there, the sun bestowing just the right amount of warmth on their faces when they stopped to watch the light shine through the diaphanous, narrow leaves of the town's pecan trees. Until they nearly tripped over her, they did not see the woman curled up in the grass, sleeping like an old copperhead.

Ginny remembers it like this: She had sniffed at the air, recognizing the scent of piss and whiskey. She stared at the lady's naked feet. Bright red polish flaked off her toenails, and her skirt hem rested above two skinned knees. Her bony clavicle rose and fell, and a thin scar on her neck reminded Ginny of the state map hanging on the wall in her first-grade classroom.

Something about that long mark made Ginny want to wake her up and tell her, Lady, you got a scar in the shape of the Sabine River on your neck. It's wonderful. But Ginny's grandma squeezed her hand tight and jerked her away from the woman, her lips rucked up and pressed tightly together. Well, she said, *that one's* been rode hard and put up wet one too many times.

For days, Ginny worked hard to figure out the meaning of those words. Sometimes she liked to imagine the lady saddled and thirsty, her skirt wrinkling beneath a wool blanket, a bit clenched in her teeth, and sweat streaming between her eyes as some old rancher rode her across the oil patch. Other times, Ginny thought about the way the woman had lain curled beneath the pecan tree, her toenails painted the exact red of the little wagon that Ginny hauled around the yard. The quickness with which her grandma had jerked her away from the woman was not so different from the way she yanked Ginny out of her granddaddy's barn when a bull started climbing up on one of the cows.

And if Grandma's hands hadn't been so full, if she hadn't had it up to here most days, with Ginny and dust and scrubbing the crude oil out of her husband's shirts, Ginny might have asked her why she said that. But she stayed quiet about it, and she sometimes thought about those two skinned knees, the scar that looked like the Sabine River, its meandering path across the woman's throat as she slept in the shade of a pecan tree. The woman had been beautiful to Ginny. She still is.

⌒

A few miles past the Slaughter Field, the derricks and pumpjacks give way to empty desert. On the other side of Pecos, the road begins to rise and fall. The horizon goes jagged, and the land turns ruddy and uneven. How lonely it is out there. How lovely.

Ginny keeps both hands on the wheel, her eyes shifting back and forth between the temperature gauge and the road ahead. She stops for gas in Van Horn, sitting in her car with her fingers wrapped around the steering wheel while the attendant fills the tank and washes the windows. Cigarette dangling from his lips, he checks the tire pressure and asks if she needs anything more. His coveralls are the same gray as Debra Ann's eyes, and there is a small oval Gulf Oil patch on his breast pocket. No thank you, she says and hands him five dollars.

He points to her back seat. You forgot to return your library book before you left town. Ginny twists around to see *Art in America* surrounded by candy bar wrappers and one of Debra Ann's graded spelling tests, the first two words *canceled* and *trespassing*, both misspelled.

At the stockyards outside of El Paso, she rolls the window up tight, her eyes and skin burning when the stench of methane gas seeps through the vents. She is ten miles from the New Mexico border, the farthest she has ever been from home.

⌒

Beauty! Beauty is not for people like us, her grandma said when Ginny tried to explain why she liked to sit and look at pictures in the afternoons. You'd do better paying attention to what's right in front of you, the old woman said. If you wanted to spend your life thinking about such things, you should have thought of that before—or been born someplace else. And maybe that's true, but it seems like a high price to pay, and maybe Ginny's not willing to make the trade—the world or her daughter—because it's clear she can't have both.

When the fan belt finally snaps on the other side of Las Cruces, Ginny's car shudders to the highway shoulder. She gets out of the car and watches the moon rise over the desert like a broken carnelian, and such has been her fear and grief and longing that, for many years, she will not remember the man who pulled up behind her car, his truck wheels grinding against the caliche-covered highway shoulder. She will not remember the words on the side of his truck—*Garza & O'Brien, Tow & Repair*—or that he fetched his toolbox from his truck and replaced the belt on the spot while she leaned against the trunk and looked at the stars, and wept without making a sound. And she will not remember what he said, when Ginny tried to give him a few dollars. Young lady, I can't take your money. Pues, good luck.

She will have seen a thousand miles of sky before she is finally able to stop moving. Flagstaff, Reno, one short and sorry stint in Albuquerque that she tries hard to forget. Weeks and months sleeping in her car after a day spent cleaning houses, or a night waiting tables. She will drive through the Sonoran Desert, its washes and ravines disappearing into box canyons, she will sit at the edge of a meadow just above the Mogollon Rim, newly covered with snow. The road that leads away is full of switchbacks so tight Ginny has to stop and back up, and hope that no one comes around the corner before she can make the curve.

There will be a bar in Reno, where the same old lady

shows up every night at nine o'clock and stays until close, her lips creased with lipstick, fingernails the color of blood, her smile as fierce and hard and true as the face Ginny sees in the mirror, most mornings. All of this is beautiful to her—the sky and sea, addicts and old ladies, musicians playing in subway stations, museums at the end of the line. She will see bridges overcome by fog, and sylvan forests teeming and dark and full of hidden water. Every place has a different kind of sky, it turns out, and much of this earth is not nearly as brown and flat as Odessa, Texas. All this wild, green beauty and still, always, a hole in her heart the size of a little girl's fist. Ginny will drive that Pontiac into the ground and grieve for it when it's gone. Never, she thinks, will I love a man the way I loved that car. And when people she meets along the way wonder about her, when they try to know her—some of them will love her, and she will love some of them, but never as much as the daughter who grows taller every day, without her—when they ask *what's your story* or *where are you from*, Ginny never knows quite what to say. Each time, she just packs up her car and drives away.

Mary Rose

Tonight the wind blows like it's got something to prove. My daughter comes to me just after midnight with another bad dream, and I do not hesitate to open the bedcovers, saying, You are safe here, we are safe here in town. I fetch the baby from his crib and bring him into bed with us, even though it will surely mean nursing him back to sleep. There is plenty of room in this bed for my kids and me. We have everything we need.

Mercifully, they are both sound asleep when the phone rings. I pick up and listen. I want to know their voices, in case I hear them on the street, in the grocery store, at the trial. Male or female, young or old, they all say more or less the same thing. You going to stand up for that spic? You going to take her word over his?

The drunker they are, the nastier they get. I am a liar and a traitor. They know where I live. I am ruining that boy's life because a girl didn't get her way. I am testifying against one of our boys on behalf of a slut—and any other foul word they can think up. I have been hearing this language my whole life without ever giving it much thought, but now it rankles.

Tonight's caller is pretty well oiled. You kiss your mama with that mouth? I ask him when he stops talking for long enough to take a breath, or swallow some more beer. Then I place the handset back on the cradle. When the phone rings again, I reach behind the nightstand and unplug it. The clock radio shines red, 1:30, just past closing time.

Guess I'm up. I pull the bedspread over the kids and place a pillow longways between the baby and the edge of the bed. The lights in the kitchen and living room are already turned on, but I flip on the rest of them as I walk through the house—Aimee's bedroom, the bathroom and hall closet. The baby's room I leave dark, apart from the small night-light next to his changing table. In the living room, I reach behind my new draperies and check the sliding-glass door that leads to the back patio. Because my new front door doesn't fit right on the doorframe, I check that too. One night last week, I went to bed thinking it was locked, but at two o'clock, when I got up to pee and check on the baby, it was standing wide open. For the rest of the night, I sat at the kitchen table with a cup of coffee, Old Lady lying on the floor next to my feet like a faithful dog. Now I open the door to make sure the porch light hasn't burned out and then push it firmly closed, lock it, jiggle the doorknob, do it all again.

The wind moves from window to window, a small animal sharpening its claws on the screens. Out at the ranch, you hear this sound and you think possum or maybe an armadillo. Here in town, you might think of a squirrel or somebody's cat. Lately the wind makes me think of animals that have not been here for a hundred years, panthers and wolves, or twisters that threaten to lift my children impossibly high in the air, only to fling them back to the earth. I turn on the weather report and stand in the kitchen smoking a cigarette, drinking one of the beers Robert keeps here. *My* beers, Mary Rose, he would say. A man doesn't *keep* things in his own house. When I exhale, I lean over the kitchen sink and slowly blow the smoke down the drain. Robert pays the rent, but I don't think of this house as his. This belongs to me, and my kids.

Last week, I thought I saw Dale Strickland's truck parked down the street and then again in the parking lot at Strike-It-Rich. Yesterday, I saw him standing in Mrs. Shepard's front yard, looking toward my house.

I have seen him in other places, too. But he is in jail. I call down there every morning and every afternoon to make sure he didn't escape or the judge hasn't decided to let him post bail.

I see Gloria Ramírez, too. Yesterday morning, when Suzanne Ledbetter knocked on the door with a plate of cookies, I stood perfectly still for a few seconds with my hand on the doorknob thinking it might be Gloria on the other side, more wreckage than child. Yesterday afternoon, when Mrs. Shepard sent Ginny's daughter to my front door with a casserole—the third that old heifer has sent over in as many weeks, I throw them straight into the trash can—I stood blinking in the doorway for a few seconds at the tall, dark-haired child standing on my porch. Debra Ann looks just like her mother, big and square-shouldered, dark-brown hair, gray eyes that look right through you. I knew your mom in high school, I said. She helped me once, when I was having a bad day. I took the dish, gave her my thanks, and gently closed my front door. Gloria could be any of our girls, I thought, and sat down right there in the hall, and cried until Aimee came and stood over me. Are you okay? she asked me. And I said, of course I am, because she is my daughter, and a child. She asked if we should call her grandma, my mother, and see if she might come over and help us out. Absolutely not, I told her. Grandma has her hands full. I reminded her of my two youngest brothers still living at home, and my dad's work delivering truckloads of water all over West Texas, and my brother's three kids who are living there while he works a rig in South America. If we call Grandma, I say, she will think something's wrong. We take care of our own business.

Who was that girl at the front door? Aimee had been watching from the kitchen window.

I don't know, I lied. Just some little girl that lives in the neighborhood.

She looked like my age. Was she nice?

I don't know, Aimee. She looked—tall for her age, big-boned. I don't want my daughter making friends. If she makes friends, she will want to run all over the neighborhood and I can't have her out there. I don't tell her that Debra Ann Pierce is the spitting image of her mama, a quiet, thoughtful girl who always had a book in her hand. I don't tell her that I cannot reconcile that teenager who stood with me in the school parking lot with the woman who has left her daughter behind.

Aimee hopped from one foot to the other, bouncing up and down like a tennis ball. Maybe I could go outside and see if she wants to ride bikes with me?

Outside. I rested my hand on Aimee's head, pushing gently so she would stop bouncing. Maybe in another month or so, I told her. Don't we have everything we need here?

I'm bored, she said, and I promised her we would be ready to have some company for her birthday in August. If you get that Daisy BB rifle you've been asking for, I said, maybe she'll come over and y'all can shoot cans in the backyard.

But Mama, it's only June! My daughter said this like I am still living in February, like I don't know the day or the month.

There's plenty of time to meet these girls, but you and me—I held her soft and pale cheeks between my hands and looked into her blue eyes—how much more time do we have together? You're going to be ten!

I am going to be the first two-digit number, a composite number, she said.

And I'm going to keep you safe, Aimee, I said. I will always keep you safe.

Day in and day out?

It has become a little ritual of ours since we moved into town. I say, I will keep you safe, and Aimee says, Day in and day out? But that afternoon she frowned and looked as if she might argue. When the baby started whimpering, revving himself up for a good cry, I was grateful for the excuse to leave the room.

It is the same cry I hear now, his cry of hunger, and

even though my breasts ache at the sound of it, I go to him. In half an hour, we will all be asleep—the baby's mouth still pulling at my nipple, Aimee pushing up against my back, her feet across my ankles, her arm trying to wrap itself around my throat. Yes, day in and day out. Always.

The clock radio reads 5:30 when I again untangle myself from the baby and head back to the kitchen. Sun's up in less than an hour, so I might as well have another cigarette and hope the baby doesn't wake up. At our old house in the desert, I used to sit outside and listen to the little creatures move in the brush while the desert turned pink and orange and gold. Once, I watched a pair of roadrunners work together to kill and eat a small rattlesnake. The noise out there was, it seemed to me, the true noise of the world, the way the world ought to sound. I felt that way right up until the morning Gloria Ramírez knocked on my front door. Even the pumpjacks switching on and trucks hauling pipe through our property didn't bother me as much as the noise here in town—honking and shouting, sirens and music from the bars on Eighth Street.

A load of towels in the washing machine has turned sour, and the kitchen table is covered with scissors, crayons, and scraps of construction paper, the remnants of Aimee's final school project, a diorama about the siege at Goliad. I clean it up while the coffee brews and I am just sitting down at the table when I remember the bucket that's catching a slow drip under the bathroom sink. After I drag it out and dump it in the bathtub, I pause for a second. When was the last time I took a bath or put my makeup on in the morning? I am letting myself go, as my mother would say, but for whom would I keep myself up? Aimee and the baby don't care, and Robert is still so mad I answered the front door and let that girl into our home, he can hardly see straight. He blames her for our troubles.

In the church where I grew up, we were taught that sin, even if it happens only in your heart, condemns you all the same. Grace is not assured to any of us, maybe not even most of us, and while being saved gives you a fighting chance, you must always hope that the sin lodged in your heart, like a bullet that cannot be removed without killing you, is not of the mortal kind. The church wasn't big on mercy, either. When I tried to explain myself to Robert in the days after the crime, when I told him I had sinned against this child, betrayed her in my heart, he said my only sin was opening the door in the first place, not thinking of my own damned kids first. The real sin, he said, was some people letting their daughters run the streets all night long. Since then, I can hardly stand to look at him.

The sheriff's deputy had taken Strickland without a fight. When Aimee called the sheriff, she gave the dispatcher an earful about the girl sitting across from her at the kitchen table and the man she could see through the window. Where is the man now? the dispatcher asked, and when Aimee said out front with my mama, they put a rush on it. The sheriff's deputy walked up to the young man and jammed the barrel of his revolver into his sternum. Son, he said, I don't know if you're stupid or crazy, but wipe that goddamn grin off your face. You are in some serious shit.

The deputy was right. The new district attorney, Keith Taylor, charged him with aggravated sexual assault and attempted murder. Mr. Taylor's secretary, Amelia, calls me every few days to tell me about a new delay in the trial or ask me questions about Gloria. Did I know her before? What did she say to me? Did I feel threatened by Dale Strickland?

You go into that house and get her, he told me. Do it right now. Don't wake up your husband who is sleeping upstairs, who is not sleeping upstairs, who is not even at home, you go in there, Mary Rose, you take that child by the arm and stand her on her own two feet and bring her to me.

And I was going to do it.

When morning comes, I walk around the house and

turn all the lights off. Robert will pitch a fit when he sees the electric bill. We can't afford to rent a house in town, he will say, especially not this year. We already have a house. Yes, but out *there*, I say, and you wanted us to move into town before all this happened, and then Robert will remind me that I used to love that old place, and that now he can't afford to be away from his cows. When he left a hired man in charge for the three days it took me to have our son and heal up enough to come home, the man took off for a job in the oil patch. Screwworms infested the animals' open sores, their ears, even their genitals. Robert lost fifty head of cattle. Shot this year's profit margin to hell, he says bitterly every time it comes up, which is every Sunday when he comes into town with a bag of candy for Aimee and flowers for me.

Thank you, I say. After I've put them in some water, we stand across the room from each other—him thinking I ruined our family, me thinking he would have preferred me to leave that child alone on the front porch while Aimee and me stood on the other side of a locked door.

Sundays, Robert looks at the baby like he's just bought a prize bull at auction. He holds my son on his lap for a few minutes, marveling at the baby's big hands—a quarterback's hands, he says—and then gives him back to me. In a few years, when he's big enough to catch a football or throw a bale of hay from the back of a truck or shoot snakes out at the ranch, the boy will be more interesting to him. Until then, he's all mine.

After the kids are asleep, I give Robert a couple of casseroles for his week's meals and he either leaves directly, or we have a fight and then he leaves. It's a relief to hear his truck door slam and the engine turn over.

I am bound and determined to keep my kids safe here in town, but I miss the sky and the quiet. Almost from the minute we moved into town, I started thinking about moving out. Not back to the ranch, but someplace as quiet as the ranch used to be, before screwworms and oil-field companies, before Dale Strickland drove up to my front door and turned me into a coward and a liar.

In my twenty-six years of living, I only have been out of Texas twice. The first time, Robert and I drove up to Ruidoso for our honeymoon. It feels like three lifetimes ago—I was seventeen years old and three months pregnant with Aimee—but I can still close my eyes and call to mind the Sierra Blanca peak standing guard over that little town. I can still breathe in long and slow and remember the pine trees, how their sharp, stinging odor grew stronger when I folded a handful of needles in half and squeezed them in my hand.

We returned home three days later after a stop to see

Fort Stanton, and for the first time in my life I noticed the way the air smelled in Odessa, something between a gas station and a trash can full of rotting eggs. You never smell it when you grow up here, I guess.

The only other time I smelled those trees was two years ago, when I told Robert that Aimee and I were driving up to Carlsbad for three days to visit an elderly second cousin he didn't even know I had. We left town to the news on the radio that nine people in Denver City had died from a hydrogen sulfide leak.

What's hydrogen sulfide, Aimee wanted to know, and I told her I had no idea. Who's the Skid Row Slasher? she asked. What's the IRA? I changed the channel to the college radio station, and we listened to Joe Ely and the Flatlanders. When we reached Carlsbad, I kept driving.

Aimee—I looked in the rearview mirror at a pickup truck that had been tailgating us for the last five miles and eased my foot off the accelerator—how about you and me go to Albuquerque?

Aimee looked up from her Etch A Sketch and frowned. How come?

I don't know, see someplace new? I hear there's a brand-new Holiday Inn downtown that's got an indoor pool and a pinball arcade. Maybe we'll drive up to the mountains and see the Ponderosa pines.

Can I have a souvenir?

No souvenirs this time, just memories. The words stuck in my throat and I eased toward the shoulder to give the truck as much room as possible. When the son of a bitch finally passed, he pulled up right next to me and laid on the horn and I nearly pissed myself. Eight years earlier, I would have given him the finger. Now, with my child sitting in the front seat next to me, I gritted my teeth and smiled.

People who live in Odessa like to tell strangers that we live two hundred miles from anywhere, but Amarillo and Dallas are at least three hundred miles away, El Paso is in a different time zone, and Houston and Austin might as well be on a different planet. *Anywhere* is Lubbock, and on a good day, it is a two-hour drive. If the sand is blowing or there's a grass fire or you stop for lunch at the Dairy Queen in Seminole, it could take you all afternoon. And the distance from Odessa to Albuquerque? Four hundred and thirty seven miles, a little more than seven hours if you don't get caught in the speed trap outside Roswell.

We had just enough time for a cheeseburger and a quick swim in the pool before bed. While Aimee was in the bathtub, I called Robert to let him know we were safe and sound in Carlsbad and my old cousin was still full of piss and vinegar. He grunted and said something about the difficulties of reheating the King Ranch casserole I had left thawing on the kitchen counter. Cover it with aluminum foil, I said, and put it in the oven. After we hung up, I sat on the bed and looked at the receiver. I was ten weeks pregnant and just the thought of another baby made me want to hang myself in the barn. Robert wanted a son, maybe even two of them, but Aimee was enough for me. I'd been thinking about trying to get my GED, maybe take some classes at Odessa College.

Three miles from our hotel, on a street lined with adobe houses, in a red-brick and cinder-block building so nondescript that it might have housed anything from a bearing supply company to an accountant's office, there was a women's clinic. It had a front door made of heavy glass and there were no windows. The parking lot could accommodate no more than a dozen cars and pickup trucks, and behind the building, completely exposed to the sun, there was a picnic table with two wooden benches and several overflowing glass ashtrays. We sat down at the table, and I explained to Aimee that she was going to stay in the waiting room while I spoke with a man about building us some new furniture for our front porch, which was the least interesting subject I could dream up. My appointment was at 10:00, but we lingered in the sun until a few minutes past the hour. There was no doubt in my mind about what I was doing, but I was loath to move off that bench. Look at that pickup truck with a rooster painted on the side, I said. Do you smell meat cooking? Is that little old lady walking a *pig*? When Aimee said she needed to pee, we went inside.

This is legal, I kept telling myself, has been for nearly two years. But it was hard to feel that way with a pack of lies, four hundred miles, and a state line under my belt. I stepped up to the window and spoke as quietly as I could, all while sliding three hundred dollars that I had taken out of my private savings account across the counter. I might have been buying cocaine, I was so covert.

The receptionist smiled and slipped the money into a drawer. She handed me a clipboard and looked over my shoulder at Aimee. Mrs. Whitehead, who is driving you home after the procedure?

No one, I said. I am driving myself.

You need somebody who can drive you home. You have somebody?

I drove up from Texas.

Ah, I see. She paused and began chewing lightly on her fingernail. Are you spending the night here in town?

We're at the Holiday Inn, I said, keeping my voice low.

The new one that's downtown? She smiled, speaking a bit more quietly, and I nodded.

Okay, good, she said. Some women try to drive all the way home, and that can cause some complications. You're lucky, she said. You'll be in for about two hours.

Two hours! I looked back at my daughter, who was sitting on a chair with a bag of potato chips and her Nancy Drew book. The woman reached across the counter and touched my hand. This happens all the time. We'll keep an eye on her.

I stood there blinking hard and trying to bring the woman's hand into focus. Her fingernails were painted the color of pink tea roses and she wore a plain gold band on her left ring finger. Thank you, I said. Her name is Aimee.

To my daughter, I smiled brightly. I'll be back in a jiffy.

Don't worry, the woman called as I pushed open a swinging door and nearly walked into another woman, a patient, standing just on the other side. We're going to have a fine time! Would you like an ice-cold Dr Pepper, she asked my daughter.

Yes, ma'am, Aimee said. Have fun with the furniture man, Mama.

We stopped at Whataburger on our way back to the Holiday Inn. Aimee watched cartoons while I threw up in the bathroom and waited for the cramping to pass. That hamburger didn't agree with me, I said when she knocked on the bathroom door. Just give me a few minutes.

That afternoon, she swam and played the pinball machines while I sat on a lounge chair and drank a couple of salty dogs. Early the next morning we headed up to the Sandia Mountains to smell the pine trees. Piñon, spruce, fir, juniper—I closed my eyes and imagined us living in a small wooden cottage deep in a forest full of creatures without intent or malice, a place where you might get hurt, but not because anything meant to harm you.

Between stopping every hour at a filling station so I could change my pads—and twice more so Aimee could throw up some of the candy I let her eat at the hotel—we didn't get home until nearly midnight. To my daughter, I said: I won't ever ask you to keep anything from your daddy unless it's really important, and this is really important. To my husband, I said: I have a bad yeast infection. Don't touch me for a while. Four months later I was pregnant again, and this time, hardly believing my own stupidity, I decided to have the baby.

When I was a little girl, time really did seem to fly. Summer days, I'd get on my bike after breakfast and in three beats of my heart, it was time for supper. Now I look at the kitchen clock and can hardly believe how early in the day it still is. It is not even ten o'clock and I have nursed the baby three times since he woke up at six. My right breast aches a little, and when I touch my nipple it feels hot and hard. While the baby quietly fusses in his crib, Aimee jumps up and down on her bed yelling, I am bored, day in and day out. I am bored!

It is the third day of summer vacation.

When the phone rings, I almost jump out of my own skin, but it's only Keith Taylor's secretary. There's been some trouble with Gloria's mother, she tells me, but they are hoping Gloria will still be able to testify. When I ask what the trouble is, she won't say. When I ask if I can see Gloria, maybe talk to her and see how she's doing, Amelia is silent for a few seconds. How are you doing, Mary Rose?

Oh I'm fine, I say brightly. Don't worry about me!

I want to tell her that my kids are safe here in town, in this house. Men call me at all hours of the day and night, and some women too, but every nasty thing they say is about them and not about me. I have my old rifle at home, and a new pistol in the glove box of my car. Instead, I thank the good lady for her call and say my goodbyes.

On the floor in front of the washing machine, the laundry is breeding like a coterie of prairie dogs. We are out of milk and eggs, and I have promised the Ladies Guild at our new church that I will be at their meeting later today. The baby screams like he's just been stung by a yellow jacket, and then, as if on cue, Aimee falls off the bed and hits her head against the dresser. A howl rises up from the bedroom. A goose egg is already starting to form on her forehead, but mostly she is pissed off that I won't let her out of the house alone, not even for a minute.

In the weeks immediately after Dale Strickland raped Gloria Ramírez, people gathered in fellowship halls, bars, and break rooms. They stood in their front yards and lingered in the aisles at the grocery store. They held court in the parking lot at the cafeteria, and distracted football devotees at the practice field. I listened to it all. The rest I got from the radio or newspaper.

Strickland's mama and daddy are back home in Magnolia, Arkansas, and if you believe the local paper and some of the more vocal citizens in town, he's a good kid. According to Pastor Rob on his usual Sunday broadcast, he had never received so much as a speeding ticket. If he ever missed a day of football practice or church, nobody in his town could remember it, and he had always been one hundred percent respectful to the local girls. His father, a Pentecostal preacher, had mailed letters and testimonials from members of his congregation to the DA's office testifying to the quality of his son's character. Rumor had it that Keith Taylor brought an extra card table into his office, just to have a place to put them all.

An editorial writer noted that the accused had, on the night in question, been awake for two straight days after taking some amphetamine tablets his foreman had given him, a common practice in the oil fields, and while nobody condoned drug use—people were still talking about Art Linkletter's daughter—the pace of work in the oil patch sometimes called for men to push themselves in unhealthy ways. Men are fighting out there, the writer noted, fighting to pull that petroleum out of the earth before the ground caves in around a well, fighting OPEC prices and Arabs. In a way, you could say they were even fighting for America.

One week later, there were two letters to the editor on the subject. The Reverend and Mrs. Paul Donnelly of First Methodist wrote of their sorrow and disgust at the way this was being handled, both in the newspaper and in town. They prayed we would all do better and they asked, What if this had been your daughter?

In the second letter, a fine, upstanding citizen reminded all of us that the alleged victim was a fourteen-year-old Mexican girl who had been hanging around the drive-in by herself on a Saturday night. Witnesses swore the girl had climbed willingly into that boy's truck. Nobody held a gun to her head. We ought to think about that, this person wrote, before we ruin a boy's life. Innocent until proven guilty. At that, I had thrown the newspaper across the kitchen, a wholly unsatisfying gesture since the pages traveled about two feet and then fell to the linoleum with a sad little rustle.

In the weeks after we moved into town, in the parking lot at Furr's Cafeteria, on the telephone with Aimee's school, and in line at the DMV while I waited to have the address changed on my driver's license, I found myself saying, I beg your pardon? Or, I'm sorry but I don't think that is true at all. Mrs. Bobby Ray Price wanted to chat about what she called *this ugly business* while we waited together in the Piggly Wiggly checkout line. Aimee was whining for some new candy she said was going to explode in her mouth. I listened to Mrs. Price talk for a few seconds and shook my head. Bullshit, I was thinking. But I didn't say anything.

By noon, we have iced Aimee's goose egg and gone outside for some air. While I stand in the front yard with the baby asleep in my arms, Aimee sulks and draws numbers on the sidewalk with a stick of chalk. The baby sighs and paws at my right breast, but the pain is sudden and stark, so I shift him to the other side, thankful when he settles down and stays asleep. We see Suzanne Ledbetter first. She wears a pair of thin white sandals and white shorts that fall to the middle of her thighs. A straw tote bag is slung over her bare shoulder, and a sleeveless white blouse shows off her red hair and pale, freckled shoulders. She looks like she got a shower this morning, I think wistfully. When Suzanne spots Aimee and me, she waves and pats her tote bag. Ding Dong, Avon calling!

Mrs. Nunally pulls up in her old Chevy and joins us. Depending on which job she is going to, Mrs. Nunally usually wears a smock or an apron over her clothes, but today she wears a long black skirt and a light green blouse with sleeves that fall to her narrow wrist. A small name tag is pinned just above her left breast. She is on her way to Beall's department store, where she works two afternoons a week. Mrs. Shepard told me that Mrs. Nunally stopped putting on makeup when she became an Adventist, but today she wears pale-pink lipstick and eye shadow that matches her blouse.

Well, look at you, Suzanne tells her. You look real pretty.

Goodness, Mrs. Nunally says, look at that baby's hands. That's a football player. The two women hover over the baby for a few seconds, making goo-goo eyes and blowing kisses. Suzanne plucks him from my arms and pulls him to her chest. Eyes closed, she sways back and forth for a few seconds before gently handing him to me. I think of my burning nipple and sleepless nights, and for a few seconds, I think about giving him back to her. Hang on, I would like to say. I'll go fetch his diaper bag.

Where's Lauralee? Aimee whines from the sidewalk, where she has been drawing a hopscotch board in a desultory way.

Swim lessons, Suzanne says. I'm picking her up in a little while to take her to dance school.

Mrs. Shepard stands in her front yard holding a water hose that is not turned on.

Is she okay? I ask Mrs. Nunally.

Suzanne leans in and lowers her voice. I heard Potter killed himself.

What? I say. Oh my God, no. It was a hunting accident. The baby sighs in his sleep and tries again to nuzzle, but the pain radiates from my nipple to my arm and I shift him to the other side.

Potter never hunted a day in his life, Suzanne says. That man couldn't shoot an animal if he was starving to death.

Mrs. Nunally purses her lips and frowns a bit. I hope that's not true, she says, for both their sakes.

When Mrs. Shepard starts across the street with her mason jar full of iced tea, Ginny's girl appears from behind a long hedge that runs along the front of Mrs. Shepard's house.

Debra Ann and Aimee stand in the front yard sizing each other up for a minute or two, then Debra Ann, who has scratched a mosquito bite so much her arm is bleeding, asks if Aimee wants to go ride bikes with her. No, I say. Y'all stay right here in the yard, please.

Oh, hell, Mrs. Shepard says. They'll be fine.

No, I say sharply. Mrs. Shepard takes a long sip of iced tea and smacks her lips.

I have already thanked Suzanne for the casserole and Mrs. Nunally for the lemon cake. Now I thank Mrs. Shepard for *her* casserole, which, I noticed as I scraped it into the trash, still has a sticker with Suzanne's name on it.

Oh, it's my pleasure, honey. Ladies, she tells us, I know a little gal who's looking for some babysitting jobs. She feels around in her pocket and pulls out three slips of paper, handing one to each of us. Here's her phone number. Karla Sibley. I highly recommend her.

Suzanne looks at the piece of paper and frowns. And from where do you know this girl?

Church, Mrs. Shepard says without hesitation.

Oh? Suzanne says. Have you returned to church, Corrine?

I sure have, Suzanne! It's such a comfort, since Potter's accident.

I see. Suzanne narrows her eyes and shifts her tote bag to the other shoulder. Well, we are all praying for you at Crescent Park Baptist.

Bless your hearts, Mrs. Shepard says.

Mrs. Nunally frowns and turns toward Suzanne. How are you feeling?

The pregnancy didn't take, she says, her cheeks flushing red. But I'm fine! We'll try again in a few months.

Oh no, Mrs. Nunally says.

You have lots of time, says Mrs. Shepard. You are only twenty-six years old.

Thank you, Corrine, but I'm thirty-four.

Really? Because you don't look a day over twenty-six— Mrs. Shepard pauses and glances at Mrs. Nunally—Do y'all mind if I smoke?

I'm sorry, I say to Suzanne.

Don't be sorry, she says. I have a beautiful, talented, and smart daughter. And look here, at what else I have! She reaches into her tote bag and pulls out a handful of Avon samples—perfume and face cream, eye shadows, even tiny lipsticks—and hands them to us.

Mrs. Shepard passes hers to Mrs. Nunally without looking at it and pulls a cigarette from the pocket of her blouse. When she exhales, the smell is so warm and rich that I want to pluck it from between her fingers and suck with all my might.

Are you still preparing for the trial? she asks me.

Yes, I am. I shift the baby again from one side to the other and glance over at Aimee. She and Debra Ann are sitting under the dead tree, talking intensely and looking over at us from time to time.

Suzanne leans forward a bit and swats at the cigarette smoke. I've heard that the girl's uncle is attempting to blackmail Mr. Strickland's family.

That is absolutely slanderous, I say before I can stop myself. That is just a terrible thing for anybody to say.

I didn't say it was true, Suzanne reminds us. Y'all know how rumors spread.

We sure do! Mrs. Shepard laughs out loud, a big, off-key, honking sound that reminds me of the homely sand hill cranes I left behind at the ranch. She arches eyebrows that, thankfully, she remembered to draw on this morning and takes several steps back from the group to blow her cigarette smoke away from the baby.

That does indeed sound slanderous, Mrs. Shepard says, but what do you expect from a bunch of bigots?

Suzanne rucks up her lips and sucks in some air.

Well, you can speak for yourself, Corrine, because I'm no bigot, but— She stops for a few seconds and looks around the group for some acknowledgment that her statement is true—Suzanne Ledbetter is no bigot. But Mrs. Shepard and I are silent, and Mrs. Nunally has already started walking toward her car, saying, You ladies have a nice afternoon. Suzanne excuses herself and begins to walk slowly, as if a little lost, down the street. Upon arriving at her house, she makes a big show of checking her mail and yanking a couple of dandelions that had the nerve to make a home in her St. Augustine. Finally, she grabs a broom off the porch and swipes at the sidewalk.

Mrs. Shepard, who apparently has nowhere else to be and nothing better to do, watches me nuzzle my son. He is new enough that I still want to sniff at him from time to time, just to know he's mine.

New baby, Mrs. Shepard says. Only thing that smells better is a brand-new Lincoln Continental. Let me have a little sniff? She holds the cigarette behind her back, leans forward, and breathes my son in. Girl, she says, I don't miss the dirty diapers, and I sure don't miss the sleepless nights, but I miss this smell.

I tuck the blanket under the baby's chin and look at her. You should have seen Gloria Ramírez. He beat the living daylights out of her. The baby jerks in his sleep, his mouth opening and closing. I lean closer and lower my voice. Mrs. Shepard, it was like an animal had got at her.

Please, call me Corrine.

Corrine, I say, Dale Strickland is no better than a feral hog. Worse, actually. They can't help themselves. I wish they would put him in the electric chair, I really do.

She drops her cigarette butt onto the sidewalk and nudges it off the curb with her foot. We both watch the smoke rise off the filter while she immediately lights another and considers her words. She smiles and tickles the baby's chin. I know it, honey. Let's just hope they get a half-decent judge. You going to testify?

Yes, I am. I can't wait to tell them what I saw.

Well, that's good. That's all you can do. Let me ask you something, Mary Rose. You getting enough sleep?

I jerk my head up from the baby, ready to tell her that I'm fine, my kids are fine, we don't need anything from anybody, but Corrine is eyeing me like a black-jack dealer watches a card counter.

I could tell her the truth, that some nights I dream Gloria is knocking on my front door again, but I don't answer it. I stay in my bed with my head under the pillow as the knocking grows louder and louder and when I can't stand listening to it anymore, I get out of bed and walk down the hall of my new house. When I pull the heavy door open, my Aimee is standing on the porch, beaten and torn up, her feet bare and bleeding. Mama, she cries, why didn't you help me?

I could tell her about the phone calls I've been getting, almost since the day the phone company turned on our new line, and I could say that some nights I can't tell the difference between being tired and being afraid.

Instead I say, I'm just fine. Thank you for asking.

Corrine starts digging through her pack for another cigarette, her third, but finding it empty, she crumples the package and shoves it in her pantsuit pocket. I could have sworn I had at least a half pack of cigarettes left, she says. Since Potter died, I can't remember a damned thing. Last week, I lost a blanket. A blanket! She looks longingly across the street at her garage door. Well, I better go move the sprinkler and fix myself another iced tea. Going to see a hundred degrees today. In June!

She has already disappeared into her house by the time I realize she left Debra Ann Pierce in my front yard. I stand there and watch the girls, who occasionally look over at me, grimace, and then ignore me completely. When the baby wakes up, I shepherd everyone into the house and lock the door. While the girls play in Aimee's room, I try to nurse him. My right breast is burning up, and a hard knot next to the nipple suggests an infected milk duct. When the baby latches on, the pain travels the entire length of my torso.

By the time we are ready to leave for the Ladies Guild, it is nearly ninety degrees out and Aimee is mad that I sent her new friend home. She sits in the front seat kicking the glove box and fiddling with the air-conditioning vent while the baby fusses on the seat between us.

Did you have fun with Debra Ann? I ask.

It was okay, she says kicking, kicking, kicking.

Stop it, Aimee. Do y'all have a lot in common?

I guess so, she says. She has a bunch of friends, but I think most of them are imaginary.

This will be my second meeting with the Ladies Guild. When we moved to town, I decided we should maybe give up our Baptist radio and find a real church. It might be good for us to be part of something, and Aimee has started to talk about getting saved. But today's meeting is a horror. The swamp cooler runs constantly, to no avail, and the heat only exacerbates the burning in my breast. When I arrive, some of the ladies are talking about having their husbands take boxes of old summer clothes out to the families living on the outskirts of town, in makeshift oil camps that have appeared overnight, it seems.

Those camps are just awful, Mrs. Robert Perry tells us. Trash everywhere and most of them don't even have running water—she pauses and lowers her voice—and full of Mexicans.

A murmur of assent goes through the room. It's terrible how they do, somebody says, and someone else reminds us that it's not all of them, just *some*, and I sit there with my mouth hanging open. As if I have never heard this kind of talk in my life, as if I didn't grow up hearing it from my daddy at the dinner table, from all my aunts and uncles at the Thanksgiving table, from my own husband. But now I think about Gloria and her family and it rankles, like an open sore that I can't stop picking at.

Aimee and the baby are down the hall in the church nursery. This is a church, I told myself when the teenaged girl squealed and plucked the baby from my arms. They will be safe here. I close my eyes and press my hand to my forehead. Maybe I'm running a little fever. My right side, from beneath my armpit to my rib cage, feels like someone took a blowtorch to it.

Mary Rose, are you all right? B. D. Hendrix's wife, Barbie, is standing next to my chair. She lays a hand on my shoulder. Someone says I'm probably worn out and then someone else mentions the awful business with the Ramírez girl, and there is another murmur of assent. It's a real shame. How on earth is Mr. Strickland's mama sleeping at night? She must be worried sick about her boy and all because of a misunderstanding.

This was no misunderstanding, I say. It was a rape, and I am sick and tired of y'all pretending otherwise. I pause and let my eyes wander around the fellowship hall. It is hot as perdition in here. Several ladies who have been fanning themselves with their copies of the charter now sit perfectly still on the edge of their folding chairs, as if they are awaiting a revelation, and I take this as a sign that I ought to continue speaking. In a few short hours, I will recognize this for the terrible error it is, but not now.

Because you can call a sandstorm a little breeze all day long, I tell them, and you can call a drought a dry spell, but at the end of the day, your house is still a mess and your tomato plants are dead and—my voice tightens up and, to my horror, my eyes begin to fill. I am not going to cry in front of these good ladies. I can still stop talking and everything might be okay, eventually, more or less.

I saw her, I tell them. What he did to her.

Excuse me, Mary Rose—the voice comes from over by the swamp cooler—I know what you *think* you saw, but last time I checked we still live in America, where a man is innocent until proven guilty.

A murmur wanders around the room, gentle bullshit passed from one good woman to another. While they are right about Strickland's constitutional rights, it seems to me they have already convicted a teenage girl. If y'all will excuse me, please, I say, and make a break for the ladies' room.

Eventually they send the treasurer, Mrs. L. D. Cowden, to check on me. Mrs. Cowden is a senior member who claims her grandmother planted the town's first row of pecan trees back in 1881—the same year the five Chinese railroad workers died in an explosion out near Penwell. A windstorm snapped all twenty-five of the first saplings in half. The story is a bald-faced lie. Everybody knows it was Mrs. Shepard's granny Viola Tillman who planted those trees, but nobody likes to admit it. Corrine was asked to resign her membership six years earlier, Suzanne told me, after a little scuffle with Barbie Hendrix. It all might have been forgiven, or at least lived with, given Corrine's deep roots in the community, but then she stopped getting her hair done on Thursday afternoons. I'm done with all this, she told the good women of the guild. From now on, I'll jack it up my own damn self, all the way to Jesus.

Mrs. Cowden finds me in the ladies' room next to the fellowship hall, hunched over the sink and trying not to cry. She leans quietly against the bathroom door while I splash lukewarm water on my face and mutter to myself. What *bullsh*— What bull. Can't even believe this.

Can I bring you a glass of iced tea? Mrs. Cowden says.

No, thank you.

Listen, she says, people know what that little gal is saying happened out there. We just don't need to be reminded of it all the time. And that word is so ugly.

I turn off the water and stand up straight to face her. You mean rape?

She winces. Yes, ma'am.

When I went into labor several weeks early with unpacked boxes at the new house and Robert losing his mind over a missing bull, Grace Cowden brought over a week of dinners and a stack of Archie comics for Aimee. She hasn't spoken a single unkind word to anybody in her life, as far as I know. I hold my hand out to her. I'm sorry, Grace.

She takes my hand and presses it to her heart. Well, I'm sorry too, Mary Rose. She chuckles gently. What a few months it has been. A preacher's son sitting downtown in a jail cell. Ginny Pierce running off to God knows where, leaving her family like that. And you with a new baby son, and a trial to boot. And this heat, it's mean as a snake.

She holds my hand while she wonders aloud if the judge might let me just write a letter or something. It might be less upsetting for my family and me. Besides—she leans in close—Lou Connelly heard the girl's mother was deported and the girl had been sent to Laredo to be with family. Heck, she might not even come back for the trial. Not unless there's some money in it for her.

I gently remove my hand from Grace's heart and turn back to the sink, my fingers working the faucet, while she yammers on. As for the Ladies Guild, she says, well, these meetings are supposed to be fun. Nobody comes to these meetings to feel bad about herself.

Mrs. Cowden says she and some of the other ladies have been thinking that I might not want to come to any more meetings for a little while, just until the dust settles and all this ugliness is behind us. Just until I start feeling a little more like myself.

Yes, I think, the old Mary Rose. I hold my fingers beneath the tap for a few seconds and watch the water meander across my skin, the smell of sulfur and dirt rising from the basin. That morning on my front porch, when he was already cuffed and sitting in the back seat of the deputy's sedan, one of the paramedics, a young man with eyes the color of sandstone, pressed his fingers against the knot on the back of my head.

The other handed me a glass of ice water that smelled like cold and sulfur. What the hell happened, they both wanted to know. And I shook my head. I shook and shook, but I could not find one word to say. The medics told me they couldn't get the two little girls to open the front door, and once they did, Gloria wouldn't let either of the men near her. I drank the glass of water, and the two men waited on the porch while I went inside and dampened a washrag and held it gently to her cheek.

You're going to be fine now, I told her, as my daughter stood silently at the edge of the room, watching. You're going to be fine, I said again, and this time I made sure to include both girls in my glance. I kept washing the child's face and telling her that we were going to be fine, we were all going to be just fine.

Out there the water flows out of the faucet ice cold, even in the summer, but here in town it comes out warm, with none of the debris and grit of well water. Clean water, clean start, clean slate. She had not cried, not even once, but when the paramedics tried to get her to climb inside the ambulance, when one of them put his hands on the small of her back, she screamed as if she'd been stabbed. We might as well have stood her up on a tree stump and driven an ax through her longways. She fought and kicked and screamed for her mother. She ran over and held on to me as if she were caught in a tornado and I was the last fence post still standing. But by then, I was worn out and heartsick, and I turned away. Even as she was reaching for me, I turned away and stepped inside my house and closed the door. I listened while the men grabbed her and wrestled her into the back of the ambulance and slammed the door closed.

And now, here in town, people are making this child out to be some kind of liar, or blackmailer, or slut. Forgive us our trespasses, all right. I cup my hands together and allow the water to pool in my palms. What will I be a part of, here in Odessa? What will my days look like now, and who will I become? Same old Mary Rose? Grace Cowden? I smile just a little and when the water begins to seep between my fingers, I squeeze them tightly together. I can drink from it, this cup made with my own hands, if I hurry up—and so I do. I slurp loudly, water dribbling down my chin while Grace makes little sounds in her throat. Again, I bend down and allow my hands to fill back up. Maybe discretion is the better part of valor. Then again, maybe it isn't. And knowing that I have failed another woman's daughter in all the ways that matter, I now want badly to be a person of valor.

And what will my great act of valor look like?

This: Just as the esteemed Mrs. L. D. Cowden

begins to talk about how I should get more rest and maybe think about supplementing with baby formula, I lift my face from the lavatory, hold up my two cupped hands, and fling the water into her face.

Grace stands perfectly still. Finally, she has nothing to say. After a few seconds she lifts her hand and wipes the water from her forehead and flicks it to the bathroom floor. Well, she says. That was rude.

Go to hell, I tell her. Why don't you go pack boxes for those poor people y'all can't quit judging?

I could have two sick kids and a pantry full of nothing, and Robert would complain about having to leave the ranch. But the moment he hears about this, he drives into town. It takes nothing for me to close my eyes and imagine the phone ringing off the hook in our farmhouse kitchen, Robert standing there with a bologna sandwich in his hand while some woman, or her husband, expresses grave concern for my well-being. After the kids are in bed, he follows me from room to room hollering and raging while I pick up Aimee's books and toys. My breast feels like someone is holding a lit torch to it. I fight the urge not to tear off my nursing bra and fling it on the living-room carpet.

Can't you even try, Mary Rose, he says. Every day, I'm doing my damnedest to keep us from losing everything out there, land my family has worked for the past eighty years. He follows me into the kitchen and watches me pull out a paper bag and start filling it with cans of food he can take back to the farm. You think you're doing our family any favors by making yourself out to be the town lunatic?

I kneel down and stare at a shelf full of canned goods, trying to do some math. I could have sworn there were still two cans of Hormel chili in there, and a can of corn too.

Robert's boot is right next to my leg, close enough that I can smell the cow shit lingering on the leather. In the last forty-eight hours, he has lost more than a dozen cows to blowflies. The ones that didn't die out-right, he had to shoot and because blowflies lay their eggs on fresh carcasses, he pushed the corpses into a pile with his bulldozer and poured kerosene over them.

I stack the dinner dishes in the sink and turn on the hot water. What do you want me to say, Robert? People in this town seem bound and determined to believe that this whole thing is some sort of misun-derstanding, some sort of lover's spat.

Well, how do you know it wasn't?

I plunge both hands into a sink full of water as hot as I can stand it. The smell of bleach wafts off the water, strong enough that I think I must have measured wrong, and by the time I pull my hands out, they are dark red.

Are you shitting me, Robert? Did you hear what they said about her injuries? They had to take her spleen out, for God's sake. For that matter, did you hear what *I* told you?

Yes, Mary Rose. I heard it, all thirty times you told it.

I press both hands into a dishrag, trying to take the heat out of them. Everything in the kitchen stinks of bleach. As calmly as I can manage, I speak to my husband. Robert, Gloria Ramírez is fourteen years old. What if it had been Aimee?

Don't you compare that girl to my daughter, he says.

Well, why the hell not?

Because it's not the same, he is nearly shouting now. You know how those little gals are.

I pick up a stack of plates that are still in the dish rack from yesterday and set them down on the counter so hard the cabinet door shudders. No, I tell him. You shut your goddamned mouth.

Robert clamps his lips shut. When his eyes narrow and his hands curl into a fist, I yank the kitchen curtains open and start looking around for my big wooden spoon. If we are going to start hitting each other, I want to strike first. And I might want witnesses, too.

Excuse me, Mary Rose, he says, but I don't believe I will shut my mouth.

He is still yapping when the phone starts ringing off the hook. Leave it, I tell him, there's a salesman that won't stop calling. The phone rings and rings, stops for a few seconds, and starts up again. Robert stands there looking at me like I have lost my everloving mind. Leave it, I yell when he moves toward the phone. It's a goddamn salesman.

After the phone goes quiet, he asks how long I'm going to keep Aimee under house arrest, and I lie and tell him she has made all kinds of new friends here on Larkspur Lane.

When he sidles up to me at the kitchen sink and asks if I don't miss him even just a little bit, I grab at my breast and tell him about my milk duct.

Jackpot.

I have watched my husband stick his arm up a cow all the way to the elbow to turn a breeched calf and then cry when neither the cow nor the calf survived the night, but one word about his wife's nipple infection, and he can't get out the door fast enough.

He takes his canned goods and one of Suzanne's frozen casseroles and pulls out of the driveway with a little honk to let me know he means it. I take some aspirin and redraw the dishwater. Across the street,

Corrine Shepard is sitting on her front porch. I lift my hand from the soapy dish tub and hold it up to the window, and she lifts hers, cigarette held aloft, the small red cherry dancing merrily back and forth in the night. Hello, Mary Rose.

When the phone starts ringing again, it takes every bit of my willpower not to run over and fetch it off the receiver. Well come on over, you bastard, I want to tell them. I'll be standing on the front porch with my Winchester, waiting for you.

Glory

Six o'clock in the morning and Alma is tired, as always, after a night spent cleaning the administrative offices and safety department, the credit union and break shacks, the bathrooms where men sometimes piss on the floor next to the toilet and trash cans overflow with rotting food and empty aerosol cans of cleaning solvent. But it is Friday and she, along with the other six women on the crew, is looking forward to collecting her pay—money for rent and groceries, money for all the little things her daughter is always needing, money to send home and, if there are a few dollars left over, money enough to buy something small for herself—hand cream, a new rosary, a chocolate bar—and maybe knowing this makes Alma and the other women feel a little less tired than usual.

The border patrol van is already parked outside the front gate, the sliding door already open and waiting for them, and because they are women, the youngest eighteen and the oldest nearly sixty with half a dozen grandchildren, and because the four agents who stand next to the vehicle are larger and stronger, and each man's service pistol is prominently displayed on his right hip, taking the women into custody is a quick, mostly quiet affair. The women will be dropped off on the other side of the Zaragoza bridge before Alma can tell her brother about the spare money she has hidden in the bedroom closet, before she can grab an extra jug of water or a second pair of shoes for the long trip back to Puerto Ángel, before she can say goodbye to Glory. Alma speaks her daughter's name awkwardly. Glory— the name she insists on. Glory, the extra beat that has been severed. She misses it.

Word of the raid spreads quickly through the community, thanks to Sra. Domínguez, who, having gone back to retrieve her sweater from a break shack, watched from the small window as the other women were taken into custody. After the van drove away, she stood there for nearly an hour, as if her feet had been nailed to the concrete floor, and then slipped quietly through the front gate at shift change. For months, people will talk about the sad blessing of

Lucha Domínguez forgetting her sweater, a lightweight cotton cardigan that she carries even in the spring and summer, not only because she is often cold but because the indigo cloth reminds her of the night sky back home in Oaxaca. Otherwise, it might have been weeks before husbands and children and sisters knew for sure what had happened to Alma Ramírez and Mary Vásquez, Juanita González, Celia Muñoz, and a sixteen-year-old girl who had joined the crew barely a week earlier, and who was known to the other women only as Ninfa, from Taxco, in the state of Guerrero.

⌐

Three days after the raid, Victor knocks on the door of Alma's apartment. Don't worry, I'm not giving up a room at the Ritz, he tells his niece as he sets two duffel bags and a sack of groceries on the carpet. The bunkhouse at the man camp in Big Lake has a leaky faucet and crickets the size of jalapeños. He holds up both index fingers and moves them gently apart, an inch, two inches, to show her how big they are, then looks around the apartment appreciatively, as if he hasn't been there for dinner at least twice a week since he returned from the war. As if he doesn't see the pockmarked and water-stained drywall, or the carpeting that curls up along the baseboards, or the window blinds so old the slats will crack in half if Glory does not open and close them with care. As if the faucet doesn't leak here, too, the tap a steady drip that stinks like rotten eggs in the summer. As if crickets don't swarm behind the walls here, too.

Los grillos, Alma had called them a few weeks earlier, and Glory rolled her eyes. Jesus Christ, how hard is it to say cricket? Ay mija, no maldigas al Señor.

Speak English, Glory said. Act like you belong here, for once in your life.

Glory watches her uncle fetch the rest of his things off the sidewalk and then step over to the sofa bed where she sleeps. He sets down a third duffel bag, along with a small wooden crate that holds two books, a bag of potato chips, a carton of cereal, a gallon of milk, and two six-packs of Coors Light. This here's nicer than my place, he says, you got covered parking here. Keep the hailstones off my El Camino, eh, Gloria?

Glory claps her hands over her ears and walks backward toward her mother's bedroom. When she reminds her uncle, he looks at her blankly. Call me anything, she has begged her mother and uncle, even the district attorney on the one occasion she sat for an interview, but not that. Now, Victor says, Why not, m'ija? It's your name. Because every time I hear it, she wants to shout at him, I hear his voice.

It is a few minutes past four o'clock and the apartment complex sings and sighs with the noise of little kids coming home from day-care centers and vacation Bible schools. Mothers and big sisters shout at them to hurry up and help with chores. Box fans hum in the open windows, pushing hot air into the small courtyard. Ranchera drifts across the parking lot, and Glory again fights the urge to go into her mother's bedroom, climb into bed, and put all the pillows between her ears and the world. Out there in the oil patch, he played his music loud, stopping to switch the channel from one country and western station to another, once to a late-night punk show on the college radio station she used to love. And why wouldn't he play the music loud? Who was out there to hear? Nobody is coming to help you, he told her, and he was right.

Glory is still in her mother's bedroom when the property manager, Mr. Navarro, knocks on the door. They cannot stay here, he tells Victor. Mr. Navarro has heard about the raid at the plant, and he doesn't want illegals living in this complex. Victor tells the man that his niece, Glory, was born right here in Odessa, at the medical center.

¿Y tú? the old man says.

Victor answers in Spanish, which Glory cannot understand. Here in Texas, her mother has always insisted, Spanish is the language of janitors and housekeepers, not her daughter, and kids who speak Spanish at school land in detention, or worse. Still, Glory knows the substance, if not the content, of Victor's words. Like his niece, he is also an American, he tells the man. He earned his citizenship serving two tours of duty in Vietnam, cabrón.

A few minutes later, her uncle knocks on the bedroom door and says he is going to find them a different place to live, a better place. So start packing, Glory.

It doesn't take long to gather up their lives. Four years earlier, Glory and Alma walked into the furnished apartment carrying three suitcases and a milk crate filled with kitchen items. Now, Glory lays her clothes in one suitcase, and Alma's in another. She folds her mother's bedspread and strips the sheets off the bed, packing them, along with their pillows and her knife, into the third suitcase. There is a wooden cigar box that smells faintly of cedar and holds photos of family back home in Oaxaca. Where the sandy beaches are white as salt, Tío says, and the red snapper tastes like butter. Glory sets the box in her mother's suitcase, nestling it between a pair of blue jeans and her mother's favorite blouse.

In the kitchen, she opens the cabinet next to the stove. Into the milk crate go Alma's cooking pot, her tablespoons and coffee cups, the chipped plates they found in the church store, and the plain wooden cooking spoon Alma carried with her across the border eighteen years earlier. It stirred beans and stews when Alma shared a one-room apartment with half a dozen other women who were sending money back home. Glory sometimes felt that spoon swat her ass when she was little, and the year she turned ten, Alma threw it across the kitchen and asked Glory to stop once and for all asking about the father she had never known. Well, where is he? Glory asked. ¿Pues, quién sabe? Maybe California, maybe dead. ¿Y a mí qué me importa?

And several years later, when Glory was taller and stronger than her mother, and Alma suspected she was skipping school, she pointed the spoon at Glory's head and told Victor to translate as she begged her daughter to use the brains God gave her to do something more with her life than shoplift beer at Pinkie's liquor store and go parking at the old buffalo wallow. It is this old wooden spoon that sends Glory to the small kitchen table in tears, where she sits cross-legged and rubs at the bright red scars on her feet and wonders how long it will be before Alma can gather up the money and nerve and opportunity to cross the river.

⌒

There are thirty-six rooms at the Jeronimo Motel, a U-shaped motor inn that sits near the intersection of Pearl and Petroleum, less than a mile from the refinery. On a hot night, if tenants blow a fuse running their air conditioners at the same time as their hot plates and televisions, they might step out of their rooms and lean on the iron railing and watch the blue-orange flames from the flare stacks. It's not much cooler out there, but there's usually a little wind blowing in their direction.

Victor pulls his long, white El Camino—El Tiburón, he calls it—into a space facing the pool. Pues, you can float there all day long, he tells his niece, who leans against the passenger door with her cheek pressed against the warm glass. It is after ten and the lot is already filled with diesel trucks, pickups, a smattering of sedans and station wagons. A small camper is parked across two spots on the other side of the pool, its yellow porch light flickering gently against the water. A woman paddles across the pool, a small wake radiating from her head and hands. When she reaches the middle, she flips onto her back and drifts in the dark, her body exposed to the air, her yellow hair floating eel-like around her face. The woman wears cut-off jeans and a T-shirt, Glory sees now, and her thick arms and legs gleam in the dark like shark's teeth.

After Victor has helped Glory carry her things to the second floor, he hands her a room key on a plastic, Texas-shaped fob. Best thing about this place, it's cheap enough that Glory can have her own room. Rooms cost twice as much at the Dixie Motel out on Andrews Highway. He gives her room 15. Which makes sense, he says, because she will turn fifteen in the fall. This year is gonna pass, mi vida, he says, and you'll feel better soon. This isn't your life.

Room 15 smells of cigarettes and grease, but there are fresh vacuum cleaner lines on the carpet and the bathroom smells like lemon Pine-Sol. A television sits on a low brown dresser that is nearly as long as the room, and the double bed is covered with a carrot-colored polyester bedspread. While Victor looks for the Coke machine, Glory strips off the bedding. She makes the bed with Alma's floral-scented sheets and the bedspread her mother bought last fall after working some extra shifts. It is covered with Texas bluebonnets, a flower Alma claims as her favorite, though she has never in her life seen a real one. Last fall Victor promised Alma and Glory that they would drive down to the Hill Country in April, and Alma could take a picture of her daughter sitting in a field that had been overtaken by the tiny purple flowers, then put it in a frame and hang it on the wall, like every other parent in the great state of Texas. Thanks, Glory told her uncle, but I'd rather stay home and read *The Scarlet Letter*. See how ungrateful she is, said Alma, and they stared at each other until Glory dropped her eyes. And now it's June, Glory thinks. We missed it.

Victor stops by with a bottle of cold Dr Pepper and a promise to bring her a doughnut before he leaves for work in the morning. When he steps back onto the landing that runs the entire length of the building, she closes the door and fastens the thin brass chain. There's a door that connects their rooms, but he says it's only for emergencies. He will knock on the front door, just like anybody else. For most of her life, Glory has dreamed of having her own room, her own door to lock, and she feels a little spark of pleasure, in spite of the horror that has brought them here.

A thin rectangle of late-afternoon sun pushes through a narrow gap in the curtains, the light falling across the carpet and catching the dust motes that drift through the air. She pulls the curtains tight and the light disappears. The window is hardly bigger than a pizza box, impossible for even a small man to climb through. Still, Glory checks the metal clasp on the window, and the piece of broomstick that someone has wedged along the jamb between the upper and lower sash. The yellow-haired woman is out of the pool now. She sits on a lounge chair with a towel around her head and a cigarette in her hand, her wet clothes clinging to her large body. The other rooms are dark, the Jeronimo Motel quiet and still.

The proprietor don't put up with any silliness, Victor told her when they pulled into the parking lot and her eyes widened at the rows of work trucks. He only rents to working-men and families. You'll be safe here—he reached over as if to pat his niece's arm but stopped short of touching her—you're gonna be okay.

Maybe he's right, but when Glory climbs into bed, she reaches under the pillow and runs her fingers across the folded pocketknife she has stashed there. If anybody comes through that door, or the window, she will be ready for him. Once, twice, three times, Glory runs her fingers across the knife's smooth steel and leather handle. She is still holding it, still running through the steps—grab the knife, press the catch, slash at the air until the knife connects—when she falls asleep.

In every dream, the desert is alive. She walks carefully, but the moon disappears behind a cloud and she doesn't see the pile of rocks, or the nest of snakes on the other side of it. When she falls and rises shrieking from the ground, they are already on her, wrapping themselves around her ankles and legs, climbing toward her belly and breasts. One curls itself around her neck and Glory feels the quick, thin flick of a tongue against her eyelash. She stands perfectly still, waiting for them to move off her, to retreat back into the dark. Moonlight shines through the truck's window. His pupils are black holes surrounded by blue sky. Time to pony up, Gloria, he says, time to pay for all my beer you drank, all this gas I used to get us here. Wait, she says. Wait! She reaches into the pocket of her jeans and wraps her fingers around the leather handle. The knife opens effortlessly and finds his gullet without fail.

Awake now in the dark, Glory moves one finger up and down the raised skin on her belly. About the width of a dandelion stem, the scar begins just below her breasts and follows a meandering path down her torso, as if she has been cut in half and sewn back together. At her navel, it curves around her belly button and continues on, stopping just below her pubic line. When she woke up in the hospital, she had been shaved and her belly was held together with a long line of metal staples. Lacerated spleen, the surgeon told Victor, probably from one of the punches she took to the abdomen. She fought, she fought, she fought. Her feet and hands were wrapped in white bandages, and her hair had been cut to the scalp, a line of stitches wandering across the crown of her head. Victor leaned down and whispered that her mama couldn't come to the hospital—too many cops, too many questions—but she was waiting for Glory at home. Listen, he whispered to his niece, you survived this. He said something else then, but Glory was already sinking back into sleep and pain, and she couldn't be sure what it was. She thought he said, This is a war story. Or maybe, this is yours.

⌒

When Victor knocks on the door at 4:30 every morning, he's holding a chocolate doughnut and a carton of milk. Keep the door locked, he says. If you need help, dial zero for the motel office. After he leaves, Glory lies in bed and listens as the parking lot growls to life. Diesel engines and doors slam. Men, still half asleep, murmur outside her door. She hears the echo of work boots on the metal stairs, and the sudden blast of a car horn when one of the workers has overslept. And she hunkers down in her covers, fingers still wrapped around the knife handle. By five o'clock, the parking lot is mostly empty. Until the kids and wives and girlfriends wake up, the Jeronimo Motel will sit quiet as an abandoned church, and it is then that Glory is able to get her best sleep.

By late morning, when kids start running up and

down the stairs and doing cannonballs into the deep end of the pool, when girlfriends and wives are heading out to work the lunch shift or pick up some groceries at Strike-It-Rich, when the woman who tries to clean the room has knocked on the door and handed her a stack of clean towels—no thanks, she says when the woman tries to come in and change the sheets—Glory has had the television on for hours. The soap operas and detergent commercials drone constantly in the background as Glory sleeps and snacks, bathes and showers, peeks through the curtain, watches a shaft of sunlight move across the floor. A couple of times she picks up the phone and thinks about calling Sylvia, but she has not spoken to anyone from school since February. And what would she say? Hello, from the stupidest girl in the world, who climbed into a stranger's truck and slammed the door shut, whose picture ended up in the paper, blowing any chance she had at getting past this.

Her uncle returns by seven o'clock every evening, carrying bags from Whataburger or KFC, and some small gift—a magazine, lip balm, a small hot plate and cans of soup so she can make lunch, peanut butter and a box of saltines, a Spanish workbook with hardly any of the words filled in that he found on the ground next to a pumpjack. Every night he brings something, and when he hands it to her, she can see that he has done his best to get the oil off his hands.

One evening, he comes home with a pair of sunglasses, a portable cassette deck, and three tapes—Carole King, Fleetwood Mac, and Lydia Mendoza. Drove all over West Odessa to find that last one, he says. This machine is portable. You can carry it anywhere, you don't even have to find a plug. He shows her where to put the batteries, how to adjust the shoulder strap.

I don't want it, Glory says. I don't want to hear any music, and if I did, it wouldn't be this crap.

Okay. Victor loads the items back into a grocery bag. I'll set them on the dresser in case you change your mind. Let me take a shower and we'll watch some TV. Soon, Victor tells his niece, Alma will be back and they will all sit down together and watch their programs. He has sent letters to their family in Puerto Ángel with their new address. It's only a matter of time before Alma writes back to let them know she is fine. Your mother will have a plan, he says. She will try to cross again in September, when the weather is cooler.

It is June, and the patches of hair that cover Glory's head are scarcely thicker than pinfeathers. Her hair, like the rest of her, is starting over. Like Brandy Henderson, the soap opera character in *The Edge of Night* who goes into hiding and disappears from the story,

Glory's life is a long pause, a stopped tape. But she is getting ready to start moving again. Come August, all she has to do is testify, her uncle says. Just put on a nice dress and walk into that courtroom, and tell the truth. I'm not doing it, she tells him. I don't care what happens to him.

⌒

It is ninety-eight degrees outside when the air conditioner switches off, ticks steadily for a few minutes, and goes silent. Within minutes, as if it has been waiting for its opportunity to strike, the heat begins to seep through the windowpane and climb in through the small cracks on the windowsill. It crawls through the narrow gap between the door and carpet, and slithers from the vent above the bed.

Glory usually waits it out in a bathtub filled with cold water, but today it is so hot the water comes out of the faucet warm, and her embarrassment about her scars and hair, her desire not to be seen, and her fear and sorrow that she has been stolen from herself, that she has been wounded, maybe fatally—all are in abeyance to something she has not felt since February. She is bored. Or at least that is what she will name it this morning. In a few years, she might call it loneliness.

This afternoon, she digs around in a box until she finds the bathing suit Victor bought for her, a simple blue one-piece with sturdy straps. She pulls it on without looking at her stomach, or her feet and ankles, or the star-shaped scar in the center of her palm.

Grabbed onto a barbed-wire fence to stop yourself from falling? Victor said when she showed it to him in the hospital. Girl, that's some army-level toughness. But I fell anyway, she said. Well, don't tell that part of your story, he said. Tell people you squeezed that fence until the barbs bent flat in your hand.

My story? No. This is not my story.

She squeezes the doorknob of her motel room tight and grips the wrought-iron railing that runs along the second-story walkway. Heart pounding, one hand on the pocket of her shorts where she can feel the knife pressing against her groin, Glory tries to act as if she goes to the pool every day, as if she walks down these metal stairs several times a day, as if she is a normal girl.

She sits on a lawn chair at the far end of the pool, still wearing the Led Zeppelin T-shirt and jean shorts she pulled on over her bathing suit. Before she left the room, she wrapped a bottle of Coke in a white bath towel that rests on the deck next to her feet. She drinks it quickly. For weeks she has been peeking through the curtains, watching the woman she saw swimming on their first night at the Jeronimo Motel. Every day she comes down to the pool with her two kids, a chubby little boy who has his mother's yellow hair and always wears the same navy-blue swim trunks, and a little girl, long and skinny as a rifle, her freckles and stringy red hair glowing in the sunlight.

Today, when they walk to the shallow side of the pool, the three of them pause and stare briefly at Glory, as if she is trespassing. The little girl lies down on a lounger and opens a thick book, and the boy jumps into the pool with his small collection of things that float—a faded plastic boat, a tennis ball, a blow-up raft that has been patched with several pieces of silver duct tape. The mother paddles up and down the pool a few times and then wraps a towel around her head and puts on her sunglasses before sitting down next to her daughter. Mother and daughter slather baby oil on their legs and arms. They lie back and wait for the sun to turn them pink, bright pink, then lobster red. They wear matching one-piece bathing suits covered with large red and yellow flowers, the girl's a little too large for her skinny body, the mother's a little too small.

They might be the homeliest people Glory has ever seen. The boy has a large gap where his two front baby teeth used to be, and the little girl picks at the skin peeling from her sunburned shoulders, covertly putting the pieces in her mouth while she reads. The mother's arms and legs are round and hairless and pink, like something plucked from a shell.

Glory leans back and closes her eyes until the sun burns her eyelids and the knife grows hot against her skin. She tucks it into the folded white towel, but puts it back in her shorts after a few minutes. As the day grows hotter, she walks to the edge of the pool and lowers the towel into the water, then wrings it out and lays it across her legs, her arms and face.

The little boy paddles his float to the deep end of the pool and hovers next to the edge a few feet from where Glory sits. You got change for a dollar? he asks suddenly, as if he is hiding a bill somewhere in his swim trunks and might pull it out, wadded up and dripping wet, to trade for a handful of coins. Glory looks at him with her mouth open, as if the fact of him, or more particularly, of his voice, has left her stupefied.

Do you speak *English*? he drawls.

T. J.! You leave that girl alone. The woman jumps to her feet and hustles across the pool deck, large and quick as a parade float caught in a sharp wind. When the towel on her head comes loose and begins to slide down her back, she tosses it on the deck. She moves fast for a woman her size, closing the distance between herself and the little boy and Glory in just a few seconds.

T. J. grins at Glory and pushes his float away from the edge of the pool. Why don't you get in the swimming pool? he says. Are ya afraid ya might get grease in the water? Afraid your back might get wet? He giggles then, shoving his fist against his mouth as if to stifle the sound. Wetback, he says. He looks like he weighs eighty pounds, and while she can't really swim, Glory thinks she could probably drown him.

The mother gets down on her hands and knees, stretches her arm across the water, and grabs at his raft. God *damn* it, T. J., you little shit. You come out of that water right now. She drags the float to the pool's edge and he is already yowling when his mother reaches down and grabs him by the arm. Standing now, she lifts her son into the air, his arms flailing, fat legs churning madly. Her strength is surprising, and wonderful.

Glory is already on her feet, reaching for her towel and eyeing the gate. She will have to walk past the woman and her son to get to it, or go the long way around the pool, past the little girl who has set down her book and sits laughing on her lounge chair.

Wait, the woman says to Glory. Can you just wait a minute? Red-faced and panting, the woman sets her son on his feet and towers over him. She wraps her fingers around the soft part of his arm and pinches so hard he yowls. You won't be able to sit down for three days if I *ever* hear you talking like that again. She tightens her grip and the boy snuffles.

You hear me? She is still holding the soft flesh of his arm.

Yes, ma'am, he says.

Get your ass upstairs and take a nap. Tammy! Take T. J. up to the room—she glowers at her son—he's tired. Glory thinks for a second the woman has said *tarred*, her accent is so thick. He's *tarred*.

The little girl is on her feet now, holding her book in the air and yelling back at her mama. It's hot in there and you promised to take me to the bookmobile.

We'll see, maybe later. Beneath her T-shirt, the woman's chest moves rapidly up and down. Y'all get to the room *now*.

They watch the little boy fuss and stomp across the parking lot, and then the woman holds out one hand. I'm sorry about that, he gets it from his daddy's side of the family. Glory shoves her hands in her pockets. I don't really care.

I'm Tina Allen from Lake Charles, Louisiana, and those two little wretches are T. J. and Tammy. My husband works on a rig near Ozona.

Glory looks at her without saying anything until Tina sighs and walks back to her lounge chair. She digs around in her purse for a few seconds. I'm going to get myself an ice-cold drink. Can I get you something?

No, thank you.

C'mon, sugar. Let me buy you a Dr Pepper. It'll make me feel better. Tina's laugh is horsey and rough, and it reminds Glory of a teacher she had hated, before, when she was a C student who dreamed of learning to play the guitar and earning her own money and calling her own shots, when the teacher called the Mexican kids her little brown refugees, when Glory and her friend Sylvia stole a box cutter from the woodshop and slashed two of the woman's tires. I wish we knew how to cut the bitch's brake lines, Sylvia said and held out her hands as if she were clutching a steering wheel. Save me, you little brown refugees! It still makes Glory laugh out loud, and miss her friend terribly.

Can I have a cigarette? she asks Tina.

Pardon me, but you don't look old enough to smoke.

Well, I am. These are the most words Glory has exchanged with anyone other than her mother or uncle since she left the hospital. She'd really love to have a cigarette, it occurs to her, and maybe sit with her feet in the water while she smokes it.

Yeah, I guess you're right. Tina walks over and holds

out a slim and pretty Benson & Hedges. Can I sit down for a second?

They sit and look across the parking lot. It is past noon and the full force of the sun is unleashed on their bodies. The air conditioners have not come back on, and the courtyard is quieter than usual, but across the road, flatbed trucks pull in and out of pipe yards and bearing-supply companies. Behind the motel lies a field, fawn-colored and scattered with broken glass that catches the light and shines green, red, blue. Behind that, lay small wooden houses with dirt yards and thin curtains that smell of noxious fumes from the plant.

Tina sucks deeply on her cigarette and then turns her face upward and blows the smoke toward the sun. I miss Lake Charles, and it weren't exactly paradise on earth. You can't throw a rock without hitting some good old boy with a bad attitude, and the bayou is full of gators and 'skeeters and rats as big as a dog, nutria, they're called—she ashes on the deck and rubs it with her big toe—but the fishing's good and some people are nice. And there's trees. Dogwood and sugarberry, cypress. I miss trees, and I miss sucking the heads off crawdaddies. Me and Terry are just here to make enough money to buy a shrimp boat. That's all I want, a fishing boat for Terry to earn a living, and for my kids to go back to school. That don't seem like too much to ask.

She smiles at Glory. How about you? You been here very long?

Glory has been listening intently to the other woman, and it occurs to her now that she is expected to say something, tell the woman something about her life, participate in the give and take. I'm here with my uncle, she says. He works in Big Lake, hauling water and mucking tanks. I'm recovering from—an accident.

Pauvre ti bête, Tina says, and when Glory looks at her, Poor little thing. Is that what happened to your feet?

Glory looks down. Dozens of thin scars cover her feet and ankles—from cactus thorns and stray pieces of steel, broken glass and bent nails, a mess of stickers and a stray piece of barbed wire, all the things she stepped on when she walked away from his truck—and her throat closes on itself.

It's okay, hon, Tina says.

Glory opens her mouth, closes it. She shakes her head and looks at her cigarette. I was attacked by a man out in the oil patch.

God damn it all, Tina says, and after a long pause, I'm sorry.

I got in his truck and went with him.

Well hell, sugar, Tina says. That don't mean jack. That evil belongs to him, it's got nothing to do with you.

They sit quietly for a few minutes and then Tina starts talking about the trees back home, the knobby-kneed bald cypress that loses its needles in the winter and can live for a thousand years, the tupelo with its scarlet Ogeechee limes. They ain't worth a damn for eating, she says, but the tree gives good honey. Tina tosses her cigarette butt toward the fence and immediately lights another. But it isn't all greenery and good fishing, she says and holds the box out to Glory. You want to hear a joke?

I guess so. Glory plucks a smoke from the box and puts it between her lips.

What's the definition of a Lake Charles virgin? Tina inhales deeply and blows three perfect smoke rings toward the sun. For a few seconds, they hang in the hot air like rain clouds.

I don't know. What *is* the definition of a Lake Charles virgin?

Tina snorts. An ugly twelve-year-old who can run real fast. She pauses and stares into the swimming pool for a few seconds. Guess I weren't ugly enough, or quick enough.

Ha, Glory says. Ha, ha. And then they are both

laughing. Sitting under the hot sun and smoking their cigarettes, laughing their asses off.

Well, it is hot as a well digger's balls out here, Tina says. I'm going for a swim. She stands up and tamps a half-smoked cigarette against the pool deck, then walks over and sets it on the table for later. She eases her large body into the water, her bathing suit hugging her large breasts and arms. You want to come in, Glory? It feels pretty good.

Within seconds, Glory's T-shirt and shorts are saturated and sagging, tugging her toward the pool's bottom, as if to say, go ahead and sink. She isn't a strong swimmer—the public pools are for the white kids and although her friends often swam in the livestock tanks they came across when they were out driving, Glory never climbed in with them—but now she discovers she can stay afloat, if she holds her arms away from her body and moves her hands in gentle circles. Eyes closed, Tina and Glory float in the pool next to each other, the sun a jackhammer against their eyelids, the heat a dead weight against their bare skin. They drift, and Tina occasionally sighs, goddamn, goddamn.

When the water pushes them close enough that Tina's hand lightly brushes against hers, Glory jerks her hand away as if she's touched a snake. In late February, one nurse held her chin and told her to close her eyes while another nurse gently snipped the stitches at the top of Glory's head. She tugged each stitch with a pair of tweezers, one by one, until they lay in thin black rows in a small bowl next to the table. And that was the last time Glory felt someone's hands against her skin.

I once burned my mother's favorite bedspread on purpose, Glory says, and I wish I hadn't. We were fighting about school. I didn't want to go anymore. I wanted to go to work with her and make some money. I wanted to buy some clothes and a guitar, maybe take some lessons.

Kids do all kinds of stupid, Tina says. Look at mine. Your mama probably didn't care one bit about a hole in a bedspread. She stretches her arms above her head. Never has Glory seen a more buoyant person.

So when are you going back to school? Tina says. What do you want to be when you grow up?

Glory lifts her hand from the water and holds up one finger. First question: never. She holds up another. Second question: I don't know. At school, she often left the building at lunch and didn't come back for the rest of the day. She and Sylvia would catch a lift to somebody's house and spend the afternoon there, listening to music and passing a joint around, watching some of the other kids slide their arms around each other's waists and wander down the hall and slip into one of the bedrooms.

Tina sighs, her large body expanding and contracting on top of the water. No school? Really? Because girl, I can't wait to get my two little angels back into school. Your mama's right.

Maybe. Glory drifts across the pool with her eyes closed, arms moving in slow circles. When the water again pushes the woman and girl close, she reaches over and takes Tina's hand and squeezes real hard. She waits, and after a pause, Tina squeezes gently back.

They will never meet again. This day will feel too big for Glory, and she will retreat back to room 15 for another week. Tina's husband will get a job making more money on an offshore rig closer to home, and after some discussion they will carry their sleeping kids to the station wagon in the middle of the night. By the time Glory carries her pocketknife and her towel and a bottle of cold Dr Pepper to the pool again, Tina will be back in Lake Charles. But Glory will never forget her kindness, or her throaty laugh, or the slippery warmth of her hand against Glory's when they threaded their fingers together and Tina asked, When did it happen?

In February, when Alma and Glory were fighting every day about homework and money. When Glory said, I want to quit school and go to work, I want some money of my own, and Alma shook her head fiercely. It was her job to work, her daughter's job to learn. When boys sometimes pulled into the alley behind their apartment and tapped the horn until Glory grabbed her rabbit's fur jacket and dashed out the door, but not before Mr. Navarro beat on the front door and hollered at Glory and Alma to stop shouting at each other. On Valentine's night, when her mother cursed Glory in Spanish while they waited for the van that would pick up Alma and drive her to work, and Glory walked into the bedroom and stood over to her mother's bed for a few seconds and then casually, as if she were standing over a flowerpot, tamped her cigarette out on the new bedspread. I can't understand you, *Alma*. You won't let me learn it and neither will the school, so speak English, goddamn you. And when, two hours later, Glory took a long, last look around the Sonic parking lot and decided she had nothing to lose. When she climbed into Dale Strickland's pickup truck and pulled the heavy door closed. When the morning is still as a corpse. When tumbleweeds newly torn from their roots are flung across the land. When the wind picks up, when it says stand up. And she stands up. When a mesquite branch snaps beneath the weight of her bare foot and she hears her uncle's voice in the slight echo that follows. Walk quiet, Glory. When she thinks she will miss this blue sky stretched tight above the earth's seam because she can't stay, not after this. When the wind is always pushing and pulling, losing and gaining, lifting and holding and dropping, when all the voices and stories begin and end the same way. *Listen, this is a war story*. Or maybe, *this is yours*.

Suzanne

On the first and third Friday mornings of every month, Suzanne Ledbetter and her daughter drive over to the credit union to deposit Jon's paycheck along with her cash and checks from selling Avon and Tupperware. To avoid the crowds of men who work at the plant across the highway and come on their lunch breaks, they arrive a few minutes before nine. While Lauralee waits in the car or stands in the parking lot twirling her baton, Suzanne fills out deposit slips for checking, savings, retirement, vacation, Lauralee's college and wedding, and one account that she records in her notebook as charity. It is an account she has had since she worked full-time selling life insurance and nobody, not even Jon, knows about it. It is her safety net. If things go south in a hurry, she will have options.

When Suzanne hands the slips and checks and cash to the teller, the woman marvels aloud, as she does every two weeks, at Suzanne's neat handwriting and tidy piles. I believe you are the most organized woman I have ever seen, the woman says, and Suzanne replies, Well, aren't you sweet, Mrs. Ordóñez, and she digs through her purse for a business card and a perfume sample. Because she prefers to sell products that make women feel pretty, she does not mention the new food storage system she has in the trunk of her car. Instead, she tucks a catalog under the woman's windshield wiper on her way out.

It is late June and the sun is murderous. Suzanne's heels sink into the black tar and gravel as she walks back to the car where Lauralee waits with the windows up and the engine running, her hair hanging in thin strands around her face. She has her mother's red hair, just as Suzanne has *her* mother's.

How much did we earn this week? Lauralee asks after Suzanne has slammed the door and pulled a tissue from her purse to dab her forehead and armpits.

Forty-five dollars. We'll have to step up our game at this afternoon's practice.

You can do it, Lauralee says. Her baton rolls off the seat and she leans over to pick it up, groaning as the seat belt cuts into her belly, kicking her mother's seat as she stretches her arms toward the baton. You're the best saleslady in Odessa.

That's because nothing feels as good as earning your own money, Suzanne says. Her deliveries are in small white bags on the passenger seat, and she keeps the vents pointed directly at them. She pulls a small spiral notebook from her purse and makes a record of her account balances. She is five dollars short of her biweekly goal. Two weeks ago, she was short by ten. Suzanne pats her armpits one last time with the tissue and then puts on her sunglasses and freshens her lipstick. Time to channel Arlene, she thinks, setting aside her notebook and taking up the legal pad where she has written her to-do list: Take Lauralee to piano lessons, drop off casserole for Mary Rose, pick up Lauralee, hang needlepoint art in L's bedroom, deliver gift bags to the ladies at the practice field, call Dr. Bauman, go to Credit union. *Check.*

They are running late, so she shifts the car into first gear and pulls out of the parking lot with her tires squealing and the transmission humming tightly. They are going nearly sixty miles an hour when they drive through the green light at Dixie and South Petroleum Street, but they catch the train anyway. Suzanne pulls to a quick stop and taps one fingernail against the steering wheel while they watch the Burlington Northern cars rattle past. When the train slows to a crawl and then stops completely, she chews her cuticle for a moment, then shifts into reverse and takes a different route. Never depend on a man to take care of you, Lauralee, she says. Not even one as good as your daddy.

I won't. Her daughter is buckled up tight, a stack of piano books on the seat next to her. Her tap and ballet shoes are in the trunk, along with her swim bag and a large plastic tub filled with Tupperware.

I got lucky because your daddy is the best man in Odessa, Suzanne says, but many don't. You are going to get everything you want in life—she tries to catch her daughter's eye in the rearview mirror—but you can't take your eye off the ball, not even for a minute. People who take their eye off the ball get hit in the face.

Suzanne is a firm believer in sunlight and bleach, and not hiding behind little white lies. The sooner Lauralee has a complete picture of their situation, the better, so she tells her: Trash, that's what people say when they talk about my family. Trash when they were tenant farmers in England, and crofters in Scotland, trash when they were sharecroppers, first in Kentucky, then in Alabama, and trash here in Texas, where the men became horse thieves and bison hunters, Klansmen and vigilantes, and the women became liars and confeder-ates. And that, she says, is why there are only three of us at Thanksgiving dinner every year. That's why nobody will be coming to town for the Bicentennial celebration. I wouldn't have those people at my table if somebody held a gun to my head—which they might.

When her daughter is a little older, Suzanne will tell her that less than a hundred years ago, they were still living in dugouts, hiding out from debt collectors and Texas Rangers, waiting for the Comanche to come and fill them with arrows. Suzanne's people were too stupid, or isolated, to know that the Red River War had been over for five years, and what was left of the Comanche people, mostly women and children and old men, were confined to Fort Sill. Until the day he died, Suzanne's great-great granddaddy carried a tobacco pouch made from the scrotum of a Mescalero Apache he murdered on the Llano Estacado. Suzanne's cousin, Alton Lee, still keeps it in an old cedar chest covered with cigarette burns and bumper stickers of the Stars and Bars.

I don't feel like going to piano, Lauralee says. It's boring.

Suzanne grits her teeth and chews the inside of her cheek. Little girl, you think you've got it bad? When I was your age, I saw a boy get eaten by an alligator. All they found of him was his little Dallas Cowboys T-shirt, and one sneaker.

Why did he get eaten? Lauralee has heard this story a dozen times and she knows what question to ask next.

Well, he wasn't paying attention to where he was going. When people don't look where they're going, alligators get them. Anyhow, the boy's mother—her name was Mrs. Goodrow and her family had been in East Texas since they were run out of Louisiana—she hung in there. She had eight other kids and no time to dwell on it, but his daddy wasn't ever the same. Or at least that's what your grandma Arlene told all of us kids. Your grandma could sell a glass of iced water to a polar bear. She could talk the sweet out of a sugar cube. And she was pretty as a field of bluebonnets, too. Five years running, she was the Harrison County rodeo queen.

I wish she was here, Lauralee says.

As do we all, honey. Stop hunching your shoulders like that, she calls as Lauralee walks away from the car, you'll get a dowager's hump. Piano lessons. *Check.*

Arlene and Larry Compton used to drag Suzanne and her brothers all over West Texas, chasing the boom. Stanton, Andrews, Ozona, Big Lake—they were always trying to save for a rainy day, but when the price of oil fell or Arlene had bounced enough checks to get the sheriff's attention, the family would rush to pack the car. Suzanne and her brothers sat elbow to elbow in the back seat while her parents smoked and fussed and blamed each other. If they hurried, her daddy said, they might be able to watch the sun rise over the swamp. Her mother said, Goddamn it, Suzie. If you don't stop kicking the back of my seat, I am going to wear you out.

Back in East Texas, they'd find some little tarpaper shack at the edge of the swamp, someplace with a landlord who didn't recognize their name—Compton, as in the Compton boys are back in town, so don't let your cats out of the house, lock your doors and hide the silver, tell your daughters to watch out—or if the landlord did know the name, he didn't care. Nobody else wanted to live out there.

Her mama was as unpredictable as the stray dogs that sometimes slipped into the yard when Suzanne left the gate open. When Daddy sent her outside to close it, she walked into the darkened yard, swearing she'd remember to close the gate next time, hoping the things she saw moving in the night were only moon shadows cast against the bare dirt. Some mornings before he left the house to look for work, when the brothers were still sleeping or they hadn't come home the night before, Suzanne's daddy would give her a dime. Make yourself scarce, he'd tell her. Your mama needs to rest.

On those days, she walked into whatever town they

were living near and spent her dime, and when the sun was threatening to go down, or she was hungry again, Suzanne went home and stood on the front porch with her hand on the doorknob and one ear pressed against the door, the wood splintered and rough against her cheek, tarpaper flapping gently on the wall next to the front door, while she tried to get a feel for what might be waiting on the other side.

⌒

If Dr. Bauman can be believed, Suzanne is unlikely to ever carry another pregnancy to term. Her womb is chock-full of fibroid tumors, he says, and the miscarriages are hard on her body, hard on her spirit, hard on her family. They might as well go in and take everything out. Call it a day, he says, if you aren't going to be using them anyway—*them* being Suzanne's ovaries. She will hardly notice the difference, he says, except she won't have her monthly cycle anymore. And won't that be a treat.

When Suzanne knocks on Mary Rose's door, she is holding a King Ranch casserole in the hand she doesn't chew on. She admires the new baby, remarking on his size and weight and length, and Mary Rose hands him over without hesitation. When Suzanne mentions her conversation with the doctor, Mary Rose says, I'm sorry to hear that, but she is looking past Suzanne, her eyes scanning the front yard and the street. They haven't spoken since Corrine Shepard practically accused Suzanne of being a bigot—a crazy notion that she got, or so Suzanne has heard, from D. A. Pierce.

Oh, please, she tells Mary Rose, I'm *fine*. There are people starving in Cambodia. Her gaze takes in Mary Rose's thin frame, the shadows beneath her eyes. You look like you're starving, too.

Mary Rose stares at the casserole dish she has found herself holding, and the baby, who is gripped like a bag of groceries in the crook of her other arm. All right, she says flatly, thank you.

I taped a little Tupperware catalog to the bottom of the dish.

Mary Rose runs a finger along the bottom of the glassware. Oh, I see.

I gave one to my friend who works at the credit union, too. Suzanne looks at a jagged cuticle and quickly tucks it behind her back. Do you know Mrs. Ordóñez?

We use Cattleman's Bank, Mary Rose says.

Well, she is just the sweetest lady. Suzanne glances at her watch. If you throw together a little green salad, y'all will have yourselves a complete meal.

Casserole, *Check.*

Suzanne has the best of intentions, but she can't stop wondering aloud how some people get to be so stupid. In the midst of any calamity, she almost always says the wrong thing. A year earlier, when a tornado wiped out a trailer park in West Odessa, killing three people and injuring a dozen more, she wondered aloud why anyone would choose to live in such cheaply made structures. The ones that survived, she told Rita Nunally, ought to be prosecuted for putting their families' lives at risk. But those homemade casseroles that mean somebody won't have to fix supper that night? Those, she can do. When the recipe calls for a can of cream of mushroom soup, she sautés fresh button mushrooms and stirs in a can of milk with a tablespoon of flour. And while her casseroles aren't exactly quiche lorraine, every one of them is a complete meal—meat, vegetable, and a pasta or grain.

Her chocolate-chip cookies are made with real butter, not margarine, and she never skimps on the brown sugar. Everything fresh, nothing canned. That's her motto. No pinto beans and corn bread for Lauralee, she likes to tell her neighbors, no babies before she's finished college. Her daughter will never eat stewed dandelion greens, alligator, rattlesnake, or collards. She will never eat catfish or carp or anything else with a mud vein that has to be removed, and there will always be a dessert course after supper, however simple it might be. Every night before dinner, she lights two small candles and sets them in the middle of the dining room table, then stands back to take in the scene. They're pretty, she tells Jon and Lauralee. They make every night feel special, even Wednesday. And in this light no one can see the bright red knot where a pimple is trying to sprout on her chin, the chipped tooth from a fall she took when she was fifteen, the cuticles she can't stop chewing.

When I was a little girl, she tells Lauralee, I would have given my eyeteeth to live in a house with carpet, and a bathtub that's big enough to lie down in, and a piano that my mother had bought by licking and posting four hundred and fifty-six *thousand* S & H green stamps. Your daddy and I are the first in our families to own a home in five generations, but someday, your house will be even better. You're going to graduate from college and buy one that is even bigger than this, with a second story and plenty of windows, so you can look out and watch the whole wide world passing by.

They have returned from piano lessons, *Check,* and Suzanne is hanging a needlepoint above Lauralee's white wicker headboard. It is the only completed project from Suzanne's brief foray into crafting the previous spring after a miscarriage, this one so early she isn't certain if it was another pregnancy that didn't take or just a particularly painful and heavy period. She has set the needlepoint in a brass frame, and thin green vines and white roses form a loose chain around the words *Tidy house, Tidy life, Tidy heart*. Clenching a leftover nail between her canines, she stands on Lauralee's twin bed, lightly tapping the frame, first at one corner, then at another, then at the first again, until it hangs perfectly straight. She steps back to the center of the bed and examines her artwork, then leans forward and pushes gently on the upper right corner. Perfect.

Lauralee sits on the carpet with her legs crossed and her shoulders hunched, listening to Gordon Lightfoot on her little pink record player. Since his album came out a few weeks ago, that damned record has been spinning 24/7, Lauralee moving herself to tears every time she hears the song about the ship that went down in Lake Superior.

See how this little needlepoint is hanging just perfectly, Suzanne says and reaches to touch her daughter's fine hair. Honey, why don't you turn that off for a little while? It's maudlin.

Maybe she and Jon can drive to Dallas to get a second opinion from a specialist. Maybe they can adopt, or the next time one of her brothers or cousins calls and asks if Suzanne and Jon can take care of their children for a little while, just until they sort themselves out, maybe Suzanne will say yes, but only if they're willing to leave them for good. If she decides to have the procedure done, she isn't going to tell anybody until it's over and done with. She will check herself into the hospital, have the surgery and be back in her own kitchen before Lauralee gets home, before the plant whistle blows and Jon comes home from the plant.

Suzanne heads to the kitchen table for her legal pad and the gift bags she brought in from the car earlier that day. When she looks out the kitchen window and spies D. A. Pierce riding her bicycle in circles in front of her house, she drops everything and rushes outside, calling, You there, Debra Ann Pierce, you come here. I want to talk to you. The child lets out a high-pitched squeak and takes off pedaling down the street, sturdy legs moving like two piston pumps. She swerves madly to dodge a truck that has run the stop sign at the corner, and keeps right on pedaling.

ᕗ

To avoid being run over by a young man with his eye on the ball, they walk along the edge of the practice field. When Lauralee dawdles, Suzanne reminds her to pay attention. You stop paying attention and next thing you know, somebody's come and towed the family car away, or you come from church one day and find all the furniture sitting on the lawn, sinking into the swamp.

She carries a plastic food container in one hand and six Avon bags in the other. Three more gift bags are hidden in the heavy purse that hangs from one shoulder. It's hot as the devil's armpit out there, but Suzanne's red hair is tucked neatly behind her ears. Her bright orange pedal pushers are freshly ironed, and her blouse is white as a magnolia blossom. Even out here on a hot and dusty football field, she wants her neighbors to say, Suzanne Ledbetter looks like she just stepped off an airplane.

Lauralee walks a few feet behind her mother with her head down and the baton cradled in the crook of her elbow. She has legs like a jackrabbit and her face is covered with so many freckles it looks like a red pen exploded on it, and although Suzanne curled the girl's hair again before they left the house this afternoon, it has already fallen. In the center of her forehead, a single, valiant curl hangs on for dear life. Stand up straight, Suzanne says, and Lauralee throws her head back, high-stepping her way across the field and clutching her baton like it's Judith's sword.

On the football field, the team is doing its first set of burpees. When they get to fifty, Coach Allen tells them to do it again. Sweat rolls down the boys' foreheads, and the edges of their pads and jerseys are dark with water. One boy falls to the ground and lies there. When somebody squirts cold water in his face, the spectators laugh. Shit, back when they played ball, Coach threw a *bucket* of *ice water* in their faces. They once watched a boy get heat stroke out there, and he didn't go to the locker room. He played through it.

Suzanne and Lauralee walk up to the bleachers where the fans sit with cold beers or plastic cups of iced tea wedged between their knees, and when someone says under her breath, God love her, Suzanne knows they are talking about Lauralee, who has drifted over to the outer edge of the practice field and begun doing figure eights with her baton.

Good job, honey, her mother calls. Try to do a reverse flash followed by a Little Joe flip.

Lauralee wrenches her arm behind her back and spins the baton until it flies into the dirt and lands with a thud. She is so talented, a woman says. I can't wait to see her in the halftime show in a few years. And she's *tall*, says someone else. Bless her little heart. Try a pinwheel, Suzanne calls out. Try a double spin. Lauralee flings the baton into the sun, spins twice, and watches the baton roll to the sideline.

Suzanne climbs up on the bleachers and hands out pink-and-white Avon bags. Each bag holds next month's catalog along with lipsticks and eye shadows, perfumes and creams and lotions. Each item is wrapped with soft pink tissue paper and carefully tied with a white ribbon no wider than a fingernail. Smiling broadly and taking care to thank each woman individually, Suzanne slips their checks and cash into a small white envelope and zips it into her purse.

Ten to one, Suzanne has a relative who owes money to at least one man sitting at the other end of the bleachers. Ten to one, her mama bounced a check to at least one of their daddies, back in the good old days. They would never hold it against her, but a woman could spend her whole life proving everybody wrong. So Suzanne keeps moving. She gathers, carries, and drops off. She volunteers, counts, plans, and falls to her knees to gather crumbs that no one else can see. There is always something that needs to be cleaned—a table, a window, her daughter's face.

Hit him harder, a booster yells. Y'all ain't going to beat Midland Lee with that attitude, says another. Two boys crash into each other with a loud smack and lie unmoving on the field for a few seconds. Oh hell, one of the boosters yells from the aluminum bleachers, you just got your bells rung a little bit. On your feet, boys, shouts the coach, and the boys slowly roll onto their sides and get to their knees and stand up.

After the Avon has been distributed, Suzanne unlocks the sides of the plastic container she sent Lauralee to fetch from the car. The lid swivels up to reveal three dozen chocolate cupcakes she's made to give to the team when practice is over. One of the women remarks on the container, and Suzanne passes out catalogs. She is having a product party next week. They should come over for pimento cheese sandwiches and iced tea. Y'all bring your checkbooks. She winks at them, just like Arlene would have.

On a good day, Suzanne's mother could talk the pithy out of a cucumber. Everyone she ever met had high hopes for her. She was a master at reading a situation and becoming whoever she needed to be—Adventist, card shark, desperate mother in need of a little help. In Blanco, she had been a practicing Catholic. In Lubbock, she spoke in tongues and walked barefoot over hot coals. For a time there, when they lived in Pecos, she had everybody believing that she had lost her sight in a gas explosion. The family laughed all the way to the county line over that one.

This all goes for Lauralee's college fund, Suzanne tells the women, and while that is not strictly true, it is true enough.

I'm sure she is going to be very successful at whatever she makes up her mind to do, one of the ladies says before turning to talk to the woman sitting next to her about the weather, the football team, the price of oil. When one woman gives an update on the Ramírez case, another wonders aloud what the girl's mother was doing while her daughter was out running the streets. Well, I'll tell you what she *wasn't* doing, Suzanne says. Paying attention.

Mmm-hmm, another woman says.

It could have been any of our daughters, says a third.

Not mine, Suzanne says. I don't take my eye off her for a minute.

And then, just as one of the linebackers stumbles to the sidelines and begins retching in the grass, Lauralee flings her baton high into the air, spins around three times, and looks up to the sky with a wide grin on her face. The baton smacks her in the eye so hard that even Coach Allen gasps. She lets out a wail that spins across the practice field like a dust devil, a high-pitched scream that is a full-frontal assault on both hearing and reason.

Suzanne runs down the metal bleachers, each aluminum row trembling as she steps hard, her purse banging against her hip, the cupcakes forgotten and melting on the back row. She grabs her daughter by the shoulders and peers into her eye. It is barely red. She is unlikely to have so much as a bump.

You're okay, she tells her daughter. Rub some dirt on it. But Lauralee wails on and on, and then everybody stops what they're doing—Coach Allen stops yelling at the team, the women stop peering into their gift bags, the boosters stop armchair quarterbacking, even the team stands still—and all of them, in what seems to Suzanne to be a single, coordinated motion, look at her as if to say, Well, do something.

I hate the baton, Lauralee yells.

Oh, you do not. Suzanne chews her finger and looks back over her shoulder at the row of boosters, still sitting there with their mouths open, still waiting for her to take control of the situation. She doesn't hate it, she calls to them.

Lauralee wails again and then falls to the ground, rolling back and forth with her hand over one eye, saying *Ow, ow, ow.*

Stop it, Suzanne whispers fiercely. You want to let these people see you cry? She pulls her daughter to her feet, walks her quickly across the field, and pushes her into the front seat of the car, all while begging her to stop that damned crying and act like a big girl, for heaven's sake. She turns on the car and points the vents directly at her daughter's face, and now she can see that the eye has begun to swell after all. She is going to have a shiner the size of a walnut.

Can we go home, Lauralee asks quietly.

In a minute, honey. Suzanne gently closes the door and walks to the back of her car, where she leans against the trunk and waits for practice to be over.

In a few minutes, the boys run into the locker room and the coaches head to their office to watch tape. The boosters climb down from the bleachers and wander to their cars and trucks, still talking about the season, the price of oil, and the concert Elvis played at the coliseum last March. And still her daughter weeps. When three men walk over to her car, one after another, each pausing awkwardly and glancing toward the front seat, Suzanne apologizes for her daughter and then reaches into her tote bag and hands each man a gift bag—one for a wife, one for a girlfriend, one for himself, though she will never, ever breathe a word about it. She smiles and winks and tucks their money into her little white envelope. She shows them the Tupperware she's got in the trunk.

Someday Suzanne is going to die, and when she does, what will people say about her? That she died owing money to half the town? That she was a mean drunk?

No and no. That she died without a pot to piss in, or a window to throw it out? No. They are going to say that Suzanne Ledbetter was a good woman, a clever businesswoman, that she toed the line. She was an angel here on earth, they will say, and our town is poorer for her loss. She looks at her list and sighs and takes up her pen and then reaches over to pat her daughter's back. You don't ever let them see you cry, honey. That's all I meant.

Lauralee sits up and wipes the back of her hand across her nose. I know.

You have to be tougher than them.

Before she met Jon, Suzanne herself certainly ducked a swinging fist a time or two, or an open hand. She dodged fingers curling around her ass, climbing up her back, rubbing her shoulders. She was twelve years old the first time a boy grabbed her breasts, but she won't tell Lauralee the details—not yet, she's still too little. For now, all she will tell her daughter, as they sit together in the car with the air conditioner turned on high, is this:

Some boy tried to grab me once, when I was just a little older than you. He walked right up to me, in front of God and everybody else, and put his hands on me.

What did you do?

Well, I picked up a two-by-four and hit him right

upside his head. Knocked him right out. He didn't wake up for three days. Needed stitches, too—fifteen, or maybe it was twenty, I can't remember.

Did you get in trouble?

Heck, no. His mama tried to send the sheriff over to ask me what happened, and when I told him, you know what he said to me? He said: Next time, make sure you pick up a board with a couple of rusty nails sticking out of it then get one of your brothers to drag him out there into the swamp and leave him for the gators. Then he gave me a dollar—which is like five dollars now. He patted me on the head and told my mama she needed to come down to the station the next day and talk with him about an unrelated matter. Suzie Compton, he said to me, you are the best thing about this place. And do you know what I did with that dollar?

Bought candy?

No, ma'am. I put it in a box that had a padlock on it, and I wore that key around my neck until I left home for good.

Corrine

When Debra Ann asks if she can borrow Potter's old army tent, which has been gathering dust in the garage for twenty years, Corrine tells the girl that she and Potter spent many happy nights in that tent, hunting white-tailed deer in Big Bend or stargazing in the Guadalupe Mountains. They took their first real vacation as a family in the summer of 1949, the three of them staring into the Grand Canyon, Potter and Corrine gripping Alice's fingers until she howled. When they drove back to their campsite, Alice stood swaying between them on the bench seat, and every time they hit a pothole, they laughed and threw their arms in front of their daughter saying, wouldn't it be funny if Alice went flying out the window? When she climbed down from the seat and fell asleep on the floorboard between Corrine's feet, Potter turned off the radio and slowed to a crawl until he could carry their daughter to the tent and zip her into the sleeping bag they had placed between theirs.

D. A. yawns and scuffs her feet, rubs her eyes and tugs on her eyebrow. Okay, Mrs. Shepard. Can I borrow it?

That's what you do when you get as old as me, you remember as much as you can, all the time. How are *you* doing, Miss Pierce? Corrine asks, and Debra Ann smiles. It is the first honest grin Corrine has seen since the Fourth of July came and went with no sign of Ginny.

I'm doing good, D. A. says. I'm going to help my friend Jesse get back home to Tennessee.

Who? Corrine starts to say, because Debra Ann is too old for imaginary friends, but she decides to leave it alone. Who knows what story D. A.'s been cooking up this summer, what kind of complicated narrative she's woven? Who can know the mind of a child?

You're doing *well*, honey. What happened to Peter and Lily?

They aren't real. Jesse's a real person.

Mmm-hmmm. Corrine reaches over and pushes the girl's hair out of her eyes. Come over tomorrow and I'll trim your bangs for you.

After Debra Ann has dragged the tent down the

street, a butter-and-sugar sandwich clutched in her free hand, Corrine pours herself a glass of buttermilk and makes a fried egg sandwich while she half watches, half listens to the news. Jimmy Carter, gas leak near Sterling City, rig counts up and beef down, not a word about Gloria Ramírez or the trial scheduled in less than a month but tonight, there is a new horror. The news-caster cuts to a reporter standing next to an oil lease near Abilene. A local woman's body has been found, the fourth in the past two years. What a thing an oil boom is for a town, Corrine used to tell Potter bitterly. It brings in the very best sort of psychopath. And if the prognosticators can be believed, this boom is only just beginning. She switches off the television and heads outside to move the sprinkler.

The summer has been dry as chalk and Corrine has made a routine of turning on the sprinklers in the morning and moving them slowly across the front yard. In the afternoons, she washes down a sandwich with an iced tea and bourbon, or Scotch, then drives to Strike-It-Rich to buy cigarettes. A few weeks earlier she pulled Potter's truck into the garage for good. Climb-ing in and out of the cab was killing her knees, and she missed the FM radio and the dark-red crushed velvet interior of her Lincoln, the sensation of feeling as if she were steering a yacht down Eighth Street. Sometimes she puts a mixed drink in the cup holder and drives around town with the windows down, facing off with out-of-state drivers and equipment haulers who cut her off when she tries to change lanes. She might hate the oil, but she loves the heat and the land, its spare beauty and the relentless sunshine. It was something she had shared with her granny, along with her fondness for having a cup of coffee and chocolate doughnut for supper.

And this, too, is part of Corrine's routine: Every night after nine o'clock, when it finally gets dark out, she sits in Potter's truck with the keys in the ignition and the garage door closed. For an hour or longer, she stays out there, wishing she had the nerve. When she goes back into the house, she leaves the keys in the ignition. She fixes another drink, lights another cigarette, and heads to the front porch. Nearly five months since Potter passed—and oh how she hates that word, *passed*, as if he just drove a little too far into the desert, as if he would soon realize his mistake, and turn around, and come back to her.

Alice calls every Sunday and talks about coming down to check on her. She wishes Corrine would think about moving to Alaska. I'm worried sick about you, she tells her mother in late July.

If I come live in Alaska, will you come to *my* funeral?

Mother, that is so unfair. You have no idea what my life is like up here.

But Corrine is not going to let this go for a long time, maybe even years. Guess not. Bye-bye, honey.

⌣

Every August for the nearly thirty years she taught English, in an overheated classroom filled with farm boys and cheerleaders and roughneck wannabes reeking of aftershave, Corrine would spot the name of at least one misfit or dreamer on her fall roster. In a good year, there might be two or three of them—the outcasts and weirdoes, the cellists and geniuses and acne-ridden tuba players, the poets, the boys whose asthma precluded a high school football career and the girls who hadn't learned to hide their smarts. Stories save lives, Corrine said to those students. To the rest of them she said, I'll wake you when it's over.

While a box fan, together with the small, cell-like window that she cracked open every morning, labored heroically to clear the sweat and bubblegum and malice out of the classroom air, Corrine let her gaze wander, gauging the reactions of her various misfits. Invariably, some little shit would pop his gum or belch, or fart, but one or two of those kids would remember her words forever. They would graduate and get the hell out of Dodge, sending her letters from UT or Tech or the army and once, from India. And for most of Corrine's teaching career, that had been enough. When I say stories, she told those tormented souls, I also mean poems and hymns, birdsong and wind in the trees. I mean the hue and cry, the call and response, and the silence in between. I mean memory. So hang on to that, next time someone's beating the shit out of you after school.

Stories can save your life. This, Corrine still believes, even if she hasn't been able to focus on a book since Potter died. And memory wanders, sometimes a capful of wind on a treeless plain, sometimes a twister in late spring. Nights, she sits on the front porch and lets those stories keep her alive for a little while longer.

There have been plenty of months and years in Corrine's life so unremarkable or so unpleasant that she can call to mind almost nothing about them. She does not, for example, remember the birth of her daughter in the winter of 1946, or much about the month afterward, but she remembers every detail of September 25, 1945, the day Potter came home from Japan, intact, if you didn't count the night terrors and his new aversion to flying. Three years in the cockpit of a B-29 was plenty, he told Corrine, I won't ever step foot in another airplane. It's been five months since Potter died, and his voice is still as sharp and clear to Corrine as a crack of thunder.

He is home on a three-day leave and they have made love for the first time in the back seat of her daddy's Ford. The two of them sit facing each other, grinning and bloody and sore as hell. Well, that was just terrible, Corrine says. Potter laughs and promises her something better, next time around. He kisses her freckled shoulder and begins to sing. *What a beautiful thought I am thinking, concerning that great speckled bird . . . and to know my name is written in her holy book.*

Corrine is ten years old and sitting in the front row at her grandmother's funeral. When her father starts crying so hard he has to hand off the eulogy to the minister, she finally understands the enormity of their loss.

She is eleven and watching a calf being born for the first time, all unsteady legs and pitiful bawls, and she thinks how much her granny would have loved seeing this.

She is twelve and her daddy comes home from a rig

with a bottle of moonshine and two fingers missing. Don't cry, baby girl, he tells her. I didn't even need those two fingers. Now if it were *these*—he holds up his other hand and waggles his fingers, and they both fall out laughing, but she is remembering what her grandmother said the first time they saw an oil well come in. Lord, help us all.

She is twenty-eight years old and a foreman calls to tell her there has been an explosion at the Stanton well. She drives to the hospital with Alice sleeping next to her on the front seat, convinced Potter is already dead, trying to figure out how the hell she is going to move through this life without him. But there he is, sitting up in bed with a shit-eating grin on his face. Ugly flash burns stain his face and neck. Honey, he says, I fell off the platform right before it blew. And the smile dies on his face. Some of the other guys didn't, though.

It is October 1929 and Corrine's father is home for lunch. A man who generally hates idle conversation—nattering, he calls it—today he can hardly stop talking for long enough to chew his sandwich. The Penn's well has come in, a surface blowout so powerful that pieces of drill pipe, caliche, and rock were blown fifty feet into the air. The well blew at nine o'clock that morning, and it is still spewing crude oil. Who knows how many barrels are flowing across the desert? The drill operator has no idea when he'll be able to cap it. This here's a historic day, Prestige tells Corrine and her grandmother, Viola Tillman. This is going to put Odessa on the map.

Corrine and Viola are already gathering up their hats and gloves when Prestige shakes his head and stuffs the last of his fried egg sandwich into his mouth. An oil well ain't no place for little girls or—he looks at Viola—old ladies. Y'all stay home. I mean it.

Corrine is tall for her age, but she still has to sit all the way at the edge of the driver's to reach the starter pedal on her father's Model T. They careen across the Llano Estacado, the little girl and old woman bouncing madly on the car seat while some of Prestige's Herefords look on, their jaws working, working. The Penn's Well is still a mile away when the sky turns black and the ground beneath the car starts to tremble. The air fills with so much debris they have to cover their mouths with handkerchiefs. Lord help us all, Viola says.

As it falls back to earth, the oil spills out across the land and covers everything in its path—the purple sage and the blue grama grass that Viola loves, the bluestems and buffalo grasses that come nearly to Corrine's waist. A prairie dog family stands some thirty yards from the growing hole in the ground, their faces lifted as they bark at one another. A small female scutters to the edge of a burrow and peers inside, and Corrine imagines every hidey hole and den within five miles filled with confused little creatures who will never know what hit them. But the fifty or so men and boys who stand around the site aren't looking at the grass or the critters, or the earth. They are looking at the sky, their faces rapt. It's going to kill every living thing, Viola says.

Corrine frowns and sniffs the air while her grandmother sags against the passenger door. Viola's face is pale, her eyes cloudy. She coughs and holds her hand over her mouth and nose. That smell, she says. It's like every cow in West Texas farted at the same time. And our trees, she cries, spotting now a stand of young pecan trees in the direct path of a river of oil. What about them?

But it's going to put West Texas on the map, Corrine says, and Daddy says this land's not worth a tinker's damn anyway. Viola Tillman stares at her granddaughter as if she has never seen her before in her life. The Llano Estacado might not be good for anything except stars and space and quiet, the winter songbirds and the sharp smell of post cedars, after even a little rain, but she loves it. Together, the old woman and little girl have steered their horses through dry arroyos and creosote forests, then sat quietly and watched a family of javelina forage through a patch of prickly pear. Together, they found and named the largest tree on their property—Galloping Ghost, for the shaggy bark that resembles Red Grange's raccoon coat. Now Viola's face is the color of cold embers, and her hands are trembling. Take me home, she tells her granddaughter.

Yes, ma'am, Corrine says.

Can you drive me back to Georgia?

In three months Viola will be dead and by then, her granddaughter will have seen enough of an oil boom to loathe every one of them for the rest of her life.

For three days the Penn's well spews an uncontrolled stream of crude oil into the air. A house-sized pool forms in a matter of hours and then quickly breaches the sides, destroying everything in its path. More than thirty thousand barrels of oil spill out across the earth before the men get control of the well. And when they finally do, the men stand on the slick platform, their hands and faces stained black. They shout and shake hands and slap each other on the back. We capped her, they tell each other. We got her.

⌒

Since Potter died, Corrine knows the night sky the way she knew the contours of his face. Tonight on Larkspur Lane, the crescent moon crawls toward the center of the sky where it will remain for an hour or two before starting its long slide toward the western edge of the earth. Only a smattering of stars remains—*The night boils with eleven stars*—and the bars have been closed for two hours. The street is dark, except for Mary Rose's house, which is lit up like a drilling platform in the middle of a black sea.

Corrine hears Jon Ledbetter before she sees him. His hatchback peels out from the stop sign at the corner of Custer and Eighth, then comes flying around the sharp curve. His windows are open and the music is turned all the way up, Kris Kristofferson's wrecked baritone shaking the car speakers half to death. A glass of iced tea sweats a dark ring on the concrete porch. Corrine's too old to sit on the ground for this long with her legs crossed, and she nearly breaks the glass when she struggles to stand up so she can walk across the street and tell Jon Ledbetter to turn down his goddamn radio.

She is halfway there when Jon turns the music down, and the street is again silent. Mary Rose's face appears briefly in the window, the kitchen light turning her pale hair white. She stands there for a few seconds, then leans forward and draws the curtain. Corrine's leg is still half asleep, and she is feeling every bit of the bourbon she added to her iced tea, but she eventually makes it across the street, where Jon sits in the driver's seat with his hands on the steering wheel, a sad song playing on the radio.

Corrine hardly knows this young neighbor, Suzanne's husband, who is always working, always driving out to the plant in the middle of the night after the whistle has gone off, but she recognizes the cant of his shoulders and the stains on his hands. Potter looked like this sometimes, in the weeks and months after he returned from the war.

When she walks up to the car, she is careful not to touch him. Keeping her voice low, she asks if he would like to come sit down on her porch for a little while, maybe have a glass of ice water or a stiff drink. She's got this same album and she'll put it on, if Jon thinks he'd like to hear it again.

⌒

The great postwar boom is just getting under way, and the war is far enough behind them that people have started to look forward to things. Corrine and Potter stroll hand in hand through the new car lot on Eighth Street. They kick a few tires and take a couple of test drives then pay cash for a new Dodge truck, and they could not be more pleased with themselves. It is a beautiful machine, a new-model

Pilothouse, flathead straight-six. Potter talks Corrine into spending the extra money for the long bed, so they can go for long drives and lie back there, and look up at the Milky Way.

⌒

The minute Corrine starts to show, the principal sends her home with a handshake and a jar of his wife's locally famous chow-chow. What in the hell am I going to do at home for the next six months, she cries in the school secretary's office, knit booties? The secretary has seen this before. Her own children have been out of the house for ten years, and while she loves them to pieces, she still wakes up every morning and thanks God she doesn't have to make anybody's lunch or help them find their homework. Honey, she says, you're going to be out for more than six months.

Baby Alice cries every night from midnight to three. Potter and Corrine don't know why, and they can't make it stop. They are so tired that Potter develops a tic in his left eye and starts hearing things that aren't there. Corrine cries and then hates herself for crying because until she became a mother, she never cried, never, never, never.

∽

Nights like this, Corrine tells Jon, she can hardly stand to be anywhere in her house. Not the living room or kitchen, certainly not the bedroom. She can't move any damned thing—not the stack of *TV Guides* sitting next to his chair, or the towel that still hangs on his hook in the bathroom. She can still see the mark on the carpet from the snuff can she spent forty years bitching about. She can still see the imprint of his thumb on his old steering wheel cover and the gentle impression of his body on their mattress. His shoes are everywhere. She can't change the television station.

Would Jon like a drink? Because she sure would.

Jon picks up a small book of poems she left on the porch. He holds it carefully with his thumb and forefinger, as if it might go off in his hand. *Live or Die.* He laughs. Is that a serious question?

Hell, yes, she says. Would you like a cigarette?

∽

All she and Potter talk about is money and the baby. Nights, they have fallen into the habit of lying in bed while they argue about everything that's pissing them off. She is going out of her mind staying at home all the time. He is working sixty hours a week and can't understand why Corrine doesn't see how lucky she is that she doesn't have to. She has discovered that she was completely unprepared for how boring motherhood is. He thinks caring for Alice and the house ought to be enough for her. Why doesn't she find some other young mothers or go to the church meetings, or something? Corrine snorts and rolls her eyes. Well, that will take care of at least *two* hours in every day, she says. All this fiddle-faddle about women staying home with their babies, if they can possibly afford to do it, is a three-foot-tall heap of Grade-A bullshit. Potter says he can't imagine what he'll say to the fellas if his wife goes to work. Corrine couldn't give two shits what the fellas think. They roll over and face their separate walls. And so it goes.

⌒

The shipping operator lost his balance, Jon tells Corrine. Maybe he was tired. Maybe he had a fight with his wife before he left for work, or one of the kids was sick, or some unpaid bill was keeping him up nights. Maybe he was working a double because a man called in sick and the shipping operator had been around long enough to know oil booms don't last forever.

When it came to overtime, he had a simple philosophy. Get it while you can.

Maybe it is as simple as this: he slipped, he fell. Because this was a job the shipping operator had done a hundred times before, and he could do it with his eyes closed, this routine check on a row of tankers parked next to the loading dock at the olefin plant, this last step before they began filling the tanks with liquid ethylene to ship to California. He was already standing on the top rung of the steel ladder, the other men told Jon, when an engineer far down the line gave the go-ahead to add an extra car, and the slack action from the coupling caused the small jolt that shook the shipping operator's hands and feet loose and sent him rolling beneath the train. And on any other day, he might have been able to scramble away from the heavy wheels before they rolled across his thighs. Might have. But thinking about it wears Jon out, and it doesn't matter now, not to this man who died tonight on Jon's watch. It is my job to keep them safe, he tells Corrine.

꿈

Alice is six months old, and she doesn't sleep. Corrine stands under a hot shower and leans against the wall, knocking her head against the tile just hard enough to make it hurt. She doesn't sleep, she doesn't sleep, she doesn't sleep.

⌒

Their new truck drives like a dream, Potter tells her, even as he fights to loosen up the gearstick. And would she just listen to this radio! This is called high fidelity! He spins the volume knob all the way to the right. When Hank Williams and his Drifting Cowboys come on, he smacks the steering wheel and whoops. *I been in the doghouse so doggone long, that when I get a kiss I think that something's wrong*— Potter falls silent.

Mm-hmm, says Corrine.

When they get home, she sends him to the store for something and lets Alice cry in her crib for a few minutes. She calls the principal at the high school. There's a boom on, she tells him, and I'm thinking y'all might need some help down there. Corrine is right, enrollment has doubled and they are desperate for an English teacher. What does Potter think about her returning to work? the secretary wants to know. Maybe Corrine could ask him to give the principal a call?

They don't fuck for months—months!—and it is Potter's fault. He has let himself go, in her opinion. After the baby came, Corrine must have walked five hundred miles to get her figure back. Living on iceberg lettuce and apples when what she really wanted was a steak and a baked potato with all the fixins. Smoking a cigarette when she might have preferred a candy bar. But Potter is a different story. He put on a few pounds during the pregnancy—thirty, to be exact—from all those nights lying in bed, sharing a dish of Blue Bell ice cream while Alice tried to punch her way through Corrine's belly. He still enjoys a bowl every evening, brings it right into their bedroom and climbs into bed with it.

And she blames the baby. Corrine loves Alice with a ferocity that shook her to the core in the days and weeks after the nurses allowed them to bring her home. That anybody would let them leave the hospital with something as fragile and important as a baby—this alone had seemed both miraculous and deeply reckless to Corrine and Potter—but as far as Corrine is concerned, there is an unbroken line of cause and effect between her daughter's birth and the fact that she can't get laid. She misses Potter holding her by the hips and looking up at her, misses his finger running along the spot of red that appears on her neck when she comes, the way it deepens and grows and covers her chin and her cheeks.

The baby is in bed and they are sitting in their chairs,

listening to Bob Wills on the radio. Corrine is trying to read a book, but she is always listening for the baby. That's something I used to do, she thinks, read books. I used to memorize poems and bring myself to tears when I recited them. I used to walk out the door and go for a long drive anytime I wanted. I used to bring home my own paycheck.

Potter is working a crossword. He sets down the pencil and watches his wife for a few minutes. Hey, he says softly, can I ask you something, Corie?

Hmm. Maybe.

What do you need?

What do I *need*?

Yeah. What do you need, Corrine, to be happy with me and Alice?

She doesn't hesitate. I need to go back to work, Potter.

Honey, you *work*, taking care of Alice and me.

Yes, I do. I'd prefer to teach English to a classroom full of hormonal rednecks.

I'm afraid teaching will be too much for you.

The second the words are out of his mouth, Potter wishes he could have them back. And sure enough, Corrine comes out with her guns a'blazing. Potter, are you shitting me? Are you shitting me right about now? I'll tell you what I need, Potter. I *need* for people to stop talking to me like I've become a bona fide idiot since I had a baby. I need for the good ladies of Odessa to stop advising me that what I really ought to do is get cracking on another baby. Ha! She slams her book closed and holds it over her head, and it occurs to Potter that she is going to lean over and hit him with it.

I need to go back to teaching, Corrine says, because I happen to like holding a room full of teenagers hostage while I read Miss Willa Cather's *My Antonia* out loud to them. Let somebody else come over here and make goo-goo eyes at Alice for eight hours every day—*every day*, Potter, and why don't you think about that for a minute, if you never once left work, what that might be like?

You were a great teacher, he says, but who is going to watch Alice?

I *am* a great teacher.

They sit and listen to the clock tick. A neighbor's dog barks. In the kitchen, their new icebox switches on, a steady hum that reaches every corner of the house. He will wish until the day he dies that he hadn't said it, but Potter has the best of intentions when he sets his crossword on the end table and walks over to sit on the carpet next to his wife's chair, when he wonders aloud, How soon is too soon to start thinking about another baby?

Alice is her first thought in the morning, her last before she falls asleep for a few hours at night, and all the hours in between. She is a flash of lightning and its aftermath, a fire bearing down on a copse of juniper and mesquite. She is love, and Corrine is completely unprepared for it. Here is a person who is, and must always be, what the whole world was made for, and without whom that same world becomes unimaginable. If something happens to Alice, if she gets sick, if there is an accident, if a rattlesnake crawls into the backyard while Alice is out there on her blanket—it is enough to drive a woman straight into the arms of the nearest church or, in Corrine's case, the bookmobile that somebody parked last week on the empty lot less than a block from their new house.

It is also Jon's job to drive over to the shipping operator's house in the middle of the night and knock on the front door and stand on the porch until the man's wife comes to the door. She didn't want to wake up the kids, he tells Corrine, so he sat with her on the couch while they waited for her sister to arrive. He kept his hands folded in his lap and his fingernails hidden. Back at the plant, he had showered and put on the clean shirt he keeps in his locker. But blood is pernicious and when he sat down on the man's couch, he could see it under his fingernails and in the wrinkles of his knuckles. The man's wife asked some questions and he told some lies—it was over quickly, he didn't suffer, he never knew what happened. Jon watched the man's wife cross her hands one over the other and push them hard against her mouth. Here's one true thing he could tell her: He wasn't alone when it happened, and he wasn't alone when he died. Jon was there, pressing his hands against the man's face, telling him that everything was going to be okay.

Alice is already walking when they decide to take the truck out on the highway, open up the engine, and see what it can do. Potter calls his father-in-law and asks if he will take the baby for the night. He has heard good things about the mountains up near Salt Flat, he tells Corrine. There is some camping up that way, but they ought to go now before spring comes and it's too hot.

Potter airs his old army tent out in the backyard and checks the seams while Alice wobbles in and out of the heavy canvas flap, singing her only complete sentence. What about me? What about me?

Corrine fills the camp icebox with beer, cold fried chicken, and potato salad and then loads three jugs of water into the back of the truck. Potter packs a fifth of bourbon, a flashlight, two emergency flares, and his service revolver in the truck's glove box. Corrine adds her pocket pistol. Potter tucks a couple of rubbers into his wallet. Corrine shoves her diaphragm, some spermicidal cream, and a wad of tissues into her purse.

While Potter feeds Alice, Corrine stands at the foot of their bed and considers a little black chiffon negligee she used to wear before the baby. It might fit, but it seems ridiculous to bring such a garment on a camping trip. After dressing in a cardigan and a swingy red A-line skirt that falls just below her knees—Potter loves this skirt—she digs around in the closet for her black heels, which she can at least wear for the drive. She sets her boots next to her overnight bag. At the last moment Corrine removes her panties, choosing instead to wear beneath her skirt only a pair of black stockings and garter belt. In nearly thirty years of living, Corrine has not once left the house without her underwear. It is delicious. She puts on her new eyeglasses, takes them off, and squints at the mirror on the dresser. She puts them back on and steps into the living room. Ta-da! She throws one arm in the air.

Potter's eyes widen. He laughs a little and holds his arms out to her. Whoa! Baby, you look just like a librarian.

Corrine's arm falls to her side. Thank you very much.

No, Corrie! Honey, I meant—

But Alice begins to wail, toddling toward her mother and holding her arms up like a tiny robber caught in the sheriff's headlights. As his wife shoves past him, Potter touches the sleeve of her sweater lightly. Soft, he says, but she doesn't hear him. Instead she goes to work soothing the baby while he stands in the doorway, one hand still reaching for his wife.

They kiss the baby and pat her and speak to her as if they are leaving on a freighter bound for Cameroon, then hand her off to her granddaddy with a page of instructions. Prestige glances at the list, folds it in half, and slides it into his shirt pocket. All-righty, then, he says. Have a great time. Don't hurry back.

They take the new highway north toward Notrees, driving past the man camps that have sprung up in the coliseum parking lot while people wait for more houses to be built. At the family camps, which are spread out on dirt lots behind the coliseum, skinny, dust-smeared kids play and fight and sprawl in the dust. Corrine watches them and chews on her thumbnail. Most of them probably aren't even enrolled in school. That's a scandal, she says. Shameful.

How come? Potter is fiddling with his new headlights, turning them on, turning them off, then back on. People have to make a living.

It's shameful that we've got people living in tents in the middle of dirt lots, Potter. Those companies ought to be doing better by them.

I think they're probably doing the best they can, under the circumstances. There are a lot of people coming here, real fast.

Oh, bullshit. Those oil companies don't care about these people, and you're kidding yourself if you think different. Besides—she digs around in her purse for a lipstick and compact—doesn't it bother you what they're doing to the land out here?

Potter punches the gas pedal. It would bother me a lot more if I couldn't put food on the table for you and Alice, if I couldn't put a little something away in case our daughter wants to go to college, like her mama did.

Corrine swipes a rich red lipstick across her bottom lip then checks her teeth in the mirror. She thinks about the panties she is not wearing. The leather seat is delightful against the backs of her knees. Be careful, she says. We do not want to get into an accident.

All right, Corrine. Potter turns on the radio and they

light cigarettes. Wisps of smoke drift out their windows as they pass pickup trucks with their beds stuffed full of men. Some will look you right in the eye. Others avert their gaze, as if they might be on the run from something—the law, the mob, wives and babies back home in Gulf Shores or Jackson or some other dismal little town with scarce work and few prospects.

They drive past rolls of barbed wire and piles of steel beams lying next to the road. A quarter mile ahead, a truck pulls over and two women jump out the back. They stand on the shoulder waving madly for a minute or two, and when another truck pulls over, they climb in. The men cheer. Corrine frowns and tucks her hands behind her knees. The lining of her skirt is sticking to her ass cheeks, and her thighs are sweaty. What is Alice doing right now? she wonders. Probably jumping up and down on her grandfather's stomach. He'll be sore for days.

By the time they reach Mentone, the sun burns at the edge of the earth. They pull over at a picnic table on an escarpment just above the shallow, sluggish Pecos. It's been a dry year, and you couldn't drown in there if you tried. Diffuse sunlight turns the water the color of mesquite bark and cirrus clouds blush overhead. They take turns stomping out into the brush to pee, Corrine tottering through the scrub, high heels sinking in the sand, as she claps loudly to scare off snakes. She knows it is foolish not to have already changed into her boots, but then, when she staggers out from behind a copse of mesquites, skirt swinging around her knees, Potter whistles.

Hello, Mrs. Shepard, he says. Girl of my dreams.

For the first time all day, maybe the first time in weeks, Corrine's face breaks into a wide grin. Hello, Mr. Shepard.

After a quiet supper of fried chicken and beer, they continue north. Night has come all the way in, but natural gas flares burn on both sides of the highway. Potter says that some nights the companies flare off so much gas a person can drive all the way from Odessa to El Paso without once turning on his headlights. They are dependable as West Texas sunshine, he says.

Wish they smelled better, Corrine says. Wish I knew what was in there.

When they turn off the highway and start toward the peaks, he switches off the headlamps and they drive along a dirt road in the dark. Flares flicker in the distance. He glances at his wife. Her eyes shine in the gaslight, a freckle on her cheek turns gold, and he begins to sing quietly. *Frankie was a good girl, everybody knows. She paid one hundred dollars for Albert's suit of clothes. He's her man, and he did her wrong.*

When he reaches across the cab and touches his wife on the knee, she jumps. They have not touched each other, not so much as a pat, since they handed the baby off to her father hours earlier.

Corrine lays her hand on top of his and gently rubs his knuckle. Are you trying to flirt with me?

Potter laughs. Yeah, maybe, a little bit.

Well, she breathes deeply. All right.

Abruptly, he turns onto another dirt road and heads for open desert. They bump along for a few minutes, their heads like fishing bobbers, as Potter peers down access roads on either side of them that are barely wider than the truck. Corrine leans forward and looks through the windshield. Where are we going?

I used to know a little rise up this way. Good place to watch the moon and stars come out. You want to stop and get out of the truck for a little bit?

All right.

A few minutes later, he pulls up next to a mesquite forest. This looks like a good place.

They sit on the tailgate for a few minutes, feet dangling while they smoke and watch a few stars come out. A smiling moon hangs just above the earth's edge, and they can see the Burlington Northern rolling across the desert, though it is too far away for the train's whistle to be louder than a moan. Potter jumps up and reaches through the passenger window, and Corrine hears him open the glove box. We going to shoot each other? she says.

Ha, ha. Funny lady. He returns with the bourbon and leans next to her on the tailgate, the bottle wedged between his thighs. He kicks at some dirt. There are a dozen things Potter might say to Corrine right now, and she thinks, not for the first time, that maybe she should have married Walter Hendrickson, the local boy who grew up to write country songs, *and* get paid to do it.

I wish you could be happy staying at home, Potter says.

Corrine stands up and takes several long strides away from the truck. When she turns, her face is a fury. Well fuck you, Potter.

Potter looks as if he'd like to take off running into the scrub. Maybe she'll get lucky and he'll fall into an abandoned well, or a rattlesnake den.

I'm going to tell you something, Potter. The only thing I hate more than being home with Alice all day long is feeling guilty about not wanting to do it. Corrine's voice breaks and she pushes her fist against her mouth. She is trying not to cry, and this makes her even angrier.

He unscrews the cap on the bourbon and takes a

long swallow, then another. Somewhere in the brush a bobwhite begins to sing. *Bob White! Not quiet! Come again, some other night.* Another answers, *Bob White, Bob White. Hooey, hooey, hooey.* Falling stars tumble across the sky—there, then quickly gone. He holds the bottle out to her, but Corrine shakes her head and lights another cigarette. He watches her smoke for a few minutes and then stands up and sets the bottle down on the tailgate. He takes his wife by the shoulders. Corrine is a tall, curvy lady, but she is still almost a foot shorter than her husband. He ducks down and looks directly into her beautiful eyes. Corrine, I'm sorry.

If he had just declared himself a Soviet spy, she could not have been more surprised. She never says she's sorry to anybody for anything, it's one of her character flaws, but Potter doesn't exactly fall over himself dishing out apologies either.

Corrine touches his face, her hand large and warm against his cheek. It has been months since she's touched him like this.

Potter, when you were flying planes over Japan, I taught English all day and then I drove out to the fields with a bunch of other women and helped load cattle onto freight trains. I was worn out every night—and I mean tired, Potter, all the way down to the bone.

Even my tits hurt at the end of the day. But I also felt *strong*. And then all you men came home and we were just supposed to get knocked up as soon as possible and slink back into the kitchen like a bunch of old cows headed back to the barn. And maybe that's all right. I guess plenty of women are just pleased as punch by the whole arrangement, or maybe they just bitch less than I do. Corrine pushes herself off the tailgate and takes a few steps into the desert. She turns and faces her husband. I love Alice. She's the best thing you and me ever did together. But hear me, Potter. I am losing my everloving mind.

She walks back over to him, and they stand side by side next to the tailgate. Some of the gas flares have gone out and the sky has again filled with stars. Corrine stands stiffly next to her husband. Her back is straight as always, but her hands are trembling.

As soon as we get home, he says, we'll start looking for somebody to watch Alice, one of those oil-field widows you can't stop reminding me about.

Well, *finally*. Thank you. She stubs out her cigarette on the truck's bumper. Can I ask you for something else?

Honey, if the principal asks me—and you know he will—I will assure him that we talked about it and agreed you should go back to work.

She laughs bitterly and rolls her eyes. He's right, of course. She will need her husband's permission, and even then they might not hire her. The thought of it makes Corrine want to spit, or break a bottle over somebody's head. Not that, Potter. I want you to talk to me.

Talk?

Like you used to, before Alice. Like we're new to each other.

She watches his face carefully, thinking that he could not look less enthusiastic if she had asked him to remove one of his own teeth with a pair of pliers.

Oh, for Christ's sake. Never mind. Corrine flips her cigarette toward a creosote, sits down with a thud on the tailgate, and kicks her legs back and forth.

Potter walks around the truck a few times. After his third revolution around the truck, he stops and stands in front of his wife. Gently, he stops her legs from swinging. Mrs. Shepard, would you care to have a drink with me?

Yes. I believe I will. Corrine picks up the bottle, screws the cap off, and takes a couple of long pulls. A bit of bourbon dribbles down her throat.

She has a lovely neck, long and slim and lightly freckled. He touches her throat with one finger, marveling aloud at the softness of her skin, a new line that traverses her throat. Did I ever tell you what a beautiful neck you have?

Not lately.

Yes. He leans over and touches the tip of his tongue to the bourbon that glistens on her clavicle. Beautiful word, that. Clavicle.

Corrine leans into him and looks up at the stars. Do you think somebody might see us out here?

Nah, we'll see them coming from ten miles off.

Wife and husband face each other. *Talk*, she thinks.

Let me taste you, he says, and presses his lips against her mouth. Beautiful lady with her new glasses and her hair up in a knot. Sweet Corrine with the warm bourbon mouth.

Corrine begins to take off her glasses.

Keep them on. Please.

She looks at him for several seconds and then takes another sip of bourbon, her throat moving a bit as she swallows. We might get carried away and forget to look for headlights.

Maybe you need another little sip of bourbon, he says. Liquid courage.

Again she drinks. She hands the bottle back to her husband. To courage.

Courage, he says. He sets the bottle down and takes her hand, pressing it first against his heart and then against the front of his jeans. You couldn't be making this any harder.

She giggles and he pulls her legs gently apart, running the flat of his hand along her stocking, his eyes widening when his finger finds her bare skin.

Why don't you stand up, Corrine, and show me those black stockings?

She walks out onto the plain, her face and hair lit by the moon, black heels and a half smile, fingers pulling gently at her skirt.

Jesus, honey. Come here. He sets her on the tailgate, the backs of her knees bumping lightly against the steel, and he pulls her to the edge of the tailgate. Lean back, Corrine.

∽

Jon hasn't had a cigarette since he was overseas, and he promised himself he wouldn't ever do it again, but when he pulls the smoke into his lungs he can feel his chest expanding, growing larger, and it is so goddamned good, it is such a fucking relief, he thinks he might cry. What do you say to a man who is dying in your arms? Do not be afraid. You are not alone.

The album stops playing. Jon and Corrine listen to

the click as the stylus lifts from the platter and settles into its stand.

He says, Corrine, would you like to listen for a little longer?

To the music? she asks.

Yes.

Will you turn the album over?

When Jon tries to stand up, he stumbles in the dark and falls against Corrine's shoulder. He tries to right himself, but she grabs his shirt and pulls him to her, as if he is a child who slipped and fell off a fishing dock, or she is a ship about to go down, or they are poor swimmers in rough seas. Corrine takes his hand and presses it to her face and after a pause, he does the same. They sit together and watch the last of the stars go out. Sun's coming up soon, one of them says. Better get home.

∽

On the drive home the next afternoon Corrine takes Potter's warm hand from the gearshift and presses it gently against her skirt, then guides it up and under, past a tiny bruise on her right knee, to rest on her bare inner thigh. They are worn out and hung over and sore as hell—and they never did make it to the mountains. Corrine crooks her neck and sticks her head out the window, trying to see herself in the rearview mirror. When they get home, all their problems will still be there. They will still be a young man and a young woman with the worst war of their lives just a few years behind them, with worries and fears and a little girl to feed and love. They will fight over money and sex, and whose turn it is to mow the yard, wash the dishes, pay the bills. In a few years, Corrine will threaten to tear it all down when she falls in love with the social studies teacher, and a few years after that, Potter will do something similar. And each time they will grit their teeth and wait to love each other again, and when they do, it will be a wonder. On this morning, Corrine's hair blows wild about the truck's cab, and a slight rash marks her lovely throat. Honey, he says, you could not be more beautiful.

Debra Ann

Jesse's stories are so much better than hers. He was in the army and he served overseas. When he came home to eastern Tennessee, he tells her, he kept his discharge papers in the front pocket of his shirt for a time, as if somebody might demand to see them, as if maybe just coming home alive made him a criminal. He said they fixed his teeth when he joined the service and after his mama saw him for the first time, she started to cover her mouth when she laughed, her big hands marked with scratches, knuckles twisted and raw, scarred from hammers and meat hooks and industrial sewing machines.

At the welcome home party, Jesse stood in his family's trailer and watched people smile and shake hands. He tried to keep them on his right side, but he still missed a lot of what they said. He nodded and grinned and let them fill his cup, and when somebody asked where Jesse had been, he said, Hell if I know, I never did learn to pronounce the name, and he thought about the two boys he had killed. The aunts talked about picking cotton or working in textile mills. The uncles talked about driving to eastern Kentucky for jobs in the mine, their eyes going soft when they saw Jesse watching them. You picked a hell of a time to come back to Belden Hollow, they said. There ain't *nothing* going on here.

And then here came his cousin Travis, pulling into the yard in a brand-new Ford F-150 that he bought in Texas. Paid cash for it, too, he said. He wore new boots and had a new nickname—Boomer, he said, because he nearly blew himself to kingdom come his first week on the job.

Because she's a kid, and a girl, Jesse doesn't tell Debra Ann what his cousin said to him next. You don't need to know jack shit about petroleum. Just do what they tell you and collect your pay every Friday. Three hundred a week, and all the West Texas pussy you can handle. Pack your rubbers, brother. Get ready to party.

Instead, Jesse tells D. A. that he drove away from Tennessee in January, with his gear on the front seat of his truck and Boomer's phone number in his pocket, and a particular kind of noise in his head, a Jesse-get-your-act-together kind of noise. He tells her when the trees disappeared on the other side of Dallas, he wondered how on earth any place could be so dusty, and brown. Even the shining blue sky turned the color of dirt when the wind blew hard enough. Sometimes, he could hardly tell which was which, sky or land, dirt or air.

And you came to Odessa, D. A. says.

Yes, I did. That foreman at Boomer's worksite took one look at me and started laughing his butt off. You don't mind small spaces, do you, Shorty? he asked me. When I said I'd been a tunnel rat overseas, Mr. Strickland gave me a twenty to go buy some boots and he told me to bring a change of clothes the next day.

My daddy used to muck saltwater tanks, D. A. says, right after I was born. He says the first time he climbed into a tank with his respirator and a broom, and a metal scraper as tall as him, he almost had a heart attack, it was so small and dark in there.

They are sitting side by side at the mouth of the drainpipe, both of them with their knees drawn up to their chests, trying not to let any bare skin touch the scorching concrete. When I climbed into that tank, says Jesse, I looked like a man. When I came out, I looked like one of them onyx statues I used to see in markets overseas. I was covered head to toe in oil. It took me twenty minutes in the field shower to get it all off my skin.

My daddy hated it. He said it made him sick to his stomach.

I guess so, Jesse says and falls silent. Back home, there wasn't anything to do but fish the Clinch River and look for agates at Paint Rock or Greasy Cove. Maybe drive over to the VA hospital once a week to see if his hearing had improved. But here in Odessa, he works. Like a man does. Jesse picks up a small piece of chalk and uses it to draw marks on the concrete.

I'm saving nearly everything I make, he tells Debra Ann, thanks to your hospitality. I'll have Boomer's money in another month or so, and he'll have to give my truck back.

He sees Boomer at the strip club now and then, sitting at the bar with the same men who threw Jesse out of his truck. They drink and watch women, and when they see Jesse sweeping up broken glass or running a mop through some vomit, they put their hands over their mouths and laugh, but they don't ever talk to him, they don't ever ask where he's living.

D. A. shows him the postcard that arrived just after the Fourth of July. They pass it back and forth, turning it over in their hands. A plaster cowboy, his hat pulled low over his eyes, leans against a sign that says GALLUP, NEW MEXICO.

But the postmark is from Reno, Jesse says.

I know it, says D. A. I don't have any idea where the hell my mother is, and she plucks the card out of her friend's hand, takes off running up the steep embankment without saying goodbye. She is rushing to leave him behind, to get somewhere private, where nobody can see her grief.

⌒

Debra Ann has never been on an airplane, never even been out of Texas, but she and Ginny used to drive out to West Odessa every month to see Debra Ann's great-grandma for an hour or two. Ginny sat on one end of the sofa and D. A. sat on the other while the old lady refilled their iced tea and talked about the Second Coming. When they were walking back to the car, Ginny would sometimes grab her daughter's hand. Why don't you and me drive over to Andrews and get an ice cream cone at Dairy Queen, she'd say. Or, you want to drive over to the sand hills and watch the stars come out, then maybe head to Monahans and get a cheeseburger at the drive-in?

They'd sit on the hood of the car and listen to the

wind blow just hard enough that they'd taste the sand in their mouths, see traces of it in the bottom of the bathtub that night, and it seemed to Debra Ann that every star in the sky had come out just for them. There's Orion's Belt. Ginny would point toward the southern sky. There's the Seven Sisters. They say seven, but there are nine, and a thousand other stars that we can't even see.

And one night, when they saw a truck coming down the same dirt road they'd driven, Ginny sat up straight, watching, her gray eyes narrow and her shoulders square.

Should we go? D. A. asked.

Ginny said, No. We have just as much right to be here as anybody else. She climbed down from the hood and leaned through the open car window to take something out of the glove box, then turned the car radio up and climbed back onto the hood. When the jazz show came on the college radio station, they listened to Chet Baker and Nina Simone, the horn, the piano, the voices drifting across the sand and disappearing behind the dunes.

Try to remember this night, Ginny said. She had tears in her eyes. The moon rose orange and big across a dozen miles of pale sand in this otherwise empty corner of the world. She smiled at her daughter and handed over the car keys. You want to drive us back to the highway, D. A.? There's about ten miles of dirt road before we hit pavement.

∽

He tells her that when a young boy stepped out of a side tunnel and stood directly in front of him, they were in an underground room so close to the water table Jesse could smell the minerals. And he had been amazed that a boy had materialized in the dark like that, though he shouldn't have been. They stood and stared at each other, two frightened boys with their mouths hanging open, and Jesse didn't see the second boy until he jammed the butt of his rifle into Jesse's left ear.

He doesn't tell Debra Ann that the echo from his service revolver was still bouncing off the dirt walls when he stood and looked at the two boys with matching holes in their chests, that he had shaken his head against the odd dullness in his bleeding ear, as if someone had suddenly thrown up a brick wall between him and the world. It wouldn't be right to tell her that he wakes up thinking about them. Were they brothers? And if they were, did their mama sit up all night long, waiting for them to come home and wondering what happened?

Jesse has saved nearly enough money to get his truck back, and he's starting to believe he might make it home before winter, when one of the dancers tells him that Boomer has moved out of town. She hands him a beverage napkin with Boomer's new phone number and address on it. He says to come on out when you have his money.

Jesse studies the phone number written just beneath the club's logo, a woman's shadowy figure, her large breasts and the bunny ears coming out of her head. *Penwell, TX, trailer behind the old gas station.*

How am I going to get out to Penwell? he asks the woman.

It's only about fifteen miles outside of town. She runs her hand gently up and down his arm. I'm sorry, sugar, I'd help you if I could. And in spite of the bad news, Jesse feels the warmth of her touch for hours.

⌒

There has been no rain for nine months, and the sprinklers run day and night. D. A. brags to anyone who will listen that she hasn't had a real bath since the middle of June. She just runs through the closest sprinkler and calls it a day. It is the best thing about not having her mother around, she tells Aimee, who says her own mother never stops watching her.

Aimee is six inches shorter than Debra Ann, with eyelashes so pale they are nearly invisible. Together, the girls run through the sprinklers in Aimee's backyard while their faces burn, freckle, and peel. When D. A.'s bangs grow so long they cover her eyes, she gets on her hands and knees and pretends to be a sheepdog chasing Aimee around the yard. They pass bags of chips, tall tales, chiggers, and a case of ringworm back and forth seamlessly. The bug bites that line their arms and legs turn into sores and scabs and scars. When their shoulders turn the color of tomatoes, they sit in the shade of the cinder-block fence and ignore Aimee's mother, who comes to the back door every few minutes and looks anxiously around the yard. Aimee says the phone never stops ringing at her house. Yesterday, she heard her mom ask somebody if they weren't tired of it yet and then slam the phone down so hard, it probably busted the caller's eardrum.

At the YMCA pool, Mrs. Whitehead sits stiffly at the edge of a lounge chair with the baby in her arms, watching Aimee jump from the high dive for the first time. When it's her turn, Debra Ann stands trembling, skinny and full of fear, for a few long seconds at the board's edge, but then she looks down and sees Aimee treading water in the deep end, urging her on, and she hurls her body into the air. In the seconds after she hits the water, before she kicks her way back to the surface, she thinks she can do anything. Aimee says she feels the same way.

Their faith is rooted in their bodies, the muscle and sinew and bone that holds them together and says *move*. They are track stars and gymnasts and Olympic swimmers who win gold medals in diving and synchronized swimming. While Mrs. Whitehead changes the baby's diaper and tries to get him to take his new bottle, they dunk each another and dive off the side. They sink to the pool's floor and sit with their bottoms pressed against the rough surface while they gaze up at shoals of children, skinny limbs casting long shadows across the water. They hold their breath for as long as they can, and when they rise from the water, gasping and sputtering, Mrs. Whitehead is standing by the pool's edge, shouting for someone to help them.

What is wrong with you? Aimee yells. She takes a deep breath and dives back into the water, skinny legs kicking hard, carrying her away from her mother.

We're okay! D. A. says. We're just playing.

Mrs. Whitehead shifts the baby onto her other hip and adjusts his hat. I want y'all to get out and come sit down for a minute, she tells Debra Ann. Please, right now.

Aimee reads the Karen Carpenter interview in *People* and vows to drink at least eight glasses of water a day, and when they are ready to leave the pool, she carries her clothing into a closed stall to change out of her bathing suit. D. A. worries aloud that her father is working too much, that she isn't cooking good enough dinners for him. Macaroni and cheese isn't really a balanced meal. Aimee says her mother doesn't sleep nights, and every time her daddy drives into town they stand in the kitchen and shout about the trial. Last week, one of them broke a lamp.

Daddy wants us back out at the ranch *right* now, she tells Debra Ann. He says he's done paying rent *and* a mortgage. My mother can be a real bitch. Aimee says that last word slowly, D. A. notices, drawing it out and letting it hang in the air between them like the scent of something wonderful, heavily buttered popcorn or a warm chocolate bar.

⌒

When she asks Jesse where he's been lately, why he hasn't felt like having any company, he says he doesn't know. Maybe it's the heat, but lately there's been a persistent hum in his good ear, a little ache that remains even after the bar is closed and the bouncer has turned off the music.

He doesn't tell her that the noise is there when one of the dancers pulls a few dollars from her roll of tips and says, Thanks, Jesse, you're a real sweetheart. It's there when he mops the floors and hauls the garbage to the dumpster, when he collects his pay and says good night to the bartender, also a veteran, who lets Jesse come in before the dancers arrive and use the dressing room shower. And Jesse appreciates that, he really does. But he still wishes the man would ask him to sit down and have a drink with the rest of the crew at the end of a long night.

He doesn't tell D. A. that the noise follows him home and lies with him on his pallet while he waits for the stray cat to wander in and curl up against his side, that it is still there in the morning when he and the cat wake up and stretch and marvel at the heat, its meanness and persistence. Instead, he says that he figured he could sleep anywhere after being overseas, but his bed feels harder than it did a month ago, and some mornings he wakes up thinking he'll never get home. Summer is here, and he still hasn't fished the Clinch River. His sister Nadine hasn't yelled at him to put on a hat before he dies of sunstroke. There are a thousand miles between here and home. I guess I'm just real tired, he says.

I know what you mean, D. A. says, because she thinks this is what a grown-up would say. I feel the same. She scratches fiercely at a nasty rash on her ankle. When it begins to bleed, Jesse stands up and goes into his hideout for a tissue. She is not allowed to go inside. Jesse has explained that it wouldn't be proper for her to see his underwear lying on the ground, or his shaving kit scattered across the top of an overturned milk crate. I've already seen it, she could tell him if she wanted to. Sometimes when you're at work, me and the cat come in and take a nap on your pallet.

You ought not to pick at that ringworm, he says. That's how it spreads. The fungus gets up underneath your fingernails and contaminates everything you touch.

D. A. jerks her hand away from her leg and stares at her fingernails for a few seconds. Tell me one of your stories, she says. Tell me about the time you caught a two-headed catfish. Tell about your sister, Nadine, and how she got baptized twice, just because she thought the first time didn't take. Tell me about Belden Hollow and trilobites.

But Jesse doesn't feel up to it, hasn't felt up to it for a few weeks. Maybe Debra Ann can bring a few more of Mrs. Ledbetter's homegrown tomatoes next time, maybe some more of them sleeping pills from Mrs. Shepard's kitchen drawer. Maybe if he could get a decent night's sleep, he'd feel better.

Maybe, D. A. says, but I think the tomatoes might be all played out for the year. She doesn't tell her friend that she's been thinking about giving up stealing since Ginny's postcard came, since she realized she could be the best girl, she could take care of every stranger who found himself stranded in West Texas, and it wouldn't make a damn bit of difference. Ginny isn't coming back to Odessa, at least not anytime soon.

They are lying in a shady spot at the bottom of the flood canal, dipping washcloths into a bucket of ice water, wringing them out, and laying them across their faces. If you need to get out to Penwell, she says casually, I could drive you out there.

You're too little to drive. Jesse laughs. He picks an ice cube out of the bucket and pops it in his mouth to suck on. D. A. sticks her hand in the bucket and feels around for the biggest piece of ice she can find. She throws it as hard as she can, and the ice cube skitters across the pavement and melts almost immediately.

Hold on, Jesse says and ducks into his hideout for a few minutes. When he comes back, he carries a wad of bills—seven hundred dollars. He needs another hundred, and then he can go out to Penwell for his truck.

Can I hold it? she asks him, and when Jesse hands the money over, she hops up and down saying, We're rich, we're rich, we're rich.

He holds out his hand and she reluctantly gives the bills back. I can bring you a rubber band to hold all that together, she says. When are you going back to Tennessee?

There aren't any jobs there, he says, but when I get my truck I can stay here for a while longer and make a lot of money working on a rig.

What he doesn't say: If he goes home empty-handed to Nadine and his mama, it will just be the latest fuckup in a lifetime of fuckups.

They are quiet for a few minutes, each of them sitting up from time to time to dip their washcloth into the bucket and wring it out and lay it on whichever part of their body is most miserable. Forehead, neck, chest.

I haven't seen our cat for a couple of days, Jesse says. We ought to give him a name.

Tricky Dick? Debra Ann says. Elvis? Walter Cronkite?

Nah, you can't give a cat a human name, Jesse says. He's a good hunter. How about something to do with that?

Archer? D. A. says. Sharpshooter?

Archer, Jesse says. We'll call him that.

She wraps the washcloth around her wrist and leaves it there for a count of five, then wraps it around the other.

It is late afternoon and the shade has moved a little farther down the flood channel. Jesse scoots over a bit and sits quietly for a moment. His mama never knew what he and Nadine were up to when they were kids. As long as they showed up for dinner, she didn't care. D. A.'s a tough little kid, he thinks. He will miss her when he goes home.

She has been watching him carefully, studying the play of emotions across his narrow face. My mama used to let me drive all over hell's half acre, she says.

She did not, Jesse says. You couldn't even reach the pedals.

Oh, yes I can. I have to sit at the edge of the seat, but I can reach them. Again, she feels around the bucket of water but all the ice has melted. She draws her finger out and traces a heart on the hot concrete. It fades almost immediately.

If you need somebody to help you get out to Penwell, she says, I could borrow Mrs. Shepard's truck for an hour. You can drive us out, we'll get your truck, and I can follow you in Mrs. Shepard's truck. If we time it right—like maybe when she's running errands—she won't even know it's gone.

If she doesn't know it's gone, that's stealing, Jesse says.

It's not stealing if you bring it back.

And if you had a wreck driving that truck back to town, I wouldn't ever forgive myself.

I won't wreck it.

Maybe if you were a little older—thirteen, or even twelve.

D. A. stands up and walks over to him. She crosses her arms and narrows her eyes. Well, I guess I'm old enough to be helping you out all summer. I guess I'm old enough not to tell anybody there's been a man living out here, eating Mrs. Ledbetter's casseroles and working at the titty bar.

⌐

The four girls lean an old aluminum ladder against Mary Rose's new six-foot-high concrete security fence, and because she has the smallest feet and is good on the balance beam, Casey sets up the targets. Every two feet she bends carefully and sets an empty Dr Pepper can on top of the wall. When she has set down a dozen cans, she walks to the end and sits with her legs straddling the concrete. The girls watch Aimee practice. With each shot, a can flies off the fence and falls into the alley. When the last can has fallen, Lauralee gathers them up, climbs the ladder, and hands them up to Casey. And they do it again.

Aimee is generous with her .22 gauge rifle, but Casey is afraid of it and Mrs. Ledbetter says that Lauralee is not to lay one finger on a firearm. So Lauralee is the record-keeper: how many shots fired, how many holes in the cans. D. A. takes a turn, but when she hits the wall instead of the cans and the bullet ricochets so wildly off the concrete and dirt that Casey gets tangled up in her long skirt and falls off the fence, D. A. decides she'll just watch Aimee.

Every day Aimee stands a little farther away from the targets, and every day she is a better shot. Aimee tells D. A. that some nights, after the rest of them go home, she and her mom stand in the backyard and practice until it is so dark out they can't see the cans.

Every morning, while the other girls are at swim lessons or vacation Bible school, D. A. carries food to Jesse and asks him if he's earned enough money to go back home. Every afternoon, she watches Aimee set the rifle against her shoulder and shoot row after row of cans off the fence.

In early August, Mary Rose stands on the patio and watches Aimee shoot forty in a row off the fence. She steps into the house for a few minutes and returns with two skeins of old crochet yarn and a small wooden awl. The girls form an impromptu assembly line—D. A. stabs a hole in the bottom of each can, Lauralee feeds the yarn through the hole and jiggles the thread until it comes out the top, Casey ties a knot to keep the can from slipping up the thread, and so on. It's a Christmas garland made of aluminum cans, Casey says, when they have a strand of twenty. They drape half the strand over the lower branches of the small elm tree that Mary Rose planted the week they moved into the house. The rest of the strand dangles in the air. D. A. runs over and gives it a hard push and jumps out of the line of fire. The girls watch Aimee hit every one of the cans before she runs out of pellets. While Aimee rests her trigger finger, Debra Ann gathers up the cans and counts the holes in them. Five shots, she calls to Lauralee, five holes in a single can. Five cans, five shots, one hole in each can. Lauralee writes it down in her notebook.

You're a sharpshooter, D. A. tells Aimee. Maybe next summer you can teach me how to do it.

⌒

Here's a good story that my mom used to tell me, Debra Ann says when Jesse tells her he's too tired to come out and sit next to her on their milk crates. If it's okay with you, he calls weakly from deep inside the drainpipe, I'll just lie here on my bed and listen to you tell it.

Is everything okay with the money? she asks and he tells her yes, he'll have it soon, but this afternoon he's real tired. It's too hot to sleep nights, and his ear has been aching. D. A. stands up and walks to the mouth of the pipe. Can I sit down here at the edge? she asks him. You'll be able to hear me better.

Jesse's voice is small. Okay, but don't come in here. I don't want no company right now.

The mouth of the drainpipe is about six inches wider than Debra Ann is tall. She steps just inside the concrete lip and slides down the curved side to sit with her back against the wall. It is early August and the day is tired and still. Even in the shade, the air burns her face and neck and shoulders.

There was this old rancher's wife who lived down by the Pecos River, she tells him, back when they still ran sheep in this part of Texas. She was a beautiful woman with hair so thick and red that when she stood in the sunlight, she sometimes looked as if she were on fire.

But she was unlucky. A blizzard came up suddenly while her children were out riding fence with their daddy, and they all froze to death. The searchers found the children in a dry wash, huddled together with their horses. Her husband was just a few feet away with his head resting against the barbed-wire fence the woman had helped him build just a few weeks earlier.

For three years, nobody saw her. She didn't come into town, not even for coffee or cornmeal. The stationmaster kept her mail in an old wooden crate behind the counter at the depot, and although a few men sometimes talked about going out to check on her, nobody wanted to interfere with her grief. And besides, it had been a bad couple of years. They all had their hands full with the Big Die-Up and the ban on Texas cattle and anyway, they figured, she was probably dead.

Finally, somebody got the idea to draw straws and send the loser out there to cut her body down or pull the buzzards off her bones, but when the sixteen-year-old boy who drew the short straw arrived at the woman's homestead, he found her very much alive and working in her garden. She was bony and sunburned, and her hands were covered with scars and sunspots. Her eyebrows and eyelashes were so sun-bleached they were practically white.

But what a garden she had! The boy had never seen anything like it. They hadn't seen a good rain in three years, but the woman had plants growing out there that nobody had seen since they left Ohio or Louisiana— peach trees and ropy cantaloupe vines, corn plants and tomatoes. There was honeysuckle below her kitchen window, and one corner of her garden had been planted with wildflowers. Hummingbirds drifted from blossom to blossom. The boy stared and stared, trying to figure it out, and after a while he noticed a deep trench running between her garden and the Pecos River. All by herself, the woman had changed the course of the river!

She sent him back to town with two baskets, one filled with melons, the other with cucumbers, and anyone who happened to be standing around the depot when the boy returned shared in a spontaneous and joyful feast. One man got out his buck knife and sliced up all the cucumbers. Another fetched his machete and split the cantaloupes in half, then quarters. The men scooped out the tender orange flesh with their bare hands and ate and ate until their chins were sticky, and their shirts were soaked through with juice. They feasted. And for a while everybody admired the woman for her green thumb and her fortitude. How was it possible to have such a garden out there in the desert?

One night, while the men were sitting around the depot drinking somebody's homemade whiskey and enjoying a basket full of peaches the woman had sent into town, one of them joked that maybe she was a witch. Maybe she had cast a spell and changed the direction of the Pecos River. Or maybe she dug a trench, one old man called from his table in the corner, but he was a known liar and lunatic, and nobody listened to him.

Months passed, and each time a man rode out to check on her, the woman sent a basket of fruit and vegetables back to town with him.

And then, predictably, there was an influenza outbreak.

Predictably? asks Jesse. His voice is hoarse and low, nearly a whisper.

Yes, Debra Ann says. That is the exact word my mama always used.

Predictably, Ginny would say, and she meant that every tall tale has to have some kind of calamity.

And because the men couldn't believe it was just bad luck, or their own stupidity, they started looking for someone to blame. How could a woman grow such a marvelous garden all by herself? How could she change the course of a river? How could she bear to go on living without her husband and her children? Any self-respecting woman would have killed herself, one man said, or at least gone back to the Midwest.

When several babies and young children fell ill and died, the woman's fate was sealed. If she was bringing death to their offspring, five of the town's men decided, they wanted to see it for themselves.

They'd started drinking before sunset and they were about half stupid.

They left the depot after midnight, and bad luck struck almost immediately. One man was so drunk he fell off his horse, struck his head on a rock, and choked to death on his own vomit. One wanted to take a detour and show the other men the strange pockets of gas between rocks where you could toss a lit match and watch the flames dance across the stones, but more gas than he expected had gathered in the crevices of the rocks and he was consumed with fire.

This left three men riding out to see that poor woman and ask her if she was a witch. When a sudden thunderstorm came barreling across the land, as if summoned out of nowhere, one man and his horse were struck by lightning. When one of the two remaining men tried to save him—not one of them was smart enough to understand electricity—he too died.

And so, after all that, only one drunk, scared, and angry man made it to the woman's door.

And do you know what happened? D. A. pauses.

What happened? Jesse's voice is so quiet she leans forward and repeats the question. Do you know what happened?

What happened? He sounds as if he is trying to speak louder, but it's a sad effort, and Debra Ann wonders if her friend is all right, if the heat and loneliness and living out here have worn him down, if maybe she's not enough to help him get back on his feet again.

Well, she says, the man knocked on her door, pounded on it really, and he was hollering at her to open up, open this goddamned door!

What happened to her? Jesse asks quietly. Something bad?

That is exactly what I used to ask my mom.

What did your mother say? Jesse wants to know, and Debra Ann closes her eyes.

Her mother pauses and stands up from D. A.'s bed, then walks over and picks up a pile of clothes off the floor. The woman picked up her lantern and opened her door, Ginny says, and in the flickering yellow light, her hair looked like a fire burning.

Debra Ann can see the circles under her mother's eyes, the fingernails she's chewed to the quick. What did the woman do next?

Ginny laughs quietly. Well, she shot him on the spot and dragged his body to the edge of her property. She walks over to D. A.'s bed and tucks the blanket around her legs and arms.

After that, nobody bothered her much. The woman spent her days working in her garden, though she never again sent baskets into town for the men to enjoy.

Evenings, she sat on her front porch and watched all the stars come out, one by one. She lived to be a hundred and five years old and died peacefully in her sleep, and by the time it occurred to anybody to ride out there and check on her, she was nothing but a pile of dusty bones in her bed.

And her garden? Debra Ann asks her mother. What happened to that?

I guess it probably died, Ginny shrugs, but it was remarkable while it lasted.

There is a rustling sound in the drainpipe and the cat ambles out of the dark, arching its back and rubbing against D. A.'s leg. After a few minutes, Jesse climbs out and sits down next to her with his arms wrapped around his knees. In the bright afternoon sun, his eyes are shining. That's a good story, he says. I'm sorry your mom left.

D. A. shrugs and starts worrying the ringworm that has spread from her ankle to her calf. I don't really give a damn one way or the other. She pulls several black hairs out of her eyebrow. What about your truck? When are you getting it back?

Jesse pulls the napkin from his pocket and shows it to her. I guess Boomer lives out there now, he says.

That's way out there in the sticks. D. A. grabs the cat and flips him on his back. Too far to walk to.

Will you look at the balls on this guy? She laughs and Jesse rocks slightly, trying to laugh along with her. He leans over and rubs the cat's belly, and they sit without talking until it's time for Jesse to go to work, and D. A. to go home and start supper.

Mary Rose

Barely nine o'clock in the morning, and already it's hot enough to wish I'd skipped the pantyhose, but I can't walk into a courtroom with my legs bare. By the time Aimee and I walk across the street to Corrine's house, my lower torso feels like encased meat. Aimee dawdles a few steps behind me, in a snit because she thought she would be testifying in court today, too. She sat with Gloria Ramírez in the kitchen, she reminds me. She called the sheriff, and she can't understand why nobody wants to hear what she has to say. Because a courtroom's no place for a little girl, I tell her for the umpteenth time. Because I'm going to tell the story for both of us.

When I hand the baby to Corrine, she leans in and stares into his eyes for a few seconds, then makes a face and hands him off to Aimee. She is still wearing her nightgown, and one side of her thin hair is sticking straight out, perpendicular to the rest of her head. Thanks for taking them, Corrine, I say. Karla's baby came down with the stomach flu.

Aimee lifts one finger to flick the baby on the forehead, but when Corrine promises an endless supply of Dr Pepper, television, and D. A. Pierce if she doesn't wake him up, my daughter pivots on her heel and heads down the hallway to the living room without so much as a goodbye. The baby is slung over her shoulder like a sack of potatoes, his little head bouncing like a bobbin, and I start to call out *Careful.* Instead, I run back across the street to fetch the diaper bag.

When I tell Corrine that Keith Taylor says I should expect to be gone most of the morning, she squints and tilts her head to the side. Her gaze is sparrow sharp, like she's maybe wondering where Robert is on a day like today, why he isn't here to drive me over to the courthouse, to help me get through this, and I want to tell her that I don't need his help. We were in trouble long before Gloria Ramírez knocked on our front door. But him resenting me for opening the door to that child? The way he blames her for what happened out there? His hatefulness and bigotry? I guess I never noticed it before, but now I cannot think of him without thinking of her. I would like to say some of this to Corrine, but here we are, standing on her porch in the heat, and my kids are already stealing some of her day.

I don't know what I'd do without you, Corrine, I say. Robert's got cows dropping like flies out there. Get it, flies? Blowflies?

Corrine's lips curve upward, her face rich with complicated lines that remind me of the old pecan wood on my porch back at the ranch, or the dried-out creeks that crisscross our property. But when I study her face a little longer, I see that it is a thin smile, a barely there smile that says, Oh cut the shit, Mary Rose. You and I both know he's punishing you for agreeing to testify in the first place.

Lady, she says instead, you look worn out.

Really, I say, because you look fantastic.

She laughs gently. Fair enough.

I'm fine—I reach into the diaper bag, pull out a tissue, and pat the sweat that's threatening to ruin my makeup—looking forward to seeing justice served.

Is that so? Corrine reaches into the pocket of her housecoat and I am already thinking about having a cigarette, even if it means standing in the heat for a few more minutes, but then she lifts her shoulders apologetically. I am losing things left and right, she says. Cigarettes, matches, sleeping pills. Hell, I even managed to lose a saucepan and a jar of chow-chow. Grief makes you stupid, I guess. She winks at me, but she's not smiling when she asks again how I've been sleeping.

I could tell her about the phone ringing day and night, the messages being left on my new answering machine, and the baby wanting to nurse every two or three hours. When he falls back to sleep, I pull my nipple out of his mouth and rise from my bed to check the doors and turn the lights on. I check and recheck the windows, listening carefully to every little sound, the wind drawing its fingers across a window screen or a pickup truck peeling out after the bar has closed or the plant whistle's solitary wail. Sometimes I think I hear a window being tugged open at the other end of the house, and I am sure somebody is coming to harm us. And every night I think the same thing—once Dale Strickland is sentenced and sent to the penitentiary in Fort Worth, this will all die down. People will get bored and the late-night calls will stop, and I will have done my part to set things right for Gloria.

I hand the diaper bag to Corrine and tell her that I haven't been sleeping well, but I expect to start doing so real soon. And by the way, I am also losing things right and left—cans of food, matchboxes, aspirin, even a couple of bath towels.

Must be something in the water, she says.

⌒

In the parking lot outside the courthouse, Keith Taylor hands me a paper cup filled with coffee that looks thick enough to clog a drain. Mr. Ramírez, the uncle? He called me again this morning, he says. She's not coming, Mary Rose.

This should not surprise me—Keith has been warning me for weeks that Victor hasn't let anyone from Keith's office interview his niece since June, that they are not even sure where she's living—but I still cry out, Why not?

Two men standing next to a tow truck look over at us. They wear sports coats over white shirts, cowboy hats, and top-dollar snakeskin boots. They stop talking to watch us for a few seconds, and then the one in the white Stetson leans forward and says something quietly in the other man's ear. The man nods in our general direction and I fight the urge to yell at both of them, Y'all have something to say to me? You two sons of bitches been calling my house late at night?

Mary Rose, I warned you this might happen, Keith

says. Mr. Ramírez doesn't want to put her through it, and I can't blame him. He raises his coffee cup and lifts one finger toward the men, a little greeting. He is tall and good-looking, known locally for his unwavering commitment to taking every case to trial and to remaining a bachelor. He is at least ten years older than me, but this morning he looks ten years younger, and about half as worn out.

She has to testify, I tell him. We stand together under the sun, me fighting the urge to yank at the waistband of my blue-jean skirt, the pavement burning a hole in my shoes. When the stenographer, Mrs. Henderson, walks past us with her arms full of file folders, Keith gently strokes his blond mustache with his index finger and puffs up his chest.

When she steps into the courthouse, he exhales and lets his shoulders fall back into their usual slight slump.

Look, Mary Rose, that girl has lost everything, even her mother, and Mr. Ramírez knows how some people around town are talking, he has to, and maybe he thinks she's suffered enough. Maybe he doesn't want to expose her to any more scrutiny.

I can hardly believe I am hearing this. That's it? You're going to let him do this?

Keith hitches up his slacks and wipes a bit of sweat

off his forehead. He looks up at the sun like he wishes he could shoot it out of the sky. Honestly, he says, I don't blame him, not even a little bit.

She ought to be in that courtroom, telling them what that bastard did to her. Can't you make her testify?

No, Mary Rose, I cannot make her testify.

Well, how come? How are we going to get justice?

We? Keith laughs. You got a mouse in your pocket? He stands still for so long that several horseflies as big as peanuts land on his shirt. His hands are large and lightly freckled, and when he swats at the flies, hot air moves gently between us.

You know what I hate most about my job?

Losing a case?

Huh! You would think so, but no ma'am. He smiles and nods again at the two men who have started walking toward the courthouse doors. What I hate most, Mary Rose, is when somebody squirts hot sauce up my ass and tries to tell me it's cool water. Pardon my French.

Keith takes a drink of his coffee and frowns—this is terrible—then he takes another. The cleaning crew that Mrs. Ramírez worked with? They've been cleaning office buildings in this town for years without anybody wanting to see their social security cards. Hell, they mopped floors and emptied trash cans at the courthouse for three years before the city council caught wind of it and got their undies in a wad. And five weeks after her daughter knocks on your front door, immigration is waiting for Mrs. Ramírez at the front gate when she finishes her shift at the plant? Bullshit, he says. Pardon my French.

He drinks the rest of his coffee in one long gulp and tosses the paper cup on the ground. We have the sheriff's report, he says, and the hospital report, and we have you. That will have to be enough.

I give him a look and walk over to pick up the cup, making a show of putting it in a trash can that is hardly more than an arm's length from where we stand. I wonder, not for the first time, if I ought to tell him about the ugly phone calls I've been getting all these months—You sure love wetbacks, don't you Mrs. Whitehead? Know what happens to race traitors, Mary Rose? Maybe I'll drive over there and rape you myself, you bitch.

I know they aren't serious, just a bunch of bigots and drunks, and Keith would likely remind me that this is a free country, people can *say* anything they want. And I don't want to ask for help, not from Keith or anybody else. What I want is to be left alone with Aimee Jo and the baby. And I want to be ready, if somebody shows up at my front door.

I'm ready, I tell Keith.

Good. Let's get inside and stand under the air-conditioning for a minute or two. He gently presses one hand against the small of my back and we cross the parking lot. Christ almighty, he says, it's hot. Hello, Scooter, he says when the defense attorney passes us on the stairs.

Keith warned me about Strickland's lawyer last week when we were practicing my testimony. He sat in the dining room and called questions through the swinging door while I nursed the baby in the kitchen.

He's a pushy little son of a bitch, Keith said after I had put the baby down and fixed us both a glass of iced tea. Pardon my French— He winked at Aimee, who had walked in behind me, a popsicle hanging out of her mouth. She stared at him like she was already planning their wedding. I'm going to be a lawyer, she said, like you. Smart girl, he said. Go to UT and study business law. Criminal law will break your heart.

When he reached over to steal her nose, Aimee batted his hand away and rolled her eyes. I'm too old for that, Mr. Taylor.

I guess you are. Anyway, he said, Scooter Clemens hails from Dallas. Highland Park. He wears a Stetson so clean you could eat a sandwich off the brim. All hat, no cattle. Keith leaned forward and looked me right in the eye. Family's been in Texas since forever. Probably got a whole cedar chest full of white hoods in the attic.

How come? Aimee asked, and Keith stumbled around for a bit before telling her, Well, for Halloween, of course.

Aimee, that popsicle is melting all over the carpet, I said. Go eat it in the backyard.

She sighed and pursed her lips together, and I could tell she was thinking about arguing, but when Keith offered her a silver dollar if she gave us a minute to talk, she couldn't get out of the dining room fast enough. We listened as the kitchen door slammed shut behind her.

Scooter Clemens is a stone-cold killer, Keith said. He's been getting boys out of trouble for thirty years. Keep your answers short. Don't let him rile you up, and whatever you do, don't look at Dale Strickland when they bring him into the courtroom.

⌒

Judge Rice is a thick-necked old Aggie with heavy white eyebrows and shoulders like a linebacker. He reminds me of the bulldog that used to chase my brother and me home from school. When he's not in court he runs cattle on family land that runs from Plainview, Texas, to Ada, Oklahoma.

When the bailiffs bring Strickland in, I hear them walk him over to his chair, but I keep my eyes on my lap. Scooter asks if they can take the handcuffs off—he ain't going anywhere, he says, in his best country voice—and I feel a little of the air go out of my chest. But Judge Rice tells him absolutely not, this man is in custody until somebody declares him innocent or guilty. I breathe out through my nose. Try not to look at him.

After we all say the pledge and the prayer, Judge Rice pulls a pistol out from under his robe and sets it on his desk. West Texas gavel, he tells all of us. Welcome to my courtroom. I look up at him, but the judge is looking over all our heads. Y'all play nice, he says, and points his gavel toward the back of the room.

I stand up and swear the oath, all while staring at Keith's face. Look at me, he said again and again as we practiced. Look at me, he says now. Tell me what you saw. I tell my story, and then we all take a fifteen-minute break. Other than the jury, there are a handful of people in the courtroom, all of them men of various ages, heights, and shapes. Keith points to a young man sitting alone on the last row. He wears a white dress shirt and a plain black tie, and his arms are folded across his broad chest. His mustache is neatly trimmed and his hair's so short I can see patches of his skull underneath. Keith leans over. That's the girl's uncle, he whispers, and I long to jump from my seat, rush to him, and ask how she's doing, where she is, why she isn't here.

I am not back on the stand for more than a minute before I recall that conversation at our house, and the last thing Keith said to me before he packed up his briefcase and admired the baby, who was awake again, and crying and rooting. Do not look at Strickland, Mary Rose. Look at anybody else in the room, but not him.

So I stare at Mrs. Henderson until she looks up and winks at me. The pantyhose have a vise grip on my belly, but instead of clawing at my skirt I fold my hands in my lap and try sending a smile the judge's way.

How are you doing today, Mrs. Whitehead? Scooter Clemens looks down at his legal pad as if he's studying it carefully.

Well, I'm just fine, I say. Thank you for asking.

I hear you've been having a hard time of things. You feeling okay?

Yes, I am. I say, But I'm wondering what the hell he's heard.

How are things out at the ranch? Y'all losing many cows to these heel flies?

Blowflies, I correct him.

Oh, I beg your pardon, Mrs. Whitehead. Blowflies. My husband has lost nearly his entire stock.

Whew! Clemens pulls a handkerchief from his pocket and dabs at his forehead. I'm so sorry to hear that. Please give Robert my regards. It's a nasty business, these bugs—he folds the handkerchief and slides it into his jacket and then turns his smile on me—I'll bet you and the children are a real comfort to him out there. Bet he loves coming home at night and seeing your beautiful face. Clemens slaps his forehead and glances in the general direction of the jury. I look at them too and realize with a start that there are only two women in the room—Mrs. Henderson and me. We don't belong here, I think. This room isn't for us.

Oh, I beg your pardon, Mrs. Whitehead, Clemens says. I plumb forgot that you and the children are living in town now.

Yes, I say. We moved to town in April. We only came to town because of *him*, I tell the court. I explain that seeing Dale Strickland, and what he did to Gloria Ramírez, made me want to take my daughter and leave. Then I mention Ginny Pierce, who might be gone for good. I talk about Raylene McKnight, who took half the family savings, two suitcases, and her ten-year-old son, and flew from Midland to Dallas to Atlanta to London to Melbourne, Australia. Imagine all those layovers, I tell the court before Judge Rice asks me to please, please, please get on with my story. Young lady, he says, I don't like complicated tales, and what does this have to do with today's task? The answer is nothing—this has nothing to do with Gloria Ramiréz. Still, I feel my face grow warm, and I think, This is my story, you old rooster. Y'all can sit and listen for a few minutes. Instead I say, yes sir, and tug at my waistband.

Well, it's a shame to let this little bit of trouble run you out of your own house, Scooter says. When this matter is settled, I hope you feel like you can go back out there and be with your husband, where you belong.

Mr. Clemens, I don't think that's really any of your—

Keith shakes his head very slightly, and I imagine what he'd say if he were standing next to me. Don't let him get your goat, Mary Rose.

How's that new son of yours?

He's fine. Thank you.

You enjoying your new house here in town—he looks down at his legal pad—on Larkspur Lane?

At the mention of my street, I glance sharply at the defense table. Strickland keeps his eyes turned toward the table in front of him, but there is a slight smile on his face. If he ever gets the chance, he will drive straight to my house. He will park his truck in my driveway, and this time he won't even have time to take his hand off the steering wheel before I shoot him in the face.

Larkspur Lane, Clemens says. Ain't that where Corrine Shepard lives?

For a man that doesn't live here in Odessa, I tell him, you seem to know everybody and everything.

He chuckles, and I want to knock his teeth in.

Corrine keeping busy?

I guess so.

I hear she's a hoot, always cutting people off in traffic, getting the ladies in an uproar at church, but I guess her family's been here since Odessa was just a pee stop on the Texas & Pacific, so y'all get to keep her. He looks over at the jury. Several men smile and shake their heads.

How have you been getting along with your new neighbors, Mrs. Whitehead?

At that, Keith Taylor sighs loudly and gets to his feet. Judge, is there some point to this line of questioning?

Judge Rice has been sitting with his head leaned against one hand and his eyes closed. Now he sits up straight in his chair and looks at me. I heard you gave Grace Cowden what-for at church not too long ago, he says.

Keith's shoulders are all the way up around his neck, and he is frowning at the notepad in front of him.

My wife is still talking about it. The judge laughs. You gals! Y'all look for trouble coming and trouble going. And speaking of my wife, Mr. Clemens, come one o'clock, I'm meeting Mrs. Rice for lunch at the Country Club. You have some pertinent questions for Mrs. Whitehead?

Scooter Clemens nods solemnly. Yes sir, thank you. Mrs. Whitehead, can you tell us how far your house is from Farm to Market, Number 182?

The old ranch road? I ask him.

Ranch road, he says. No, ma'am, I mean FM182.

Okay, I shrug. Everybody out here calls it the ranch road.

Well, Judge Rice doesn't. And neither do I. He looks at the jury like they have just shared an inside joke, and my pantyhose suddenly feel real tight against my belly, still loose from my pregnancy. I think about Aimee Jo and my new son, barely four months old, both of them at home with Mrs. Shepard so I can come do my civic duty, talk about this awfulness. I didn't ask for this trouble. It came to me. I didn't go looking for it. Then my breasts begin to itch and burn because I haven't fed the baby in nearly four hours, and I start to worry that

I might be shamed in front of these men if my milk should leak through the Kleenex I tucked into my bra. So I tell Scooter that Farm to Market wasn't what I meant to say at all. Everybody knows you call it the ranch road, unless you're from someplace else, which I guess he is, since his boots don't look like they've ever stepped in a single cow patty. The jury starts laughing, and I remind them all that I was the first to see Gloria Ramírez alive that Sunday morning.

Ranch road, Clemens says. Okay. Mrs. Whitehead, on the morning this little Mexican gal—he looks at his legal pad—Gloria Ramírez, knocked on your front door, what did she say?

Say?

Yes, ma'am. What did she say to you?

Well, she didn't say anything, I tell him.

Not even one word? Mr. Clemens glances again toward the jury, and I do the same. I recognize three of the twelve men from around town. They look kindly and bemused, as if they feel sorry for me.

She asked for a glass of water, I tell him, and she said she wanted her mama.

Had she been drinking the night before? Was she hung over?

I doubt it, Mr. Clemens. She is a child.

Well, she's fourteen—

Yes, I interrupt him, and that makes her a child.

Clemens smiles. Well, one girl's fourteen is another girl's seventeen, least that's what my old daddy always said.

I want to leap off the stand, grab a chair, and break it across his face. But I sit and listen and twist my hands into complicated knots.

Did she tell you she had been molested?

Excuse me?

I'm trying to be delicate, Mrs. Whitehead. Did Gloria Ramírez say she had been raped?

I *saw* her. I *saw* what he did to her.

But did the young lady tell you she'd been raped, Mrs. Whitehead? Did she use that word?

That child did not even have her shoes. She walked three miles in her bare feet, just to get away from him. Jesus Christ, he hit her so hard he ruptured her spleen.

Judge Rice leans forward and speaks quietly to me. Ma'am, please do not take the name of the Lord in vain in my courtroom.

Are you shitting me? I want to ask him. Are you shitting me right now? But I look down and try not to tug at my pantyhose. Yes sir, I say.

It says right here—Scooter consults his goddamn legal pad again—that Miss Ramírez had puncture wounds and abrasions on her hands and feet that were consistent with falling. Could she have damaged her spleen when she fell?

Instead of waiting for my answer, he reminds me that I have sworn to tell the truth, the whole truth, etcetera, and because he wants to make sure we're all clear on this, he speaks slowly, as if I'm a child. Mrs. Whitehead, I am asking you a simple yes or no question. Did she say he raped her?

Yes, I say. She said that.

She used that word?

Yes, she did.

Keith Taylor grabs his bottom lip between his thumb and index finger and starts pulling at it. He looks like he's about to cry. I look to the back of the courtroom where Mr. Ramírez is sitting, but he is looking down at his lap.

Well, pardon me, Mary Rose, Clemens says, but that's not what you said in any interview up until this minute. You telling us a little story now?

No, I say. I forgot until just this minute.

I see.

At this point, Keith stands up and asks to speak with me privately. Judge Rice denies the request—it's getting late and he needs to go to the little boys' room—but he says Keith can come up to the stand if he wants to. Keith crosses the room in about four long strides and stands in front of me. Mary Rose, he whispers, you have to tell the truth.

She did not use those exact words, I tell the court. But she didn't have to. It was obvious to anybody with two eyes to see.

Clemens smiles like he's just won the office football pool. So you *did* tell us a little story. How about this gentleman sitting over here? Mr. Strickland. Did you see him that morning?

Yes, he came to my front door, too.

What did he want?

He was looking for her.

He was worried about his girlfriend?

She was not his girlfriend. She is a child and he is a grown man.

Hmm, Scooter says. I don't think Miss Ramírez ever told him her age. He stretches her last name out, all while looking at the jury, making sure everybody hears it.

So he was looking for this young lady who had gone out with him the night before?

She was scared to death when she turned up at my door. He would have killed her.

How do you know? Did she tell you these things?

She didn't have to. I *saw* her.

Did Mr. Strickland threaten you? Clemens asks.

He yelled at me to go inside and get her. He called me a bitch.

Mrs. Whitehead, Judge Rice says, *please* don't use that language in here.

So he was hung over—Clemens looks again at the jury, like every one of them is a fraternity brother—as I imagine quite a few of us were, the morning after Valentine's. And he was a little short-tempered because they had a squabble and his girlfriend wandered off?

Objection, Keith Taylor says, and Judge Rice says, Naw, Keith. Come on, now, you know better than that.

Objection, Judge! He's trying to create a different story.

That's your objection, Keith? Clemens's smile doesn't even come close to reaching his eyes. He's a snake. If you turned the air conditioner up high enough, his heart rate would plummet.

Is this not what we do? he says. Do we not consider whether there's enough evidence to make a decision *beyond reasonable doubt* before we ruin a young man's life?

But I have had enough. I say, She is a child, you piece of shit.

Clemens walks over, sits down at his table, and puts his head in his hands. Judge Rice knocks his desk with the butt of his pistol and speaks so quietly that everyone in the room has to lean forward. Mrs. Whitehead, it's clear to me how hard this has been on you and your family, but I promise you, if you cuss in my courtroom one more time, you will spend tonight in a jail cell. Do you understand me?

Yes.

Yes, what? Beneath those white eyebrows, Judge Rice has turned red as a beet.

Yes, I say.

Yes, *what*?

I know what he's looking for. When I was a girl just a few years older than Aimee is now, there was a time when I got into some pretty good squabbles with my daddy, mostly because I wouldn't stop arguing with him about every little thing. There came a day when we both had had enough and we stood across from each other in the driveway, him asking questions and me looking him right in the eye. I was still about half tickled that I was tall enough to do it, look him in the eye, and I folded my arms across my chest when he asked a question.

I said, Yes.

And he said, Yes, what?

And I smirked, Yep.

He slapped my face. Yes, what?

Yes. He slapped me again. Yes, what?

Yes.

When he slapped me a third time, I told my daddy what he wanted to hear—yes *sir*—but I never forgot it and I never really forgave him. And I vowed I'd never hit my own kids. Now I look around the courtroom, searching for somebody to stand up with me, to help me make it through this morning. Mr. Ramírez nods slightly, and I wonder what his life here in Odessa has been like since this happened. I wonder about Gloria's mother and how long it will be before she sees her daughter again. Nothing is more important than this, certainly not my pride. So I look at the judge and I ruck up my lips, and I smile. Yes, *sir*.

But he's not done. He says, It is painful to see a young woman—a mother—use that language in a court of law.

Yes, sir.

Thank you. Did that young man threaten you?

Judge, he was like—nothing I have ever seen. It was like the devil himself drove into my front yard. I have never in my life seen such evil.

Clemens is back on his feet. Objection! It's a yes or no question.

Did he threaten you, Mary Rose, or your family?

No. Sir.

Good girl, Clemens says, and Judge Rice leans back in his chair. He crosses his hands behind his head. Mr. Clemens, do you have any more questions for this young lady?

Just one more. Mrs. Whitehead, were you pointing a gun at Mr. Strickland?

I see Keith sigh in his chair, shuffle some papers around, and lean forward. But I do not look at Strickland. Yes, I was.

⌒

Victor Ramírez is already standing next to his car with his hand on the door when he sees me running across the parking lot. We've got ten minutes before we have to be back in court and even though I've hardly run more than a few feet, I am out of breath. I glance down, just to be sure there's no milk on my blouse, and then step close to Mr. Ramírez, as if standing close to him might make me feel better.

I'm sorry, I say. I want to help Gloria.

Glory, he says and stands looking at the sky, as if I haven't said a word.

Can I see her and talk with her, ask her if she's okay?

A small chuckle rises in his throat. No, ma'am, he

says. No, you may not. He opens the driver's side door and sits down. When I try to grab the door, he gently pushes my hand away.

Are you leaving?

Yes, ma'am.

Please, Mr. Ramírez, make her testify.

You people won't hear what *Glory* has to say. Do you understand that, Mrs. Whitehead? Then he pulls the door closed and starts the car and drives away.

Keith stands up and gives his collar a few good tugs. Mary Rose, can you describe for all of us one more time what Gloria Ramírez looked like when she showed up at your front door that morning?

Yes, I can.

Well, let's make it quick, Judge Rice says. If I keep the missus waiting and they run out of that prime rib special, I'll be sleeping outside with my horses tonight. The courtroom erupts with laughter. Dale Strickland laughs, a flat and hollow sound that sets my teeth on edge. Even Mrs. Henderson cracks a smile. Me and Keith Taylor are the only two people in that room who are not laughing.

On my way back to my seat, Strickland reaches out

and presses his thumb lightly against my hand. The hair stands up on my arms. A door opens in the back of the courtroom, and a thin shaft of light illuminates the dust motes floating in the air between us.

Keith is moving fast in our direction, but the rest of the court is quiet, or not paying any attention. Or maybe there is plenty of noise and everyone sees, but this is how I will remember it: a silence that makes me want to scream for days.

Mary Rose, Strickland speaks so softly I can barely hear him. His thumbnail scratches gently against my palm. His hands are still cuffed, and I feel the metal against my wrist. Mary Rose, he says—how I hate that he knows my name—I want to tell you how sorry I am for the trouble I've brought to you and your family. He smiles, mouth closed, lips pressed tight. When this is all over, he says, I hope to see you again under better circumstances, maybe at your ranch or here in town.

He has spoken so quietly, I'm not even sure I've heard him correctly. But I am about to learn something else about Dale Strickland—he's smarter than me. Because when I answer him, I make sure everybody in the courtroom hears it. Well come on over, I tell him. I will look forward to blowing your fucking head off.

She's crazy, someone says, and then everyone starts talking all at once, a quick murmur that rolls like thunder across the courtroom. Dale Strickland grins at me, and then Judge Rice slams the butt of his pistol against his desk. His lips are a tight seam. I sure hope your husband can take care of that baby without you tonight, Mrs. Whitehead, he says, because you are in contempt.

Fine, I tell him, I'm not afraid of you, old man. And the bailiff leads me away.

I won't spend the night in jail—just six hours in the holding cell. Long enough, Judge Rice says when he stops by the cell after the court closes at four o'clock. You ready to go home, young lady? You learned your lesson?

Yes, I tell him.

Yes, what?

Yes.

He looks at me for a long moment, and I wonder if we are about to have another standoff, but he shakes his head and walks out to the reception area.

By the time they find the keys and let me out, my blouse is soaked through, my breasts so heavy with milk, I can barely stand up straight. My purse is pressed tight against my shirt when I walk past the officer at the desk, and I can hear them laughing all the way down the hall. They are still laughing when I step out of the station and close the door behind me and walk across the parking lot to my car.

⌒

By the time I get to Corrine's house, the baby is so frantic that I tear a button off my blouse, trying to get him settled. He screams and paws at me, his sharp little nails leaving long scratches on my breasts. When he latches on, we both sigh and close our eyes, our bodies loosening.

Back at the house, my daughter doesn't say a word while I open some cans and get dinner on, not a word while I nurse the baby for the second time in as many hours. When I stay put in my chair while the phone rings and her daddy leaves a message on the new answering machine, she is quiet then, too. It is an easy bedtime.

At dusk Corrine walks across the street and we settle in. I make a pitcher of salty dogs and carry it, along with the vodka, out to the patio. Corrine grabs an ashtray. We turn out the porch light and leave the patio door cracked open, sit out in the backyard under the darkening sky. It is tinged purple, a sign that there might be a dust storm coming our way.

So, Corrine says, where the hell were you all afternoon? She strikes a match and her eyes glitter in the brief light. Tonight, there's a small wind loose in the world, and it can't make up its mind about which way it wants to blow or how big it wants to be. Every match that flickers and dies feels personal, like a closed fist.

Well, I think, here's my chance to reach across the darkness and tell somebody the truth. But the story I tell Corrine is a comedy about a lady with leaky tits who sasses a judge and lands herself in the pokey. I set the scene for her, me telling Strickland that I'd happily shoot him and Keith Taylor saying, oh shit, and Judge Rice banging his pistol against his wooden desk so hard we thought the wood was going to crack, and I tell the story so well that Corrine laughs and laughs. That is one of the best courtroom stories I have ever heard, she says. I'll remember it until the day I die.

So will everybody in this town, I say.

She hands me the bottle and I add some vodka to a glass half filled with grapefruit juice. Don't worry about it, she says. They'll move along.

Oh, sure. People will forget all about it in a week or two. We both laugh. We both know this is going to follow me around for years, and Aimee, too. She will be the girl with the crazy mama who spent an afternoon in jail. This day will change the two of us. Now when we play cards, I will make her fight for every win, and when she loses, I will make sure she knows why—and not always in the kindest of ways. We will spend hours in the backyard shooting cans off the fence, and when she starts whining that she's tired, she wants to go play with Debra Ann or one of the other girls on the street, I will tell her to run into the alley and gather up the cans. Set them on the fence, and do it again. Do it again, I'll say. Again. Again! You must be able to hit your target on the first shot.

I will make her daddy drive into town when he wants to see her, and it will be twenty years before I again walk across that spare, beautiful land out at the ranch, before I sit on my old front porch and watch the sun go down, nothing but a dirt road standing between me and the sky, the only noise coming from cows and birds, the occasional coyote. And in a few years, when I catch Aimee sneaking out of the house at night and driving out to the oil patch with her friends, I will slap her so hard the red mark will still be there when she wakes up the next morning. I will not apologize for years, and by the time I'm ready to say I'm sorry, every word between us will be a bullet in the chamber.

The sky is black now and the backyard is dark, except for our two cigarettes and the diffuse light from the kitchen hovering at the edge of the concrete.

You going to answer that? Corrine asks when the phone rings.

Hell no, I say. I bought a machine that does it for me. It cost me nearly two hundred dollars and I had to order it from Dallas.

We listen as the machine switches on and my voice drifts across the yard.

My God, Corrine says. Will wonders never cease? I'd never have to answer the phone again. She grabs my fly swatter, snaps it against the table, *got him*, and reaches for the vodka.

The wind shifts direction and the refinery stops being something you can forget about. We sit up straight, pinch our noses, and wait to see what the wind will do next. Keith Taylor's drawl pierces the darkness. This is Keith Taylor, he begins, and we both grin. Oh girl, Corrine says with her thumb and index fingers still holding her nose, if I were thirty years younger. Giddy-up. And we break out laughing. I laugh so hard I can feel my shoulders loosening, the sharp blades relaxing.

I've got some news. He pauses, and we hear him crack a beer open. He is quiet for so long that I start to wonder if he set the phone down on the table and wandered off, or if the machine isn't working.

It was all over by four o'clock, he says. Simple assault. Probation and a fine to be paid to the Ramírez family. These cases are hard, he says. I'm sorry, Mary Rose. He was out by five o'clock this afternoon. The machine switches off.

Corrine and I sit there in the dark without saying anything, but I can guess what she's thinking. Because did anybody believe for a minute that he would be convicted? Anybody but me?

I'm sorry, she says, but I'm already on my feet and heading inside to check the windows and doors, and my kids. On my way back, I fetch Old Lady out of the hall closet, check to make sure it's loaded. When I step onto the patio and Corrine sees me holding the rifle, she stands up with a groan. She pulls two cigarettes out of her pack and sets them on the table.

If you've got something to say to me, I tell her, then go ahead and say it. But don't you dare tell me not to be pissed off.

Hell no, Corrine says. Be pissed off. I'm pretty sure it's the only thing that gets me out of bed in the morning.

The wind is picking up, and for the first time, I wonder if there's going to be some rain in the next couple of days. Corrine puts her hand on Old Lady and gently rubs her thumb across the walnut stock. That's a beautiful rifle, Mary Rose. Potter had one like this. I sent it up to Alice when he died. Sometimes they're so pretty, you forget what they can do. Anyway, it's hard being alone with two kids all day, every day. Ask for help, if you need it.

I laugh. Did you?

Beg your pardon?

Did you ever ask for help?

No, Corrine says. The wind catches several loose strands of her thin hair and blows them across her face. She turns to go home, wobbling against the table and nearly tripping over one of my extension cords.

Grabbing the cord, I tell her to hang on. I walk over to the outlet and plug it in. Light floods every corner of the backyard. Good Lord! Corrine's hands fly to her face and she blinks hard. It's like a prison yard back here.

Six white extension cords are stretched across the back patio, each of them connected to an aluminum spotlight. Sterling lights, my granny used to call them. She set them out when coyotes were eating the chickens. My backyard is filled with great circles of light, the darkness barely clinging to the edges. I can see everything.

After Corrine has left, I stand out there with the light streaming through my skirt. I know I can't fire Old Lady out here in the backyard, not this time of night, so I grab Aimee's .22 rifle. I line up Dr Pepper cans on the back fence and smoke one of Corrine's cigarettes. Then I shoot the cans off the fence one by one, listening as each can strikes the dirt in the alley. When Debra Ann's cat comes along, I sight him through the aperture. He is stalking a locust along the cinder-block fence, batting it with his paw until it falls into the alley. I switch the safety off, and wonder what that might feel like, to destroy something just because you can. After the cat wanders off, I stand out there in the dark looking at the stars and listening to the wind pick up, and when the baby wakes up and starts crying, hungry again, I set down the gun and go to him.

Debra Ann

The sky turns the color of an old bruise, and they can see the dust cloud coming from fifty miles away, blowing through the main streets of towns even smaller than Odessa, places like Pecos and Kermit and Mentone. The red haze seizes tumbleweeds and small stones and sparrows, anything that can be picked up and carried for a while before being flung back to the earth. When the wind comes barreling across those thirsty plains, the sun disappears and the cloud covers everything—water tanks and cattle pens, the cooling towers at the petrochemical plant, oil wells and pump-jacks, the sorghum fields split in half by unpaved farm roads. Outside town, cattle huddle together as wild-eyed cows bawl for calves whose scents have been secreted away by the wind. At the plant, men climb down from the towers and run like hell for the break shack. Roughnecks leave their drilling platforms and cower in their trucks, three men sitting thigh to thigh in the front seat. Or if they are new on the job or the youngest on the crew, or if they are Mexican, they lie beneath a heavy tarp tossed hastily over a truck bed, four or five men crushed together, ass to balls, trying hard not to rub up against each other.

On Larkspur Lane, D. A. stands in the front yard watching a thousand-foot cloud rise up from the earth. Tumbleweeds and newspapers roll hard down the street. Branches tear themselves from pecan trees and power lines jerk as if they are in the hands of a mad puppeteer. A screen flies off Mrs. Shepard's bedroom window, lands on a bed of pansies next door, then picks itself up and disappears end over end down the street. Debra Ann walks over to Aimee's house, and they stand in the yard with Lauralee and Casey, their eyes and hair filling with grit, their clothes pressed stiff against their bodies. Later, they will learn that five people died when a tornado tore through a mobile home park in West Odessa. At the plant where Mr. Ledbetter is on shift, a man fell from a cooling tower and broke his neck and died almost instantly.

Dirt blacks out the sun and the sky changes from an old bruise to a ripe plum. The storm bears down on

the girls, and still they stand outside in the front yard.
Mrs. Shepard opens her front door and shouts, What
in the hell is wrong with you girls? Get inside! And
still they stand. But when they feel a slight pause in
the wind and everything grows still, when they look up
and see the sky turning lavender—a sky hand-painted
for twisters, Mrs. Ledbetter calls it—when the birds
stop singing and the wind begins to sound like a train
rushing toward them, they run for Aimee's house.

Yesterday, Jesse earned the last of the money he
needs to get his truck back, and D. A. told him that all
they needed was the right moment. Now she looks out
Aimee's kitchen window and wonders what he's doing
right this second, if he's thinking what she's thinking.
Lauralee calls home and listens for a minute or two
while her mother yells. There will be a whipping waiting for me when this is over, she tells the other girls.
Casey calls the bowling alley to let her mother know
where she is, and D. A. calls the guard at the front gate
of the olefin plant where her dad has just taken a job.
It'll be a little less money, she knows, but he'll be home
earlier and he'll get Saturdays off, mostly. Maybe that
will make things better, she tells the girls, and they nod
their heads. Maybe so.

They huddle in Aimee's kitchen peering out the
window, watching for funnel clouds, and eating every-

thing they can find. When the phone rings, Aimee's mother rushes into the kitchen and grabs the receiver. It is the middle of the day, but she is still in her nightgown. She grips the phone in her hand and listens, wrapping the cord around one finger and watching it turn dark red. It's over, she says tonelessly. Why are you still calling me? She places the receiver gently on the hook.

At the other end of the house, the baby begins to fuss, but Mrs. Whitehead makes no move to go to him. Instead, she pulls a cigarette from the pocket of her nightgown and lights it. The girls, including her own daughter, might be strangers, Debra Ann thinks, for the way Mrs. Whitehead is looking at them. D. A. checks the clock on the stove. Just past one o'clock.

Mama, Aimee says, why didn't you yell for me? It's a bad storm. Maybe even a tornado.

Mrs. Whitehead walks to the kitchen sink, pulls the curtain back, and gazes out the small window. So it is, she says and tugs the curtain firmly closed. So it is. She studies her cigarette for a few seconds and flicks the ash in the sink. She picks up a glass and pours some iced tea from a pitcher on the counter.

Are you sick? Casey asks, swaying from side to side, her long skirt nearly brushing the kitchen floor.

Nope, Mrs. Whitehead says. She takes a sip of her tea and stands looking at the glass. Her hair is lank and close to her head, her eyes luminous and ringed with shadows. It is not unlike the way Debra Ann's mother sometimes looked when she was having a bad week, when Debra Ann would follow her from room to room, asking questions. Do you want to hear a joke? Do you want to watch some TV or sit in the backyard, or lie down in your bed while I read a book to you? If it was a bad enough week, Ginny might stop talking altogether. She might spend hours in the bathtub, turning the tap back on to keep the water hot, slowly turning the pages of her *National Geographic*, sighing loud enough that D. A. could hear her through the closed door. Today, Aimee's mother looks like a reed in a windstorm, Debra Ann thinks, hanging on, hoping she can bend enough to survive.

Maybe I am sick. Mrs. Whitehead lets out a short, barking laugh. Maybe I am just bone-tired.

Aimee looks at the other girls and they lift their hands, palms up. What's wrong, Mama?

She tells the girls that Judge Rice handed down the sentence yesterday afternoon. A year's probation, she says, and five thousand dollars to that girl's family.

The girls all gasp. Five thousand dollars? D. A. says. That's a fortune.

Yeah, Casey says, he'll feel *that* in his pocketbook.

Girls, Mrs. Whitehead says, stop it right now. Y'all don't have any idea what you're talking about.

Justice is served, Debra Ann calls out. Ha! Lauralee laughs, and they all high-five each other.

Oh, shut up. All of you girls *shut up*.

One year of probation, she says, and her voice is a rupture. Five thousand dollars. Jesus. Fucking. Christ.

If a diamondback had just slithered out from under the kitchen table, the girls could not look more shocked. Aimee takes two steps back with her hands in the air, as if her mother might shoot her. Mama, that's heresy.

Oh honey, it is not. It's blasphemy. And really, who the fuck cares?

She hurls her glass of iced tea across the kitchen where it slams against the wall and shatters spectacularly. Rivulets of iced tea roll down the flowered wallpaper and gather on the linoleum. The baby begins to scream from the other end of the house, and she slides to the floor as if somebody stole her backbone. I don't know what to do with myself, she says.

D. A. doesn't know what to do either, none of them do, but they are old enough to know it isn't right to stare. So they turn away, four girls pivoting almost in unison to face the wall. They wait, and when some minutes have passed and Mrs. Whitehead still has not moved from her place on the kitchen floor, Debra Ann picks up the phone to call Mrs. Shepard. She listens and then taps the receiver a few times. Phone's dead, she says. Wind must have knocked out the line.

You're wrong, Aimee's mama says. It was just working.

No, ma'am. It's out now.

Aimee's blue eyes are huge and her cheeks are white as a sheet of paper. What are we going to do?

The baby's scream pierces the air and disintegrates into a steady, mournful wail that makes D. A. want to clamp her hands over her ears. I'm going across the street to get Mrs. Shepard, she says. She walks over to Aimee and hugs her tightly. I'm going to Penwell with my friend, but I'll be back soon.

After Debra Ann has gone, Aimee kneels next to her mother. Can you get up off the floor, Mama? Maybe have something to drink? But Mary Rose keeps her hands pressed stiffly against her thighs. I don't think so, honey.

And when Mrs. Shepard walks through the door a few minutes later, still wearing her house slippers, she looks around the kitchen, her eyes taking in the broken glass, the iced tea all over the wall and floor, and the three girls leaning uneasily against the door-frame while the baby howls like someone has set him on fire. Mrs. Shepard claps her hands sharply together. You girls go get that goddamn baby and take him to Aimee's room. She bends down so she's eye level with Mary Rose, who is crying so hard her whole body shakes with the strength of it.

None of the girls have ever seen a grown woman cry this hard, not even at a funeral, and they are all too young to recognize it as rage.

Mrs. Shepard rubs the younger woman's arm and rests one hand in the center of her back. Okay, she says, you're going to stand up now and come sit down at the kitchen table.

Aimee's mother shakes her head.

Honey, I can't bend over like this for one more minute. Now get up.

Without a word, Mary Rose stands and walks over to the kitchen table. She sits down and lays her head against the oilcloth, her shoulders moving in time with her sobs. Corrine wipes the tea off the wall and sweeps the glass into a corner. Just for the time being, she says, we'll clean it up in a few minutes. After she pours two glasses of iced tea and carries them to the table, she looks over and sees the girls still standing in the doorway with their mouths open. Why are y'all still here? Corrine says. Go get that goddamned baby before he bursts a blood vessel.

The girls walk down the hall to Aimee's bedroom, the wind shaking the house like it wants to fling them out the windows and into the yard. They sit on the floor and make goo-goo eyes at the baby, and Casey suggests they play *O Mighty Isis* because Isis can master the wind, and Lauralee says they ought to play *Incredible Hulk*, because he can turn his rage into a force for good. Aimee doesn't want to play anything. She just sits and looks from her baby brother to the window, and back again. She tells the other girls she has been thinking about probation—what it means, or what she thinks it means. Dale Strickland can still go anywhere he pleases, he can eat ice cream whenever he wants, and go see a football game. What about Glory Ramírez? What happens to her? And what about them?

Half an hour will pass before Corrine comes into Aimee's room with a bottle for the baby. She looks around their little circle, three pale, round faces and the baby grabbing at his sister's hair. Where the hell is Debra Ann? she asks them. Why isn't she in here with you girls?

Corrine

Between the wind blowing and the baby crying, between air filled with enough dust to suffocate a bull and Mary Rose refusing to open her goddamned curtains, not even for two minutes to let some sunlight in, Corrine couldn't have heard or seen Jesse and D. A. pulling the garage door open and backing the truck out. Now she stands on the dusty concrete with clenched fists and sweaty armpits, staring at the empty spot where Potter's truck used to be. All that remains is a puddle of fresh motor oil.

Mary Rose runs across the street, still buttoning her blouse, purse knocking against her hip bone. Her shoelaces are untied and she is not wearing socks. When she sees Corrine standing in the empty garage, she stops abruptly. Where is Potter's truck? Where's Debra Ann?

I don't know. Still hung over from the salty dogs, Corrine presses her fingers so hard against her eyelids that she sees stars. She tries to recall the last time she sat in the truck. When did she last listen to Bob Wills on the radio and shift into neutral before turning the key and hoping for the nerve to stay put for as long as it took? When was the last time she stared at the gauges for a minute or two before sighing and turning the truck off and going inside to fix herself a glass of iced tea? Two nights ago. And then, as always, she left the key in the ignition.

Mary Rose hurries into Corrine's kitchen and holds the phone receiver to one ear. Propping the door open with her foot, she quickly taps the switch hook, listens for a couple of seconds, and taps it again. How much gas is in the tank? she calls through the open door.

Less than half, I think. Corrine scans the garage. Everything is in its usual place, other than the empty space where Potter stored his tent. Boxes of Christmas ornaments are labeled and lined up on the shelf next to the rest of their camping gear. His rakes and shovels are stacked in a corner, covered with a fresh layer of gray dust, and just like that, Corrine sees him walking across the backyard with some animal lying in the center of the shovel blade—a garter snake or mouse or sparrow. She sees him digging a hole, a goddamned grave for every little creature. He should have outlived me, she thinks. He was so much better at life.

Corrine walks to the center of the garage and turns in a slow circle, her gaze lifting and falling as she again scans the room. Potter's truck is gone, the phones are out, and although the dust storm has passed, the air is still so thick with particulate and heat that her lungs feel as if they're caught in a steel press. The puddle of fresh oil again catches her eye, and then she sees the piece of paper lying next to it on the concrete.

Mary Rose steps out of the kitchen and stands with one arm outstretched as Corrine hands the page to her. It is a napkin from the strip club, folded in half, and although the words beneath the logo are slightly smeared, the women can make out the words *Penwell* and *gas station* and, on the other side of the napkin, a name. *Jesse Belden.* Rocking slightly, with one arm folded across her belly, Mary Rose leans forward until her hair scrapes the floor. We have to go get her.

She runs back to the kitchen and starts pounding the phone switch so hard Corrine can hear it in the garage. When Mary Rose returns—still no phone, goddamn it—her face is the color of old embers, or the fine gray dust covering Potter's workbench. That's out near our ranch, Mary Rose says. Her blue eyes go flat. I know who took her.

You know this man, Mr. Belden? Corrine glances at the note. Debra Ann spoke of him once or twice, but I thought he was one of her imaginary friends.

That's not his name, Mary Rose says flatly. I know who he is. She runs back across the street and disappears into the house. Less than five minutes later, she is standing in Corrine's driveway, rifle clutched in one hand, several loose cartridges in the other. I told the girls to stay put and call Suzanne Ledbetter the minute the phones are back on, she says.

Corrine holds out both hands, palms up. We need to put that in my trunk.

Mary Rose shakes her head. We have to go.

Drops of sweat roll down her forehead and her hair lies flat against her neck. Corrine is standing less than a foot from her neighbor, close enough to catch a whiff of grease and body odor, and to see that her pupils are enormous, an eclipse ringed by her pale blue irises. We don't want to scare anybody, Corrine says, and I have my pistol in the glove box if we need it.

He's going to kill her, Mary Rose says, and for a moment Corrine thinks she may be right. But D. A. has seemed fine this summer, purposeful and busy, she has even stopped pulling out her eyebrows. If this man hurt her in any way, there were no signs. And there is something else eating at Corrine—a note Debra Ann showed her earlier in the summer. *Thank you for helping me. I am great full.* Where's this from, Corrine had asked the girl, and D. A. said he was part of her summer project.

We don't know anything, she tells Mary Rose. Debra Ann said he was her friend.

Well, what the hell does she know? Mary Rose shouts. She's a little girl and he's a—her voice breaks and goes hollow—monster.

Bastard, Mary Rose spits the word out, as if she's just swallowed a glass filled with vinegar. The rifle is clenched in her hand, knuckles streaked white and red. She is lit with rage and purpose.

Deadly, Corrine thinks. She takes a deep breath and tries to sound calm. We don't yet know what the situation is. Debra Ann might be running away.

What in the hell is wrong with you? Mary Rose looks at Corrine as if the old woman has lost her mind. Strickland wanted Aimee, but he got D. A. instead. And it's my fault.

Whatever air Corrine has wrestled into her lungs disappears completely, and she reaches toward Potter's workbench. When she shoves aside the gardening tools and presses her hand flat against the table, the dust and cobwebs that have gathered over the long spring and summer take flight. Heat and dirt again fill her lungs and she coughs into her shoulder. I can't do this, she thinks.

Let me put that weapon in my trunk and I'll drive us out to Penwell. She stands up straight and reaches for her neighbor's hand, but Mary Rose jerks away from her. Whose side are you on, old woman?

Please, Corrine says. Again she reaches out, but Mary Rose is already running back across the street, where she leans the rifle against her car and digs wildly through her purse. When she finds her keys, she grabs Old Lady and sets it on the passenger seat. She drives off without so much as a glance in Corrine's direction.

꩜

The Whitehead Ranch is three miles south of Penwell. Close enough to walk to, as Glory Ramírez did, and if you had walked those miles with her, you might have grabbed onto the barbed-wire fence that separates the railroad track from the makeshift grave, a single row of large caliche stones piled one on top of the other, and the smaller, unmarked grave that is only a few yards away—a dog that belonged to one of the workers, an infant killed by fever, a small child who got bit by a rattlesnake. And if you weren't paying attention, or you were looking behind you, you might have fallen over the pile of rocks, as Glory did. You might have watched the wind move through the grass with the same dread in your belly. You might have looked back at the place you had walked away from and opened your mouth, only to find you were unable to speak. It is at the smaller grave where Glory sat down and picked the gravel from the palm of her hand, and it is there Jesse Belden hoists D. A. Pierce onto his shoulders and braves those wild grasses still being whipped and tugged by the last of the dust storm, so she can see the gravesite she's been telling him about all summer.

⌒

Corrine is an unrepentant leadfoot, accustomed to going at least twenty miles over the speed limit even when she's in no particular hurry. Now she drives down the I-20 like death itself is chasing her. The speedometer's needle trembles between eighty and eight-five miles an hour, but Mary Rose's white sedan is moving faster, and the distance between the two cars grows until the younger woman is at least a half mile ahead.

With the storm moving south at ten miles an hour, the women drive into a cloud of red dirt and bone-colored caliche dust. As they approach Penwell, the wind turns fierce and Corrine's car begins to shake. The motion roils her stomach, reminding her that she has not eaten today, that she is thirsty, that she drank too much last night and every night since Potter died, that she is an old woman completely unprepared to stop the world from coming apart at the seams.

When they were standing in Corrine's driveway and Mary Rose spat out that word—bastard—her voice was flat as the land Corrine is looking at now, and her heart fell to her feet. She has heard this tone of voice a few times in her life, usually but not always from a man or group of men. And although Mary Rose is angry and afraid, and there's a little girl driving around with a man they don't know, it occurs to Corrine why Mary Rose's tone of voice sounds so familiar.

It is not the ginned-up, high-pitched rage you hear when a crowd burns a book or throws a rock through a window or plants a kerosene-soaked cross in somebody's yard and sets it ablaze. The flatness of Mary Rose's speech, the hollow affect, the cold and steady tone of voice—all are fear and rage transformed into wrath. Hers is the voice of someone whose mind is made up. All that's left to do is wait for the little spark that will justify what is about to happen next. All her life Corrine has watched this poison move through her students and their parents, through men sitting at the bar or in the bleachers, through churchgoers and neighbors and the town's fathers and mothers. She has watched her own kith and kin pour this poison into their best glassware, spoon it onto the plates and bowls their ancestors hauled in wagons from Georgia and Alabama, all while proclaiming that they worked for everything they ever got and nobody ever gave them nothing, they earned it, living and dying in that refinery, in those fields, and they can't do a goddamn thing about the people who control the purse strings and hand over their paychecks, who can put them out of work with a wink and a nod, but they sure can point a finger at somebody else. If they say it long enough, in enough different ways, they might stop seeing the child of God standing on the other side of those words, or buckling under the awful weight of them. Whatever gets you through the night, or helps you turn your back so you can keep up the lie. Whatever lets you light the match or throw the rope over a strong branch, and still be home in time for dinner and the football game. And while Mary Rose maybe has better reason than most of these fools and sinners to open the door for unbridled wrath, Corrine also knows this: one way or another, it will eventually kill you. But goddamn, you can do some damage on your way out the door.

Corrine presses the accelerator and tries to close the gap between her car and Mary Rose's. At ninety-five, her Lincoln shakes and roars like a jet. When Mary Rose slows down to make the sharp turn onto the access road and then guns the engine, what feels like an acre of dust is thrown onto Corrine's windshield. She slams on the brake and slides onto the dirt road with one last look in the rearview mirror, and for the first time in her life she wishes that a state trooper would put down his newspaper or lunch and pay attention to her for one blessed minute.

It is nearly three o'clock, less than an hour since Corrine stepped into her garage and well past the time of day when she mixes up her first whiskey and iced tea and heads for the front porch. When her hands begin to shake, another reminder that she has absolutely no business being out here, she laughs and beats her fist against the steering wheel. She should have driven directly to the police station, or stopped by the 7-Eleven and asked if their phone was working. All she wants—all she has wanted since Potter died—is to be left alone, to slowly drink and smoke herself into the sweet hereafter. But here she is, an old lady with busted lungs and a dead husband, driving all over hell's half acre in a Lincoln Continental, going to save the world. It is so ridiculous that Corrine knocks her fist against her forehead and laughs until tears draw streaky lines through the dirt on her face. Well shit, she thinks. Here I am.

Corrine is right on Mary Rose's tail when they roar through Penwell, a fusty little town on an otherwise empty stretch of earth interrupted only by pump-jacks and railroad tracks and a single row of telephone poles that looks as if it stretches to eternity. There are seventy-five or so permanent citizens, many of them living in trailers they hauled from Odessa and parked among the remnants of the original pecan-wood oil derricks. All that remains of the old gas station and dance hall is a stack of lumber and broken glass, and piled-up tumbleweeds against a rusty sign lying on the ground. DANCE TO-NIGHT.

Two little boys are standing on the side of the road, and they cheer as the women blow through a traffic light that hasn't worked in forty years. They pass the gas station without seeing any sign of Potter's truck.

On the other side of town, the road veers south and starts running alongside the railroad tracks. The asphalt disappears and the road deteriorates to a dusty mess of ruts and tumbleweeds. The dust cloud is still ahead of them, mostly, but the wind is unreliable. It dives and dips, seizes the cars and shakes them fiercely before letting go suddenly. When Mary Rose swerves to miss a piece of pipeline that has fallen across the road, Corrine does the same.

Mary Rose hits the brakes a second time, veering madly and leaving Corrine to stare down a mama armadillo ambling across the road with her four pups. She slams her foot against the brake pedal and jerks hard to the right, her face hitting the steering wheel with enough force that stars swim at the edges of her vision.

The two cars careen toward the edge of the road and come to a stop. Potter's truck is parked up ahead, and a second, older pickup truck is next to it. Corrine taps her horn and tries to pull up next to Mary Rose, but the road is narrow and Mary Rose will not look at her, so Corrine reaches across the wide expanse of her front seat, opens the glove box, and sets her pistol next to her cigarettes. If they get out of this situation with everybody still alive, she is going home and smoking that whole pack. She is going to drink herself half stupid, and then sleep for three days.

Mary Rose's car rolls slowly down the road until they are only a few yards from the two trucks, and it is only then that Corrine spots the man and girl walking side by side along the railroad tracks. He is small and thin with stooped shoulders and black hair, nothing at all like the man whose pictures were all over the news in the wake of the attack on Gloria Ramírez. Debra Ann's bangs are in her eyes and she is wearing her favorite terrycloth shorts and sparkly pink T-shirt. In one hand the man holds a jug of water and oh, what Corrine wouldn't give for a little sip of that. His other hand is gently folded around D. A.'s grimy fingers.

Corrine rolls down the window and leans out to shout at them, but she sees Mary Rose's car door swing open and lays on the horn instead. It is a long unbroken wail, not so different from the plant whistle, and it gets their attention. Jesse and D. A. stop and turn around, and after a brief pause, he bends down to say something to her. The child shrugs and rubs her eyes, and looks at her feet.

Mary Rose jumps out of her car and runs toward them, the rifle bouncing against her shoulder, bullets spilling onto the ground behind her. Corrine's heart jumps as if she's just grabbed an electric fence. She has been living across the street from this young woman for months, watching her grow thin as a mesquite leaf, noticing the dark shadows under her eyes when she sits on the front porch and watches her daughter as if she might disappear at any moment.

A few weeks before the trial, while the girls were giving the baby a bath and the women were having a cigarette on Mary Rose's back patio, Corrine thought she saw in her neighbor's eyes, ever so briefly, something that might have been despair.

Do you need anything? she asked Mary Rose.

No, Mary Rose said, I guess I don't.

When was the last time you got a good night's sleep? And Mary Rose let loose with a laugh that was more snarl than anything else. Well, she said, I'm one of those women who has to get up and pee every ten minutes, pretty much from the day I get pregnant, and the baby's three months old, so I'd say it's been about thirteen months since I slept through the night, give or take.

Honey, what about Robert? I know he'd come into town and help out, if you asked him to.

Robert's busy with his cows. Mary Rose looked out at her lawn and kicked at one of the half dozen extension cords that were spread across the patio. And I don't want him here anyway.

She walked to the edge of the porch and stepped on a large black spider. Keith Taylor was over here the other day helping me get ready for the trial, she said, and he asked me about living here in town, if I didn't miss being with my husband, and I didn't know how to answer him.

One of the girls shouted inside the house and both women stopped talking, ears pricking in expectation of being needed for one thing or another, being asked to solve the next domestic situation, however large or small, but the girls chattered for a few seconds and went quiet.

Because when I ask myself what is lost between Robert and me, Mary Rose paused and looked at her hands, turned them over and over. Well. How would I even know? Shit, I got my first cheerleading outfit when I was still in diapers. All of us did. If we were lucky, we made it to twelve before some man or boy, or well-intentioned woman who just thought we ought to know the score, let us know why we were put on this earth. To cheer them on. To smile and bring a little sunshine into the room. To prop them up and know them, and be nice to everybody we meet. I married Robert when I was seventeen years old, went straight from my father's house to his. Mary Rose sat down on a lawn chair and leaned her head against the patio table and began to cry. Is this what I'm supposed to do? she said. Cheer him on?

Corrine stood and waited for the crying to stop, but it went on and on and after a while Corrine, embarrassed for her neighbor, touched Mary Rose's shoulder. Call me if you need anything, she said, and let herself out through the side gate.

Corrine has run less than ten feet when her lungs seize and tell her *no*, no ma'am, should have thought about this twenty years ago. She doubles over in the desert, breathing hard, then stands up and takes a few steps. Her whole face aches from hitting the steering wheel, and a knot is rising on her forehead. She vomits a little into the sand, nothing but bile and water, and wonders if she might have a concussion.

Mary Rose is far ahead of her now, and Corrine begins to shout Debra Ann's name again and again, each word a new challenge to her aching lungs, her parched throat and bruised head.

D. A. and Jesse watch the two women, one far ahead of the other and moving fast, the other lumbering behind like an old heifer, wishing she'd listened to Potter all those years when he said haranguing teenagers all day long wasn't real exercise, no matter how many hours a day she was on her feet.

Let her go, Strickland. Mary Rose's voice is a steel

rod, and it pierces Corrine to the core. That's not him, Mary Rose, she yells. It's not the same man.

Mary Rose stops running and looks at the young man. Corrine knows her friend is close enough to see him clearly. They both are. See there, Corrine calls. That's Mr. Belden.

Debra Ann frowns up at Jesse, and they see him stoop down a bit to gently take her by the arm. He stands up straight and waves toward the women.

Thank God. Corrine takes a step toward them.

No, Mary Rose says quietly. She lifts the rifle she calls Old Lady and snugs it against her shoulder and squeezes the trigger.

⌒

The rifle report tears the day in half. Debra Ann and Jesse fall to the ground and lie without moving. Mary Rose gazes at them calmly. Her head is cocked slightly to the side, as if she is trying to solve a problem. I missed, she says flatly. I fucking missed.

Both D. A. and Jesse are crying now, both of them repeating what's going on, what's going on, and although Jesse's voice is louder and deeper than Debra Ann's, it is still very much the voice of a child who does not understand.

Debra Ann, Corrine yells, get up and come here *right now*. The girl rises wraithlike from the dirt and hits the ground running.

Mary Rose pops the cartridge out of the rifle, bends down, and grabs one of several bullets that lie scattered at her feet. After she slips a bullet into the chamber and pumps the bolt closed, she stands perfectly still, watching. She is tracking him, Corrine sees, waiting for him to make his next move. She's a good shot. If she fires again, she will not miss. And as if reading Corrine's mind, Mary Rose yells at Jesse, Next time I won't miss.

Corrine reaches Mary Rose at the same time as Debra Ann. He's my friend, she says, I'm *helping* him.

He hurt you, Mary Rose says.

No. Debra Ann yanks convulsively at her eyebrow, tearing at the thin hairs and flinging them to the ground. He's my friend.

Are you okay? Corrine asks, and when Debra Ann nods, she says, What in the hell are you doing?

I'm helping him go back home. D. A. swipes the back of her hand across her nose and rubs a string of brown snot against her shorts. He needs his truck, and I drove him out here.

Oh, honey, says Corrine.

I was coming back. Debra Ann's face turns red. I wasn't stealing Mr. Shepard's truck. I know you love it.

She starts to cry. Nobody cares what happens to Jesse, she says. Or me.

And she is right, Corrine sees now. Debra Ann and Jesse need so much more than anyone has given them. A whistle blows in the distance—the refinery maybe, or a train that is still several miles away. The wind whips their hair around their faces and makes it difficult to hear. In the water-starved desert, the cactuses have turned black and folded in on themselves. Mesquite beans, gray and shriveled, cling to their trees or lie in piles around the trunks, and Jesse Belden lies in the dirt making small noises in his throat, a small and frightened critter, a young man who has seen firsthand how a bullet can tear a body to pieces.

You stand up, Mary Rose tells him. Get up and hold your hands in the air.

He can't hear you, Debra Ann yells. Her face is covered with dirt and tears, and there is a small scrape on her cheek. He can't hear—her voice breaks—this is my fault.

Get up, Mary Rose yells. Get up now.

Jesse rises to his knees and rocks a little as he clasps his hands to his head.

Mary Rose, Corrine says. *Stop.*

I missed my chance before. Her voice is full of sorrow. Corrine grabs her arm, shaking it hard enough that the gun wobbles. You stop this, Mary Rose. This is not the same man. She seizes Debra Ann and holds her out to Mary Rose like an offering. Look. She's fine. See?

He's not well, Mrs. Whitehead, D. A. says. I'm responsible for him.

I want to go home, Jesse calls to the women. I want Nadine.

D. A. makes as if to run back to him, but Corrine grabs her by the arm and shakes her hard. Go sit down in my car, lie down in the back seat, and don't you dare look out that window.

Yes, Mary Rose says quietly. Tell her not to look out the window.

They are the most terrifying words Corrine has ever heard in her life, and it occurs to her that she wants to sit down in the middle of this dusty field, and close her eyes, and go to sleep. She imagines Potter standing beside his truck in a field not far from where they are now. He left the house before dawn, she's sure, because he would have wanted to see the sun come up one more time. He never missed a chance to watch the sun rise. They could be standing in the middle of the smelliest, most gutted corner of the oil patch and he would watch that burning star hoist itself over the earth's edge. What color of red is that, he'd say to her. What color, that sky? Those clouds? Another glorious day. He'd smile. What shall we do today, Mrs. Shepard?

Corrine doesn't want to make a grab for the rifle and risk it going off, so she reaches for the barrel and covers her friend's hand with her own. What are we going to do, Mary Rose?

Tears mark a slow path through the dust that has gathered on Mary Rose's cheeks, and still she stands with the rifle aimed at Jesse Belden, safety off, her finger coiled tight around the trigger. I want some fucking justice, she says.

I know, honey, but you don't want to shoot the wrong man.

Wrong? Mary Rose says. We don't know what he's done, or will do, but we know that he sure as shit won't be held accountable for it.

Corrine rubs her thumb gently across the hand holding the rifle barrel and then moves it gently up Mary Rose's arm. The stock is pressed tight against Mary Rose's shoulder, her arm taut as a violin string. She is trembling with rage.

In wrath may you remember mercy, Corrine thinks. Mary Rose, if you shoot this man, you will never be the same. And neither will Debra Ann, or me.

Every day, I wait to pick up the phone and hear his voice on the other end, Mary Rose says. Every night, I wait for somebody to come through my front door and hurt my kids. He is *out*. They didn't do one god-damned thing to him.

I know. But this is not your man.

Corrine would have done anything to be with Potter on the morning he chose to die. Not to stop him—she knows damned well what he was facing, how hard his death was going to be if they let the illness run its course—but she could have stood with him and watched the sun come up. Don't be afraid, she could have told him. You're not alone.

Thanks for putting up with me all these years, she would have told him, and all my petty bullshit. Potter would have laughed and pointed out some little critter scuttling through the brush. See there? A family of blue quail. See the little hatchlings, nine of them in the clutch? Ain't that sweet, Corrine?

And it is sweet, she sees now. Potter knew it all the way to the end. How could she have thought so little of the world? How could she have taken herself out of the equation, she wonders, always looking askance, tearing so much down, giving so little back? She will grieve him until the day she dies, but that is going to be a long time from today—for everyone standing in this field, if she can help it.

It is just past three o'clock. The sun and heat are without mercy, and the wind blows hot against their faces. Jesse Belden kneels quietly in the dirt with his hands on his head and his face turned toward the earth, a prisoner who has been waiting his whole life for this. *This is the soldier home from the war. These are the years and the walls and the door*— Where are those words from? What song, what poem, what story? When she gets home, she will try to find them. If need be, she will take every book off the shelves. Home without Potter, home with a goddamned stray cat and a motherless child, home with a young woman whose face is a mess of gray dust and tears and rage, whose finger is still on the trigger. Home with this young stranger kneeling in the dirt.

Corrine keeps her hand on Mary Rose's shoulder. We are going to drive back to town, she says, and ask Suzanne to stay with the kids a little longer. We'll sit out in my backyard and have a stiff drink, and we will figure this out.

What the hell is wrong with this place? Mary Rose's voice is barely more than a whisper. Why don't we give a shit about what happens to a girl like Glory Ramírez?

I don't know.

Mary Rose looks across the field at Jesse Belden. I want to kill someone.

Not this man. Corrine laughs gently. Maybe another time. She wraps her hand around the rifle's barrel. Her arm wobbles under its weight as she lifts the gun out of Mary Rose's hand and sets it on the ground and nudges it away with the toe of her sneaker. You're not alone, she says.

Don't be afraid, Corrine calls out to Jesse and Mary Rose, and D. A. Pierce, whose face is pressed against the window of Corrine's car, a small and pale witness, trying to understand what it means when Mary Rose walks over to Jesse and helps him to his feet, when she tells him how sorry she is, how easy it is to become the thing you most hate, or fear. I never knew, Mary Rose tells him, and I wish I still didn't.

∽

They drive back to Odessa slowly, Corrine and D. A. leading the way in the Lincoln, followed by Jesse in Potter's truck. Mary Rose brings up the rear, her white sedan so covered with dust it is barely indistinguishable from the fields they pass. Tomorrow morning, Corrine tells Jesse, she will drive him back out and they will pick up his truck, which they left parked next to the gravesite of those railroad workers. They will make sure he gets home to eastern Tennessee. Your sister is there, right? Yes, ma'am, he says quietly, and my mom.

When they arrive at Corrine's driveway, Jesse pulls Potter's truck behind her car and sits looking through the windshield while she brings him a glass of water. His hands are still gripping the steering wheel when he falls asleep, but when she looks out the window a few minutes later, the truck is empty and he is gone. She will find him in the morning, take him back to Penwell, give him some money, and make sure he gets home.

Corrine steers Mary Rose across the street and hands her off to Suzanne, who opens and closes her mouth a half dozen times before pressing her lips together and saying nothing. If any of this gets out, Corrine knows, Mary Rose is likely to find herself locked up in the hospital at Big Springs.

Slowly, Corrine walks back across the street and draws a hot bath for Debra Ann, who will soak for nearly an hour and leave so much sand and dirt in the tub that Corrine will wonder aloud when this child last bathed.

With soap? Debra Anne says.

Corrine is sitting on the floor outside the bathroom with her back against the door and her legs straight out in front of her. Everything hurts—her knees, her ass, her tits, every damn thing. If you steal anything from me, ever again, she tells the girl, I will send you packing—straight to Suzanne Ledbetter. She'd just love to get her hands on you.

I won't, D. A. says. Can you come wash my back?

No, honey. Mrs. Shepard just wants to sit here quietly for a minute or two.

I can't reach it, and it itches.

Corrine sighs and tries to stand up, but her back rebels. She rolls over onto one side and lies there panting, then uses the wall to pull herself up. When she steps into the bathroom, D. A. is hunched over in the bathtub, her round shoulders and back covered with chigger bites and open scabs. Long, ugly scratches mark the places she can reach. Everything else is a mess of dried blood and infected skin. Corrine grabs a washcloth and dips it in the bathwater and then, kneeling on the floor, she rubs it gently against the child's skin. From now on, she says, you can come over any time, as long as it's after ten a.m., and I will always answer the door. The little girl sighs deeply and closes her eyes. That feels good.

We'll need to doctor these bites. Corrine wrings out

the washcloth and sets it on the edge of the bathtub. You can come anytime and take a hot bath and watch television, she says, and I will make sure there's plenty of Dr Pepper in the house.

All I ask in return—Corrine pauses for a few seconds and pushes Debra Ann's damp hair out of her eyes—is that you don't tell anybody about Mrs. Whitehead firing that gun. We don't want anybody to suffer more than they need to.

D. A. nods and slides down into the bathtub until she is flat on her back, pretending to float in a lake, her brown hair fanning out on either side of her face. She never wanted anybody to suffer.

⌒

There are thunderstorms on the heels of that dust cloud. It will rain for three days and when the gutters on Larkspur Lane overflow, the canal behind Corrine's house will fill in less than hour, washing away everything that Jesse decided to leave behind—his skillet, the blanket Debra Ann brought when he was cold and the medicine she brought when he was sick, even that old tomcat who, just a few minutes before the flood, was seen chasing a juvenile bull snake deep into the pipe.

On the other side of the street, Mary Rose's alley floods and water seeps under the fence, rising gently toward the back patio until it covers the half dozen extension cords that are still plugged into the outlet. For a few days, she will stand at her sliding-glass door and wonder if the yard is electrified. She will tape the back door closed and keep a close eye on her daughter.

By the time the water recedes and everything dries out, Jesse will be home. His first letter will come in September, a single page with the words *Dictated to Nadine* written above the salutation. He will describe the long, boring drive back to eastern Tennessee—whether you take the southern route or the northern route, he says, it's all the same ugly—and his joy upon seeing his mother's little trailer in Belden Hollow. He promises to send a letter every month, and he hopes D. A. will do the same.

He will fish the Clinch River and try to find work in his hometown, and when the money that Corrine gave him runs out and there are still no jobs, he will throw his duffel bag into the back of his truck and head down to Louisiana. He will work the oil fields and offshore rigs in Lake Charles, Baton Rouge, Petroleum City, then drive over to Gulf Shores to work as a shrimper. Construction work in Jackson, corrections at the prison in Dixon, farmhand in the Florida panhandle, then on to New Orleans, where he discovers that he is finally old enough to grow a beard that will help keep him warm in the winter months. He will not live to be very old—too much working against him—but each time a stranger shows him a bit of kindness, he will remember Debra Ann, and the way he ends every letter to her, however long or short it may be.

Thank you for the kindness you showed me, when I was in your hometown. I won't ever forget it. Love, Jesse Belden

Karla

We lose the men when they try to beat the train and their pickup trucks stall on the tracks, or they get drunk and accidentally shoot themselves, or they get drunk and climb the water tower and fall ten stories to their deaths. During cutting season, when they stumble in the chute and a bull calf roars and kicks them in the heart. On fishing trips, when they drown in the lake or fall asleep at the wheel on the drive home. Pile-up on the interstate, shooting at the Dixie Motel, hydrogen sulfide leak outside Gardendale. Looks like somebody came down with a fatal case of the stupid, Evelyn says when one of the regulars shares the news at happy hour. Those are the usual ways, the ordinary days, but now it is the first of September and the Bone Springs shale is coming back into play. Now we will also lose them to crystal and coke and painkillers. We will lose them to slipped drill bits or unsecured stacks of pipeline or fires caused by vapor clouds. And the women, how do we lose them? Usually, it's when one of the men kills them.

In the spring of 1962, just after natural gas fields were discovered out near Wink, Evelyn likes to tell new hires, one of her waitresses clocked out, rolled up her apron, and carried it with her into the bar to knock back a few with the regulars. The woman's car was still in the parking lot when Evelyn locked up that night, and it sat there for nearly a week before they found her body. At an abandoned oil lease, Evelyn says, because that's where you always find the bodies. Bastard set her on fire too. You don't get used to knowing something like that.

Evelyn is small and wound tight, with forearms like sisal and a beehive the color of ripe plums. The next gas fields will be even bigger than Wink, she tells us at the weekly staff meeting. Start your engines, gals. Get ready to make bank. Keep your eyes peeled for the next serial killer.

⌒

You raise a family in Midland,
but you raise hell in Odessa.

This is a family place. We keep our jewelry and makeup tasteful. We wear red-checkered blouses that match the curtains and tablecloths. Our denim skirts hit just above the knee. Our ropers are brown with pink stitching. When we bend over a table, we smell of soap and cigarettes and perfume. A few of us leave, but most of us stay.

All you have to do is smile, we tell Karla Sibley on her first day of training, and you can make big bucks, maybe the best money in town, and still keep your shirt on, ha, ha!

The dinner salad gets two slices of tomato, we tell her. Salad dressing is served in a ramekin on the side. Ranch, French, blue cheese, and Thousand Island. Memorize them. We serve beer in ice-cold mugs, iced tea in quart-sized mason jars, and surf 'n' turf on our signature Texas-shaped metal platters. Always keep your sleeves turned down, even in the summer, or the metal will leave burns that turn into scars. Like this, we pull up our sleeves. See here?

We send her home early so we don't have to split the tips, but before she goes Evelyn gives her a pep talk. Karla, darlin', an oil boom can mean earning a month's rent on a single Friday night. It can mean a down payment on a car and a little scratch in the bank. We can post bail, help one of our kids dry out, pay for a semester at the junior college, all on one week's tips. So when a customer tells us to smile, you can bet your right tit we do it. Our lips curl upward like somebody just pulled a string. Our teeth are paper white, our dimples parentheses.

After closing time, when the tables have been scrubbed down and the floors are swept and we've rolled enough silverware to feed the U.S. Army, we have our shift drink and then walk to our cars in twos and threes. We wait for long enough to make sure nobody has a flat tire or dead battery. We come prepared, with jumper cables and Fix-a-Flat in our trunks. We carry pistols and Mace in our purses. Evelyn, who is left-handed, keeps one little snubbie in her purse and one in the glove box of her Ford Mustang. Behind the bar, she keeps an antique electric cattle prod, for the usual trouble, and a Wingmaster, for when things get out of hand.

Two o'clock in the morning and still nearly ninety degrees out. The recent rains settled the dust, and now the clouds are moonlit and pale and empty as old churches. There's the usual light traffic on the drag, but if Evelyn is right about the Bone Springs shale, or the Ozona platform, it will be bumper-to-bumper in a few months, with license plates from all over the country and hungry men with cash in their pockets. Something to look forward to.

⌒

Monday through Friday, Karla's mother works the line at a bearing supply company, but she's happy to watch the baby at night. New hires work the lunch rush for the first month, Evelyn tells her, so Karla hires a sitter for Diane and takes four shifts a week. In the storeroom where we sit at a folding card table and eat our shift meals, she tapes an index card to the wall with her phone number—I will pick up <u>any</u> nights or weekends. Thanks, Karla Sibley. Someone draws a line through her last name and writes, Darlin'! And below that, Smile! Because it doesn't seem to come naturally to her.

While Karla waits for somebody to call in sick, she drinks her weight in coffee and counts her tips and tries to remember to smile. She reminds herself that she lost her last job, a sweet bartending gig at the Country Club, because she couldn't get along with the regulars. Corrine Shepard doesn't count, management told her. Our male patrons think you don't like them. So Karla rolls extra silverware at the end of each shift and rubs the ice machine until she can see, if not her own face clearly reflected in the stainless steel, then at least the indistinct shadows of her mud-brown curls and wide forehead, the dark smudges beneath her eyes from sweating through her black eyeliner and having a baby at home that still doesn't sleep through the night.

The oil reps come in for lunch smelling like they came straight from the cologne counter at Dillard's. They wear Polo shirts and khaki pants. If they drove in from Houston, they stopped in San Angelo and bought ostrich or alligator boots. If they came from Dallas, they stopped at Luskey's or James Leddy's. Everybody wears a Stetson, and everybody's got a checkbook in his shirt pocket.

They carry cardboard tubes filled with topographical maps, and after lunch, they spread them out on the table. The new fields are here and here and here—they point to vast sections of grazing land, or land that used to be good for grazing—three billion barrels of oil and enough natural gas to set the whole world on fire twice. The infrastructure is already in place, they tell wildcatters and hard-up cattle ranchers, or it will be soon. The oil reps talk easements and cattle guards, wastewater ponds and extraction wells and spill contingencies. They talk about a newly discovered shale in the Delaware Basin, natural gas fields out near the Bowman

Ranch. They buy and sell water and promise to close the gate behind them so the cows don't get out on the highway. They nod their heads and promise to remind their men that a good bull is worth three months' pay. When they close a deal, they take out their checkbooks and lift one finger in the air and Karla brings a round of shots.

She pays the sitter and helps her mother with the mortgage. She opens a savings account for Diane. On her day off, she drives out to see a 1965 Buick Skylark that was advertised in the *American*. The storage facility is just outside the city limits, six corrugated metal buildings across the field from the Full River Gospel of Life Church, a confusing name since the closest river is the Pecos and it generally looks like everybody in the county went down and took a shit in it at the same time. It was her mother's car, the woman tells Karla, and it's been in storage since the crash of '72. It can be a little sluggish on the highway, she says, but it's got eight cylinders and 5,000 original miles. For two hundred dollars cash, it's Karla's.

Karla climbs into the front seat, a palace of gold crushed velvet that still smells of the old lady's tobacco and baby powder and wintergreen gum. The back seat looks big enough to pitch a tent in, and Karla is already imagining Diane bouncing around back there as they drive down the highway to their next life. The woman hands her a set of car keys—one for the ignition and driver's side door, one for the glove box, one for the trunk. When Karla turns the ignition switch, the engine burbles and dies. She turns it a second time. The engine roars and rumbles and vibrates from her ass all the way down to her foot resting on the gas pedal. Oh, *hell* yes, she thinks. Would you take $150 for it? she asks the woman.

⌒

Why did God give oil to West Texas?
To make up for what He did to the land.

⌒

Nights are money, we tell Karla when she picks up her first dinner shift. After nine o'clock, it's mostly men with wallets full of cash and hair still damp after stopping by the house for a hot shower. Karla, darlin', we tell her, they can run the hot water until their skin peels off, and they will still smell like stale farts in a closed room.

We tell her which men don't mean anything by it—a joke, an arm snaking around her waist, a marriage proposal—and which men do. Listen to their damn stories, we say about the first group. Laugh at their damn jokes. About the second group, we say never let them get you alone. Don't tell them where you live. And watch out for that one—we point to Dale Strickland sitting at the end of the bar, getting drunk all by his lonesome—he's a pervert with a thing for brunettes. Buckle up, gals, Evelyn says. It's going to start getting busy any day now.

Karla tells us Diane's daddy is in the navy and stationed in Germany, but we spend some time rolling silverware together and the lies fall away PDQ. It doesn't matter who it was, she tells us, some boy from Midland.

What matters? Diane napped today and Karla got a hot shower before her shift. She shows us the Polaroid took that morning. Karla has russet-colored hair and eyes the color of sandstones. Constellations of freckles cover her nose, and her round cheeks mark her as still barely out of childhood. A black tank top shows off more freckles on her shoulders. The baby, dressed in head-to-toe pink, stares doe-eyed at the camera, her little cheek crushed against her mother's. Four months old today, Karla tells us, her name means divine. She's beautiful, we tell Karla, she looks just like you.

⌢

The women's clinic in Santa Teresa is three hundred miles north, just across the border at Las Cruces, and back then Karla shared a car with her mom. She thought about taking it anyway, but even if she could get there, she would have to spend the night, and how would she explain this to her mother? And what if she were pulled over in one of those little towns between Odessa and El Paso? She had heard stories about those sheriffs, how they knew what girls were up to, when they spotted them driving down the interstate by themselves, how they made girls follow them back to the station and wait while their fathers were called. Game over.

At eight weeks, Karla drove over to the health-food store and bought tinctures of black cohosh and cotton root bark from a woman with frizzy hair and a muumuu so electric it ought to have come with a seizure warning. Put this in hot water and drink a lot of it, the woman said. *Gallons.* You ought to be peeing every ten minutes. If you run out, come back and get more.

Karla drank until she was bent in half with cramps. The tea tasted like dirt and mold, and when she puked and shit, her mother sprayed Lysol in the bathroom and asked what the hell she'd been eating. She went to band practice and wrote a paper on *The Rime of the Ancient Mariner*. In gym class, she stood with her arms at her sides while dodge balls hit her square in the belly until Coach Wilkins yelled at her to get the hell out of the way. In the locker room, she stared at the shower floor. *Water, water, every where, nor any drop to drink.* And not a drop of blood anywhere, she thought. In bathroom stalls all over school, she studied wads of toilet paper and the crotch of her panties. But the pregnancy stuck. It stuck, it stuck, it stuck. *My uterus is a painted ship,* Karla thought, *and I am waiting for the trade winds.* Ten weeks, fifteen—and then she was at twenty and it was too late to pretend anymore.

The woman at the health-food store introduces herself as Alison and asks Karla if she's breastfeeding. When Karla explains that the labor and delivery nurses didn't think it was a good idea, since she needed to get a job ASAP, Alison gives her several joints and tells her to stay away from booze and crystal. It is fall now and Alison's muumuus are the color of wildfires and whiskey. Coffee and weed is the best possible combination of drugs for a single mother, she tells Karla. Don't let yourself get busted. Never share. Never tell anyone, not even your boyfriend—

especially not him. Don't buy paraphernalia. Instead, roll joints and tuck them in a pack of cigarettes, never in a plastic baggie.

You're going to be fine, Alison says. Just don't start thinking you've made all the big decisions you're ever going to make.

Does Karla love her baby? Yes, fiercely. Diane's got a big, strong name and a grin that could melt the devil's heart. When they are alone together during the day, Karla hardly wants to set her down for a moment. But becoming a mom has taught Karla plenty of things. That she can get by with less sleep than she could ever have imagined. That it doesn't take her long to be able to hear herself think at the end of a nine-hour shift, just a short detour through the desert on her way home from work and a little time looking at the stars. That you can love someone with all your heart and still wish she weren't there.

We wish we had known you back then, a couple of us tell her later. We could have loaned you a little money if you were short. One of us would have driven you up to New Mexico. We wouldn't have told any of the prayer warriors.

⌣

What do you call a single mother who has to be up
early in the morning?
A sophomore.

⌒

When she gets home from work, Mrs. Sibley changes
into a pair of sweats, clasps her granddaughter between her knees, and stares into her big blue eyes.
Well then, Miss Diane, is this all there is to it? She
feeds and bathes and rocks her granddaughter and
holds her on her lap so they can watch Oral Roberts
together.

Mrs. Sibley's got a scrap of her late husband's
great-great-great granddaddy's gray uniform framed
and hanging in the hallway next to his daguerreotype,
and a cedar chest full of pictures from the old family
plantation, and she can't for the life of her figure out
how her family got from there to here in just a few
generations—here being stuck in West Texas, trying
to keep the dust out of your eyes and a roof over your
head while Mexicans and feminists take over the
world.

When Karla comes home from her shift, she stands
in the dark behind her mother and child, watching the
television's blue light play across their sleeping faces.

Time for bed, she says, and carries Diane to her crib. Karla loves her mama, but she worries that Mrs. Sibley's fear and hatred will eventually kill her. What will happen to her mother when she and Diane are gone? After her mother and daughter are tucked in, Karla stands out in the backyard and smokes a joint and imagines a different story for herself, one where she tries a little harder to get to that clinic in Santa Teresa.

They are flaring off casinghead gases at the refinery tonight. The sky is pale, the stars countable. If Karla closes her eyes, it's easy to imagine her hometown in another fifteen years, or fifty, or a hundred, or whenever they've pulled everything they can from the ground. It's easy to imagine all the drilling equipment gone, the derricks and pumpjacks packed onto flatbeds and driven to some new desert, or coast. She sees her hometown without the churches and bars and the practice field at the high school, without the stadium east of town, or the car dealers who said they were closing down for good during the last bust, or until the next boom. She sees it without the hospital where everyone she knows was born, and everyone will go to die, quickly, if they're lucky.

Maybe this year everybody's talking about the Bone Springs shale and the Delaware Basin, but when the price of oil drops, the parking lots will empty out and the man camps will lie abandoned, nothing but rusting beer cans and broken windows and snakes under the beds. But here in town, curtains or drapes or old T-shirts will still cover the windows of little brick houses, and little wooden houses gone to wrack and ruin. There will still be tricycles turned over in the front yard, empty Dr Pepper bottles and sun-bleached toys, tennis shoes with the laces gone, laundry hanging in the backyard, and windowsills covered in sand. And there will still be a woman somewhere who refuses to give up. Every night before dinner, she wipes sand off the kitchen table. Every morning, she sweeps the porch clean. She sweeps and sweeps, but there is always more dust.

You can leave town, Mrs. Sibley tells her daughter, but if you go, I won't be able to help you no more.

⟡

How do you walk from Midland to Odessa?
Head west and stop when you step in shit.

⟡

Dale Strickland is plenty drunk when he finally pays his bill and stands up from the booth he's occupied for nearly three hours. We watch him walk to the little boys' room, and when he stops in front of Karla, we can hear him from over here. Hey there, Valentine. You look like you just lost your best friend.

One of us starts to head over and tell her she has food up in the kitchen. Like we've done countless times before, for other women and girls, some of us for thirty years. Smile, he tells her. Why don't you smile? You got a piece of coal stuck up your ass?

Karla leans toward him, and we can see her mouth moving next to his ear. We will never find out what she says, but Strickland draws back his arm and takes aim at her face. He swings and misses and staggers. When he draws his arm back a second time, Evelyn starts shouting for some of the regulars to get him the hell out. Karla is still standing next to the hostess stand with her mouth hanging open, like maybe in her seventeen years of living, no one has ever before tried to hit her.

How do you think this is going to go? Old West justice? Those men take Strickland out to the parking lot and beat him so badly that he never again shows his face around these parts? Well, sure. They'll rough him up some. But we all know how this goes: We will all laugh and say good thing he was too drunk to land a punch, and Evelyn will eighty-six him for a couple of weeks, or until he comes in and apologizes to Karla.

Nobody wants to overreact and make this worse than it needs to be, Evelyn says. We don't want to let things get out of hand. When things get out of hand, people start reaching for their guns, and we don't want anybody reaching for his gun. And we couldn't agree more. But how nice it must be for Dale Strickland and his kind, we say when Evelyn goes into her office and closes the door, to move through the world knowing everything will work out for them in the end.

To Karla, who cannot remember to smile, we say: This is our bread and butter. We don't have time for this shit. But we promise ourselves that she will never again have to wait on him, even if it means trading for a good table in our own section, and Evelyn slips her some extra money and tells her to take a few days off, as is her custom in these situations.

The rain has already started when we walk to our cars. All night, great sheets of water pour out of the sky, settling the dust and rinsing the smell of the oil patch away. It drops nearly three inches of water before the storm moves out of town at sunrise. When the rain stops, we take a deep breath. We check for broken windows and keep an eye out for downed electric poles. When the birds start to chatter and sing, we step out of our houses and look up to see nothing but blue skies.

How long does it take a couple of Mexican oil-field workers to get a table at Evelyn's place on a busy Friday night?

That's no joke. Evelyn walks over with two menus, all smiles and the new orange tint of her hair glowing like a runway light. You boys got your papers? one of the regulars calls from the bar, and Evelyn shoots him a look. Better start packing your bags, the regular says, and some of us laugh and some of us look at the ceiling and some of us look at the floor, but not one of us says a word.

Our great-granddaddies drove men from their beds with bullwhips and fire, dragged children out of beds by their feet and made them watch their mamas being pulled into the fields by their hair. Some of our daddies and brothers still keep a bullwhip under the front seat. Our great-grandmothers feigned frailty until it was stitched to their hearts. Some of us still do the same. To speak up would require courage that we cannot even begin to imagine.

Are we guilty? We are guilty as sin, guilty as the day is long. If we ever stopped and thought about it for very long, and we try not to, our guilt would be as bright and heavy as sunlight in August. Come sit down at the bar and take a long look around at all of us unrepentant sinners—con artists and liars and dreamers, bigots and grifters and murderers—and know there is still time for every one of us to be saved, bless our hearts. But God help you if you should have the misfortune to cross paths with one of us before that happens.

Hey Evelyn, one of the regulars says after those hungry, bewildered men have been seated at a booth as far away from the bar as possible, here's a good one for you. Why wasn't Baby Jesus born in West Texas? Because they couldn't find three wise men or a virgin.

⌣

Tonight, the lights from several new drill sites keep the stars at bay, but Karla darlin' stands in the desert and looks upward, watches the harvest moon rise behind the cooling towers at the petroleum plant. She keeps her face turned up to the stars—her mother says there used to be more of them—because there is not much else to look at, because looking at the sky might mean the difference between living and dying. There's sleet and ice in the winter and tornados in the spring, fires at the plant. But the sky won't show you a gas leak or a chemical spill in the water table, or how to steer clear of a young man just a couple of weeks out of jail and looking to make somebody pay.

After the men had finished with him, one last kick to the kidneys just because they could, they said Dale Strickland sat on the gravel for a while and then staggered to his truck and drove away. And Karla thought she had dodged a bullet. People think it's all snakes and scorpions out there in the oil patch, but hell, those are the most harmless things in the county. At least the rattlesnakes let you know they're coming, most of the time.

Why didn't she smile at him? Maybe because Diane still doesn't sleep through the night and Karla is bone-tired. Maybe because she is seventeen years old and already a mother, for now and forever. Or maybe she just didn't fucking feel like smiling. And what was Karla doing out there in an empty field, all by herself in the middle of the night, when she knows that's no place for a girl? She was looking at the stars and smoking a joint, killing a little time on her way home after nine hours of smiling so hard she thought her teeth might shatter.

⁓

What's the difference between a
bucket of shit and Odessa?
The bucket.

～

He was lit up like a Christmas tree, the sheriff says when he comes in during happy hour to ask us a few questions. Whoever ran over him took the time to hit him twice, once with the front bumper, once with the back. Took his wallet, too. Do y'all have any idea what might have happened?

Evelyn looks up from the booth where she's making the schedule for next week. Maybe he got out of his truck to take a leak and was stumbling around out there in the dark, trying to find his way back— she shrugs—and the other driver didn't see him until it was too late. Maybe he picked up a hitchhiker and there was an argument over pitching in for gas. Maybe he was pushed. Maybe he finally met someone who was meaner than him, or had more to lose. She shrugs again. Guess it's just one of those things.

Well, he suffered, the sheriff tells us. He wandered around in the oil patch all night and most of the next day. When we found him, he was covered head to toe in red mud and chiggers. Scorpions got at his ankles, and he has a bump on his head as big as a baseball, and two broken arms. The doctor says it's a miracle he's alive.

That's just terrible. Evelyn takes the sheriff's arm and leads him to a booth. I wouldn't wish that on almost anybody.

Y'all had some trouble with him over here recently? The sheriff looks over at us. We all shake our heads. We think about the red mud on Karla's bumpers and the new dent in her driver's side door, the bounce in her step. And we are grateful that she has the day off.

Just the usual shenanigans. Evelyn hands him a menu. Probably wasn't the first time somebody ran him over, probably won't be the last. Hard to think of that one as a child of God—she laughs—or any of us for that matter.

Well, he doesn't remember anything, the sheriff says. That's how hard they hit him.

Maybe that's for the best, Evelyn says. A blessing in disguise.

When the sheriff leaves, she goes into her office and shuts the door. After closing time, she sits down with us and drinks enough Manhattans to decide she'll sleep on the cot in her office. Gals, she tells us, I am getting too old for this shit. When we put on our jackets and get ready to leave, she stands in the doorway and watches us walk to our cars.

⌒

What's the first thing a girl from Odessa does when
she wakes up in the morning?
Finds her shoes and walks home.

⌒

Nights, we watch Karla sort her money into piles—
one for school, one for baby Diane, one for her
mother. When her diploma from the alternative high
school comes in the mail, we celebrate by letting her
have a glass of wine after closing. When she turns
eighteen in November, Karla tells us, she and Diane
are heading to San Antonio. Maybe she'll take a class
or two at one of the colleges there.

They have more than one? we ask. How come?

Except for the chandelier hanging above the booth
and a thin light shining from under Evelyn's office
door, the place is dark. We have finished the side work
and counted out our banks, and now we sit together
in the big booth. What do you want to be when you
grow up? we ask Karla. Nurse? Teacher? Librarian?
Philosopher? Ha, ha! She says she wants to do something beautiful and true, something that will blow the
lid off the world. Aha, we think, a dreamer.

I've got this, she tells us. I can do this.

And why not, we think. She's a smart girl.

Here's a little bit of money, we say on her last day of work. Three hundred dollars, and a grocery bag filled with clothes our babies outgrew years ago. Here's a hug and a kiss, and a little pistol for your purse. Carry it with you always. You might never need it—you probably won't—but if you do, shoot to kill.

Good luck to you, Karla darlin'! Just as sure as we are standing here, you are a thief and a wannabe murderer, but we are rooting for you. We will miss you when you go. Keep an eye out for us in your rearview mirror. Watch us grow smaller and smaller, watch us disappear.

∽

Why don't girls from Odessa play hide-and-go-seek?

Because nobody would go look for them.

∽

This place. Flat earth, flat sky. How long does it take for an oil derrick to rust away in a place this dry? How to describe the way home? A ribbon of brown with an asphalt hem, each sewn to the other with a thread of fury? While the wind riffles her hair and a waning moon rises over the oil patch, Karla Sibley stands in her mother's backyard and listens for the baby. Yesterday, she turned eighteen. Tonight, their bags are packed and loaded into the trunk of a car that Karla already loves as if it were an old grandmother. By the time they return to Odessa, Diane will stand nearly a foot taller than her mother. They will walk from one end of that town to the other, and no one will know who they are.

Glory

Because sometimes she wakes up swinging, knife in hand, her finger already on the catch, Victor has learned to stand on the other side of the room when he calls to her. M'ija, he says, taking care not to use the name she hates. Time to wake up. Sometimes he calls her after the birds he loves most—wren, for the plain gray bird that will build her nest anywhere, even under pumpjacks or next to railroad tracks, or cantora, after the brown-headed cowbird that builds no nest of her own, preferring instead to leave her eggs in those of other birds. Singing, singing, always singing, morning, noon, and night. You would too, Victor tells his niece, if you tricked someone else into doing all your work. This afternoon, Glory is drowsing under one of her mother's light blankets, her breathing regular and steady, when he calls her phoebe, for the fierce little flycatcher that sings her own name. *Phoebe, phoebe, calling faint and far away.*

Time to go, his voice is quieter than usual. Time for you and me to get the hell out of Dodge.

They have been planning their departure since the middle of August when Victor returned from court and rapped on her door, hat clenched between his hands, the collar of his best white shirt ringed with sweat. In preparation for the trial, he had trimmed his thick mustache and run the shaver over his head. He had scrubbed his hands for so long that the cuticles cracked and bled. There were dark circles under his eyes, and his hands trembled slightly when he walked into Glory's room and set his hat on the dresser.

Did he pay? she wanted to know. Did he pay for what he did?

Victor listened as the man in the room next door flushed the toilet and turned on the shower. Yes, he lied, Dale Strickland's gonna pay for this every day for the rest of his life.

Now it is early September, and Victor has returned from a meeting at the district attorney's office when Glory asks again if Dale Strickland paid for what he did. He pats the front pocket of his pants where five thousand dollars, most of it in Benjamin Franklins, is held together with a rubber band. This is her money, but she doesn't know it yet. When they get to Puerto Ángel, he will give it to Alma. Here, he will tell his sister, for a nicer place to live and a few pieces of furniture, and school tuition for Glory. He looks away from the small shape huddled under the bedcovers and lets his gaze fall on the single heroic ray of sunlight that has pushed its way through a thumb-sized gap in the curtains. He will let her keep on believing that Strickland is at the state prison in Fort Worth, that he'll be farting dust by the time he gets out. They'll have to roll him out the gate in a wheelchair, Victor says, with a new set of false teeth and a bag full of extra underwear.

I hope he dies there, she says and hunkers a little deeper into Alma's sheets. The heat broke early this year, and although Glory still turns on the air conditioner in the afternoons when she comes in from the pool, it is only for ten or fifteen minutes, just long enough to drive the stuffiness from her room. The recent storms settled the dust and smashed records for precipitation. On the street where Glory and her mother used to live, the Muskingum Draw flooded. Little kids floated on old tires from one end of town to the other, and when the water grew shallow and sprawling, when they could see the buffalo wallow ahead, now thick with mud and water moccasins, they stood and wrested their tires out of the water. Outside town, the flash floods eventually settled into ravines and gulches and cattle crossings. If Glory looks closely when they drive through the desert this afternoon, Victor says, she will see flowers she's never seen before—butterfly daisies and buffalo bur and cactus blossoms the color of fresh snow.

When she was little, maybe four or five, a rare snowstorm passed through Odessa overnight. At dawn, Alma woke her daughter, and they went outside to see the ice crystals that covered the ground and sidewalks and car windows. It was the first time either of them had seen snow, and they stood in front of their apartment, mouths agape. When the morning sun cleared the roof of their complex, the ice began to sparkle and shimmer in the light. Make it stay, Glory begged her mother, but by noon, the snow had turned to red mud and soggy grass, and Glory blamed Alma—as if her mother could have stopped the sun from rising and the day from growing warmer, if only she had tried harder.

Glory rises from her bed and starts packing. I hope he suffers, she tells her uncle again. Victor nods and curls his fingers around the money in his pocket. Take it, you lazy wetback, Scooter Clemens had said, pissed off that Strickland hadn't shown up to do his own dirty work. He slapped the bills on Keith Taylor's desk while Keith sat frowning and looking out the window, saying nothing. After everyone had signed the agreement,

Victor stood with his hat in his hands and imagined his large thumbs pressed against the man's throat. But of all the things Victor learned during the war—that living to see another day is almost always a matter of stupid luck, that men who know they might die any minute can learn not to give a shit about who's the All-Star and who's the Mexican, or that heroism is most often small and accidental but it still means the world—the greatest lesson was this: nothing causes more suffering than vengeance. And Victor has no taste for it, not even as the sole witness to his niece's suffering.

He picks up an empty suitcase and sets it on the bed. Phoebe, he says again, that son of a bitch is going to pay for this every day until he's dead. Believe it.

And maybe he will pay, one way or another, Victor thinks, but that's got nothing to do with him, or Glory. The cops and lawyers and teachers and churches, the judge and jury, the people who raised that boy and then sent him out into the world, to this town—every one of them is guilty.

They load their suitcases and boxes into the back of El Tiburón, covering everything with a tarp weighed down by red bricks. It is just after four o'clock when they walk over to the motel office, and the desk clerk is counting his drawer when they hand over the keys to their rooms, first the young man, then the girl who comes downstairs every day around noon wearing the same Led Zeppelin T-shirt, towel in one hand, bottle of Dr Pepper in the other, and lately, a portable cassette player slung over one shoulder. In a few hours, the boy will wish he'd stopped what he was doing for a minute and thanked them for always paying their bill on time, wished them good luck wherever they were headed next.

⌣

The road map, when Victor lays it across the steering wheel, is two feet wide and three feet long. He folds it in half, then quarters, and then again until it fits easily in Glory's hands. He points to the bottom edge of the fold, his index finger lightly tracing the border, a pale blue line that wanders between the two countries, its gentle bends and turns becoming sharper and more complicated as it meanders toward the gulf. It is a line that grows thinner each time the map is revised, Victor has noticed, the river diminished by dredging and fences and dams. It's been at least a hundred years since old ladies sat on their porches just a few feet from the river's edge and watched steamboats carry passengers to and from the Gulf while live jazz or country or Tejano drifted across the water, the music lingering long after the boats had passed by.

Two hours south of Laredo, there's a ferry at Los Ebanos, Victor tells his niece. It can carry a dozen people and two cars on each trip across the river. Victor runs his index finger along a series of state highways and back roads marked by black lines wending their way across the desert and through the Chisos Mountains, stopping at Lake Amistad and picking up again on the other side only to spend another six hundred miles wandering back and forth across the border. Victor fetches the map from his niece's hand, flips it over, and points at the jagged edge of land hugging the sea. And then we drive down to Oaxaca and Puerto Ángel, he says, fifteen hundred miles and roads so bumpy your nalgas will hurt for a week. He glances at his watch and looks toward the western sky. He does not want to be driving through this part of West Texas at night with Glory in the car, if he can help it. If we hurry, he says, we can be in Del Rio before dark.

⌒

On a two-lane highway somewhere between Ozona and Comstock, along a stretch of road so remote that they haven't seen another car for nearly an hour, the El Camino starts hesitating on accelerations. When Victor swears and pumps the gas, the engine coughs and sputters like an old man, but they press on for another fifty miles. The sun is hovering just above the horizon when he mutters something about a clogged fuel filter and starts looking for a wide spot where he can ease the car off the road. Glory is half-dozing in the passenger seat with her cheek pressed against the warm window, trying to imagine what her mother's hometown might look like, whether it will be much different from the old photos Alma keeps in a cigar box. Her hair has grown out enough to look like she means for it to be that way, and there is a fine sheen of sweat on her neck, even as the coming night threatens to send temperatures plummeting.

While her uncle curses and fiddles under the hood of El Tiburón, Glory steps outside and stands on her toes until she loses her balance. She'd love a cigarette, but Victor says a girl her age has no business smoking. Instead, she walks to the back of the truck and lowers the tailgate. She pulls a pack of gum out of her pocket and stuffs three pieces in her mouth. When she sits down, the metal is warm against the backs of her legs. Sweat gathers along her bra line and waistband, and she rubs hard at her eyes. ¡Pedazo de mierda! Victor tells the car. You'll never be a classic.

A dead armadillo lies on the gravel shoulder a few feet away. Above the animal's crushed armor, two buzzards circle lazily overhead. When the wind picks up just enough to gently lift the hair on the back of her neck and Glory notices that the wind is blowing the animal's smell away from her, she lifts her face to the empty blue sky and breathes deeply.

Díos mío, Victor mutters, a flathead screwdriver tucked behind his ear. He tries to clamp a hose with a pair of pliers, but when he shuts the fuel line off and gasoline vapors rush to fill his nose, he staggers away from the engine, choking and spitting. Sit tight, Glory, he gasps, we'll get her fixed up. He tinkers for a few more minutes and then pokes his head out the side of the car's hood. Go fetch me a stick about four feet long and this wide—he holds up his pinkie finger to show her the width—so I can run it down the fuel line and clear the blockage.

Glory climbs onto the bed of the El Camino and stands up to face the big bunch of nothing that surrounds them on all sides. They haven't seen a pumpjack since Ozona, and there are no buildings out here, not even a little farmhouse in the distance. The only signs that people have ever been here is the barbed-wire fence that runs along the highway for as far as she can see, and an open gate about fifty yards away. This is different, she tells herself when her heart starts hammering against her sternum. Out there in the oil patch, the earth was an empty table. Here the land is rocky and uneven in some places, flat and bald and red-faced in others. In the loosely scattered cactus patches, tiny blooms cover Texas barrels and fishhook and lace-spine. On the highway's shoulder, a purple tansy no more than an inch tall or wide has shoved its way through a narrow crack in the caliche, a joyful noise in the midst of all that brown, and as Victor promised, there is a patch of buffalo bur with its bright yellow flowers and tough dark green leaves. When the plant dries out in a few months and its shallow roots begin to wither, the wind will tear it from the earth and send it rolling and tumbling across the land, a dead and dying conflagration of sticks and leaves set rootless upon the world—a tumbleweed. This is not the same place, Glory says out loud when the thin black hairs on her arms begin to prickle and stand up. He is locked up in Fort Worth.

The shoulder is narrow so she keeps an eye out for traffic and snakes, and a goddamned stick. When she reaches the open gate, Glory stops and peers past the cattle guard. A thin layer of fresh gray dust covers the metal grates and a horny toad stands in the middle watching a line of fire ants cross its path. Just beyond, a mockingbird sits atop a strand of barbed wire and sings a complicated song, some of the notes its own and some stolen, and who can tell. The air has begun to cool, but Glory can still feel the sweat running down her back when she walks to the center of the cattle guard and peers through the steel grates, half expecting something to reach up and sting or pierce or strike at her legs.

After the storm, a surge of water had rushed across the desert and filled the ravine, a flash flood so sudden as to catch a family of blue quail unawares, but now there is only garbage and rusting beer cans and shotgun casings. Her legs are damp against the heavy denim. The sneakers she wears are thin enough to be pierced by a piece of barbed wire or a cactus needle, and her socks barely cover the new scars that crisscross her feet and ankles. Standing now in the middle of the dirt road, listening to the steady drone of cicadas, she watches a pair of tumbleweeds roll aimlessly across the desert. There ain't jack shit out here, she thinks, and a murmur of rage rises in her throat, a low burble directed at her uncle for bringing her here. When a roadrunner emerges from the brush and scampers across the road in front of her, Glory reaches into her pocket and curls her fingers around the knife she carries with her always.

Another fifty feet up ahead, dead and dying mesquite are lined up next to the dirt road like parade-goers. Knowing the branches will snap off easily, she moves quickly, her anger pressing her forward, a warm hand in the center of her back saying *Go*. When she hands Victor the damned stick, she will tell him that she wants to go back to Odessa. He can go back to work and she will lie by the pool watching her scars turn darker, scarlet and shiny against her brown skin, and they will wait until Alma is able to make her way back to, and across, the border. Trying to scare off any animals that are surely hiding in the brush, she stomps hard across the earth and sure enough, the vibrations startle several little critters—a rat and a couple of blue quail, a family of prairie dogs already holed up for the night.

Glory is only an arm's reach from the mesquite when she hears the clicking of a baby's plastic rattle, a maraca filled with dried beans, the terrifying *chica-chica-chica* as fifteen hollow rings of cartilage knock against one another. An old diamondback comes gliding across the desert floor, a shallow wake forming in the sand behind her. She is thick-bodied and long, six feet of heavy muscle and skin marked by brown diamonds that taper to a brilliant series of black and white stripes. Her head is flat as an old wooden spoon and each of her sharply curved fangs is as thick and long as Glory's index finger. She has already scented the girl when she stops in the middle of the dirt road and wraps herself into a tight coil. When she uses every bit of her scarce strength to raise her head and flick her tongue in the direction of Glory's bare legs. When she tries to discern how big a threat this animal is to her and the ten young snakes she is about to deliver.

The old snake is weak enough that a strike, even if she could land it, would surely be a dry bite, but Glory can't know this—or that the snake will only live for a few more hours, just long enough to watch the last of her young emerge from its amniotic sac and unfold itself against the pale earth, its body a bright shimmer of black and gold lit by the full moon.

Glory stands with her fingers curled around a pocketknife that might stop a man but is entirely insufficient to this moment, and although she was hoping to stay angry enough to claim some space of her own and fight for it, now's not the time and this is not personal. This is the sun threatening to go down and one hell of a big rattlesnake blocking her path. She watches the snake and the snake watches her, tongue flickering, rattles shaking steadily against the air, an unrelenting buzz and hum. When the snake lowers her head and uncoils her long body and glides slowly into the brush, Glory counts to a hundred and listens for whatever might come next, and when her heart has stopped hammering against her breast, she tears a limb from a mesquite tree and heads back to the highway.

Glory and Victor won't make it to Del Rio in time

for sunset. When she returns to the El Camino, her uncle has removed the fuel filter and sprayed it down with Chemtool. While they wait for the filter to dry, they sit on the hood watching the sun go down and listening as the coyotes get revved up for the night. The harvest moon, when it rises, is blood red and beautiful against the darkening sky. Try floating with your ears under the water, Tina had said to Glory as they drifted across the swimming pool that afternoon. Listen for long enough, she said, and the sounds from the highway will blend together. A truck hauling pipeline or water, a flatbed turning onto the highway, the crank of a pumpjack slowly winding itself up, they will all start to sound alike. You can tell yourself you're hearing anything, Tina said, her large white arms floating next to her like buoys. And will you look at that sky? It's a wonder, a damned wonder.

On the other side of Comstock, they cut south to State Highway 277 and drive along the border through Juno and Del Rio. At Eagle Pass, the road to El Indio turns to gravel and then dirt, and the border pulls them closer. Victor drives quietly, keeping an eye out for a cop's flashing lights in the rearview mirror, occasionally glancing at his niece in the passenger seat. Is she okay, this child who has never been more than fifty miles from the town where she was born?

Are you okay? he asks.

Fine—Glory rolls her eyes and smacks her gum and blows a bubble as big as her face—but next time, go out there and get your own damned stick.

He smiles and keeps his eyes on the road ahead, lightly scanning the narrow shoulders for armadillos and coyotes, maybe the occasional bobcat. A set of headlights appears on the horizon, and he watches it grow brighter and larger as it draws near. When a cop passes them, Victor looks in his rearview mirror to see if the car has pulled onto the shoulder and begun to turn around. Victor won't be coming back to this beautiful place, Texas. For him, it is a diseased limb, to be quickly removed before the rot reaches his heart— something he had managed to forget in the years after coming home from Vietnam and finding work and keeping an eye on Alma and Glory. Although, he muses now, his homecoming from Southeast Asia should have been a good reminder. He had stepped off a Greyhound bus in downtown Odessa expecting to be met by his sister and instead came face-to-face with his old boss from the gas station.

The man wore his work overalls and a Shell cap, and to Victor, it seemed like no time at all had passed while he was overseas. Old Kirby Lee hadn't changed a bit. On seeing the younger man, he pulled Victor into a big bear hug, his icy blue eyes flashing with pleasure. Well shit, Ramírez, you lucky spic. Looks like you'll live to drink another Tecate, or three. And there was Victor breathing in the scent of gasoline on the man's gray overalls, hugging his old boss back tight, tight, so tight the man began to squirm in his arms, and all the while Victor was thinking, He don't mean anything by it, he don't mean it, he don't mean it. I made it home alive.

Victor drives on, the lump in his throat large enough to insist on silence. He is thinking about a summer when he picked grapes in Northern California. His fingers bled every night, and the hours were long, but he loved the country, and the woman who drove him into the city one Sunday to eat chocolate at the pier and walk through the park at dusk. He will miss thinking that he might run into her again, sometime. He will miss movie theaters and Blue Bell ice cream and brisket. He will miss a steady paycheck and the sun setting over the sand hills in Monahans, and he will miss hearing the odd, ugly cries of the cranes when he is sitting on the bank of the skinny and shallow Pecos River, a cold beer in one hand, his bird book in the other. The birds in Mexico will be more or less the same, but the river will be different. He will miss it.

Why don't you tell me one of your war stories? Glory looks worried, and for an instant, Victor wonders if he has been talking out loud. Maybe in a little while, he tells her.

Are we still in Texas? she asks when they drive through El Indio, a village without a stoplight, gas station, or a single sign written in English. Yes, Victor nods. This is Texas.

Tell me a story about Texas, she says, or Mexico.

There are a dozen stories Victor could tell his niece. So many! But tonight he can only think of the sad ones. Ancestors hanged from posts in downtown Brownsville, their wives and children fleeing to Matamoros to spend the rest of their lives looking across the river at land that had been in their families for six generations. Texas Rangers shooting Mexican farmers in the backs as the men harvested sugar cane, or tying men to mesquite trees and setting them on fire, or forcing broken beer bottles down their throats.

They did it for fun, Victor could tell her. They did it on a bet. They did it because they were drunk, or they hated Mexicans, or they heard a rumor that the Mexicans were teaming up with some freedmen or what was left of the Comanche, and they were all coming for the white settlers' land, their wives and their daughters. And maybe sometimes they did it because they knew they were guilty, and having already traveled so far down the path of their own iniquity, they figured they might as well see it through. But mostly, they did it because they could. Río Bravo, Victor's papi had called it—furious river, river of villains and desperadoes—and Papi hadn't meant him and his. He meant whatever lost souls lynched hundreds of men, and a few women, in the years between 1910 and 1920. He meant the Texas Rangers who in the summer of 1956 loaded two of Victor's uncles onto a cattle car, along with twenty other men, and dropped them off in the Sierra Madres with a single jug of water and a one-liner—Y'all fight it out amongst yourselves, boys. Look in any ravine within fifty miles of the border, Victor could tell his niece, in any small wash or depression, look under any skinny mesquite that might bring some small relief from the hot sun, and you will find us there. You could build a house with the skeletons of our ancestors, a cathedral from our bones and skulls.

Instead, he tells her about her mother's village, and how the sea is so crowded with red snapper, they jump into fishing boats just to get a little elbow room.

Unimpressed, Glory again pops her gum and blows a bubble so large that when it eventually pops, she has to peel it off her face. Tell me a *good* story, she says.

An opossum meanders off the shoulder and steps in front of the car. Victor taps the brake and swerves gently, relieved not to feel the thud beneath his tire.

Okay, he says, here's one that my abuela used to tell us kids. I'll take you to her gravesite when we get to Puerto Ángel. It's a sad story, he warns.

Is it a Texas story?

Yes.

Then tell it.

Near the end of the Red River War, when the Comanche and Kiowa had already lost but nobody was willing to admit it, a group of warriors came upon a rancher's house. They broke down the door and found the rancher and his wife gone, but a baby sleeping in a basket next to the bed. They thought about stealing the baby, but it was late in the day and they were tired, and while they would take women and small children, babies were more trouble than they were worth. So they carried the basket out into the yard and filled the baby with arrows. Poor thing looked like a porcupine when they were done—Victor pauses and glances at his niece who stares at him with a look of delighted horror on her face—that's how your abuela described it, not me.

Pues, the rancher and his wife came home—they'd only been down at the creek washing some bed linens— and discovered their baby. The poor thing was so thoroughly shot through with arrows that they had to bury her basket and all. A regiment of Texas Rangers

heard about this. Half the regiment was old Confeder-
ates and the other half was old Blues, but they were one
hundred percent in agreement that there was a score
to settle, so they rode around the Panhandle until they
found an Arapahoe woman with *her* baby. They figured
they'd riddle the child with bullets and call it even. But
some of the men didn't feel right about this. Filling a
baby with bullets was barbaric, they decided, and these
men were not barbarians. Instead, they decided, they
would deliver a single shot to the baby's forehead. But
they didn't account for how large the cartridge, or how
small the baby, and they were shocked when the baby's
head split like a melon—again Victor pauses—that too
was your abuela's phrase, not mine.

Now the two groups of men were even, but the whole
affair had been much uglier and messier than anybody
expected and no one was really surprised when both
babies began to haunt the men. Every town they rode
into, every camp they set up—there were the babies.
The men would spend their days killing each other and
dragging their wounded off the field, and there would
be the babies hovering at the edge of things, watching them. When night fell, the babies would begin to
cry—an ungodly, agonizing wail that didn't stop until
the sun came up the next morning.

And the mothers must have died not long after their

babies, because suddenly there were two young women hanging around the campfire and they weren't nearly as peaceful as the babies had been. They shrieked and howled, their skirts rustling when they jerked men out of their tents and pulled them by their feet into the campfire. They untied horses and sent them flying across the plains, leaving the men stranded. Some of the men killed themselves, but most of them wandered around out there until they died from thirst or choked to death in one of the dust storms the mothers had wrought. When the women hurled lightning at the men, prairie fires spread so quickly they couldn't outrun them. When rain and ice came down on the men's heads, they drowned in flash floods or froze to death. Within five years, every man on either side was dead, and the mothers, having settled the score, took their babies and returned to the grave.

And this is where your abuela would lean forward and shake her finger at your mother and me and say, No matarás. Glory, you better start cracking those Spanish books if you're going to live in Mexico. Victor leans forward and peers at a small group of lights ahead. Laredo, he says. You want to stop for a bite to eat?

But Glory doesn't answer. What kind of woman, she wonders, would tell such a story to little kids? The kind Glory wishes she had known.

The lights of Laredo rise up and grow brighter. They drive quietly and after a while, Glory scrounges around in her backpack for her cassette player and a tape. She slides the tape into the player and hits play. Lydia Mendoza, the Lark of the Border, Victor cries out, and she is surprised to hear a tremor in his voice. *Una vez nada más en mi huerto brilló la esperanza . . .*

Glory rolls down her window and chews her lip. The recording is grainy and the words are hard to make out, but she understands a few words, *nada más* and *esperanza*—there was always at least one Esperanza in every classroom at Gonzalez Elementary—and now Glory is holding her arm out the window, spreading her fingers apart so the wind streams through them. She is glad she's not dead, but she would give a lot to be able to haunt Strickland for the rest of his life. Hope shines, she thinks the singer may have said, but Glory can't be sure and she doesn't want to ask her uncle, whose eyes have begun to glisten in the dark, and maybe it doesn't matter on this starry night. Maybe the woman's voice, and the gentle scratching of her fingers on the guitar strings, is enough.

They arrive in Laredo after midnight, where they grab a bite at the truck stop and take turns napping in the parking lot. But only for an hour, Victor says. He wants to be at the crossing before sunrise, and they are still nearly two hundred miles away.

Once they leave town, they drive so close to the border they are not always sure whether they are in Texas or Mexico. The sky is black as hematite, and the names on the road signs are no help—San Ygnacio, Zapata, and Ciudad Miguel Aleman—each marking a wide spot in the road named for stolen rivers or local war heroes or ranchers who died young.

Are we still in Texas? Glory asks every few minutes.

Yes, he tells her.

How about now?

Pues, who knows? Texas, Mexico, it's all the same dirt.

She tells him about the rattlesnake, how large it was, how it moved like a river. She does not tell him that she had only been that afraid on one other occasion in her life. That snake must have been six feet long, she says, and as thick as my leg.

No shit? Victor says. You're going to be a legend. Glory Ramírez, the girl who stared down a fifteen-foot rattlesnake.

It wasn't fifteen feet long, she says. There's no such thing as a snake that big.

Who cares? That's how a tall tale works, mi vida.

Most of the stars are gone when they turn off the highway and drive past half a dozen little wooden houses in the still sleeping village of Los Ebanos. At the ferry, five men sit on folding chairs outside a small, festive shack adorned with beer signs and Christmas lights. Another man leans against a two-hundred-year-old ebony tree, the red cherry of his cigarette beating back the dark. A steel cable thick as a man's fist is wrapped around the tree. It stretches across the Río Bravo and encircles its twin on the other side, where a dozen men and women are already standing on the ferry. It is a border crossing that has been unmanned for as long as anyone can remember. In dry years, in the places where the river becomes barely more than a stream, cattle wander back and forth in search of the sweet blue grama grass. Men and women work on one side and live on the other, and kids sometimes reach their tenth birthdays before they figure out which side of the river they belong to.

Tonight, most of these women and men will cross the river again, heading home to the sounds of water birds and wrens and starlings, cattle and coyotes, ocelots and bobcats. They will listen to music drifting back and forth across the water, Tejano and country, ranchera and norteño, and from the living-room window of one old woman who puts on a record every night just before sunset, pours herself a glass of whiskey and sits out on her front porch to watch the sun go down, jazz—Billie Holiday and John Coltrane, and the doomed boy from the dead center of Oklahoma who could make a horn *sing*.

No one asks any questions when Victor and Glory drive onto the ferry at Los Ebanos. No one asks to see any papers. Boxes of produce are stacked in the middle of the wooden platform, along with several steel pipes and a pile of lumber. A skinny yellow mutt stands atop the wood and looks across the river. There is so little space between the two sides, Glory sees now. Even after the recent rains, the river is not much wider than a four-lane highway, not much farther than the distance from her door at the Jeronimo Motel to the swimming pool. And sure enough, when a man on the other side calls across the river to say they are ready, and the men standing on the ferry grab the cable and begin to pull, one hand over the other, the journey is hardly longer than the time it takes Glory to braid her mother's hair before she leaves for work in the evening, or for Alma to look through her purse in the morning for a handful of change to give to her daughter. Crossing the river is enough time to sort through a stack of bills in search of a letter from home, to walk down the hall and check on the kids, to flood the engine on a car bought with military pay. It is enough time to stare down an old snake in the desert, to start wondering what comes next. When they reach the other side and one of the men sets down two thick wooden planks for their wheels to pass over, Victor and Glory look straight ahead. Neither of them looks back at Texas.

They drive south with the windows rolled down and the sun in their eyes. Glory sits with her legs crossed. At the Río Bravo Delta, also known as the Laguna Madre, they will turn west and start driving into the heart of her mother's country. If they move steadily forward, they can be in Alma's hometown for the Feast of St. Michael at the end of September. Imagine, Victor tells her, you and me and your mom standing at the water's edge with our feet in the sand, lanterns burning on the deck of every fishing boat in the harbor, a thousand candles floating among them. Can you see it, phoebe?

No, she tells him. She rubs her thumb against one palm and then reaches down to touch her feet and ankles. Victor calls them battle scars. Something to be proud of. It means you fought hard, means you came home from the war. Can you see that?

Not yet.

Try.

She rolls her eyes and looks out the window, but she is trying to imagine her scarred feet moving steadily forward, carrying her where she needs to go. Away from a pickup truck parked in the middle of the oil patch. Across the desert and up a road to someone's front door. Down a flight of metal stairs where she pressed her hands against rough concrete and lowered her body into the water, where she pushed away from the side and learned that if she moved her arms in gentle circles, she could drift until she touched something solid.

Glory looks at the two small scars on her hands, one in the center of each palm, the body doing its work. In a year, they will have flattened and grown softer. In two, they will be gone. But the scars on her ankles and feet will thicken and grow longer, dark red cords that tether her to a single morning. The girl who stood up and fell back down, who grabbed onto a barbed-wire fence and stopped herself from falling again. The girl who walked barefoot across the desert and saved her own life. She can't imagine any other way to tell the story.

Acknowledgments

For the gifts of money, time, space, and quiet, I am indebted to the National Endowment for the Arts, the Rona Jaffe Foundation, the Illinois Arts Council, Hedgebrook, and the MacDowell Colony as well as the Barbara Deming Memorial Fund, Amy Davis, and Writers Workspace, Chicago.

Two chapters appeared in earlier versions as short stories. Many thanks to the editors at *Colorado Review* and *Baltimore Review* for publishing "Valentine" and "Women & Horses."

For writing lessons, wisdom, and encouragement, I want to thank Chris Offutt, Marilynne Robinson, Luis Alberto Urrea, Lan Samantha Chang, James Alan McPherson, Connie Brothers, Deb West, and Bret Lott.

For their brilliant insights, endless patience, and steadfast support, I am indebted to Helen Garnons-Williams, the copy-editing and production heroes at Harper, and all the good people at Georges Borchardt, Inc.

I will be forever grateful to Samantha Shea and Emily Griffin, who believed in *Valentine* from the beginning, and worked tirelessly to make it better. Thank you for loving books, and for loving mine.

For reading my stories, and sharing yours. For watching my kid so I can write. For moral support and encouragement, particularly of the early sort—Caroline Steelberg, Skye Lavin, Karyn Morris Brownlee, Jon Chencinski, Mildred Lee Tanner, Ellen Wade Beals, Joan Corwin, Rochelle Distelheim, Tammi Longsjo, Christie Parker, César Avena, Tim Winkler, Ellen McKnight, Chris Pomeroy, Mike Allen, Casebeer, Mark Garrigan, Tim Hohmann, Seth Harwood, José Skinner, Joe Pan, Johnny Schmidt, Nick Arvin, Jeremy Mullem, Steve Yousha, Tayari Jones, Rebecca Johns, Brandon Trissler, Michelle Falkoff, Dan Stolar, Jessica Chiarella, Amy Crider, Bergen Anderson, Nick Geirut, Lindsay Cummings, Kelly and Jason Zech, Nathan Hoks and Nikki Flores, Chad Chmielowicz and Katie Wilson.

For being family—Cary and Jorge Sánchez, David

and Christopher Erwin, Grace Sliger, Maria González, Mary Logan Erwin and Curtis Erwin, and most especially my parents, Tom and Carol Wetmore.

For signing on as godmothers and aunties. For writing stories and songs and poems. For riding along with me through cornfields, around the ranch, across the desert, to the sea, and home. For keeping the faith and helping me keep on—Bryn Chancellor, Julie Wetmore Erwin, Judy Smith, Stephanie Soileau, and Megan Levad.

For songs and love and adventures, and for the sacrifices you've made—Jorge Sánchez and Hank Sánchez.

About the Author

Born and raised in West Texas, Elizabeth Wetmore lives with her husband and son in Chicago. This is her first novel.